"Gripping, revealing, and devastating, *The Wolf Den* made me ache for its women and their simple dreams. This novel left me breathless."—Rebecca F. John, author of *The Haunting of Henry Twist*

"An utterly gripping story. It humanises the men and women who had their humanity taken away from them, and helps to remind us that the brothels of Pompeii were far more than seedy tourist attractions."—Daisy Dunn, author of *In the Shadow of Vesuvius*

"Textured, alive and sweary historical fiction, depicting a vivid city full of life with nuanced characters, giving voice to slaves who had few choices."—Kate Sawyer, author of *The Stranding*

"*The Wolf Den* gives a voice to the forgotten women of Pompeii with a portrayal of slavedom that is so visceral that Amara's story was simultaneously utterly compelling and difficult to read. Whilst Harper doesn't shrink from laying bare the grim realities of life in the Wolf Den, she does so with such wit and compassion that this is not a tale of oppression, but of resilience, and of female friendship formed in the most harrowing of circumstances."—Sonia Velton, author of *Blackberry & Wild Rose*

"A rich and moving story about the women of ancient Rome, set in the brothels of Pompeii."—Laura Shepherd-Robinson, author of *Blood and Sugar*

"I read a lot of great books, but *The Wolf Den* by Elodie Harper took my breath away. A journalist's eye for the truth, a storyteller's art with words, and a feminist's love of sisterhood and solidarity set among the underclass of slaves in Pompeii. Cannot recommend highly enough."
—Samira Ahmed, presenter, BBC *Front Row*

THE
WOLF
DEN

ELODIE HARPER

UNION SQUARE
& CO.

NEW YORK

UNION SQUARE & CO.

NEW YORK

First published in the UK in 2021 by Head of Zeus Ltd.
This 2022 paperback edition published by Union Square & Co., LLC.

ISBN 978-1-4549-4654-0
ISBN 978-1-4549-4655-7 (e-book)

For information about custom editions, special sales,
and premium purchases, please contact
specialsales@sterlingpublishing.com.

Manufactured in the United States of America

2 4 6 8 10 9 7 5 3

unionsquareandco.com

Originally typeset by Divaddict Publishing Solutions Ltd.

Original cover illustration and design by Holly Ovenden
Cover typography US/CAN edition by Melissa Farris

To my brother and my sisters by birth and marriage,
Eugenie, Ruth and Tom, with all my love

Author's note

Lupanar in Pompeii had two meanings for the Romans—both "brothel" and "den of wolves," just as the word *lupa* could mean both "prostitute" or "she-wolf."

74 CE

FEBRUARIUS

1

"Baths, wine and sex make fate come faster."
—Roman maxim

She holds her hands up as if in prayer, steam evaporating from her skin. The water laps at her neck as she lies back into its warmth. Laughter and female voices surround her, a confusion of sound echoing off the stone. She filters it out, focusing on her fingers, turning them, watching the water drip down, the steam rise. They could be anybody's hands, she thinks, they could belong to anybody. But they belong to Felix.

Then another's fingers interlock with hers, breaking her reverie. Victoria drags her upward, out of the water.

"Amara! You're getting your hair wet! You can't lie back like that!" Victoria's nails pinch her skin as she tries to revive the curls now plastered to Amara's shoulders. "They're like rat's tails. What were you thinking?"

Anxiety surges through her. So much rests on this afternoon; she cannot believe her own thoughtlessness. "I don't know, I . . ."

"It doesn't look so bad." Amara turns to face Dido who has slid over to join them, a slight frown on her gentle face. "You can hardly notice."

"The men aren't here for hair anyway." It's a less friendly voice this time. Drauca, Simo's most valuable woman, is watching them from across the narrow pool. She rises up out of the water, lifting her arms, and sways. The dark waves of her own hair glisten like a raven's plumage. Behind her, through the curved windows, the sea looks flat and gray. It's impossible not to stare. Amara thinks of the statue of Helen of Troy back in Aphidnai, back when she had another name, another life.

"Venus Pompeiana!" Victoria gasps, grabbing Amara in exaggerated astonishment.

"The goddess walks among us! Oh, shield my eyes from such glory!" Drauca scowls, dropping her arms with a splash. Victoria laughs. "As if nobody else here has a pair of tits," she says. Though not loud enough for Drauca to hear.

"She is beautiful though," Dido says, still staring at their rival. "And she's been here before, hasn't she? Maybe the men will prefer her, maybe—"

"Apart from Drauca, what do *they* have that we don't?" Victoria interrupts, casting a scathing look at Drauca's three companions. They are taking up most of the pool, splashing about with theatrical laughter, more posed than playful. "You can tell they're all barmaids. Maria has arms like a litter-bearer."

Amara isn't sure they have the right to sneer, given their own lowly status as brothel whores. She-wolves. A familiar knot tightens in her stomach. "I wonder what the men will be like," she says.

"They'll be . . ." But Victoria doesn't finish her thought, something behind Amara has caught her attention. "Hey!" she calls. "Let go! Let go of her!" She starts wading through the water toward an old woman who is pulling at Cressa's arm, trying to drag her out of the pool. Victoria stares up at the woman as she successfully hauls a dripping Cressa out onto the side.

The woman leans down and points a gnarled finger in Victoria's face. "Felix? You Felix?" Nobody replies. The stranger looks at them all, grouped together. Beronice has swum over too, mouth slightly open in surprise. "Felix whores out!" The old woman says impatiently, waving her hand toward the door, motioning for them to leave. Cressa tries to remonstrate, but the old woman pushes her backward. Simo's women have stopped splashing and laughing. Amara senses rather than sees that they are all at the far side of the pool. "Felix whores *out now*," the woman repeats, jabbing her finger at each of them in turn. When no one moves she grabs Amara's arm. "Out! Out!" she shrieks. "Get out now!"

Stone scrapes Amara's skin as the old woman yanks her against the side of the pool. Hard fingers dig into the soft flesh of her upper arm with a grip that's surprisingly strong. She pushes herself up onto the hot tiles, shaking herself free. The woman continues shouting, threatening to call Vibo if they don't move quickly. The mention of the bath manager's name finally convinces them. Felix's women clamber naked out of the water and hurry through to the next room, shivering at the sudden plunge in lighting and temperature. A cascade splashes down into the cold pool, the noise competing with the old woman's shouts to hurry. Amara clutches at the bright blue wall to steady herself, trying not to lose her footing, squeezing against paintings of sea creatures, the open mouth of a fish huge by her face as she passes.

Victoria is the only one of the five still arguing when they arrive at the bath's changing rooms. They didn't come in this way. Rows of polished wooden lockers are topped by paintings of lovers indulging in every possible sexual position. The women's clothes have been dumped in a heap on the floor.

"Hurry, hurry!" their tormentor demands, throwing a cloak at Beronice who still looks as stupefied as she did in the pool. Amara needs no further encouragement. She bends down and begins rifling through the mass of material, handing a yellow toga to Dido who is shivering badly, perhaps as much from fear as cold. Dido is new to slavery, and every indignity seems to hit her like a knife to the heart. Victoria is the only one who doesn't rush. She is still fastening her toga long after everybody else is dressed, gazing at the old woman with pure hate. When Victoria finally looks away, Amara sees the woman make the sign of the evil eye.

A final poke with the bony finger between the shoulder blades and Amara and the other women are bundled outside into the baths' private courtyard. Drizzle hits their faces, and the wind from the sea is cold. They stand in a huddle, already damp beneath their togas and cloaks. Amara glances around, surprised they are alone, then notices two men sheltering under the colonnade, a pair of incongruous, hulking shapes against the wall's painted nymphs and roses. One of the men strides over, face thunderous. It's Thraso, Felix's steward.

"What's this? What's happened?" His hands are balled up, ready to fight. Amara steps back. She knows how hard those fists can fall.

"Better ask him," Amara says, pointing at the other man left standing in the shadows. "Isn't he with Simo?"

"Somebody double-crossed Felix," Victoria adds, as Thraso swivels round. "Simo's women got to stay; we were all thrown out before the men arrived. Bit convenient don't you think?"

Thraso doesn't wait to hear more. He charges across the yard, swinging at the other man's head. "Balbus! I'll fucking kill you! You fucking liar!"

Balbus dodges, missing the full force of Thraso's punch, though he still catches a blow to his ear, making him stagger. Thraso grabs the man's shoulders, smashing his skull into Balbus's nose. Balbus roars, breaking free, clutching his bloodied face. Thraso attacks him again, and the two men fall to the ground, throwing punches, biting and screaming. The women watch, unsure what to do.

"Felix isn't going to like this," Beronice says, stating the obvious.

Amara glances sidelong at Victoria, hoping for a sarcastic remark, but Victoria looks away.

There's a commotion from the doorway. A group of male slaves rush out, forcing the women to scramble aside.

They run over to the brawling pair, trying to intervene, one taking a kick in the face. Vibo, the bath manager, comes out next, huffing, his portly figure swathed in a green toga. He manhandles Cressa out of his path in his haste to reach the fight.

"Enough!" he shouts. "Or you will answer to your masters for disobedience!"

The two men finally roll apart. Thraso is the first to stand, Balbus has to be helped to his feet by two slaves.

"Are you trying to close down my business?" Vibo demands. "Brawling on my doorstep like dogs in the gutter? I should have you both whipped!" Balbus mutters something, but Amara cannot hear what he says. "I'm not interested!" Vibo shouts. "Clear off now, both of you. And take that rag bag of whores with you."

The women don't wait for anyone to move them on. They cross the yard before Thraso can reach them. Amara notices he is limping. Balbus came off worse but must still have landed several hefty blows. Thraso's lip is split and he's cradling one arm. Nobody is foolish enough to ask him how he is feeling.

The women climb the steps up to the tall gate, Victoria leading the way, Beronice at the back, not quite quick enough to avoid Thraso's angry slap. They all know why he's lashing out. It's the prospect of Felix's rage when they get back to the brothel. Amara can feel the fear building, a lump in her throat she cannot swallow.

Stepping onto the street is like rejoining a fast-flowing river. She grips Dido's hand, and they force their way through the crush of people, heading up the hill to the

Forum Gate. The stones are wet and slippery. The first time Amara came to Pompeii was with Dido. It can only have been a few months ago but feels longer. They traveled in on this road, together, after Felix had bought them at the slave market in Puteoli. The weather was warmer then under the clear blue skies of late October. She remembers Felix buying ripe figs for the journey. The fruit smelt so sweet, its insides pink and shining when she split it open, sticky on her fingers. It was almost a moment of happiness. If happiness could exist in a world where she had been bought and sold. Amara still wonders at this act of kindness from Felix. They were not to know, then, how uncharacteristic it would be.

A man carrying a heavy basket of fish on his head shoves past, turning his shoulders into the crowd like a weapon. They follow him under the high archway into the dark, echoing tunnel, the road growing steeper and the crush more intense. Amara glances back to see Cressa, a look of resignation on her face, lugging the puffing Beronice up the hill. Thraso is almost out of sight behind. His leg must be giving him a lot of difficulty or he would be berating Beronice's slowness. Victoria, of course, has darted ahead. She is the only one of Felix's five women who was born in this town, and although a slave, she owns the place in a way that none of the others ever will.

Inside the town walls, the road evens out but also becomes wetter, water sloshing over Amara's shoes. Dido helps her up onto the raised pavement, two fabric sellers muttering at having to shuffle out of their way. A man heaped in garlands of myrtle, offerings for the Temple of Venus, presses close.

"For your goddess? For love? One penny for two. Good price. Bring you good fortune." He is holding the leaves so close to Dido's face she instinctively puts her hand up to draw across the veil she no longer wears.

Amara pushes the garlands away. "No."

The crush thins as they reach the Forum, absorbed into its vast space. Hawkers act like stones, breaking the eddies of the crowd. Some passers-by dawdle to look or haggle, others stride past. At the far end of the square sits the Temple of Jupiter, incense rising from its steps. The building wavers in the heat before the smoke fades out over the blue mountain behind. Amara thinks of her father, of the way he would smile when she asked him if he believed in the gods. *Stories have power whether we believe them or not.* She shuts out the memory of his voice.

The others are still looking round for Thraso. Dido points him out, sweating his way through the crowd.

"Is his nose broken *again*?" Beronice asks. "He looks awful."

"Worse than usual? Are you sure?" Victoria replies. "I think maybe Balbus knocked it back the right way."

Beronice misses the joke. "No, he looks AWFUL!" she insists, raising her voice even louder to make her point.

Cressa shakes her head. "He'll hear you."

Thraso catches up, snapping at them to move it, and they all weave across the square. A group of sailors, probably just docked at the port, whistle as Amara passes, one gesturing what he'd like. She smiles at him then lowers her eyes. The men slap each other and laugh.

The road leading downhill from the Forum is overflowing with rainwater, its surface a broken mosaic of red and yellow, reflecting the painted buildings that line its banks. The women stare as a team of soaked litter-bearers trudge their way through, water sloshing over their knees, their lucky cargo raised up high, safe behind thick curtains. Amara notices the body of a dead dog wedged between two stepping stones, held there by the weight of the stream rushing past. Not all the filth is getting washed away by the morning's downpour. The women pick their way laboriously along the walkway, turning left into a narrow street that winds round to the brothel. The space to move shrinks further, but the crowds are thinner here too.

As a child, Amara would have enjoyed the thought of returning home out of the wet, of sitting with her mother in front of the brazier, their maid bringing them hot wine with spices to warm up. But the looming bulk of the brothel doesn't give her any sense of homecoming. There's no hot drink waiting, just Felix and his anger.

They huddle outside the building, pressed single file against the wall, keeping dry under the overhanging balcony. Thraso looks almost as nervous as the women.

"You two," he points at Victoria and Amara. "You had plenty to say for yourselves at the baths. You can explain it all to Felix."

The others slink inside, Dido looking back anxiously. Victoria touches Thraso's good arm, inclining her head. "I'll tell Felix how hard you fought," she says, gazing up at him with a sincerity so earnest Amara almost believes her. "You defended his honor. That will mean something."

Thraso cannot quite bear to show gratitude to a whore but nods curtly. He glances at Amara, clearly expecting something similar, but she cannot think of anything ingratiating to say. Victoria stares at her, eyes widening with warning. "Yes," she says at last, nodding at Thraso. "You did. Very brave." Her Greek accent sounds thick through fright.

Thraso knocks on the wooden door leading to Felix's apartment above the brothel. It's answered by Paris, his permanently sour expression topped by a mono-brow. Standing in the doorway, Amara catches a whiff of the latrine hidden in the darkness of the stairwell. She used to feel sorry for Paris, for the loneliness of his young life, shuttling between scrubbing his master's floors upstairs and servicing customers in the brothel below. But Paris has shown no indication that he wants the she-wolves' company or friendship.

"Felix," says Thraso, waving at him with impatience.

"He's with a client, so you'll have to wait."

Paris turns and climbs the stairs. They follow, emerging onto the narrow, covered balcony that surrounds Felix's flat. It makes her think of a spider's web, the way the walkway circles her master's rooms, slowly drawing you further in, not cutting straight to the center. Amara can hear an unfamiliar male voice, too faint to make out all the words. Though she catches one phrase: *pay you*. Paris gestures for them to go through to the small waiting room.

Thraso sits heavily on the bench by the brazier, barely leaving space for the two women on either side. They squash in next to him. The balcony lets in daylight but also cold air. The warmth from the fire is feeble. Amara's heart is thumping. It doesn't help knowing Felix is currently squeezing some poor debtor for every last penny just down the corridor. Thraso stares straight ahead as if mesmerized by the small tongues of flame near his feet. She can feel the fear coming off him.

Amara stares at the wall. No gamboling nymphs or lovers here. Everything is painted in a geometric pattern of black and white. The sharp-edged lines turn and interlock in an endless maze that's hard to follow round the room without feeling dizzy.

They sit and wait, not talking, time stretching out. It starts to rain more heavily, water beating down on the roof. It's impossible to tell over the noise whether Felix and his client are still doing business. Then Amara sees a downcast figure pass the doorway, hears him thud down the stairs. Nobody gets up from the bench.

Paris sticks his head around the door. "You'd best go through."

Thraso rises, stalking past him. Amara and Victoria follow.

2

"She reeks of the soot of the brothel!"
—Seneca, *Declamations* 1.2

The room is large, dominated by red. Their master is sitting behind his desk. He doesn't rise as they enter. If he is surprised by their arrival so much earlier than expected, he gives no sign. Felix has half Thraso's bulk but twice his strength. His wiry frame is all bunched muscle. Amara knows there is no softness anywhere on that body hidden beneath the folds of the pale toga. Nothing to give the lie of tenderness when he holds you.

"That was a quick orgy," he says. "The rich boys couldn't keep it up for long then? But they paid you double, of course." Felix looks at Victoria. "That's what you're here to tell me, isn't it, my darling? How much money you made." Felix is smiling, but Amara can feel his anger vibrate through the sarcasm. The room grows darker. She knows without looking that Paris has just closed the door to the balcony.

Victoria opens her mouth, but Thraso jumps in. "It was Simo," he says. "Simo betrayed us . . ."

"He must have been in it with Vibo," says Victoria. "All Simo's girls stayed in the pool, but some old crone dragged the rest of us out. She *forced* us. She said it was Vibo's orders. That fat slug! We never even saw the punters—"

"Balbus was in on it too," Thraso interrupts. "I thrashed him for you, the lying little—"

"Thraso only stopped because Vibo made him!" Victoria says. "And Drauca was sneering at us; she knew, I'm sure she did . . ."

Amara watches Felix as Victoria and Thraso babble on, falling over themselves to shift the blame as far away from themselves as possible, shoveling it aside like shit from a latrine. She knows that if the boss doesn't interrupt, they will soon start blaming each other. Felix listens in silence, absorbing everything, his anger visibly growing. If there were a way of making herself smaller and less noticeable, she would shrink to the size of a dormouse.

"And you?" Felix turns sharply to Amara, catching her off guard. "Do you have nothing useful to say? Or are you just going to stand there like a dog?"

"It's . . . it's like they said," she stammers. Felix waits for her to continue, radiating rage. Behind him, the wall glows red. The only sound is the heavy drumbeat of water above. Amara knows her master is just moments from erupting. If she doesn't fill the silence, there will be nothing between her and the rain of blows that fall. "The old woman forced us out of the baths," she says. Her eyes avoid his face, skirting instead to the fresco that frames his desk. She tracks up the black plinths, reaching the bulls' skulls painted at the top. "She used your name. She only wanted the women

belonging to you. It was an insult aimed solely at you."
Victoria gives a stifled gasp. Amara glances over, sees the
fear in Victoria's face then looks quickly away. "I don't
think it was an insult from Vibo. What would he have to
gain?" Nobody replies. Amara continues, talking to the
small bag of coins resting on the desk by Felix's right hand.
"Simo must have bribed him. It's the only explanation.
Simo's got a nice little deal going on at the baths right now,
why would he want to double the women and halve the
profits?"

The rain is still falling, and she is almost out of courage.
Nobody has ever frightened her more than the man in front
of her. Amara looks up from the desk. She always avoids
staring directly into his eyes, and so now, when she does,
his expression surprises her. *He is listening.* For one brief
moment, she sees him. It's enough.

"I don't think it's Vibo you want to punish," she says,
her voice a little steadier. "He could be valuable. If Simo
can pay him off, so can you. That way we could still make
money at the baths *and* show we won't be put off so easily."
Felix raises his eyebrows. She has surprised him. Amara
tries to let go of her fear, imagines it rising from her body
like steam, evaporating. "As for Simo, I'm sure you could
teach him a lesson. Doesn't he run a bar? Perhaps it will
become less attractive to customers."

Felix's expression has barely changed, but she knows the
worst of his anger has passed. "You bark a lot for such a
little dog," he says. He nods at Thraso's swollen, bloodied
lip. "And what did you do to Balbus in return for this?"

"I broke his nose."

"More than that, I hope." Felix rises from his seat, and the two women step backward. Thraso stays still. Felix clicks his fingers at Victoria. She hurries over. He runs his hands over her, feeling her body, rearranging her clothes, a critical look on his face. It's not a man touching a woman, but a salesman checking his goods. He slaps her backside, hard. "Will you make me as much money as Simo's whores? Hmmm? Will you?" He gestures toward Amara without looking at her. "*That one* thinks so, but I'm not convinced." He takes Victoria's chin between his fingers. "What were you doing at the pool today? Gawping round the place like peasants at the games? Slouching about on your flat arses?"

Victoria can't shake her head; Felix is holding her too tightly.

"I've seen Drauca. That whore has the finest ass in Pompeii. And what do you have? What sort of tits are these?" He lets go of Victoria, pushing her face away. She sways but stays upright. "Simo may have paid Vibo off, but would Vibo have thrown you out if he thought any of you could fuck like Drauca?" He pauses, daring them to answer but neither do. "Our friend Simo's been bragging he sells the best cunt. So *you*"—Felix jabs a finger at both his women—"need to show Vibo he's talking shit. Vibo gets to fuck you whenever he likes, however he likes, no charge, all part of the service. If you're not his favorite girls after that, I'll know why." Amara glances at Victoria, trying to judge her reaction, but her face is blank as wax. "*Get moving!*" Felix shouts, making them both jump. "I want five denarii *each* from you lazy, fucking whores. Tell the others they'd better put some effort in."

Amara almost stumbles over Paris in the doorway in her haste to get out of the room, but Victoria is still quicker. They scuttle along the balcony, shoving their way down the stairs. Victoria reaches the bottom first. She turns round, blocking the door so Amara can't get back into the street. Amara steadies herself against the wall, jolted as much by Victoria's obvious anger as the sudden stop. "Why did you *do* that?" Victoria whispers. "Felix would have dropped Vibo. Why ask him to send us back? What sort of *idiot* are you?"

"Think of the money," she whispers back. The pair of them are rammed together at the bottom of the smelly, dark stairwell. "Think of all the rich men! Not like the dregs who come here."

"You're crazy. What do you think they're going to do? Turn up at the baths with bags of gold? They go there to screw, not find a bride!" Victoria's whisper grows louder with exasperation. "And now we have to put up with Vibo!"

Amara wants to explain that she's willing to try anything, no matter how far-fetched, however horrible, *anything* that might get them out of the brothel. Paris's sharp voice calls down. "What are you both doing?"

"Leaving," Victoria says, pulling the door toward her. They slip out into the rain and, within a couple of paces, are back inside.

Even though the sky is murky and overcast, it is another level of darkness in the brothel. The shutters in the small cells are locked to keep out the damp and the air is thick with smoke from incense and oil lamps. The space is not that much smaller than Felix's apartment above, but to Amara, it feels as narrow as a tomb.

Fabia is slopping out, trying to stop the latrine from overflowing with rainwater. The stench, never pleasant at this end of the corridor, is worse than usual. She looks up briefly to greet them, then bends back down to her task. Fabia used to work here as a she-wolf before she grew too old. She even gave birth to the wretched Paris in one of the cells. Fabia barely earns her keep now, but so far Felix has not thrown her out on to the streets to fend for herself.

"What did Felix say?" Cressa asks, as she and the other women emerge from Beronice's cell.

"He's going to give it another go with Vibo," Victoria says. "He wants to persuade him to take us back at the baths, which means the smelly prick will be coming here, and we've got to give him whatever he wants." She folds her arms, and Amara is expecting her to tell everyone whose fault this is. But she doesn't.

"Vibo's coming here?" Beronice says. "But he can't be!"

"Is he that bad?" Amara asks. Any lingering satisfaction she felt at impressing Felix is fast disappearing.

"You two not had him yet?" Cressa asks. Amara and Dido shake their heads. "He's the *worst*. Practically strangled me last time." She raises a hand to her throat, as if remembering his fingers around her neck.

Amara looks at Victoria, full of remorse, but she ignores her. "And the best part," Victoria says, "is that we've all got to earn Our Glorious Master five denarii *each* by tomorrow."

Cressa groans.

"Was he joking?" Beronice asks, her face hopeful. She's never very good at spotting when anyone is being humorous.

"Not joking," Victoria replies. "Safe to say he was *not* in a jolly mood."

"But we'll never manage it!" Beronice wails. "That's far too much."

"We'd better get as close to it as we can." Cressa's gaze wanders over to Fabia, still sluicing the latrine. "Though Venus herself would struggle to pick up punters in this weather."

"I'm not going fishing without food," Victoria says. "We can start at the Sparrow, have something to eat, and maybe after that, the rain won't be so bad."

The five women set about extinguishing most of the oil lamps to save fuel and limit the smoke. The constant smelly fug indoors means the paintings Felix recently paid for—endless sex scenes emblazoned round the top of the walls—are already smeared with soot. The picture above Amara's cell, of a woman being taken from behind, has a new grimy shadow across the bed. She bends down to put out the terracotta lamp burning beneath it. Like every other light in the brothel, it is modeled in the shape of a penis, flames flickering from the tip. One or two even have a small clay man attached, brandishing an enormous fiery erection. Felix finds it amusing, says the lamps get the customers in the mood. Amara hates them. As if they don't have enough cocks to put up with.

Gallus, Felix's freedman, is guarding the main door, directly opposite the Elephant. A tall, broad-shouldered man, he's better looking than Thraso, though just as brutal in a fight. He grasps hold of Beronice's arm as they try to pass. "Hang on," he says. "You can't all go out at once. One of you has to stay behind. What if I get a customer?"

"Can't you just come and grab one of us from the Sparrow?" Victoria says. "We'll only be up the road."

"No," Gallus replies. "You know Felix's orders." He gives Beronice a shove. "Back in there."

"What a shit," Victoria mutters, as they hurry along the pavement. "We'll have to take her something back."

"And Fabia," says Cressa. "She's looking so thin." The presence of the older woman, barely hanging on to existence, is like the shadow of a future none of them want to face. For Cressa, who is several years older than the rest of them, Amara suspects Fabia's fate is even more frightening.

The noise from the tavern opposite is loud even at this time of day. A gigantic mural blazes with color on its outside wall. It's an elephant surrounded by dancing pygmies and draped in snakes for good fortune. Underneath reads the boast: *Sittius Restored The Elephant!* The four women don't stop to go inside. Picking up customers at the Elephant isn't impossible, but Sittius rents rooms as well as serving food and wine. In this weather, his guests are more likely to head upstairs with one of the women who work at the inn than troop to a brothel in the rain.

The Sparrow is only a few paces further away. Its painted sign is drenched and darkened by the rain, but Amara can still make out the small bird surrounded by flowers, sitting on its innuendo-laden message. *The Sparrow is Satisfied, So may You be!* Nobody is loitering in the small square outside today. Instead, the stones shine white in the wet. When Amara first arrived in Pompeii, almost every scrap of pavement in front of the bar seemed to be taken up by drinkers, most standing and talking, some scribbling messages on the wall. She's seen graffiti about Felix on there before, even some reviews of the brothel. Plenty about Victoria. Nothing about her. She's not sure whether to be grateful for that or not.

They scurry inside, stamping their feet on the floor to shake off the rain. Victoria saunters over to the bar. She leans against its marble top, undoing her cloak and letting the edge of her yellow toga slip from her shoulder. There are whistles from a table in the corner.

"Busy morning, ladies?" The landlord, Zoskales, has a cloth draped round his neck and his face is shining with sweat. There's almost no room for him behind the counter, the wall is stacked with wine jars from floor to ceiling, but Amara's never seen him knock anything over. She has no idea what brought Zoskales all the way to Pompeii from Ethiopia, a place so distant she finds it almost impossible to imagine its existence. He likes to joke to customers it was love of his wife. Amara almost never sees her at the bar, more often in the street, harried by their three small children. She makes an unlikely Siren, luring her man halfway across the world.

"Not as busy as we'd like," Victoria says. "Anybody here need entertaining?"

"I'm sure if there are, you'll soon find them." Zoskales replies. Business between tavern and brothel is always brisk. "I'll get Nicandrus to bring you hot wine and stew."

The women make their way to a table near the two wolf-whistlers. Amara feels a flicker of fear. She would have crossed the street to avoid men like this in her hometown, her mother no doubt tugging her along to walk faster, whispering at her to look down. The two men are already drunk, dressed in the stained, weatherworn clothes of traveling traders. She sees the one closest to them is missing his four front teeth. His companion has a thick beard, curled and dressed with cheap oil to hide the gray.

Amara takes a seat on a bench by the wall, and Dido joins her. Victoria tries to pull up stools for her and Cressa, but the man with the missing teeth catches hold of her wrist. "Plenty of room for you to sit here." White spittle pools in the middle of his lips as he speaks. He spreads his legs out, slapping his knee. His companion snorts with laughter.

"Hope you aren't bothering the ladies." Nicandrus arrives with the tray. His tone is light, but he walks deliberately between the tables, forcing the man to let go.

"Oh, they're no trouble." Victoria smiles sweetly at the man who just grabbed her. She sits down, moving her cloak so he can see up the length of her thigh, before swiftly covering it. She smiles at him again, and he stares back, flushed. *First fish caught*, Amara thinks.

Nicandrus puts the bean stew down in front of Dido. "You look cold," he says.

"It's so wet out," she replies.

"Hope this warms you." He hovers, obviously hoping she will say something more. Amara has noticed the way Nicandrus watches Dido, seen his nervousness whenever an aggressive customer gets too close to her. She almost loves him for it.

"Nicandrus!" Zoskales bellows across the bar. "The wine won't serve itself!"

Dido bends her head to eat. She is hopeless at fishing. A few short months ago she was a respectable girl from a small suburb of Carthage, never leaving the house with her head uncovered, betrothed to a man chosen by her father, a secluded life of raising children and keeping house stretching out in front of her. Amara feels a pain in her chest. She has been enslaved longer than Dido, but not so long she doesn't remember the agony of losing her own freedom.

"You're not from Pompeii," Victoria says to the two traders. She is making quick work of her stew, dabbing with the bread around the rim, never one to let a potential customer slip away.

"Did you travel by sea?" Cressa says. "I've always wanted to travel by sea." She sips her wine, gazing at the bearded man as if he were the god Poseidon deigning to visit the mortals on shore.

"No. We came over from Puteoli," he says. "In the meat business. Goats, mainly."

"Bet *you* like a bit of meat," his companion adds, poking Victoria in the leg, the string of saliva between his lips lengthening as he grins. Victoria laughs, covering her mouth prettily with one hand, as if he just said something witty. Amara tries not to wince. Always the same. Why do men never have anything original to say to a prostitute? This pair are moments away from bragging about the size of their cocks.

The toothless man slaps his knee again, and this time Victoria perches on it. Cressa takes a long draught of wine, draining her cup to the bottom, then rises and drapes herself over his companion. Victoria nestles herself back closer against Toothless who is breathing heavily, but Amara notices she is careful not to let his hands wander too far up inside her clothes. There are limits to what Zoskales will tolerate in his bar.

The bearded man is kissing Cressa who breaks away to steal another sip of wine, this time from his cup. He gives her a slap, meant playfully perhaps, but hard enough to make her spill red liquid down her front. "Dirty little she-wolf," he says.

Cressa exchanges a quick glance with Victoria who bends to whisper in her lover's ear. After a pause, all four rise, the men a little unsteadily, and they leave the bar.

"That was fast," Nicandrus says, coming to collect the plates and glasses. "Even for Victoria." He has switched to speaking Greek, both his and Amara's mother tongue. Dido speaks it too, though Amara suspects Nicandrus doesn't realize that Punic, not Greek, is her first language.

"Felix told us to make five denarii each by tomorrow," Amara replies.

Nicandrus winces. "What brought that on?"

"It didn't go well at the baths this morning."

"Sorry to hear that," he says, looking at Dido who still hasn't spoken. "I hope nobody gave you trouble."

Dido shakes her head. Nicandrus smiles at her before heading back to the kitchens with his stack of dirty dishes.

Amara looks round the room, trying to see if there are any other potential customers. Three men engrossed in a game of dice ignore her, another drinking alone at the counter scowls when she finally manages to catch his eye.

Lunchtime is never the easiest hour. Victoria and Cressa did well to find a pair of willing men.

"We're going to have to go further afield, aren't we?" asks Dido, her slim shoulders sagging at the thought.

"There were a few sailors hanging around the Forum earlier," Amara says. "And the rain's easing off. It might not take us too long."

Dido looks at her, her eyes dark. There's a grief deep enough to drown in, if you let it rise unchecked. Amara never will. She stands up, waits for Dido to join her, holding out her hand with the poise and confidence that belonged to her other life.

3

"All other animals derive satisfaction from having mated;
man gets almost none."
—Pliny the Elder, *Natural History*

The sounds of Victoria entertaining the toothless man—
and his appreciation—are loud in the street. Felix gave
Victoria the room by the main door for precisely this reason,
knowing she would be a good sales pitch for passing trade.
Gallus slouches by the wall, looking bored.

"Can you give this to Beronice and Fabia?" Amara asks,
handing him half a small loaf. "We're going to try our luck
in the Forum."

"Sure," Gallus stuffs the bread into a fold in his cloak.
She hopes he won't eat it himself.

The air smells fresher after the downpour, though it's
left the narrow road looking more like a canal. Amara and
Dido walk carefully, holding their cloaks up to stop the
hems trailing in the water. In the winter, their profession
is harder to tell on sight. Hidden underneath the outer
layer, they wear togas, the uniform of men and prostitutes.

Amara used to feel naked without swathes of fabric shielding her body from head to foot, but over a slippery pavement when agility matters, it's almost a relief to have her legs free.

The journey gets easier when they reach the wide main street, the Via Veneria, which leads back to the Forum. They switch to walking side by side, rather than single file. Amara takes Dido's hand, squeezing it gently. "You can't look down all the time," she says. "I understand it's difficult, but we're meant to be attracting men's attention, not avoiding it."

"I know," Dido says. "But it's really hard."

"Not really. Your face is already doing half the work for you. You're easily the most beautiful woman in Pompeii." Amara has never seen anyone as lovely as Dido. Though it's a loveliness shot through with fragility, like the exquisite glass statue of the goddess Athene she remembers from her childhood. It was so precious her parents kept it high out of reach.

"I hate it," Dido says. "I *hate* men staring. I hate it when . . ." she trails off. "I guess I'll get used to it, all of it, eventually."

"No. Just endure it. Never get used to it."

They pass a shop selling jewelry, stopping a moment to admire the cut glass and cameos. "My mother wore a stone like that," Dido says, pointing.

"The red one?"

"Yes. She was wearing it the last time I saw her."

Amara knows the rest of this story. How pirates swept through Dido's hometown, stealing people to sell as slaves. Dido was kidnapped along with her younger cousin, her uncle killed trying to defend them. Her cousin died on the voyage from Carthage to Puteoli. Dido, like Amara, was completely alone when they first met, lined up, side by side, at the slave market. Amara wants to tell Dido that she may see her mother again one day but finds she can't. She doesn't believe it's true.

They have lingered too long. The shopkeeper comes out to try and persuade them to try on a string of cheap beads, becomes offended when they refuse. They hurry off toward the Forum at the top of the hill. It's even more crowded than earlier, the street sellers have wasted no time setting up again after the rain. Amara leads Dido toward one of the wide colonnades surrounding the square. "Just smile at everyone," she says. "Pretend you're Drauca."

"Is that what you do? Pretend you are someone else?"

"I am someone else. Amara isn't even my real name; Dido isn't yours."

They walk slowly arm in arm along the brightly painted walkway. For all her bravado, Amara's heart is beating fast. Nobody pays them much attention. Expensively dressed men, perhaps meeting to discuss the upcoming elections, brush past as if they are invisible. Hawkers ignore them, too busy with their own selling. They've no time to buy what the women are offering, not at this time of day. Undeterred, Amara suggests they try another circuit.

They walk again, pausing more often this time. Amara looks everyone in the eye, unwittingly carrying herself with the assurance of a young man rather than a flirt, while Dido occasionally manages a shy smile. They don't quite hit the mark, neither looking like prostitutes nor respectable women, but this time, a few glance at them out of curiosity. They loiter at a stall for leather shoes, catching its sharp scent of freshly tanned hide. The seller demonstrates the suppleness of a pair of sandals, twisting the straps in his fingers. One man starts to haggle and another, perhaps the customer's friend, stands waiting. Amara brushes lightly against him, as if by accident. He looks up and sees Dido who manages, somehow, not to look down. For a moment, Amara thinks he is going to see through them, realize they are two frightened women who haven't any idea what they are doing. But that's not what he sees. Encouraged that Dido hasn't walked off, he leans toward her. "Too rough for your lovely little feet, surely?"

"We don't have far to walk," Amara answers. "Only a street away." She stares straight into his eyes so he cannot mistake her meaning. "Why don't you and your companion join us?"

They are standing so close he can slip his hand inside Dido's cloak. She stiffens, gripping Amara's arm until it hurts. It takes all Amara's willpower not to slap him. She thinks of Felix, thinks of what he might do if they have nothing to give him tomorrow.

"That's enough," Amara says, more harshly than she intended. The man drops his hand, surprised. She forces herself into a false, lopsided smile. "Nobody handles goods for free, not if they aren't buying."

The man looks them both up and down. "Maybe later, *ladies*." He turns his back.

They walk away from the leather stall. This time it is Amara gripping Dido; she feels as if her legs are going to give way. "Do you need to sit down?" Dido asks. She shakes her head. "I had a bad feeling about him," Dido continues. "It's just as well."

"I shouldn't have let him touch you," Amara says. "I should have told him to fuck off."

Dido laughs, taking her by surprise. "The shortest-lived whores in the business. What an opening line that would be. *You can ALL fuck off!*"

Dido's laughter is contagious and soon they are both shaking, trying not to snort out loud, overtaken by hysteria. They clasp their hands round a pillar, swinging and leaning back, giggling like children. Neither care that they are attracting contemptuous stares, suddenly it doesn't seem to matter.

Eventually, they both calm down and straighten up. "Come on," Amara says. "Back to the beast hunt."

They walk with more confidence this time; Dido isn't even having to force her smile, although the men aren't to know it's at their expense. They stop by a group dicing near an archway to the indoor food hall. The air is heavy with the smell of meat and spices. They stand at the edge of the circle and watch. "Good throw," Amara says, as one man scores a six and scoops up a small pile of coins. His friend slaps him on the back.

The players seem to be split into two teams. They all look like out-of-town traders, speaking with a wealth of accents and languages as they argue over the money. Amara and Dido pretend fascination with the game, slowly leaning more toward the winning side, ingratiating themselves. A flask of wine is passed round, and Dido accepts a sip.

"Throw for us." One of the men pulls at Amara's arm. "Go on, you throw." The winners are in good spirits. After the game, they will need to spend that money somewhere.

Amara squats down and takes the dice. "For Venus," she says, looking up sidelong at the team who've claimed her. She rolls a five, higher than their rivals had just managed. The men cheer.

"It doesn't count," says one of the losers, face scrunched in anger, watching eager fingers rake through his last few coins. "You can't get a whore to throw."

"You can get a whore to do whatever you like," Amara retorts. "That's the whole point."

Her new friends fall about laughing, one slipping his arm round Amara as she stands up, but her opponent is unamused. "Cheating little Greek," he spits. The loser gathers up his remaining money, gesturing at his three companions to do the same. They hurry away, and Amara and Dido are left with the winners. Five men whose attention has now turned from dice to other games. Her heartbeat quickens. She would prefer not to be outnumbered like this.

"Pompeii has brought you good fortune," Dido says, inclining her head in a way that reminds Amara of Victoria. "It pays to serve Venus in the goddess's own city."

"You're from Africa," one of the men says, noticing her accent.

"Venus has a wide dominion," Amara replies. "And the road to her house is short, if you care to join us." The man who urged her to throw the dice still has his arm tightly round her waist, his fingers kneading her flesh. There is no way she and Dido could fight this gang off if the men decided to cut the transaction short by taking without paying. The food hall is still being repaired from earthquake damage, and there are plenty of deserted arches where building work has paused.

Dido steps away from the group. "We share a home with three others," she says. "Five women! Such a happy chance. You must celebrate with our friends; the goddess of love deserves some thanks after all."

The men exchange glances, perhaps weighing up the possibility that they are going to be led into a den of thieves by a honeyed bait. "Perhaps you've seen our home?" Amara says. "We live by the Elephant."

"The Wolf Den!" one of them laughs. "We've got an invite to the town brothel!"

"Is that what you are?" The man holding Amara loosens his grip, turning her toward him, so he can see her face. "A little Greek she-wolf?"

His skin is tanned, cracked across the cheeks from being out in all weathers, and there is a mark at the bottom of his chin where it must have been nicked by a knife. She knows this man will be no stranger to violence, but then, none of them are. Amara decides to roll the dice again. She leans in to kiss him lightly on the lips then pushes him away, darting just out of reach. "Wolves from Greece, Carthage, Egypt and Italy," she says over her shoulder, beckoning him to follow. "All worshippers of Venus Pompeiiana."

Dido swiftly joins her, and they hold hands, walking down the colonnade toward the Via Veneria, aware the men are close behind. "We need to get there quickly," Dido whispers, her eyes wide with fear.

"Don't run," Amara says. She looks back over her shoulder, smiling at the man who until recently had her in an iron grip. He and the other dice players look flushed with excitement rather than anger, enjoying the thrill of the chase.

They weave past the shops and the grand houses on the Via Veneria. The road is still flooded with water. One of the five players, a short, brawny man with a patched cloak, grabs Dido and makes as if to throw her in. She screams and the men roar with laughter. The man sets her back down as a mule cart approaches, and Amara seizes her hand, dragging her further along the pavement.

Amara doesn't think she has ever been happier to hear the raucous chorus from the Elephant as they round the corner to the brothel. She feels ready to collapse with relief at Gallus's feet. He collects the money from their five customers. As Amara steps over the threshold, she glances down at his left hand for the signal. Three fingers. Only three women are in. Amara's heart contracts.

Beronice is waiting in the corridor, wreathed in smoke from the lamps.

"There's Egypt!" shouts the short man, grabbing her roughly round the hips. "Where are the other two?"

"On their way," Amara replies, draping her arms round the man with the marked chin. "Fabia will go and fetch them." The old woman scurries past her, hood pulled up to her face, and darts into the street.

"For fuck's sake, you promised five!" The two men left without women are furious.

Amara's customer has already pulled off most of her clothes and is pushing her toward an empty cell. He breaks from kissing her to catch hold of one of his angry companions, drawing him closer. "Stop complaining! You know I always share."

The stone bed is hard against Amara's back; there is a terrible ringing in her ears, the rush of blood pounding in her head, the smell of the strange man too close to her, his grip even tighter than she remembers in the Forum, the movement she cannot stop and cannot control. She is drowning.

Amara tries to focus on the curtain pulled across the doorway, count its folds until he has finished, anything to quell the unbearable panic. But the second man is blocking her view, his face contorted. He grips her thigh, stopping her from twisting away. She cannot scream. She cannot breathe. Terror is crushing the air from her lungs. Then the curtain opens. Cressa slips inside the room.

"No need to wait," she whispers, running her fingers through the second man's hair.

He pushes her off. "I want that one." He points at Amara. Cressa moves so she is standing between them.

"No, you don't." Cressa slides her hands around his hips, pulling him closer. He tries to resist, but the lure of her naked body is too much. He gives in, allows Cressa to lead him away. Cressa glances back as they leave. The kindness in her eyes speaks another language, reaching Amara across the darkness.

Amara starts to cry. The man with the scarred chin collapses heavily against her. He is finally finished. For a moment, she is forced to lie squashed beneath his weight, then he raises himself on his elbows and steps back from the bed. Amara pulls her legs in toward herself, unable to stop weeping. For a moment, the man stares at her, and she cannot tell if the look of disgust is for her or himself. He leaves without speaking.

4

"Take one who through long years would slave for you;
Take one who'd love with purest loyalty."
—Ovid, *Amores* 1.3

Nighttime at the brothel passes like a scene from Hades: the endless procession of drunken men, the smoke, the soot, angry shouting, pottery smashing, the sound of Dido weeping, the pungent smell of Victoria's potion as she washes out her insides, the rasp of Beronice's snoring. When the hour is too late for even the most dedicated Pompeiian to venture out in search of sex, Amara lies alone in the darkness of her cell, unable to sleep, suffocated by rage.

She is woken the next day by Victoria's singing. It's like music from another world, the light earthy voice full of hope and good humor. She sits up in bed.

"Couldn't you let us sleep in for once?" Beronice shouts.

"Look at the sunshine," Victoria calls back. "It's like the Festival of Flora!"

Amara smiles in spite of herself. She swings her feet onto the floor, wrapping the blanket round her shoulders.

Beronice and Cressa are already out in the corridor, yawning and rubbing their eyes. The three of them head to Victoria's cell. Amara glances up as she goes in. The painting of two lovers above the door shows the woman on top, a gift from Felix to his hardest-working whore.

"You woke us up!" Beronice says. Victoria is already dressed and styling her hair. It falls in a waterfall of curls about her shoulders. She does not look like a woman who has been up all night, indulging men and deflecting violence. Her eyes are sparkling at the prospect of a new day. Amara has never met anyone like Victoria.

"Where's Dido?" Victoria asks. "She can't have slept through you lazy lot yelling and complaining."

The four of them head to Dido's cell. She is lying on the bed, her face to the wall. Cressa sits next to her, bends and kisses her on the forehead. It is not only Amara and Nicandrus who feel protective of Felix's youngest she-wolf. "It's morning sweetheart," Cressa says.

Dido sits up. Her face is wet, and her eyes are red from crying. Cressa hugs her, stroking her back. "Were they shits?" she asks.

"One of them broke all the lamps," Dido says, pointing to a pile of pottery shards that she's swept into a corner. "He really frightened me."

"Nasty, *shitty* little man." Cressa's voice wavers and for a moment Amara thinks she is going to struggle to keep her composure.

Victoria sits on the other side of Dido, quickly taking over. "You can't let *him* bother you," she says, smiling. "Not Mr. GarlicFarticus."

"What a stupid name," says Beronice, looking doubtful. "He can't *really* be called that."

"But he is!" Victoria insists, her face solemn. "It's Mr. GarlicFarticus who runs that fast-food place near the baths!"

"He *was* kind of smelly." Dido looks a little brighter as she starts to play the game.

"And garlicky. And farty." Victoria nods. "Yes, definitely him. Mr. GarlicFarticus."

"I never knew he was called that," Beronice says, wonderingly. "I thought he was called Manlius."

"Of course it was Manlius, you idiot!" Cressa snorts.

They all laugh. Even Beronice smiles. Amara wonders for a moment if she might have played dumb on purpose.

"I think we should write him a message on the wall," Victoria says. "In case he ever comes back." She bends down and hands a shard of pottery to Amara. "What shall we say? I know! *Thrust SLOWLY.*"

"Shall I write it in Greek?" Amara asks.

"What's the point in that?" Victoria retorts. "We want the smelly idiot to read it, don't we?"

Amara scratches the motto on the wall. They all sit looking at it when she is finished, smirking with satisfaction.

"I'll tell you who does thrust slowly," Beronice says, her face sly. She pauses, making sure all four are giving her their full attention.

"Go on then," Cressa says. "Who is this Apollo?"

"Gallus." Beronice beams. "I love him."

"*Gallus?*" Victoria shrieks. "He's a terrible lay!"

"You've not even slept with him!" Beronice says, wounded. She looks round at her friends' embarrassed faces. "Have you?"

"We all have, sweetheart," Cressa says kindly.

Beronice flushes. "Well, it's *me* he loves. He told me he will buy my freedom one day. He loves me! He's going to marry me, so I don't have to do this anymore. We spent a whole hour together when you were all out fishing. He's really kind and loving and gentle and caring. He even asked what I wanted!"

Amara struggles to picture the oafish Gallus being any of these things. She is about to ask Beronice if he gave her the bread yesterday but decides the answer might be too painful.

"Beronice," Victoria says, her voice low with warning. "You didn't fuck him for free, did you?" There's silence. Beronice pouts, not meeting anyone's eye. "You idiot!" Victoria hisses. "What if Felix finds out? You can't spend your days rolling around with Gallus for nothing! He has to pay Felix. The prick's just playing you; he's *using* you!"

"He doesn't want to pay because he's saving up to buy me!" Beronice says, stung. "And who's going to tell Felix? Not any of you I hope!"

"Of course none of us would tell Felix," Amara says. "But are you sure Gallus isn't taking advantage?"

"He loves me," Beronice repeats stubbornly. "He told me he's never met *anyone* as kind as me, that he can really talk to me, because I listen, and I care about him." Victoria rolls her eyes. "Why do you have to make everything dark and ugly and twisted?" Beronice snaps at her. "At least I have better taste than *you*." The last word is said with such venom that Amara is surprised, but before Victoria can retaliate, Cressa interrupts.

"Nobody is trying to ruin things for you," she says to Beronice. "We just want you to look after yourself. That's all." Beronice frowns and turns away from her, not willing to be won round yet.

Cressa widens her eyes at Victoria, tilting her head at Beronice, willing her to make amends. Victoria sighs. "Of course we're happy if Gallus loves you," she says. "But you need to make him pay. He's stealing from Felix! That's much too risky—you know it is. For him as much as you."

Beronice looks crestfallen. "That's just typical of him," she says. "Putting himself in danger for me."

Victoria looks as if she might explode at this version of Gallus the Hero, but Cressa changes the subject. "Does anyone know how much money we made last night?"

"Thraso took over at the door," Victoria replies. "I spoke to him before turning in. The last count was just over sixteen denarii."

"That's a relief," says Amara, thinking of Felix. "It's not as far off as I thought it might be."

"We've got to pay to replace those though," Dido points at the broken lamps.

Cressa bends over to look at the heap of smashed-up clay cocks. "That's at least three."

"Four," Dido says.

"We'll have to pay for them ourselves," Victoria says. "We can't ask Felix for the money, not after yesterday." Amara feels some of the darkness from last night returning.

Felix gives them such a paltry allowance, barely enough for food, especially when they chip in for Fabia. None of them are ever going to save enough for their freedom that way. "It can't be helped," Victoria says, as if she can hear Amara's thoughts. "We'll make it back."

Amara stares at their fresh graffiti. *Thrust SLOWLY!* It doesn't seem as amusing anymore. Cressa gets to her feet. "We should head to the baths, get cleaned up. Unless you lot want to waft about stinking of man all day."

It's a mid-morning ritual at the brothel, their trip to the women's baths. Amara suspects she isn't the only one who finds it emotionally as well as physically cleansing. "I'll stay behind," Victoria offers. "Somebody else had better go for the lamps."

There's a pause. "I'll go," Amara offers. She is just as desperate as the others for a wash, but she owes Cressa for rescuing her, Dido had a terrible night and Beronice was trapped inside most of yesterday. Although given her affair with Gallus, this may not have been such a sacrifice after all.

"Take my savings," says Cressa. "We can split the cost when you get back."

Fabia is sweeping the floor when they step out into the corridor. Not for the first time, Amara wonders where she slept that night. She has found her huddled on the back doorstep before, wrapped in nothing but her cloak. The old woman smiles at them. "Don't you all look beautiful," she says.

Fabia helps the four who are going out to tidy up their hair. Even though they are not fishing, Felix hates his women to wander about town looking a mess. "You'll never need paste for your lips," Fabia says to Amara, as she straightens up her yellow toga, fastening it with a cheap pin. "They're bright as pomegranate seeds. You're so lucky." Amara wonders what Fabia looked like when she was young. Her face is not just lined, but beaten, like the ruts in the road where the carts have repeatedly run over the stones. It can't help that she has such a shit for a son.

"Can I bring you back anything to eat?" Amara asks.

"Gallus brought me some bread yesterday," Fabia replies. "Don't you worry."

Thraso is slumped half asleep on the doorstep when they leave. His lip looks a little better than yesterday, but his nose is still swollen. He asks where they are all going and heaves himself up to check whether the tale of broken lamps is true. Once his surly permission has been granted, they set off. Amara says goodbye to the others a few paces down the road at the entrance to the women's baths then makes for the pottery shop on the Via Pompeiiana, Cressa's leather purse tied around her waist.

Last night was dry, and the water level on the road has dropped. It no longer resembles a canal. Instead, the wet surface shines silver in the glare of the late morning light. The town is already busy. It's not often Amara has an excuse to venture out by herself. She lingers as she passes the doorways of Pompeii's wealthiest homes, stealing a look inside whenever a tall wooden door is left ajar. She catches the sparkle of fountains, glimpses of winter gardens and elaborate mosaics which sweep up to the edge of the street. Her parent's house in Aphidnai was not so grand, but some of the homely touches—a woman sitting spinning in the atrium, a sleeping dog—remind her of what she has lost.

The potter's shop is not too far along the Via Pompeiiana. It's impossible to miss with its huge mural of Venus surrounded by lamps on the front wall. The painting picks out the warmth of the flames on the goddess's features, the light reflected in her eyes. Behind her is a pink shell and the pale blue of the sea. Small potters work at her feet, shaping lamps and statues, feeding a tiny kiln, a miniature representation of the business Amara is about to enter.

The shop front is shallow and apparently empty. Through a doorway at the back she can see slaves and the red glow of the kilns. Somebody will be back in a moment. Around her, every possible surface is lined with lamps. She turns to look, careful not to knock into anything. Some are beautiful, so much lovelier than the ones she is here to buy. Amara picks up a small glazed light from the nearest shelf, gently stroking its surface with her finger. An image of Pallas Athene is stamped on it, an owl's face on her breastplate.

"That's one of mine."

She looks up. A slave is watching her. Amara hurries to put the lamp back, embarrassed. "Sorry."

"No, I mean I designed it." The slave laughs. "I don't *own* any of them." He is very good-looking, Amara realizes. Slim with dark hair and a friendly, open face. *He looks nothing like Felix*, she thinks. Then she wonders why the comparison would even matter to her. He walks over, takes the lamp back down from the shelf and turns it over. "That's my mark," he says, touching a symbol on the back, the Greek letter *M*. He has a Greek accent too. He almost sounds like he could have come from her hometown.

"Is Pallas Athene your goddess?" Amara asks, switching to Greek.

He is delighted. "Athenian?"

"No, I'm from Aphidnai." She smiles back.

"The town with the beautiful Helen of Troy."

"You've been there?" Amara stares at the potter's slave, wondering who he might have been if they had met in their past lives. Did he ever go to her father when he was sick? Was he always enslaved?

"I spent a little time there when I was a child. Many years ago now. I'm from Athens. From Attica."

Attica. So much in a single word. Pride in where she's from, pain for what she's lost. Home. It feels closer, suddenly, standing next to this stranger. "What happened?" she blurts out. "Why are you here?"

He looks startled. Slaves do not usually ask each other about the past without invitation. Nobody wants their grief dragged up unexpectedly into the light.

"My family ran out of money," he says. "And I was the last thing they had to sell." His voice is unchanged, and he has the same easy manner as before, but she can feel his sadness. Amara wants to tell him that she understands, that the story of her life is the same, but she can't find the words. He looks embarrassed by her silence. "Is this the lamp you wanted?" he asks.

She blushes. Her cloak is hiding her gaudy toga. He has no idea what she is. And now she is going to have to ask this beautiful Athenian stranger for a load of cock lamps.

"My master lives opposite the Elephant," she says slowly. There is a flicker of understanding on his face. She plows on. "My name in this country is Amara. I used to worship Pallas Athene, but since I was brought here, I have been subject to Venus. I have no choice. She is the goddess my master serves."

"Amara," the stranger says, putting his hand over hers, stopping her from continuing. "I understand. None of us has a choice here." They stare at each other. Then he moves away, as if only just noticing he is touching her.

"Menander!" a voice calls from the back. "What are you doing out there? I only wanted. . . . Ah, I see, a customer. Forgive me, forgive me." Rusticus, the potter, is standing in the doorway. He frowns at Amara, trying to place her. She stares back. In her mind's eye she sees his large naked ass, bobbing up and down, glimpsed through a half-open curtain. He is one of Victoria's regulars. "Well." He chuckles, recognition finally dawning. He turns to Menander. "No wonder you were taking your time." He leans one elbow on the counter, his previous posture of respectful service gone. "And what can we do for *you*, little wolf."

Amara is so hot that she feels on fire. "Four lamps, not glazed, of . . ." She stops, not wanting to say the words. "Of Priapus." Rusticus smirks, enjoying her humiliation. She has a flash of anger and defiance. "So that will be four cocks," she adds loudly. There's a snort. She turns and stares at Menander. Is he *laughing*? He sees her face, and his expression changes instantly.

"I'm sorry, I didn't mean . . ."

She sweeps past him to the counter, as if he hadn't said a word. "My master does not like to be kept waiting," she says

46

coldly to Rusticus, as if she has been sent by the emperor and not some small-town pimp.

"Of course," Rusticus replies, snapping his fingers at Menander who hurries to gather up the cock lamps from a shelf in the corner. Amara says nothing. She stands rigid, bristling with fury, as Menander wraps the lamps in pieces of old cloth, tying them together to make it easier for her to carry. He is trying desperately to catch her eye, but she refuses to look at him, even when he hands the bundle over. Rusticus is struggling not to laugh. "Never mind," he says in a mock whisper to his slave. "Maybe you can save your pennies and speak to the fine lady for longer next time."

Amara hands over Cressa's money and strides out of the shop without thanking either of them. She walks quickly along the street, clutching the lamps to her chest, hating herself. She is no different from Beronice, swallowing Menander's charm, as if he would be interested in *talking* to a she-wolf. Life at the brothel is hard enough, without making a fool of herself.

5

"Grab your slave girl whenever you want:
it's your right to use her"
—Pompeii graffiti

When she gets back, it's Paris on the door. The way he stands, scrawny chest puffed out and legs akimbo, makes him recognizable long before she reaches the brothel. It's rare for Paris to be put on door duty; he's far too slight to make a convincing guard. He looks years younger than his age and is desperate to grow a beard, hoping that then Felix will finally release him from his duties as a prostitute. The only person in the world who loves Paris is his mother, Fabia, and he treats her with a cruelty that makes Amara's heart ache.

"Felix wants you," he says as she approaches.

"Did he say why?"

Paris shrugs, trying to imitate Thraso's easy indifference. Instead, he looks like a petulant teenager.

Amara hurries into the brothel. "Felix is asking for me," she says, handing the bundle of lamps to Victoria before she can open her mouth for a greeting. "I've not even had a bath. He *hates* that. He's going to be so angry!"

"You can borrow some of my rose water." Victoria nods toward her cell as she starts unwrapping the lamps. "Just help yourself. And try not to worry. He almost never asks for a full service, not at this time of day."

Amara finds the small bottle in Victoria's cell, dabs a tiny amount of the rose perfume on her neck. She knows one of Victoria's customers gives her various potions as a tip and doesn't want to take too much. The thought of climbing the stairs to see Felix again makes her feel nauseous. It had confused her when she first came to Pompeii, why he wanted any of his women. He never seemed prompted by desire, let alone anything more tender. After a few weeks, she understood. All of them are afraid of him, both dreading his summons and dreading being ignored. Like everything else about Felix—it is the exercise of power.

Victoria comes into the cell, pinches her cheeks to give them more color and fusses with her hair. "What if it's something else?" Amara asks. "What if he's angry with me?"

"It will all be fine," Victoria says. "I promise. Just don't keep him waiting."

Paris lets her in, taking the keys from his cloak as they stand together in the street. "You're to go straight through to his study," he says, shoving the door open and walking off, as if stopping to talk to her would add a terrible burden to his busy day.

Amara is left alone in the hallway, surprised not to be sent to the bedroom. She wonders what Felix might mean by it. She walks up the stairs and creeps round the corridor to the end. She stops, knocks gently, then carefully opens the door. To her confusion, she sees he already has company. She is about to step back, but Felix raises his hand in a gesture for her to stay. His client turns round to see who it is. When he understands he's being watched by a prostitute, he flinches. "If this isn't a good time . . ." he says.

"Please continue," Felix replies, offering no explanation for the presence of one of his women. Amara slides into the room. "You were explaining why you want to take out a second loan without paying for the first."

"I can offer you this," the man says, taking out a pair of earrings. "They belong to my mother-in-law. Pure silver, made in Herculaneum."

Felix takes the earrings, examining them briefly, before dropping them on his desk. "This will cover the previous debt. What about the new loan?"

"They're worth far more than just the first loan!" the man protests. "This should cover at least half the value of the next one too!"

"They cover the first loan, but not the interest."

"Please, Felix," the man says, lowering his voice. "Please be reasonable. I can get you more money as soon as the shipment is in. Just give me a little time. You know I always come through."

Felix sighs, like a disappointed father. "We've been doing business for so many years Celer. And still you take me for a fool." He points at the earrings. "I'm assuming Salvia wants them back?" Celer is silent. "And I imagine it would be a terrible shock for your parents-in-law if my men had to turn up at their fabric store *uninvited* and take back what you owe me in yards of silk?"

"Felix, *please*, you can't, you know that I—"

"You can have ten denarii," Felix says. "Until the shipment comes in. Then if you've kept up with the other payments, we can consider that second loan."

"But that won't cover the earrings!"

"These"—Felix says, picking up the jewelry and dangling them at him—"are for the first loan. The offer of ten denarii is pure generosity on my part. Take it or take nothing."

Amara watches as Celer signs another contract, scratching his name in the wax. Felix looks bored. When Celer is finished, Felix folds the tablets and takes out the money from a drawer. Celer thanks him, his voice almost inaudible. His face, when he passes Amara, is flushed with humiliation.

Felix and Amara are left alone. He files away Celer's agreement, ignoring her for some minutes while he's busy at his desk. She knows better than to open her mouth.

"Yesterday, I asked what happened at the baths," he says, finally looking up. "I didn't ask for advice. What made you offer it?"

His tone has not changed since he spoke to Celer. She can read nothing in his face. "I must have misunderstood what you wanted," she says.

"No, you didn't." He waves her lie away with a flick of his hand. "And then you recommended I do a deal with Vibo, a man who's hated by every whore in Pompeii. Why?"

"Vibo is the only way into the private baths," Amara says, trying to match his blank face with her own. "We can earn more money there. The men are much richer."

"So you want to suck a superior class of cock, is that it?" Felix laughs. She knows better than to react to his sarcasm.

"What a selfless whore you are. I can't believe you're trying to make me richer." He glances at the silver earrings which he left out on his desk. "You can't think you would see that extra money? You're not as smart as you look if you imagine I'm going to share the profits." Felix beckons her closer, his manner conspiratorial. "So tell me, what was it about?"

Amara is wary. "I don't know."

"Come along," Felix says, "I'm not going to be cross. I'm asking because I'm interested. So tell me."

Amara twists her hands, still uncertain what to say. They have never had a conversation like this. Often when she sees Felix, he doesn't talk at all. Except, of course, to tell her afterward how bad her performance was, how he cannot imagine why any man would pay money for *that*. Even though she hates him, his contempt is still wounding. It hurts, the way he touches her as if she were nothing. And now he's gazing into her eyes as if he's interested in what she has to say, as if what she thinks is important. All her instincts tell her it's a ruse, but she's desperate for it to be true. Perhaps she can reach him.

"Why did you buy me?" she asks. "I was sold as a concubine. I'm educated, play the lyre. I know that cost you more. If you didn't want all those skills for yourself, then why? What sort of investment am I if I grind out the rest of my days in the cells downstairs?" Amara thinks of Gallus, of the self-assured way he stands when he's getting customers to pay up at the door. She tries to hold herself a little taller. "I could make you a lot more money than that, if you let me."

For an unbearable period of time, Felix says nothing. Amara waits, the fear she has tried to squash mushrooming in the silence. "Why did I buy you?" He rests his elbows on the table, cupping his chin in his hands. It's a gesture of familiarity, almost as if they were equals. "It wasn't for your marvelous tits; let's be honest, we've both seen better. And I wasn't dazzled by your beauty." He pauses, letting his words sink in as he looks her up and down. "You weren't much prettier than all the other girls standing naked in a row. You're no Dido." Felix stares into her eyes. "But I couldn't look anywhere else from the moment I saw you. There you were, being auctioned off as a common whore, but you could have been the goddess Diana, from the way you held yourself. As if at any moment, you would call on your hunting dogs to tear apart every man who had *dared* to see you naked."

Felix crosses from behind the desk. Amara watches him walk toward her, forcing herself to stay still, even though she wants to back away. When he is very close, he puts his hands lightly on her neck. "And you would, wouldn't you? *Tear them all apart.*" Felix tightens his grip, pressing down on her throat. "Would you like to tear me apart?" Amara struggles to breathe, and dark spots form at the sides of her vision. Panic seizes her, and she puts her hands over his, unable to supress the instinct to claw them away. He lets go, and she collapses over the desk, gasping for air. "Do you know what happens to people who betray me, Amara?" She nods her head, unable to speak. "You do, don't you? You didn't hesitate to encourage me to punish Simo." Amara is slowly getting her breath back but doesn't dare stand upright. She stays crouched over the desk, leaning as far away from him as possible. "You are not the goddess Diana." Felix circles round her. "Or *Artemis*, as you Greeks would have her." He draws out the foreign words, mocking her accent. "*Porna eis*. You are a common whore. Even if you do play the lyre." He pushes her down on the floor so that she is kneeling in front of him. "And I own you. Don't ever think you are cleverer than me."

In the women's baths with Victoria, the steam cannot hide her tears. Amara wants to dive under water, for it to swallow her so that she never has to surface. She stands by a large communal basin, sweating in the heat. Victoria gently wipes Amara's face, cupping cool water in her hands, splashing her friend's cheeks.

"You can't let every encounter upset you like this," she says, her fingers gentle on Amara's skin. "It's just fucking. It's just your body; it's not *you*. You're strong. I know you are."

It's noisier and more crowded than at Vibo's, and the decoration is nothing like as grand, but even without a huge warm pool to soak in, the women's baths are still more relaxing. Men cannot come here, not even Felix. "It's not every encounter. Felix is different," Amara replies. "It's not just what he does, though that's bad enough. It's what he says. How does he know what will hurt the most?"

Victoria splashes herself with water, sloshing it over her neck and arms. "Felix is different, you're right." She is jostled by a pair of matrons flanked by slaves carrying private tubs. The matrons settle themselves nearby, taking pains not to look at the women at the basin. They saw how Victoria and Amara rubbed each other down earlier, too poor to have attendants do it for them. "You might be rich," Victoria mutters, too quiet for the other women to hear. "But look at your arses." Amara doesn't laugh. She would exchange beauty for money in a heartbeat. "I know what you mean," Victoria continues. "Felix gets under your skin. He does it to everyone. It's not just you."

"I thought he was going to kill me."

"Oh, he would never do that!" Victoria says indignantly. "Think of the money he would lose!" She peers at Amara's neck and its faint row of bruises. "Very unusual for him to leave any marks though. You must have made him really angry."

"Everything makes him angry!" Amara says. "Just looking at him sends him into a rage. He's impossible."

"You did go on and on yesterday, telling him what to do. He hates that."

"I gave him good advice," Amara says. "What was there to be angry about?"

"Sweetheart," Victoria says. "He does not want advice from his whores."

"He told me I can't even . . ." Amara falters, shame preventing her from repeating exactly what Felix had said. "He said I don't give him enough pleasure. That I should ask *you* about it, because you know what you're doing."

"He said that?" Victoria is clearly pleased by the compliment.

"He said you're the only one who really knows what they're doing," Amara says. She does not add what else

Felix said. That Victoria was half as pretty but had ten times the skill. "I think he actually enjoys it with you. He didn't say so, but I got that impression."

"So he should," Victoria says. "I put the work in. Not that you don't," she adds, quickly. Amara is surprised at how happy praise from Felix has made Victoria. It saddens her to think of the power he has. Two more matrons and a teenage girl bump up beside them at the basin, talking loudly about the elections. One of their husbands is standing. The girl, probably a daughter, looks bored and uncomfortable. She glances shyly over at the two beautiful she-wolves, clearly unaware of who they are. "I think we'll save the advice on technique until we get home," Victoria says. "But you shouldn't be too upset. He might have been angry today, but over time, he will like you better for not being a coward. He likes a bit of spirit." She blushes, looking for a moment as shy as the young girl beside them. "He's told me before that's why I'm *his favorite whore*." She says the last words quietly, close to Amara's ear, so their neighbors can't hear.

Amara suddenly feels claustrophobic in the hot, crowded room. She steps away from the basin. Victoria follows. "The only reason *I'd* want to be his favorite," she says, glancing over her shoulder, "is so he wouldn't see the knife coming when I kill him."

Victoria laughs, thinking she's joking.

6

"If anyone wants a fuck, he should look for Attice;
she costs 16 asses"
—Graffiti near Pompeii's Marine Gate

The winter sky is clear, the sun high overhead, and although there is little warmth from its blinding light, the brightness is cheering. Amara enjoys the feeling of being clean, even takes some pleasure in Fabia doing up her hair. The old woman's fingers are deft and gentle. In a different life she could have been a skilled maid serving a grand mistress. Amara tries to let go of the morning's pain. *Like the bruises*, she tells herself, *the humiliation will fade.*

They discuss where to go fishing and decide on the harbor. It's always good for customers, and the walk will be a pleasure in the sunshine. Cressa offers to stay behind. "I've got Fabia for company," she says, refusing the others' gratitude. "We can put our feet up together; it will be lovely." Fabia looks thrilled by the compliment. The old woman is as starved of affection as she is of food. Amara knows Cressa is in for a dreary afternoon of sitting in the dark, hearing endless tales of the wretched Paris's childhood.

"Cressa's so kind," Amara says as they start off down the street. "She's a born mother."

"Don't ever say that!" Beronice looks horrified.

"Why not?"

"Cressa *is* a mother," Victoria answers, hurrying them further away from the brothel. "She had a little boy. Felix sold him last year when he was three." Amara and Dido gasp, and Victoria nods, her expression grim. "We were all amazed he let her keep him that long; it would have been kinder to have exposed the baby when it was born. Before she got attached."

"That's terrible!" Dido exclaims. "Poor Cressa."

"He was called Cosmus," Victoria says. "Sweet enough child. Fabia used to have him when we were working. Cressa adored him. I didn't think she was going to survive when Thraso took the boy away. Felix had to lock her upstairs, she was screaming so much. She was up there for days. And then after she came down, she never spoke about Cosmus again."

"I don't think she can bear to," Beronice says.

Amara thinks about the way Cressa saved her from the dice player, her kindness, her endless patience with Fabia. She is amazed Cressa has any compassion left to give after losing her child. "But she's always so thoughtful," Amara says. "I would never have guessed she carried all that grief. I had no idea."

Beronice and Victoria exchange glances. "I think she finds ways of drowning it out," Victoria says. "You must have seen how much she drinks."

"You can't blame her though," Beronice adds quickly. "And she doesn't drink that much. Not really."

"That's why I always use my herbs at the end of the night," Victoria says. "Kill off everything inside before it can take hold."

They have reached the Via Veneria and walk in pairs along the wider pavement. Victoria and Amara in front, Beronice and Dido behind. Victoria changes the subject from Cressa, as if eager to leave their friend's sadness behind. She points out the clothes of the wealthy women who pass them by, admiring the styles she likes, laughing at the ones she doesn't. The journey to the harbor is short, but the roads are so busy it takes a while to arrive. The closer they get to the sea, the fresher the air becomes. Amara can almost taste the salt.

They stop to buy their one meal of the day at a roadside stall outside town. Victoria chooses, picking out bread, olives and anchovies, the dried fish stiff with brine. After walking a little further downhill, they reach the water. It is even busier here, merchants are unloading, there's the yell of sailors and the scrape of cargo, and the constant slap of the waves against the stone walls. A little way off from the busy docks, a colonnade stretches round in a semicircle. From its roof, statues of the gods look out at incoming ships, while in the water itself, at the center of the harbor, is a giant marble column. Venus Pompeiiana stands naked at the top. She gazes out over the vast expanse of blue, the guardian of her town.

The she-wolves find a sunny patch on the colonnade, dangling their legs over the side. They eat their food quickly to avoid the gulls that swoop overhead. Victoria watches a troop of oar slaves walk up onto the docks for a brief respite. They stand bent and blinking in the light. "What a miserable life that would be." Victoria says. She stretches back, palms resting on the warm stone, her face to the sun. "Who is luckier than us in Pompeii right now? All this time to enjoy ourselves, no back-breaking loads to carry." She swings her legs up. "I shouldn't even be alive. You know I was a rubbish-heap baby? Left out to die in the shit and the fish guts. But here I am. Here we all are."

"Here we all are," Amara says. "Four penniless slaves, sucking off idiots for bread and olives. What a life."

Victoria laughs. "So bitter! You can't still be mad about Felix," she says. "That was ages ago."

"Not just Felix," Amara replies, looking at one of the larger merchant ships navigating its way into dock. She thinks about her own voyage over from Greece. The cold nights out on deck under the stars, rammed together with other slaves. The smell of vomit, the weeping, the terror of what awaited should they survive the journey. "You started life on a rubbish heap," Amara says, "but I had a home. I was a doctor's daughter. I had a *life*." She has never told anyone in Pompeii—except Dido—about her past.

"Your father was a doctor?" Beronice asks in surprise. "What are you doing in a brothel?"

The doctor's daughter. The role she inhabited for the first half of her life. A cocoon as warm as her parents' love, shielding her from the world. "He died," Amara says. She knows the others will respect her silence if she leaves it here, but now she's opened the door to the past, she doesn't want to close it. "My mother struggled on alone for a few years, helped out by family. Then her cousin, our main protector, died too. We sold everything we owned." She thinks of her home, of each beloved object being stripped away. The valuable glass statue of Athene was the first to go. By the end, they only had one plate left, not even beds to sleep on. "It was too late to marry me off. There had been no dowry to start with, and by then, we were destitute." Amara doesn't want to recount the end of the story, but now it's impossible to stop. They are all looking at her, waiting for her to finish. "So she sold me."

Dido is upset. Amara already knows she finds this impossible to imagine, but for Beronice and Victoria who were born into slavery, it is less shocking. "Who did she sell you to?" Victoria asks.

"A local man called Chremes. One of my father's former patients. My mother thought he would be more respectful because he had known my father. Chremes promised her I would be a protected house slave, that eventually I could regain my freedom." Even then, as a girl with no experience of men, Amara had suspected that this was a lie. She had seen the sly way Chremes had looked at her as a child, complimenting her father on such a *fine* daughter. His eyes made her uncomfortable although she could not name the reason. "My mother asked Chremes to buy her too. He refused." Amara cannot bear to think of her mother any longer. "So, it's not just Felix," she says. "He's not the only man I hate."

"These fish are so salty." Beronice stands up. "I'm going to the water fountain for a drink."

The others barely notice her leave; they are too caught up in Amara's story. "Chremes *obviously* had you as a concubine," Victoria says, her understanding of the world a thousand times sharper than Amara's mother's. "I just don't understand why he sold you. You're young; you're beautiful. He can't possibly have got bored that quickly."

"His wife Niobe was jealous. She insisted." Amara prefers not to remember that Chremes never even said goodbye, or the moment she understood Niobe had sold her not as a house slave, but as a *whore*.

"I don't like to disrespect your mother," Dido says. "But I can't understand her. Better to have starved together. A woman's honor is the most precious gift she has." She looks out to sea, as if she half expects to see the North African coastline instead of endless blue. "Every day I want to be home—I dream of it, I see it, I hear my parents' voices. But it's impossible. The shame of who I am now. If I went back, it would *kill* them."

"My parents didn't believe all the stories of the gods," Amara replies. She looks at Dido's earnest face and for once feels distant from her. She thinks of her father's work, of his patients—those he saved and those he didn't—and of the agony of his own death when he knew he was leaving his family behind. She understands the grief Dido feels at the loss of her innocence but doesn't share the profundity of her shame. "We only have life, nothing else matters beyond that," she says. "Not honor, not anything. My mother sold me to ensure my survival."

"And you're *alive*," Victoria says. She reaches over to take Amara's hand, her grip fierce. Then she smiles, lifting the darkness of the conversation. "But I still think I win this one. You say men are the worst, but it isn't true! The worst person in this story is that bitch, Niobe. Chremes was just like any other fool, thinking with his cock. Men are so predictable." Amara looks at Victoria, her profile backlit by the sun, chin raised. *Unconquered*, she thinks, *like her name.*

"How do you know you were a rubbish-heap baby?" Dido asks.

"That's what the other slaves in the house told me," Victoria replies. "I was the only one who never had a mother." She shrugs at Dido's horrified face. "It's not that bad. Lots of slaves don't have any parents. Though I did ask why not once, and the cook told me she picked me up when she went to the dump one morning. Thought I was dead until I started screaming. Nearly dropped me with fright." Victoria glances at Amara. "Your mother was wrong to think being a house slave is a better life than being a concubine. Ask Beronice about her first mistress in Alexandria, if you don't believe me."

They turn round to where Beronice was sitting then realize she is still not back. "She's been a long time getting a drink," Dido says.

"Shit," Victoria scrambles to her feet. The others follow. They never make solo trips to the harbor, a group is always safer. So many men who have been cooped up at sea are roaming around, suddenly released on shore, hungry for what they can get. A recipe for violence.

The three of them walk swiftly along the colonnade toward the water fountain, calling Beronice's name. There's no sign of her. They go back along the waterfront and the docks, ignoring the whistles and attention from the men they should be trying to catch. "Perhaps she went for more food?" Amara suggests. They head toward town, walking through the narrow alleyways of the fishermen's quarters. It's almost empty here, most of the men are out at sea. They are about to turn back when they hear a woman screaming.

"Beronice!" Victoria yells. They run further in, and there, under an arch in a narrow side street, is Beronice. She is on her knees trying to fend off two men. Victoria starts shrieking, making an astonishing amount of noise for one small woman. Amara and Dido join in, yelling as loud as they can. "*Murder, murder*!" Victoria wails. A few doors open. The two men back off.

"For fuck's sake," one bellows at the screeching trio. "She was selling!"

"And *you* weren't paying!" Beronice shouts back, getting to her feet.

Both men look round, unhappy at the sudden attention. One spits at Beronice. "Fuck you, you lying Egyptian whore!" He scrabbles in his leather purse and throws down a coin before running off, his companion close at his heels. Beronice bends to pick up the money.

Victoria runs over to her as she straightens up, but instead of embracing her, she slaps Beronice hard across the face. "What the fuck were you doing?"

"There was only one customer!" Beronice protests, clutching her cheek. "Then his friend tried to get in for free."

The few people who had ventured out to see what was going on realize it's just a women's brawl rather than the excitement of a dead body. They head back to their lives, grumbling at the false alarm. "You could have been killed!" Dido says. "Why would you do that?"

"It's for Gallus! I don't want him getting in trouble for not paying." Beronice's three friends gawp at her. She is wide-eyed, her hair wild where one of the men must have grabbed it. She puts both hands to her chest with passionate sincerity. "He *loves* me," she says. "Don't you understand? He loves me."

Victoria stands with her hands on her hips, facing Beronice, ready for battle, but the sight of her foe clutching her heart like a tragic actress turns her anger into amusement. "Beronice, you amaze me. Of all the whores in the world, you're the only one stupid enough to pay her own customers." She turns and the rest of the women follow, heading back to the harbor where there are still men waiting to be caught.

7

"The whole place rang with their theatrical laughter,
while we were still wondering why this sudden change
of mood and looking now at each other, now at the women."
—Petronius, *The Satyricon*: "Quartilla's Brothel"

The days pass, the weather grows warmer, the Sparrow's vegetable stews become more varied, campaign slogans spring up across town for the March elections. Life in the brothel rolls on in all its bleak monotony. Amara tries to learn from Victoria, watches how she charms men, attracting the same locals back time after time. Rusticus the potter, Phoebus the perfume seller, Manlius from the fast-food store. All of them tipping her with gifts and treats rather than money, goods that Felix won't take. Amara observes Victoria's every movement, until she knows her friend's face and body better than her own. She even tries to copy the way she moans.

She gets better at pretending, but Amara is never satisfied. The desire to escape takes hold, its roots digging deep under her skin, breaking her apart. There are days when even fear of Felix doesn't crush the urge to run away. What stops her is the certainty she would die on the road.

The only person who hates life in the brothel even more violently than Amara is Paris. His continued presence in the cells twice a week is a strain for everyone.

"I don't think I could bear it if Gallus had to do that," Beronice says. All of them save Paris and Cressa are "unoccupied," hanging about in the smoky corridor, trying to ignore the sounds of Fabia's son and his customer sweating it out nearby. They are supposed to be naked, but the March nights are still cold, so they huddle together wrapped in blankets. "I just couldn't look at him the same. For a man to be on the receiving end. The shame!"

"Oh shut up," Victoria says. "Think what Gallus might say, if that's the way you're going. *I couldn't bear MY precious cock in her mouth; think of all the OTHER cocks she's sucked!*"

"It's not the same thing at all!" Beronice says. "Gallus would *never* say that about me." She fusses with her hair. "Though he does get jealous, obviously."

"What does he say?" Dido asks.

"He says he'd like to kill all the grubby men who lay a finger on me. That's why he's going to buy me. So he can have me all to himself. Then *nobody else* will be allowed to touch me. Not even . . ." She breaks off, unable to say their boss's name, but looks up at the ceiling so they understand who she means. Beronice smiles. "That's how much he loves me."

Amara doesn't *disbelieve* Beronice when she says these things. She is a bit on the dim side though surely not a liar. But it's a struggle to picture Gallus coming out with these flowery phrases. Does he clasp his breast too? Kiss the hem of Beronice's robe? He's clearly a more enterprising little shit than he looks. Absolutely none of the other she-wolves —not even Dido—have ever considered the possibility Gallus might be genuine rather than devious.

"Does he tell you how much his mother would have *adored* you?" Victoria asks.

"Yes!" Beronice says. "He does! He told me I remind him of her, that I have the same kind eyes, that . . ." She stops when she realizes the others are trying to suppress their sniggers. A man reels in through the doorway, no doubt fresh from one of the nearby taverns. Beronice stalks toward him, almost bundling him into her cell in her hurry to get away from her friends. "You're all just jealous!" she shouts, before dragging the curtain across with a scrape.

"You shouldn't tease her so much," Amara says.

"I know, I know. But she's too easy to tease."

"Like his *mother*!" Dido is still incredulous at Gallus's love talk.

"What a weasel," Victoria says. "He's got no shame at all." A stifled, not altogether happy, yelp comes from the direction of Beronice's cell. Beronice herself is ominously quiet. "She's really cross, isn't she? That one won't be bringing his cock back here in a hurry."

"In this way." It's Thraso's voice. "We'll make sure you're well entertained."

The women look at each other, suddenly alert. Thraso doesn't normally give the punters an introduction. A large figure steps over the threshold, flickering into view in the light of the oil lamps. A cloak, a flash of green. Vibo.

"Oh!" Victoria gasps, flinging off her blanket. "Who is this vision? He must be for me!"

"Felix said to be sure to fuck the one called Amara." Vibo's voice is not friendly.

"But of course! You can't have just one woman." Victoria is already winding herself round him, kissing him, helping him off with his clothes. She glances back at the others. "You must have three! Look!" She snaps her fingers. For a moment, Amara cannot think what to do. Then she grabs Dido's hand, spinning her round. It's not the most graceful move, but the pair of them end up pressed against Vibo in a bare-limbed tangle which she hopes will give him the right idea.

"Three? All at once?" He doesn't sound altogether certain. "Two would be fine."

"You *must* have us all!" Victoria whispers, her voice husky, as if tormented by desire. "You can't be stingy, keeping yourself to just *two*. Not when we *all* want to fuck you. You *have* to let us all fuck you!" She lets out a whimpering moan.

It is the most ridiculous performance Amara has ever seen. She cannot believe the man will fall for it. But Vibo's expression softens, and he pulls Victoria to him, clasping her backside. "What a naughty little wolf you are."

Victoria needs no further encouragement. She has maneuvered Vibo into her cell, disrobed him and laid him out flat on his back, all by the time Amara and Dido are drawing the curtain. The bath manager is hung like a snail, but Victoria shrieks in rapture at the sight, leaping nimbly on top. Vibo groans.

"Oh! Don't be greedy!" Amara squeals. She flings herself at Vibo squashing her breasts in his face.

"But *I* want to sit there!" Dido tries to push Amara aside, panting in her efforts to clamber up onto the bed.

Victoria is bouncing away vigorously, determined not to let the ordeal last longer than necessary, and Vibo, gasping for breath, is not entirely thrilled by the idea of being completely buried under a pile of women.

"No, no," he says to Dido. "You two enjoy each other. I'd rather watch."

It's not the first time Amara and Dido have had this request. They writhe about theatrically, trying not to meet each other's eye. Vibo doesn't last long. Taking their cue from Victoria, all three reach a crescendo of screams at the proper moment then drape themselves over the beached bath manager, sighing with fake contentment. Amara is just on the verge of getting a dead arm from lying in the same position for so long when Vibo heaves himself up. "You are," he says, his sweaty face glistening with pleasure, "the most wonderful girls. *Wonderful.*"

"Oh, thank you," Victoria breathes. She takes Vibo's hand and kisses it as if he were the emperor. "We *adore* you."

"We do, we do!" Dido says, rolling over and gazing at him with delight.

Amara doesn't trust herself to speak, so lets out what she hopes is a seductive sigh. Victoria slowly helps Vibo into his clothes. They all crowd round the door of the cell to give him lingering kisses goodbye, feigning desolation at his departure. Vibo leaves the brothel in a much better mood than when he came in.

Dido is about to start giggling, but Victoria puts her finger to her lips. "Not yet," she says. "Wait."

They sit huddled together on the bed, leaving enough time to be sure that Vibo has really gone. Then Dido whispers in a small voice, "*We adore you!*" and the three of them collapse with laughter.

It's no longer Thraso on the door when they saunter out in their cloaks to see if Vibo left a tip. Gallus greets them with a grin. "I don't know *what* you ladies did, but for saying that was supposed to be a free fuck, he just doubled the night's takings."

Victoria lets out a whoop of triumph. "And for that," she says, laying her head on Gallus's shoulder in an intimate gesture that would make Beronice seethe, "we deserve a little break at the Sparrow." He hesitates. "Oh, come on!" Victoria punches his arm. "It's quiet! You've got three in. We'll just stir up some customers and bring them over."

"Go on then." Gallus sighs.

"He's not so bad," Dido whispers to Amara as they head across the road. "Maybe Beronice is right about him."

"She's got kind eyes like his mother?" Amara asks, raising an eyebrow.

Dido grimaces. "Or maybe not."

The Sparrow is packed. Lamps are hanging from the doorway and the rafters, shining off the brass pots Zoskales has fixed to the wall. It's a confusion of light and noise. Nicandrus is busy serving drinks and has been joined in his duties by Sava, a house slave who also works nights as a waitress. Zoskales is telling a long-winded story about his wife at the bar, making the customers laugh.

Victoria is not here to fish, whatever she told Gallus. She shoves her way to a free spot at a table where three men are dicing. "How much are you playing for?"

"How much are you selling for?" one of the men snorts, trying to put his hand on her thigh.

Victoria waves him away in irritation, all her usual flirtatiousness gone. She is a serious gambler, aided by her own weighted dice. "I can raise three asses."

Amara and Dido watch Victoria muscle her way into the game, the men eventually giving way to the force of her determination to play. "She's going to win," Amara says. "They won't know what's hit them."

Nicandrus spots Dido. He smiles, beckoning them across the room, forcing some other customers to make space for the pair of them on a bench. "Hot wine? With honey?" He is already heading to the bar.

"Thank you," Dido says.

"Here for the night?" It's one of the men who made room for them. His question is friendly rather than suggestive. He has a pleasant face and black hair that's graying at the temples. There's a small reed flute on the table in front of him, his fingers just resting on it as if to keep it safe.

"We might be if you play," Amara says.

He laughs. "Are you singers?"

"Yes."

Dido shoots her a look. Both women were taught music at home, but the respectable songs they're familiar with are unlikely to be bellowed out in a bar. "Honored to meet two fellow musicians," the man says. "I'm Salvius." He points to his companion. "This is Priscus."

Priscus bows his head in greeting.

"Amara and Dido. May I?" She picks up the flute. "My father had one like this," Amara says. She does not add that, for her father, it was the very least of his instruments, that she herself had learned to play the lyre.

She hands the flute back to Salvius who puts it to his lips and starts to play. He's more skilled than she expects. It's a popular tune from Campania, a few lively verses about a shepherd longing for his love. Priscus starts to sing, encouraging the women to join in. Amara listens a few times to catch the words then sings with him. She has a strong, clear voice, and some of the customers break off talking and begin clapping in time.

When they come to an end, the cry goes round for more. Salvius starts piping again, a famous tune about Flora and the spring. "Sing with me," Amara says to Dido. "You know this one!"

Dido's voice is not as strong as Amara's though much sweeter. She begins hesitantly, but as they repeat the song again, joy takes her over. Her face is lit up in a way Amara has never seen before. Nicandrus is gazing at her, still holding the honeyed wine, not daring to put it down in case he breaks the spell. Priscus pushes the table back, urging the women to stand up. "Another song!" he shouts.

Salvius plays festival music, perhaps guessing their unfamiliarity with local folk tunes. Amara and Dido sing together, and for the first time since coming to Pompeii, Amara is almost happy. Some of the customers leer, and one shouts at them to get their tits out, but mainly, everyone is enjoying the music too much to be a nuisance. Eventually

Salvius grows tired and puts down the flute, promising to start again when he's had a drink. Priscus turns animatedly to Dido, leaning across Nicandrus before he has a chance to say anything, asking which other tunes she knows. She sits down politely to answer him.

"That was beautiful." Amara turns at a familiar voice, one she cannot immediately place. It is Menander, the potter's slave.

The blood rushes to her face. "What are you doing here?"

"You said you worked nearby." He leans closer so she can hear over the noise. "This is the second time I've been in here, hoping to catch you. And now I have."

"Only two visits? Not very determined."

Menander laughs. "I'm a slave. Rusticus is a generous master but not *that* generous."

His mention of the potter reminds Amara of her humiliation in the shop. She glances over at Victoria, still deep in her game, wonders if the master jokes to the slave about his own visits to the brothel. "Lucky you," she says coldly.

"I wasn't laughing *at* you," he says. "But it was very funny, the way you stared him out like that. I've never seen a woman do that before." He pauses. "You were magnificent."

"So I asked for four cocks *magnificently*?" Amara says, trying not to laugh. They are standing close together in the crush. She takes a sip of the honeyed wine, already a little drunk on singing and attention. "Good to know."

"You stood your ground. *That* was magnificent," Menander replies, switching to Greek. "The cocks were incidental."

"I wish they were."

She says it to make him laugh, but Menander catches the dark undercurrent. His eyes meet hers, and she understands that he shares her grief, that her losses are also his. He puts his hand over his heart in greeting, bowing his head, as if they have only just met. "My name is Kallias," he says. "I am the son of Kleitos, the finest potter in Athens. One day, I will take over my father's business and sell my work all over Attica, including the beautiful town of Aphidnai. What is your name?"

Nobody in Pompeii has ever dared ask her this. It's the last remnant of privacy, of self, that a slave who was once freeborn possesses. Their real name. It's so loud in the crush that she almost has to shout, but still, she doesn't hesitate to give this boy from Athens what he asks for. "My name is Timarete," she says. "I am the only child of Timaios, the most learned doctor of Aphidnai, and the most loved. To him, I am both a daughter and a son."

"You see," Menander says, lightly brushing a curl of hair from her face. "Incidental."

"But I'm also Amara." She switches back to Latin, playfully moving his hand away. "Because otherwise I would never have set foot in a tavern, still less have sung for a crowd of men or talked to you!"

Menander smiles and is about to reply when Dido grabs her arm. "Amara! Is that Gallus?"

The familiar figure is bent over the gaming table, gesticulating at Victoria who is trying to scramble her winnings together while she argues with both him and the other gamblers. He smacks his head on a low-hanging oil lamp as he stands up, looking furiously round the room. He spots Amara and Dido. "Get back *now*!" he shouts.

A few drinkers turn round to discover who he's yelling at, see the two she-wolves and laugh. "I might come along with you," one slurs, getting to his feet. "Pretty little lips. Maybe you'll sing for me." He says this to Dido, obviously thinking Amara is already with a client.

Menander takes hold of her hand, covering it with both of his. For one moment, she is afraid he will ask to join her at the brothel. He leans in, lowering his voice. "Please take care of yourself, Timarete."

8

*"This truly is a Golden Age; for gold
High place is purchased; love is bought and sold."*
—Ovid, *The Art of Love* II

"Almost two denarii! That's how much I won. Those dice are the best investment I ever made! And you should have *seen* the other players' faces. Perfection."

Victoria is gloating about her victory at the gaming table. All of the women, save Dido, are sitting on the stone bench that hugs the walls of the warm room, listening to her boasts without huge enthusiasm. This section of the women's baths is always a gossip chamber, and a low babble of voices swells up to the vaulted ceiling. Cracks fan out across its surface and the stucco is chipped. When everyone's clothes are removed, it's harder to tell who is citizen, freedwoman or slave; the she-wolves might almost be mistaken for a group of young wives.

Amara usually finds the warm room a pleasant break before braving higher temperatures, but instead of feeling relaxed in the heat, her every sinew is knotted with tension. She found the aftermath of the bar unbearable. The claustrophobia of being back at the brothel, forced to put up with the parade of drunken men and their endless, thankless demands, felt infinitely more painful after her brief time with Kallias. *Menander*, she tells herself, *his slave name is Menander. Just like yours is Amara.*

"And then early this morning Felix asked for me for the second day running! A whole *hour*. That's how long he had me working for him. And I don't like to boast," Victoria says, "but I made him last *ages*. I think a few tricks even took him by surprise." She could not look more pleased with herself if she were Psyche recounting a visit from Eros. "I think that must be the longest time he's wanted to spend with anyone."

"I don't know why that's something to brag about," Beronice says. Her cheeks are shining in the heat, which makes her look cross, and strands of hair are stuck to her face with sweat. "Felix is such a *chore*. And he's always such an ungrateful bastard afterward. Hardly worth the effort. Not like Gallus. *He* always . . ." Beronice sees the others smirking and stops herself. She looks down at her feet and heaves a sigh, obviously desperate to share all the pent-up devotion in her heart but reluctant to face the ridicule. Amara feels sorry they've teased her so much.

Victoria smiles slightly but doesn't say anything. Amara realizes Felix must have complimented her. *He understands perfectly how to manipulate us all*, she thinks.

"I don't think Felix has sent for me in weeks," Cressa says. She is slumped against the wall, arms folded over her breasts, hiding the stretch marks.

"Lucky you," Beronice retorts, entirely missing the anxiety in Cressa's voice.

Amara edges away on the bench and closes her eyes. Even outside the brothel, its wretched, violent world wraps round her like a shroud. She tries to tune out her friends' voices, listening to another conversation.

"... *you can't let your sister make demands like that! Tell her you don't have the money.*"

"*I can't, her husband's family are impossible. I don't know what they'll do to her.*"

"*You don't mean ...?*"

She half opens her eyes, taking in the two women speaking beside her. They are seemingly without attendants and both have tired, careworn faces. One of them is sitting so close to Amara their thighs are almost touching. Her dyed red curls have smudged along her hairline in the heat. She is constantly fiddling with something on her left hand. A cameo ring.

"You've heard the rumors about his first wife," says the redhead. "And the slaves are too frightened to talk. Fulvia says he beat her on their wedding night. What sort of monster does that? And always complaining about the dowry, even though he spent every penny."

"Gellius will never notice if you take a bit more out of the takings, I suppose."

"Even Gellius is going to notice eventually. And no point asking him for help. He barely moves his fat arse out of the tavern. All day I'm sweating away behind that counter. Just so he can drink the profits."

"I'm sorry that I can't help either," the other woman fans herself. "I would give you the loan myself, but my husband keeps me so short. And business is always worse at this time of year."

The redhead's face falls, and Amara knows that she must have been hoping her friend would put up the money. She recognizes that look of humiliation, shot through with resentment. It reminds her painfully of her mother. After Amara's father died, her mother asked everyone they knew for help, measuring out what she could afford to entertain her guests in exchange. How far would a handful of dates stretch? Would her father's former patron be offended by the chipped plate? When the visitors were captive in the house, she would recount the hardships of widowhood, holding back tears while trying not to sound too desperate. Amara would sit quietly, head bowed at her mother's instruction, watching the flow of sympathy and money slowly dry up. By the end, her mother would have accepted a loan from anyone, whatever the terms.

"Forgive me, mistress," Amara says in a low voice. "But I may be able to help you." The two women turn in surprise. She tilts her head politely without being too servile. Let them wonder if she is freedwoman or slave. "I act as agent for my master, he understands the little difficulties we can all face. I would be happy to ask if he would be willing to arrange a loan. Discreetly, of course."

"And why would your master employ a woman as his agent?" It's the redhead's stingy companion. Her face is hard and suspicious.

"The contract would be drawn up by his steward," Amara says, thinking on her feet. She will need to ask Felix for Gallus, not Thraso. No point scaring this pair away at the last moment by turning up with a thug. She smiles at the redhead who seems less hostile than her friend. "But it's easier for women to do business with each other. We have so many concerns men are incapable of understanding."

The redhead is twisting her ring, over and over. "You say he is discreet?"

Amara nods. "As am I."

"I run a fast-food store," the redhead says. "He can't be turning up, asking for me. My husband wouldn't like it."

"You need only deal with me," Amara says. She shoots a look at the sour-faced companion who is shaking her head. "That's the advantage of a female agent."

"I don't like it Marcella," says Sour Face. "Who is this girl? What's her master's business?"

"Forgive me," Amara replies. "But *discretion* is the cornerstone of my master's business. Loans are not his main concern, and he takes great care not to expose his clients." She turns back to Marcella. "If you want to secure a loan, tell me the amount, and I will meet you with the proposed agreement and my master's steward at the Temple of Apollo tomorrow morning."

"Don't do it," Sour Face hisses. "Fulvia will just have to look after herself! You've done enough for her as it is. She's a married woman now; she's not your responsibility."

"She's my sister," Marcella says. "I can't just abandon her! I promised our mother."

"I don't want to be party to this," Sour Face says, standing up. "I'll meet you in the steam room." She walks off without looking back. Marcella watches her go, shoulders hunched with anxiety.

"I understand your hesitation," Amara says, lightly touching her arm to return her to the present. "But sometimes we have to take the opportunities Fortuna grants us."

Marcella chews her lip, staring at the floor as if the answer will be written across the small diamond tiles. "Twenty denarii," she says at last. "That's what I need. And I can bring a necklace as surety."

Amara knows exactly where Felix will be at this time of day. There's an unspoken rule among the women to steer clear of the Palaestra, precisely to avoid him. She hopes he isn't so angered by her presence that he doesn't listen to her proposal. She goes over the details of the deal in her head as she walks swiftly along the Via Veneria. Surely, he will see the opportunity it offers?

It was difficult to hide her reasons for needing time off from her friends, but an offer to stay in for the entire day in return eventually secured their help without too many questions. They had set out as if in pairs, to fool Thraso, then met up again so that Dido wouldn't be alone. She didn't ask Amara anything, just pressed her hand and begged her to be careful. Amara knows Dido imagines she is going to see Menander, as if love could be the only possible reason for secrecy. Her friend's naivety feels like a reproach. Amara knows Dido would never try to make extra money without telling the others. Even Victoria is open about her gambling. Amara walks faster, guilt pricking at her heart. It's not a feeling she can afford, not if she wants to escape from the brothel.

The Palaestra is at the opposite end of Pompeii, a public park surrounded by a forbidding walled enclosure. Amara tells herself her breathlessness is due to the long walk, rather than nerves. A couple of men slouching by the entrance break off their chat to stare at her as she passes through the gate. Inside, she is greeted by high, piping voices. A gaggle of young boys sit learning their letters at the corner of the colonnade. She skirts between them, attracting a disapproving look from their schoolmaster. It's clear he knows what she is.

Only men are permitted within the exercise grounds. She hopes Felix is on the track rather than in the pool, as brazening her way past the tall plane trees that surround it would be impossible. She waits at the very edge of the track. It's warm here, the sun high overhead. The Palaestra is open to the public for a few set hours and is always crowded. Young men jostle each other, running circuits. She picks out Felix as he sprints past, bare torso shining with sweat. He doesn't see her. She watches him as he runs the length of the grounds. His movements are so fluid and graceful, he looks like a stag in a herd of cattle. It's painful, now, to remember how she felt when he bought her. Her sense of relief that at least he was attractive. What a limited imagination she had then when it came to human nature.

The second time Felix passes, one of his cronies spots her staring after him and smacks his arm, laughing. The men slow down. They stop just off the edge of the track, looking back at her. Felix is flanked by three others. There's so much she doesn't know about his business or his life. Could these be clients? Friends? Rivals even? Fortunately, whoever the other men are, they seem to find the idea of Felix being trailed by a jealous, lovesick whore hilarious.

"You didn't fuck her hard enough," one says, slapping him on the back. "She wants more of your dick."

"Maybe she'll pay *you*."

Felix shrugs them off, but the attention doesn't seem to have annoyed him. He jogs toward her. His friends whistle and call after him, yelling out their advice before starting up their circuits again. Felix stops, resting his hands on his thighs to get his breath back. "What's this?" He looks up, amused and curious, not a hint of his usual cruelty. Perhaps Victoria really did put him in a good mood.

"I've got a proposition for you," she says, trying to sound as relaxed as he does, but failing. Felix straightens up, wiping the sweat from his eyes. "There's a woman called Marcella. She runs a fast-food store near the theater, lots of business, regular income. But her husband drinks too much, and there's nothing to spare for a loan to her sister. She needs twenty denarii."

"And you want me to do this friend of yours a favor?" Felix sounds incredulous rather than angry, but she knows his rage can rest on a knife edge.

"No, no!" Amara protests. "I only met her this morning at the baths. It's a business deal."

"You came all this way, interrupted my day, to do a deal for twenty denarii?"

"But it's not just *this* deal, is it?" Amara says. "Women are never going to come to you; they're not even allowed to. But women still need money. So what do we do? We talk to each other; we lend to each other. But if Marcella, or anyone else, does business with me, she does business with you."

Felix's friends run past on the track, whooping. He swears, making them laugh. They keep going, and he turns back to her. "And what do *you* expect to get from this?"

"Same commission as we all get for sex," she replies. "I know Victoria gets extra because she brings in more business, and that's only fair. But if I get you more money through loans, rather than men, what's the difference?"

"How did you leave it with this woman, with this Marcella?" Felix sounds dismissive, but she knows he's interested. He has the same look on his face as he did when he took ownership of her and Dido at the slave market. The sweet anticipation of making money.

"I told her I would be at the Temple of Apollo tomorrow morning with your steward, Gallus, and a contract. She doesn't know about the brothel; I thought it best she sees the cash before I tell her who you are. Once the money is in her hands, once she can smell it, she won't be able to say no."

Felix grins at her, a look of such genuine warmth that she understands for a moment why Victoria is so addicted to pleasing him. "Amara, do you have *any* idea what happens to people who can't pay me?"

She thinks of Celer begging Felix for money, of the threats that her master made to Celer's family business. *Marcella will be able to pay*, she tells herself; *nothing bad is going to happen to her. I won't let anything bad happen to her.* "I can guess," she says.

"Enough of the fucking lover's chat!"

Felix's companions have stopped running and are stretching at the side of the track a few feet away. The amusement value of their friend's tryst is obviously wearing thin. "Your girlfriend can suck you off another time," says one, wandering over. He has a mark down the length of his face, a white line that his beard refuses to grow through. "You should try *my* dick," he says to Amara, rocking his pelvis. "You won't be wanting him to fuck you after that."

Felix laughs, but Amara senses he is irritated. More, she suspects, at being asked to hurry his business along than at any slight to his manhood. "Your cock's so small, none of my whores can even find it," Felix says, pulling her toward him, one hand at the small of her back, the other cradling her face. He kisses her, long enough for the others to start whistling, then slaps her on the backside in an obvious sign of dismissal. "Mind how you go," he says, already walking away. "I can't have anything happening to *my favorite whore.*"

9

"'Tomorrow I'll start living,' you say, Postumus: always
tomorrow. Tell me, that 'tomorrow,' Postumus, when's it coming?
How far off is that 'tomorrow?'"
—Martial, *Epigrams* 5.58

The cell is the cold, dark of nighttime, even though the sun is still bright outside. Stone walls muffle the noise from the street, making it seem more distant. Amara catches the odd word as voices, raised in argument, pass her window. The hustle and excitement of the Palaestra feels like another world. Lying here on the hard bed, the air still stale with last night's smoke, she could have passed into Hades, the kingdom of the dead.

The only color on the walls is the light reflected through Victoria's treasured bottles of perfume, lined up carefully on the windowsill. Everyone uses Victoria's cell when they work alone here; it's the biggest and closest to the street. Outside the door, she can hear Fabia sweeping the corridor. The old woman must have scrubbed the entrance to the cell several times over, desperate to be invited in for company and food.

Amara thinks of Cressa and heaves herself upright, swinging her legs off the bed.

"Would you like to share some lunch, Fabia?"

There's the clatter of the broom dropping. The old woman scurries inside. "Only if you have some to spare."

Fabia sits beside her, watching as Amara portions up the bread, olives and cheese. She says nothing, but her eyes follow every morsel like a starving dog waiting for a careless guest to drop a crumb from the table. The bones of Fabia's thin hands bulge through her skin as she clasps them together. Amara suspects she is having to physically restrain herself from starting to eat before all the food has been shared out. Lunch with Fabia is never enjoyable. Either you have to eat at the same speed, meaning it's over too quickly, or endure her agonized staring while she watches you finish. Amara chooses to eat quickly.

Fabia tears into the bread first, demolishing it in a few mouthfuls. It's not clear how she manages to chew so fast without choking. Amara is never going to be able to keep up. "I always liked this cell best," Fabia says, worrying away at an olive, extracting every last scrap of green flesh with her teeth. "It used to be Mola's. She's long dead now. That there, in the corner, is where I used to draw for Paris."

Amara follows the line of her pointing finger to the very bottom of the wall. She squints and the crude scratch marks take on the shape of a dog. "It must have been hard, raising a child here."

"My little boy," Fabia says. "He didn't always hate me. Everyone made such a fuss of him when he was small. All the other girls, they doted on him." She discards another olive. "But the old pimp, the master here before Felix, he rented him out to work in the kitchens across the way when he was four." Fabia pauses, contemplating the remaining bread and cheese on her knee. "I wish he'd sold him. But he never did. My boy was too pretty." She gives in to hunger, gobbling down the last scraps of food, sucking her fingers and wiping them on her knees. "That's what I tell Cressa. It's better if they're sold. Then you can imagine things turned out well for them. Better the heartbreak now, than later."

Amara has barely said a word but still has a small pile of food left. She eats it as fast as she can, conscious of Fabia watching. "Is this the only brothel you worked in?" she mumbles through a mouthful of cheese.

"I suppose," Fabia replies. "I started as a house slave. Had two little babies for the master, not that he cared, the ungrateful shit. Two little girls I never got to see grow up. After the second child, I thought he'd let me marry another slave in the household, the odd-job man. I quite liked him. He was kind, anyway. But then he died, and the master rented me out. It was only guests, family members, that sort of thing. But once they do that, rent you out I mean, you know they'll sell you on." Amara thinks of her time as a slave in Chremes' household. It does not cheer her to see parallels between her past and that of the destitute old woman beside her. "You didn't start life as a slave, did you?" Fabia asks, perhaps sensing her discomfort. "I can always tell."

"How can you tell?"

"You still act like you matter."

Amara knows Fabia doesn't mean to be hurtful, but still, her last mouthful of food feels like a stone as she swallows it. "That bread was dry, wasn't it?" she says, changing the subject. She reaches down to pick up the jug by her feet. "Would you mind fetching us some more water, please? Also, I think the other cells will need some more for this evening."

Fabia takes the jug. She looks at Amara, the hunger still in her eyes. "What does it *feel* like?"

"What does what feel like?"

"Being free. What does it feel like?"

What did it feel like to be Timarete? Amara's past life blazes into her mind's eye, with all its love, innocence and hope. "When you see a bird flying," she says, "that moment when it chooses to swoop lower or soar higher, when there's nothing but air stopping it, that's what freedom feels like." She pauses, knowing that this isn't the whole truth. The memory she tries to keep buried, the agony of her last day as a free woman rises to the surface. "But hunger feels the same, Fabia. Whether you are slave or free, hunger is the same."

Fabia nods, satisfied. Hunger is something she understands. She leaves the cell, and the sound of her footsteps is swallowed up almost instantly by the thickness of the stone. Amara stays sitting on the bed, conscious of the world washing past the walls outside, even though she cannot see it. Out there, over unimaginable distance, her hometown still exists. People she knew: her neighbors, her father's patients, the baker who always spared her bread, Chremes, Niobe. All the figures of her past will still be living out their lives in Aphidnai. But not her mother. Amara knows that her mother is dead.

She knew it on her first day as a slave. After the trauma of saying goodbye, Chremes took her to his bedroom. But instead of stripping her naked as she had feared, he seized the small bundle of belongings she had brought with her. Amara watched, bewildered and afraid, as Chremes rifled through her father's old leather bag until he found what he was looking for. Inside, her mother had hidden the money she had been paid for her only child. A well-known trick, Chremes said as he counted out the coins, for naive parents selling their children. A way to give them a head start toward buying back their own freedom.

Amara stands up. She doesn't want to remember the rest of that day. Everything her parents had hoped for, every gift they gave her, including her mother's last desperate act of love, has been taken from her. Timarete no longer exists, except as a brief reflection in the eyes of a boy from Athens. She will have to survive as Amara.

One relic from the past is here with her. Her father's battered, moldering bag is hanging from a hook on the wall. When the leather was bright and flexible, he would take it to visit patients, all his herbs and instruments parceled up inside. She lifts it from the wall. Sitting back down on the bed, she counts out the savings she has managed to collect at the brothel. At most it's enough for a few day's food. Nothing like the enormous sum she would need to buy herself from Felix. Amara tries to calculate the number of Marcellas she will have to bring him to get anywhere close. It's impossible. Not unless her value drops over the years like Fabia's. Then she might well only be worth the price of a week's bread. Amara doesn't pursue that thought. Perhaps she will earn more at the baths, if Vibo ever has them back? For a moment, she allows herself to daydream about meeting a fantastically wealthy patron, a man who would be fascinated by her conversation, somebody who would want her to *charm* him and not just screw her.

"Beronice?" It's Gallus, calling softly from the corridor. Amara walks to the doorway and sticks her head out. "Oh. It's you." He's disappointed. No free fuck for him today.

"We thought it was Thraso on the door, so I agreed to stay in."

"Felix swapped him onto the night watch," Gallus replies. "Is Beronice coming back later?"

"Only if she has a customer."

"Right." Gallus looks uncomfortable. Amara feels irritated by his awkwardness. She's had sex with the man at least twice, surely a brief conversation is not too taxing. "Does Beronice talk about me much?"

She studies him, trying to work out if it's a trick question. Perhaps he wants to discover if Beronice has exposed his financial dishonesty toward Felix. But she can see nothing in his face other than hopefulness. Amara relents. "She loves you."

"Well," he says, looking smug. "I knew *that*." He saunters back to the door.

She retreats into the cell, amused in spite of herself. Victoria and Dido will enjoy that story later. The walls surrounding her are covered in the same predictable attitude. Gallus is hardly alone. She runs her fingers over the scratches. *I fucked loads of girls here!* She remembers the man who scrawled that message; he had been keen to tell her how she compared to her friends. He works at the laundry. What's his name again? She should remember it; he visits regularly. Amara realizes she knows exactly what sort of blow job the man likes, but not what he's called.

She scans the walls, reading all the familiar phrases. *Hey Fabia!* That one makes her wince, thinking of how little life changes. *On 15th June, Hermeros, Phileterus and Caphisus fucked here.* She is happy to have missed that particular night—handling a group of men is usually hideous. She passes on to happier messages. *Hail, Victoria the Conqueror! Victoria, Unconquered!* The praise makes her smile. She wouldn't be surprised if Victoria dictated it herself. Amara squats on the floor, looking for her favorite scrawl. An anonymous act of rebellion half-hidden at the base of the bed. *Felix takes it up the arse for 5 asses.* She wonders what happened to the woman who wrote it.

Another message catches her eye, its letters large and jagged. *I FUCKED.* She stares at it. The words look like an act of physical aggression, a reminder of her own powerlessness. She opens her father's bag, searching for the broken stylus she once picked up in the street. It has already come in useful. She used it to draw a bird in her own cell the other day, a small act of defiance against the endless fucking and sucking that hems her in. She walks over to the message, starts to gouge into the stone, her hand shaking with anger. A man's profile takes shape, the letters of the boast becoming his forehead, transforming his own words into a slave brand.

She steps back to look at her picture. But all her rage was spent in the carving, and now it's done, she finds that staring at a branded face doesn't make her feel better. Victoria will probably hate it. She flops down on the floor. How long is it since she left the Palaestra? One hour? Two? The day feels endless.

Amara leans back against the stone bed. At home, she would have had actual books to read: her father's medical texts, natural history, poetry—verses of idealized love, rather than the crude variety now splattered all over her walls. She starts to recite Odysseus's meeting with Nausicaa from memory, but the sound of her own voice makes her feel even lonelier. She remembers singing a version of that story for her parents. Amara closes her eyes. She holds her arms out, imagining the shape of her old lyre, moves her fingers over the nonexistent strings.

"First door on the left!" It's Gallus. He is warning her to expect company as much as giving directions to the customer. She scrambles to her feet. A stranger appears in the doorway, making the cell even darker. Amara smiles at him, tilting her head the way Victoria does, letting her cloak slip off one shoulder.

"You'd better be worth the money," he says.

Amara hurries to draw the curtain behind them both. "But of course," she says in a husky voice that nobody in Aphidnai would recognize. She lets the cloak drop to the floor, waits to see the impact her body has on him. Then she beckons the strange man over to the bed, unsure if her feeling of light-headedness is due to dread or relief from boredom.

10

*"Sextus, you say their passion for you sets the pretty girls on
fire—you who have the face of a man swimming underwater."*
—Martial, *Epigrams* 2.87

The noise grows, like the buzz from a hive, the deeper
they push into the crowd. It isn't an official market day
at the Forum but, as always, various chancers have arrived
here early with their wares bundled up in blankets to spread
on the pavement. Gallus and Amara weave between the
makeshift stalls, heading for the towering bulk of Apollo's
Temple. At the steps to the god's sanctuary, a salesman is
beating on a copper pot, bellowing out its price. Several
more metal pots and jars, in varying sizes, are stacked in
piles by his feet.

It takes Amara a while to recognize the woman she is here
to meet. Marcella looks more formidable in her clothes. Her
red hair is no longer smudging her skin. Instead, the curls
are piled up neatly on her head. She looks at Amara with
sharper eyes than she did at the baths. Amara knows she cuts
a much shabbier figure in the full glare of the marketplace.

She is afraid she looks like what she is: a prostitute working for a loan shark.

"Is this the steward?" Marcella nods at Gallus. He looks even more disreputable than usual, having tipped an absurd amount of oil into his hair. It's a style he's newly copied from Felix, but where the boss achieves an air of slicked-back menace, Gallus looks more like he got soaked in the street by a slave slopping out an upstairs room.

"Yeah." Gallus sidesteps to avoid an ironmonger shoving past with his tray. Amara worries he might start a row, but he catches her eyes and thinks better of it. Felix made it clear that Amara was to be in charge of the business side of this deal, a role reversal neither Amara nor Gallus quite know how to navigate.

"We brought some surety." Another woman, standing just behind Marcella, steps forward. She must be Fulvia, the younger sister. Blonde as her name, she is thin and fragile-looking. When the copper seller starts clanging his pot again, she flinches.

"Let's see." Amara holds out her hand before Marcella can intervene. Fulvia is clearly the weaker of the two. She smells of need and desperation. Amara tries not to imagine why she might want the money. Fulvia unwinds a long rope of amber beads from her neck, placing it carefully into Amara's palm. The stones are perfectly round, a couple shot through with twisted, sparkling strands. It is years since she has touched anything this valuable.

"It more than covers the loan," Marcella says.

She's correct, but Amara is not going to concede the point. "Not the interest though." She gestures at Gallus to hand her Felix's wax tablets. "This is my master's proposal." She gives the tablets to Marcella. "And here's the money." Gallus fumbles at his belt for the purse, nearly dropping it. Amara snatches it before it falls, handing it to Fulvia while her sister pores over the agreement. As Amara anticipated, the feel of the money in her hands has a physical effect on Fulvia. She looks close to tears.

"This rate is very steep," Marcella says, frowning. "I'll be paying almost double the value of the loan!"

"We can be flexible about the time period," Amara says, unsure if Felix will agree but eager to seal the deal. She can persuade him to extend the repayments later, she tells herself. Just as long as Marcella signs.

"Marcella, please," Fulvia begs. "Please think about what he'll do if I don't have the money."

"But this is too much!" Marcella hisses back. "You're risking mother's necklace and all for a rate that's going to punch a giant hole in my accounts."

Fulvia clutches the purse to her chest. "Please, I'm *begging* you. *Please.*"

"Let me look at it again."

The two women huddle anxiously over the tablets. Fulvia's distress makes Amara feel edgy. She understands the terrible, ceaseless pressure of never being able to make as much money as you need, of knowing you are running out of things to sell. After all, it's the reason she's here herself. "If it's too much . . ." she begins, gesturing for Fulvia to give back the coins.

Marcella puts a hand out in front of her sister, preventing Amara from stepping closer. "Alright, I'll sign it," she says.

"I'll sign. But tell your master he needs to give me a few more months." Amara and Gallus watch as Marcella scratches into the tablet with the stylus. "Where is your master's business?"

"Opposite the Elephant Inn," Gallus replies, taking the tablet and snapping the wooden frame together. Fulvia and Marcella exchange glances.

"Not the . . . ?"

"I will visit to take the first payment in two weeks," Amara says with a bow.

She and Gallus head back swiftly through the Forum, leaving the two unhappy sisters to their recriminations. "I'll take that," Gallus says, gesturing for the amber necklace. He stuffs it into a bag as they walk.

"Don't scratch the beads."

"Least of our worries," he replies. "What were you doing telling that poor bitch Felix would give her more time?"

"What difference will another month make if he gets the money?"

"This is Felix we're talking about."

The guilt Amara had been trying to ignore starts to surface, making her feel sick. "I'll think of something," she says. Gallus shakes his head. "What will you tell Beronice?"

"I won't tell her anything!" Gallus snaps. "I'm not a fucking *woman*. I never talk about Felix's business. And neither should you, not if you want to live out the year."

They almost miss the turning off the Via Veneria with their bickering. Amara waits to let Gallus go first, and they walk in single file onto the narrower pavement. To her surprise, as they round the corner, she sees Felix standing in the street outside the brothel.

"Get a move on," he calls, as they hurry to meet him. "Fabia's gone to round up the others. You've all got another chance with Vibo." He peers at Amara, frowning. "Do something with your hair; you look like a slut." He turns his back on her, taking the tablets from Gallus. "All signed?" Gallus nods. Amara waits for Felix to acknowledge her part in the transaction or ask what happened, but when he sees she is still standing in the street, he loses his temper. "What are you staring at?" He grabs her by the hair, pulling her toward him before shoving her back toward the brothel. "I told you to fucking move!"

The splash of the warm water as she slides into the pool brings back memories of their last ill-fated visit. On the domed ceiling above her, light ripples over an elaborate mosaic. It's Europa, her naked body wreathed in flowers, being carried across the sea by the god Jupiter in his form as a bull. Amara had forgotten how opulent this place is. Beronice drops down heavily beside her. The light on the ceiling dances, reflecting back the waves she's made. All Felix's women are more flustered than usual. Victoria wouldn't let them leave until everyone's hair had been styled, so instead of having messy curls, they are flushed and sweaty from rushing to make it in time.

"Already had a busy morning, ladies," Drauca calls. She is draped languidly against the side, both arms resting on the ledge of the large open window at her back. Simo's other two women, Maria and Attice, are floating either side of her like a pair of bodyguards. A third woman, whose name Amara doesn't know, lurks sullenly in the corner.

"We're always in demand," Victoria replies.

"I'm sure you must have picked up a few tricks at the Wolf Den," Drauca says. "But have any of you had a man in water?" None of Felix's women reply. "Just try not to drown. That's my advice."

"Is she serious?" Beronice whispers, as Drauca and Attice laugh. "I don't want some idiot sticking my head underwater."

"She's just being a bitch," Amara says, though the threat of drowning has done nothing to calm her own nerves. It's an ugly secret she carries, the panic which so often threatens to overwhelm her. A terrible sensation of being unable to breathe, unable to move. The horror began that first time with Chremes and has never left her. It's bad enough when it happens with a customer in her cell. She couldn't bear the humiliation of crying here, in front of Drauca.

She looks round the room for the others. Dido and Cressa haven't joined them in the water but are sitting on a marble bench not far from the side of the pool. Felix sent for Dido this morning while Amara was in the Forum. The thought makes her feel guilty in ways she cannot explain. Dido hasn't said what happened, but Amara knows she is upset. She looks like a wounded bird. Not that the customers will care. Dido's vulnerability always seems to attract the greediest men, like wasps to honey.

"I suppose coming here makes a lovely change for *you*," Victoria says to Drauca. "A break from all that slopping out and changing the sheets when customers have pissed in them." She turns to Beronice and Amara in mock sympathy. "Imagine working all hours in a bar *and* having to screw the customers! Exhausting!"

"Fuck you," says Attice. "At least our master isn't a total shit. When was the last time Felix-the-tight-arse let *you* keep any tips?"

"You're right he does have a tight arse," Victoria replies. "A *hard*, tight arse, like an apple. Such a shame we have to serve a master who looks like Apollo. I'd *so* much rather be squashed under fat old Simo with his bad breath and bald patch."

"Yeah, must be brilliant for you all," Maria says. She points at Dido, raising her voice. "That one looks like she's loving life."

Dido turns her face away, in no mood to fight back, but Cressa is angry. "Why don't you just keep your big mouth shut?" She flaps a hand at Maria. "As if *you*'ve never cried over a man. Sure, Felix is a dick. So is Simo. Big deal."

"Simo might be a dick," Drauca sighs, turning her pretty face to look out over the sea as if she's bored. "But at least he tips. *That*'s the point."

"I suppose he gave you extra to have us thrown out last time," Amara says, still annoyed at the thought of being cheated. "Shame that didn't work out for you."

"Oh," says Victoria. "I don't think it was the *money*." She stands up on the steps where she has been sitting in the water, nimbly hopping up onto the heated floor. She flexes her body, not in the coy way Drauca does, but like an athlete, showing off her strength as well as her beauty. "Are you scared of the competition? Afraid those legendary tits of yours aren't going to look as good next to mine?"

"I think you'll find the men are looking for Venus not Hercules," Drauca sneers. Simo's other women laugh, but Amara can see Drauca is rattled. She stares at Victoria who is now doing backflips, a small crease on her beautiful forehead.

"Shut up!" Beronice hisses. "Listen." The women fall silent. An echo of male voices reaches the pool.

"Here they come." Victoria splashes back down into the water. She is flushed with excitement. It's not about sex, Amara realizes, looking at her. Her eyes take on that same look at the gaming table. The ferocious will to win.

Six men walk through an archway encrusted with colored shells, bare feet slapping on the stone. Their faces are red, and their bodies shine with sweat. They must have come from the steam room. Amara watches as they drift toward the pool, chatting, unhurried, not yet acknowledging the women's presence.

Drauca may have picked the most scenic spot, but Victoria, sprawled over the steps, beats her by proximity. "You're new," says a young man as he eases himself into the water next to her.

"Victoria," she breathes in his ear, twisting herself round his body like a vine. She starts kissing him to forestall any further conversation.

"Lucius got a lively one," laughs another man, following his companion down the steps. He wades toward Drauca. "And how's my lovely girl?"

Amara realizes she has unconsciously shrunk back against the side, away from where the customers are getting in. She thinks of Felix, of Vibo, of all she has gone through to get this second chance. There's no point wasting her time by allowing nobodies like Maria and Attice to upstage her. Swallowing down the feeling of dread, she swims toward two older men who are sitting talking at the side of the pool, their thin legs dangling in the water.

"So I told him, at that price, we will look for another supplier. People need bread, but the city won't pay for grain at any cost . . ." He trails off, noticing Amara leaning against the side next to him. "Not now." He shoos her away. "Maybe later." She freezes, not sure what to do.

"Maybe this one doesn't speak Latin," says the other man. He turns to her, enunciating slowly, as if she is stupid. "You. Greek. Whore. Yes?" The man's white hair is stuck to his head in sweaty tufts like a newborn duckling. His pale eyes stare at her with a lack of focus, as if he doesn't expect to see anyone looking back.

Amara thinks of her father. The crooked way he would smile when he talked about the power of the Roman state. *Everything they have is borrowed from us, Timarete. Always remember that.* "I am from Aphidnai," she replies, speaking fluent Latin. "Twelfth city of Attica, once the home of Helen of Troy." She inclines her head graciously, one hand over her heart in greeting, her father's smile on her face. "In this country, I am called Amara. I wish nothing other than to be of service to you both."

Duckling Head is not charmed. "Aphidnai didn't keep hold of Helen for long, if your myths are true."

His companion laughs. "Don't be so bad-tempered Gaius." He looks at Amara with more interest. She looks back under lowered lashes. He is old, it's true, but not entirely unattractive. His square jaw and iron-gray hair at least make him more prepossessing than his rude companion. She glances downward. There are gold rings on his fingers, the flesh around them swollen in the heat. Her heart flutters. Could this be the patron she has been hoping for? Can he see how much she has to offer? In her imagination, she leaps forward in time, sees him devotedly draping her in jewels, entranced by her every word . . . "You have a pretty mouth, Amara from Aphidnai. Don't waste it talking to him." He parts his legs in a not very subtle sign of what he wants. Of course, it's not *interest* in his eyes. It's nothing more than the drunk look of lust she has seen so many times before. Amara hesitates, the disappointment of reality taking a few seconds to dissipate her fantasy. Then she bends her head to oblige.

Duckling Head harrumphs in annoyance. "Not very entertaining for *me*, and now you've gone and taken the last pretty one."

"Don't make a fuss," groans his companion. "That fat one over there isn't doing anything. It's not like you have to look at their faces anyway!"

The men shout at Maria to join them. Amara finds it distracting to have to work next to her. Duckling Head does nothing but complain, threatening to shove Maria's head under the water if she doesn't make more effort. It seems Drauca's warning wasn't a joke. The rage Amara feels is blinding. For a moment, she thinks of Felix. Imagines what it must be like to have the power to act on your anger rather than bury it.

Amara's customer—whose name she still doesn't know —finishes with a whimper. He pulls his legs up out of the water and rises unsteadily. He waits for Duckling Head then helps him get to his feet. They walk off without offering any thanks.

"Is it always like this?" Amara asks Maria.

"Like what?" Maria snaps, wiping her face. There are red marks on her cheek where her customer must have dug his fingernails into her skin.

Amara glances round the luxurious room which is now reverberating with the women's fake gasps and moans. Victoria is the loudest, but she seems far more interested in what Drauca is up to than in the man beneath her. The two women are showing off and out-performing each other, their customers the unknowing recipients of their rivalry. Amara looks over at the window then looks away—she isn't sure she wants to know what two men are doing with Beronice over there. Dido and Cressa have the easiest deal, giving a double massage to a man sprawled over the bench they were sitting on.

"I thought maybe . . ." Amara trails off, silenced by Maria's angry, uncomprehending stare. She isn't sure what she would say anyway. That she was hoping for a watery symposium, impressing rich men with her conversation like the courtesans of Greek high society? Her humiliation feels worse for being self-inflicted. Better to expect nothing than be made a fool.

There's laughter as three more customers walk into the baths from the steam room. This time, Amara doesn't wait. She leaves Maria, wading toward the men. It isn't Victoria she imitates as climbs the steps, water dripping off her. She remembers the way Felix moved at the Palaestra, the sharp lines of his body as he ran past his rivals, the violence and the rage.

She stalks toward the men, interrupting their conversation without apology. "I am Amara of Aphidnai," she says. "Twelfth city of Attica, home of Helen of Troy. Which of you imagines he may command my attention?" The three men look at each other, amused but not entirely sure how to respond. The illusion of power she has created is fragile; she knows any one of them could force her if they choose to. Rather than frighten her, the knowledge makes her even more aggressive. She holds out her hand to the most confident-looking man, the one she hopes will have the least to prove by humiliating her.

"Who could refuse such an Amazon?" he says, smirking. He takes her hand and follows her to an empty bench.

Amara has learned more than enough about the mechanics of sex to understand what will give pleasure. All that matters now is severing herself completely from her body. She runs through the repertoire, the line between fear and anger stretched taut across her heart. The only time panic threatens to pull her into the present is at the end when he tries to wrest her onto her back. She cedes control, telling herself it will be quicker that way.

Afterward she doesn't wait to see if his reaction will be gratitude or indifference. She turns her back and walks to the pool. Down the steps, the water rises past her waist then higher as she plunges all the way in, swimming to the window. Amara looks out to the sea. If she didn't know the scene behind her, if she couldn't hear it, she could imagine that the horizon stretching out ahead belonged to her. Instead, she knows that she is as confined here, in the air and the light, as she is in the narrow darkness of her cell.

11

*"Do you regard yourself as chaste just because
you are an unwilling whore?"*
—Seneca, *Declamations* 1.2

Amara holds Dido as she cries. They sit huddled together on Dido's narrow bed. Over her friend's heaving shoulder, she can read the *Thrust SLOWLY!* command she carved into the wall. She cannot imagine now why it ever seemed funny. Beside it, the curtain is half-drawn to give them a little privacy. She doesn't dare pull it across completely. Victoria's voice is loud in the corridor, praising some man to get him in the mood. At any moment, they will be interrupted by a customer. The women have no time for themselves at night, not even for grief.

"I can't live like this," Dido gasps out between sobs. "I can't go on. I can't bear my life; I can't bear it."

"But you did so well at the baths earlier," Amara says, stroking her hair. "Second most popular after Victoria. All those tips." At the time, she had felt a stab of jealousy, but now she wishes Dido had out-earned her by twice as much.

She holds her closer. "You just need to keep thinking about making enough to escape. Nothing else matters."

"We're never going to escape!" Dido says, pushing her away. "This is it! It's all our lives will ever be." Her voice is rising, almost hysterical. "If I had any real virtue, I would have killed myself before allowing any man to touch me!"

"Please don't," Amara says. "Please don't say things like that."

"Everything good about me died in this cell; Felix made sure of that," Dido puts her hands over her face, either to stem the tears or to blot out the memory. "Eight Denarii. That's what he was paid for my virginity. That's what my honor was worth."

"You didn't have any choice," Amara says. "It's not your fault."

"Do you know what he told me this morning?" Amara doesn't reply. She had suspected Dido's despair might have been prompted by their pimp's cruelty. "He asked me if I thought my mother was dead. I said I thought she must be. Then he said I shouldn't worry. If she was as beautiful as me, the pirates wouldn't have killed her; some man was probably fucking her as a whore somewhere, right at the same time as he was fucking me." Dido starts crying again. "He doesn't leave you anything; he has to destroy everything."

Amara stares at the smoke billowing from one of the clay lamps in the corner of the cell. A savage, grinning little Priapus, one of the models she bought from Rusticus. It has almost burnt out. If she were Victoria, she would tell Dido not to pay attention, to ignore Felix. "I wish I could kill him for you," she says, her voice flat. "I've imagined it enough times. But

I know what happens to slaves who murder their masters." In the flickering glow, the whites of Dido's eyes shine. Amara shrugs. "Better than killing yourself, if you have to end it all." She cannot read the expression on her friend's face. "So you see, you're not such a bad person, are you? I know you've never thought of hurting anyone. Not even Felix."

"Perhaps I should have."

"No." Amara takes her hand. "You are one of the kindest people I've ever known. It's why I love you so much."

"More than the potter's slave?" Dido wipes her face with her free hand. "I know that's who you went to see the other day."

The smoking lamp stutters out. Next door, they can hear Beronice's customer shouting, presumably with pleasure. The busiest hours of the night are approaching. Amara glances at the curtain. Every second alone is time they have stolen. "I didn't go to see Menander. Though I wanted to."

"Where then?"

"I went to see Felix at the Palaestra."

Dido looks more shocked than when Amara confessed her longing to murder him. "But *why?*"

"For money. Because I'm trying to act as his agent, arranging loans for desperate women. They're not quite as desperate as me, but still, I'm not proud of it." She shifts herself up further onto the bed, crossing her legs. "Either we choose to stay alive, or we give up. And if it's living we choose, then we do whatever it takes."

"I'm not as strong as you."

"You're stronger," Amara replies. "You lost *everything* in a single day. I had years to get used to my losses. I cannot imagine what it was like for you—one moment safe with your family, the next dragged off onto that ship. All the things you saw. But you survived."

Dido picks at the fabric on the bed, not looking up. "Sometimes I think I brought it on myself." She tugs a thread lose and winds it round and round her finger. It digs deep into her skin. "I didn't want to marry the husband my father chose for me. I was complaining about him to my cousin before the pirates attacked. Until then, being tied to an ugly man who sold *cheese* was the worst thing I could imagine."

Amara almost wants to laugh, but Dido's stricken face stops her. Before she can think of what to say, Thraso sticks his head round the door. "Some fucking drunk just threw up in the corridor. We need more water."

"What about Fabia?" Amara says.

"She's already trying to clean it up, she can't do everything. Anyway, why are you moaning? You've barely sucked a cock all night, you lazy bitch." Thraso takes a step forward, but Amara jumps off the bed before he can raise his hand to slap her.

She ducks past him, grabbing the bucket from the doorway. "I'm sorry. I'm sorry; I'm going." Dido picks up one of the oil lamps and hurries after her. The stench hits them as soon as they leave the cell. They step around the vomit splattered on the floor, bumping into Fabia as she straightens up.

"I'll need that bucket as full as you can manage," she says, flicking an angry look at the culprit.

The sick-stained drunk is pawing at Cressa, trying to persuade her to take him into her cell, even though he can hardly stand upright. "So pretty . . ." he murmurs, insensible to her look of revulsion.

Amara and Dido take the back way onto the street, passing the door to Felix's apartment. Dido goes ahead, holding up the clay lamp to show the way. The flare sends their shadows lurching. At first the light and noise from the Elephant follows them, but soon, they are enveloped in almost total darkness. Moonlight picks out the bare shape of the houses, leaving unknown pools of black. Amara's heart beats loud in her ears. She has always hated being out in the dark.

They walk slowly and painstakingly, taking care not to stumble. Wooden shutters seal up the shops and houses that they pass. If it's not to visit a tavern or brothel, few people venture out at this hour. Unless they are thieves. Amara knows their poverty is no protection, plenty of men would steal what Felix sells. She glances up at one of the bolted windows. There's little chance anyone would rush outside to help a screaming woman at this time of night.

The well is at the end of the street. "Hold it up for me," she whispers to Dido, nodding at the lamp. Amara leans over the side, putting her weight into the groove in the stone, sunken under the pressure of so many hands. The flame flickers over the carved face as she cranks the arm of the well. Water pours from the stone mouth. It has never seemed to take so long to fill a bucket.

"Somebody is coming!" Dido hisses.

Amara straightens up, not wanting to leave her back exposed to whatever is approaching. She and Dido press together. There's the brisk clip of feet, more certain than their mouse-like shuffle up the street, and soon, a single flame bobs into view. It's a man with a bucket. Nicandrus.

He looks startled. "What are you doing out here?" The light from Dido's lamp shakes wildly. Her hand is trembling with fright. Nicandrus puts down his bucket with a clank and rushes over. "It's alright," he says, putting an arm round her to hold her steady. "It's alright." He looks at them both shivering in their togas. "You've not even put your cloaks on!"

"We didn't have time, we . . ." Amara trails off. What is there to say? That they ran off half-dressed because they were afraid of Thraso?

The sudden kindness is too much for Dido. All her emotion, already so close to the surface, spills over, and she starts to cry again. Nicandrus gently takes the lamp from her and hands both lights to Amara. "It's alright," he says, holding her close. "You're alright."

It's not alright, Amara thinks, feeling foolish as she illuminates the pair of them, huddled like lovers in the dark. *Nothing about our lives is alright.*

Dido buries her face in his shoulder in embarrassment. "I'm sorry," she says.

"You've nothing to be sorry about, nothing at all." And indeed, Nicandrus looks far from sorry at the situation. "Why don't you take my cloak?" He says, unfastening it. He looks over at Amara. "I mean, you can both share it, maybe?"

"I think I'd better keep hold of the lamps."

Nicandrus wraps Dido in his cloak. He takes his time, smoothing it over her shoulders, reluctant to let go of her.

"I can get the water," he says. He heads to the well, starts refilling their bucket. It takes him half the time to work the pump that it took Amara. He hauls their pail out and clanks his own into the trough. "It's not safe for you both out here, Zoskales would never send Sava out at this time of night."

"Zoskales isn't Thraso," Amara replies. "Or Felix."

"I know." Nicandrus lifts out the second bucket. "I'm sorry." He looks at them both—Dido muffled in his cloak, Amara standing rigid with her two lights like a lamp stand. "I wish I could. . . . I wish . . ." They stare back at him, waiting for him to finish. "You don't deserve any of it," he says to Dido, as if Amara wasn't there. He picks up both buckets. "I guess we should get going. Zoskales always moans if I take too long."

Amara hands Dido one of the oil lamps and sends her ahead. Nicandrus follows, and she takes up the rear with the second light. It's brighter with two flames, and although one skinny man would be small protection against thieves, it still feels safer with Nicandrus than it had without him.

At the back door to the brothel, Amara is prepared to slip inside and give her friend a moment alone, but Dido stands on the threshold, blocking her way. She passes Amara the lamp, her hand no longer shaking, and takes off the cloak, giving it back to Nicandrus. Then she leans over and grabs the bucket from him, holding it like a shield across her front, spilling some water on her shoes. "Thank you," she says, not looking him in the eye.

All three stand in the doorway. It's painfully obvious that Nicandrus wants to hold Dido, to kiss her, anything to recapture the intimacy at the well. But it's also obvious the moment has passed. "Anytime," he says bowing his head, before turning and walking back to the tavern.

Amara feels sad, watching him go. "I think he was hoping for . . ."

"I know what he was hoping," Dido says.

"Don't you like him? I think he really cares for you."

"I do like him."

"Then why not?"

Dido turns to her. Her face is drawn. "I can't bear any man touching me. They all feel like Felix." She is gripping the bucket. "Even when he had his arms round me, when I wanted to hug him back, I kept thinking he was going to hurt me."

Amara is about to answer, to say Nicandrus would never hurt her, but then she realizes she doesn't know that for sure. Perhaps he is like other men, after all. "I understand," she says.

They step inside the brothel. "At last," Fabia exclaims, taking the bucket from Dido. She sloshes it over the floor and starts to brush the vomit toward the front door. A man, who has been hovering at the entrance, dances to avoid the splash.

"Fucking watch it, you old crone!" He looks up at Dido and Amara. "Which one of you is mine?" Amara feels like she has met this man a thousand times before, even though his face is not familiar. Disheveled, drunk, no doubt rough with his hands. She thinks of Cressa, of the way her kindness once reached across the darkness, of what that had meant when she was afraid.

"My cell is here," she says, pointing to the open door.

The man staggers his way over the wet floor, avoiding Fabia's busy, darting brush. Dido leans in toward her, speaking quietly so he cannot hear. "Thank you."

The customer pushes between them, and Dido turns away. Amara follows him into her cell, drawing the curtain. He sits heavily on the bed. "I'm Publius," he says.

"Lovely to meet you Publius," she says. "I'm Amara."

She starts to undress, taking her time, not to titillate him but to give herself a small delay. This is where Victoria would be running through her patter to get him in the mood. But there is no need. Publius is looking at her naked body in wonder. "You're lovely," he says.

Amara almost feels sorry for him, this man who cannot see her bitterness. She smiles. "Thank you." She walks to the bed and kneels on the floor, unfastens his boots, easing them off his feet. "You're tired," she says, without thinking.

"It was a long day at the bakery," he replies.

She carries on undressing him. At least he is not such a monster as the wealthy old men at the baths. The memory brings a flush to her cheeks. All that effort and she barely made a denarius in tips. If anything, the day has shown her rich men are meaner than poor ones. She cannot believe she was stupid enough to think a place run by a man like Vibo would ever provide her with a way out.

Amara climbs up onto the bed beside Publius. She thinks of brokering the loan in the Forum, the feeling she had when Marcella signed. Not just guilt but elation. She lets Publius kiss her, lying passive as a stone. It's supposed to be her making the effort here, not him, but he doesn't seem to care. The anger that is always just beneath the surface of her skin flickers into life. Why should he care? He's lucky to be able to touch her at all.

She hears Felix's voice in her head. *And you would, wouldn't you? Tear them all apart.*

He seems nice enough, this Publius, the baker's man. Perhaps he has a wife at home, a family. Would she tear him apart? Amara doesn't even have to ask herself the question. She rises, looking down on her breathless lover, eyes glittering orange in the lamplight. If the only way out requires working with Felix, then so be it. Whatever it takes.

APRILIS

12

"Celebrate the power of Venus, girls of the street; Venus is
appropriate for the earnings of women who promise a lot.
With an offering of incense ask for beauty and popular favor,
ask for seductiveness and words that are fit for fun. And give
your mistress pleasing mint along with her own myrtle, and
bonds of reed covered with well-arranged roses."
—Ovid, *Fasti* IV

Amara is caught in a river of women, unable to break
from the flow, even if she wanted to. There are so many
of them, they have burst the banks of the pavements and
spilled over into the road. Mud is splashing up her legs, but
she doesn't care. They are a noisy crowd, singing, laughing,
wrists and ankles jingling with bells. The sweet smell of
mint mingles with the reek of sweat. She would never have
suspected Pompeii had so many prostitutes.

Out of sight at the front of the procession, musicians
blow their shrill pipes, and her blood pulses to its beat.
She squeezes Dido's fingers. The kohl she drew around her
friend's dark brown eyes has smudged a little but that only

makes them look wider. Neither have watched the Vinalia before, still less taken part. The April festival of whores and wine is hardly an event a respectable girl would attend, or even try to glimpse from the window.

Plenty of others are watching though. People stand bunched together outside shopfronts or hang out of balconies to see the women pass. Men loiter at the edges of the procession, drinking and shouting, vying for a chance to grab a kiss or maybe more. Amara knows Felix, Thraso and Gallus will be weaving through the crowds, keeping watch, even when she cannot see them. After all, the women aren't just here to celebrate but to sell. Everything in Pompeii turns to making a profit.

"Keep up!" Victoria yells, looking back over her shoulder. She is almost naked and has dressed her hair in myrtle, Venus's own flowers. Amara knows how much this day means to Victoria. To spend your life classed as *infamia*, unable—even if you win your freedom—to rub off the taint is a shame that can eat into your bones if you let it. But the Vinalia upends the usual order. Today, they own the streets. Nobody can deny the whores' importance to Pompeii's most powerful patron.

"Look at the goddess!" Beronice says, pointing. As the road to the Forum rises, they can see the plaster statue of Venus more clearly. Carried on a platform, she stands above the crowd as an immortal should, swaying on the shoulders of her temple's slaves, draped in garlands. "I'm going to ask her to help me marry Gallus," Beronice says, glancing round, trying to spy her lover in the crowd. "He's bought me roses to give her."

"Gallus *bought* them?" Amara asks.

"Well, he's going to buy them," Beronice replies. "When we get to the Forum."

"He'll be lucky if the sellers have any left," Cressa says.

Beronice doesn't reply; she has seen her beloved and rushes to the edge to be closer to him. "Won't Felix notice?" Dido asks, watching her with an anxious frown. "She's not very subtle."

"Probably useful for him," Cressa says. "All that foolishness keeps them both obedient."

At the Forum, their river hits a bank of humanity. Hawkers ride slipstreams through the crowd, balancing trays on their shoulders, selling everything from garlands to hot pies. And of course, wine. Venus isn't the only deity worshipped at the Vinalia, it's also a day to thank Jupiter for Campania's fruitful vineyards. Although she cannot see it, Amara knows the faithful will be pouring wine on his altar, a sacrifice to please the most libidinous of gods. Although looking at the state of the worshippers, she suspects even more has been poured down their throats. Those who aren't already too drunk, cheer at the women's arrival, pressing toward them. The surge brings their procession to a standstill. Ahead, the musicians blast on their pipes more insistently, driving the men back from the goddess. Amara feels a hand grip her arm and whips round. Felix.

"Keep close," he says, as if she has any choice with his fingers digging into her flesh.

"What about the others?" she asks, realizing she can no longer see Beronice or Victoria. Cressa is stuck with Thraso.

"Gallus has them," he says, looking down at her and Dido. "Just concentrate on getting to the temple."

They shuffle forward, so slowly it's almost painful. Felix's presence stops her from getting trampled but also squashes her excitement. His hand on her arm, steering her along, owning her, makes this day more like any other, not the brief moment of freedom she had imagined. In her sweaty fingers, the sprigs of mint and myrtle are already wilting. Fabia went out early to buy their offerings but didn't bring back any roses. Felix thinks they are overpriced.

At last, the goddess reaches the narrow road that leads to the temple. The plaster Venus dips and jerks as the slaves carry her over the uneven stones. The women follow, squeezing into the passageway. The mud is even deeper here, and Amara doesn't like to imagine what might be in the damp sludge she is squelching through; everyone is packed so closely together she cannot see her feet. Getting through the arch into the temple grounds feels like she is being pressed through a sieve. On the other side, there's a little more room to breathe.

Amara has never been here before. The precinct is enormous, perhaps half the size of the Forum, and although the temple itself is only part built, the vast colonnade which encircles it on three sides gives the illusion of opening out onto the sky. In spite of the crowds, from this position, high up on the edge of the hilltop, she can see the glittering sweep of the bay, the blue haze of the mountains. She stands, mesmerized. The first time Amara saw the sea was at the harbor in Piraeus, waiting to be loaded onto the cargo boat with all the other goods. The water had looked dark and frightening then, the savage kingdom of monsters which kept Odysseus from his home, just as she was being taken from hers. But here at Pompeii the sea looks different. From this height, it has the illusion of calm, a burnished silver mirror, reflecting the sky.

Blasts from horn pipes and flutes draw her attention back to the ceremony. The slaves have carried their painted Venus up the steps onto the dais and set her in front of the altar. Facing the crowd, the goddess of love's eyes are thickly lined with black, giving her a staring, watchful look. She is naked apart from gold jewelry encircling her arms and the garlands draped around her neck. Behind her, the temple is a half-finished shell. Worshippers aren't usually allowed in here, but the priests seem to hope today's offerings will encourage the goddess to bless the construction work. Amara catches sight of Victoria and Beronice squashed beside Gallus. Beronice is leaning against her lover, and Amara realizes with a jolt of surprise that she is clutching a single pink rose to her cheek.

More blasts on the pipes, and the ceremony begins. A waft of smoke drifts toward Amara and she breathes in. It smells sweet with the tang of cinnamon. Priests are burning incense, making offerings of grain and wine. One miscalculates the strength of the flames and an attendant has to step in to protect the goddess from flying sparks. People in the crowd murmur and exchange uneasy glances. *Surely that's not a good sign?* Amara looks up at Felix, but his face is impassive. She supposes he can't be especially pious, or he would have bought them better garlands.

The women are called on to approach the steps. For a moment, Amara wonders if Felix is going to come too, but he releases her arm and gestures for her and Dido to go ahead. Cressa joins them, lips moving in prayer, and they walk forward arm in arm. Amara wonders what Cressa is asking for. She looks down at her own crumpled offering. All the prayers of her childhood were to Athene; she doesn't know what she should ask her new mistress, doesn't know how much she believes in the gods at all.

Temple slaves guard the base of the steps to prevent over-zealous worshippers getting too close to the altar. Some of the women are weeping, raising their arms to the statue, milking the moment, others simply drop a sprig and leave. Victoria and Beronice are already at the front. Beronice lobs her rose so hard toward Venus, one of the attendants reprimands her. Victoria is uncharacteristically quiet, unweaving almost all the myrtle from her hair. She kisses it and lets it fall. Cressa lets go of Amara's arm and pushes ahead. Amara and Dido hang back, uncertain.

"What do we ask for?" Dido whispers.

Amara looks up at Venus. It's the closest she has been to the statue. Those painted eyes, so black and wide apart, don't just look watchful but angry. She is not only the goddess of love, Amara thinks, this is a deity who drives men to madness, a destroyer of warriors, author of the fall of Troy.

"We ask her for power over men."

Amara pulls Dido closer to the steps. She takes her sprig in both hands, crushing it to release the scent. *May men fall to me as this offering falls to you, Greatest Aphrodite. May I know love's power, if never its sweetness.* Amara drops her mangled garland on the ever-growing pile of heaped offerings from the desperate whores of Pompeii.

13

"Learn singing, fair ones. Song's a thing of grace;
Voice oft's a better procuress than face."
—Ovid, *The Art of Love* III

Felix's women loiter at the entrance to the Forum, trying to decide which way to go. The Vinalia has taken hold like a fever. Clumps of drinkers stand around, while street musicians and performers stoke the excitement, urging people to dance. At the edge of the square, wine sellers are busy behind their stalls, making sure nobody goes short. Their master has given the she-wolves permission to stay out until evening—an unheard of amount of freedom. As if to prove his point, Felix has already abandoned them and wandered off to join a group of men. Amara isn't sure what to do with herself.

"Don't just stand there!" Cressa says, shooing her and Dido toward the nearest wine seller. "Make the most of it!" Cressa buys herself two flasks of honeyed wine, keeping one in reserve, while she knocks back the other.

"Shall we share one?" Amara suggests. The wine is expensive, the sellers' obviously pricing in the captive audience and the loss of some of their flasks. Even on a festival day, Amara is reluctant to spend a single penny she might save for her future. Time enough to drink when she's a free woman.

"I can get the next one," Dido agrees as Amara takes a flask from the seller's outstretched tray.

"For fuck's sake!" Victoria laughs, elbowing her. "Live a little! You're not old women yet." She makes a point of buying herself a drink, rolling her eyes at them both as she hands over the money.

"That's the spirit, goddess," the seller says, looking Victoria up and down. She has a small piece of cloth tied around her breasts, another round her hips. Her legs and waist are bare. "It's not often I get to sell to Venus herself," he continues, smacking his lips. "For a kiss, you can have the next for free."

"Done," Victoria says. She downs the flask and thumps it back on his tray, making the dark liquid in the other jars wobble.

"*You* don't miss a trick."

"Do you want that kiss or not?"

He leans forward eagerly, but Victoria steps back. "Drink first." She points to Amara. "My friend will hold it for me."

He obliges then takes hold of Victoria with one arm, holding his tray out with the other. Before Amara can warn her, the wine seller's hand has reached the knot at Victoria's back. He yanks the material down, trying to expose her breasts. She shoves him off, and he lets go, anxious to save his tray.

Victoria laughs. "These will cost you more than a flask of wine," she says, hoicking the material back up again.

"If you're in the mood later, you can find me at the Wolf Den. That's if you can afford it." She takes the wine from Amara, and the three of them push deeper into the crowd. "Best way to get a drink at the Vinalia," Victoria says. "You shouldn't have to pay for more than one."

"Beronice doesn't seem to be paying for *any*," Dido says. "I just saw Gallus get her a flask."

"So he should," Victoria replies. "He's had enough free fucks off her." They stop to join a small circle that's formed around a flute player. A woman is dancing to the music, the men clapping and cheering as she lowers herself to the ground, her backside and thighs quivering. "Drauca!" Victoria exclaims. They stand and watch for a moment, but Victoria is restless. "Here, you can keep this," she says, handing her drink back to Amara. She shoves her way to the center of the circle, ignoring the catcalls, and stands in front of her rival. "I'll show you how to move, bitch!"

Victoria flings herself into the dance, bumping and grinding, shaking herself at her yelling audience. Drauca only hesitates a second before joining in. The flute player ups his tempo, piping so fast it seems impossible the dancers will be able to keep time, but they do. One of the men throws his drink at the women, and others follow, screaming encouragement. Red liquid shining on their skin, dancing with the ferocity of wolves, Victoria and Drauca look less like whores and more like the fevered acolytes of Dionysis about to rip each other limb from limb.

"There you are!" Beronice heads toward them. She is draped over Gallus like a garland, her cheeks shining. Nicandrus trails after them both, holding a small bunch of roses. "We've been looking everywhere for you!" She stands on tiptoe to see what all the nearby shrieking is about and recognizes Victoria. "*Such* a show-off! And she's taken *all* her clothes off! Do you like it?" She turns anxiously to Gallus. "I can dance like that for you, if you like? Do you want me to? Would it turn you on?"

Gallus answers by seizing her and sticking his tongue down her throat.

Neither of them look likely to break for air anytime soon, so Nicandrus pushes in front. "These are for you," he says to Dido.

"Thank you." She takes the roses and holds them to her heart. "You're always so kind."

"I'll be back in a moment," Amara murmurs, half expecting Dido to protest. But perhaps the honeyed wine or the atmosphere has taken the edge off her shyness. She is pleased to see Dido smile as Nicandrus bends to say something to her.

Amara has no idea where she wants to go. The flask of wine Victoria gave her is warm in her hand, and she sips it, wandering slowly through the square, stopping now and then to listen to various players. She wonders if Salvius might be here with his pipe.

The crush is not as intense as in the procession, and the noise of so many competing musicians, the cheers, the laughter, echoes off the stone and rises into the warm air like an offering to the gods. It's the first time Amara has been completely alone like this in a crowd. She looks briefly at the people she passes, not to attract unwanted attention but to get a sense of those around her. Has she been with any of these men? It's hard to know. In the brothel, she tries not to focus on their faces.

Amara walks a little faster, back toward the area where she left Dido, aware that she doesn't want to drift too far from her friends. She is so intent on her purpose that she almost misses him. Menander. He is walking in her direction, staring at all the women he passes, his brow creased with worry. Then he sees her.

"There you are!" he says, his face lighting up. "I *knew* I'd find you." His joy and the lack of effort he makes to hide it warm her like wine.

"I bet you say that to all the women at the Vinalia." She laughs.

"You know that's not true, Timarete."

The switch to Greek, as always, hits her harder. "Rusticus is a generous master," she says. "Letting you wander about a wine festival at will."

"He is generous. But only to a point. I have an hour, that's all."

Amara cannot look away from his face. She thinks about her prayer to Venus Aphrodite. *May I know love's power, if never its sweetness.* Perhaps the goddess is punishing her for her arrogance. "Let's not waste it then," she says, reaching out to him.

They walk hand in hand through the crowd, not saying anything at first, not even sure where they are going, carried along on a current of shared happiness. "I've been to the Sparrow three times since I last saw you," he says. "That's every evening I've had off. The barman told me you usually only visit during the day."

"But you kept coming?"

"Of course! A small chance of seeing you is better than none."

The thought of Menander waiting for her just over the road, while she is powerless to join him, is almost too painful. "I'm sorry I wasn't there," she says.

"Does your master give you any time off for the games? I think he must do; the first game in July is traditionally for slaves too."

"July?" Amara asks, horrified at the thought of a date so far in the future.

"Can't you wait that long for me?"

She knows he is teasing her. He has the same air of confidence she remembers at their first meeting when he claimed the lamp in her hands as his own. She smiles, not wanting to give him everything at once. "I expect so."

They reach the end of the Forum. A musician is playing a slow, melancholy tune on a lyre. Amara watches, imagining the vibration of the strings under her own fingers. "I used to play," she says. "My father liked me to sing in the evenings. Though only in private," she adds, hoping he will understand that in Greece, unlike Pompeii, she came from a respectable house.

"Why don't you ask him to let you borrow it?" Amara laughs, thinking he is joking. "Why not?" he presses. "It's the Vinalia. You should be free to demand what you like."

Amara is spared from answering when she spots Dido, now standing alone. Beronice and Gallus are nowhere to be seen. "There's my friend," she says, pointing. "We should join her."

"I remember her," he says. "She has a beautiful voice."

Amara introduces them both again. She is pleased to see Dido pretend not to remember Menander. He would never guess they have both spent more hours poring over his name and character than priests divining entrails on an altar. "Where's Nicandrus?" she asks.

"He only had a few minutes to spare; he just came to give me these."

The musician on the lyre begins a jauntier song. A couple beside them cheer and start dancing. Dido sways to the music, holding her roses.

"I have to leave soon too." Menander looks at Amara. "Will you have one dance with me?"

"I'm not sure I know how." She thinks of a family wedding she attended back home, the childhood glee of spinning round and round with her cousins. "I've only ever danced with women."

He takes both her hands and pulls her closer to the lyre. "Everybody's drunk," he says. "We can make it up." She hesitates, but the clapping, the twirling, the stamping, are infectious. Amara and Menander link arms, turn, stop and clap, faster and faster, over and over, until she collapses against him in laughter. The musician ends his tune with a flourish, holding out the lyre and bowing.

"Ask him now," Menander says. "I want to see you play before I leave."

She looks at the lyre with longing but shakes her head. "I can't."

Menander lets go of her and heads over to the musician. She sees him greet the man then turn back and gesture toward her. They have an urgent exchange. The musician nods and beckons her over.

"How could I refuse such a request," the musician says to her in Greek, as she approaches. Amara looks at Menander, wondering what he can have said. "Of course you must play." He hands over his instrument.

For a moment, Amara feels nothing but panic. Her mind is blank, she cannot remember a tune, cannot remember how to play a note. She looks up and sees people staring, curious, waiting to hear what she will perform. Dido is watching too. "Sing with me!" Amara calls to her, desperation in her voice.

Dido hurries over. "What are you doing?" she whispers. "We can't sing here!"

"What about that love song Salvius taught us?" Amara's cheeks are burning at the prospect of handing back the lyre, unplayed.

"I don't think I can remember it," Dido says, but Amara has already started strumming the strings with the plectrum. The first notes strike her as shockingly discordant. It's an unfamiliar instrument, with seven strings, not ten, and it takes her a while to work out which chords will recreate the Campanian folk song. She is concentrating so hard on getting the music right that she forgets about the crowd, even about Menander. With every touch to the strings, her confidence grows a little, and the music sounds a little sweeter. She launches into the first verse. To her relief, Dido joins her.

The crowd clap and several sing along, prompting them to remember the words. She is conscious of Menander smiling, nodding encouragement, but it's hard to keep sight of him with dancers swirling and stamping past her. Instead, she looks at Dido. The performance has lent her the confidence of a stranger. She is holding herself with a boldness she never manages walking the streets. Amara catches her eye, and they start to sing to one another. It becomes a conversation, the passing of a look, a gesture, a feeling, even as they sing the same words. They repeat the song, but this time Amara stays silent when Dido sings the role of the shepherd, and understanding her, Dido leaves the role of the woman to Amara. They tell the story as a duet, playing up the comic element, Dido ever more pleading, Amara increasingly absurd in her proud rejection. At the end, Dido feigns collapse of a broken heart, sending a ripple of laughter through the small crowd.

Amara laughs too, looking for Menander, hoping to find his approval. She cannot see him. His absence jolts her, but she is too caught up in the moment for sadness to swallow her. Two young men at the front are clapping and chanting, demanding another song. Others join in. Amara looks at the crowd, at the faces watching her. It is a power she has never felt before, this sense that she might shape the expectations of others, hold their desires in check, or release them. She bows.

"We are celebrating the goddess of love," she says, her voice loud. "Perhaps you would allow us to sing a hymn to our mistress, Aphrodite?" She makes no effort to hide her foreign accent, deliberately calling Venus by her Greek title. The two men at the front yell their approval, and Amara turns to Dido, speaking quietly. "If I sang a verse to you in Greek, line by line, would you be able to sing it back to me?"

"I think so."

Amara strikes the lyre with the plectrum, the chords swift and insistent. The notes take her back almost instantly to Chremes's house, and the way he watched her in the lamplight with the greed of a fox waiting for its prey to falter. This was not a song she learned as a child. The memory is bitter. Amara imagines herself back at the feet of the painted Venus, breathes in, remembers the feel of the myrtle crushed beneath her fingers, its sweet scent.

Aphrodite, subtle of soul and deathless,
Daughter of God, weaver of wiles, I pray thee
Neither with care, dread Mistress, nor with anguish,
Slay thou my spirit!

Dido listens intently, her eyes never leaving Amara's face. She repeats each line back at a lower pitch, her voice catching the haunting quality of the song. It's not a tavern favorite, like the folk tune, but their audience is eager to enjoy themselves, swaying to the music, some even clapping as they pick up the rhythm.

At the second verse, one of the young men gives a sudden shout of recognition, slaps his companion on the back. Amara looks at them both more closely. One wears an expensive brooch at the fastening of his cloak. It is bronze, inset with red stones. She smiles, beckoning them toward her. The pair are drunk, but not insensible, and notice her flirtation. They draw a little closer, catcalling. Behind them, she sees a more familiar figure. Not Menander, but Felix. He is flanked by Thraso, watching her and Dido with an expression that she would mistake for fascination, if he were any other man. Perhaps he understands, finally, what they might be worth.

They reach the last verse and just as she hoped, the two young men push themselves forward. "Sappho?" one says, laying a hand on her arm. "A little grand for the Vinalia, isn't she? Whose women are you?"

Felix slips between them, swift as smoke. "The girls are mine," he says, bowing low. Amara has never seen him speak with men of this class before. He is slighter than the two drunks, but she knows who would win in a fist fight.

"Perfect for Zoilus, don't you think?" The man says to his companion, barely acknowledging her master's presence.

The other laughs hysterically, slapping his thighs. "You have to, Quintus! You have to!"

Quintus smiles at Felix, the sort of grimace the rich reserve for servants. "How much to rent the pair for the evening?"

"The whole night?" Felix asks. Amara understands he is playing for time, trying to assess how far he can push it. She feels the warmth of Dido's body press closer to hers. Their proper role in this exchange is silence, but there are other ways to communicate. She answers with a brief brush of the fingertips.

"Of course the whole night, man! We want them to adorn our esteemed host's party!" His companion again collapses into guffaws. "You must have heard of Zoilus?" Quintus continues with a smirk. "Foremost freedman in Pompeii."

Felix is himself a freedman. Amara suspects that neither Quintus, nor his friend, have any slaves in their own ancestry. Her master inclines his head graciously. "For such a host," he says. "Fifty denarii."

The man called Quintus doesn't flinch. "Done."

"Of course, if you want the lyre as well," Felix replies. "That will be another twenty."

Even Quintus is not such a fool as to miss the fact he's been tricked, but he clearly doesn't wish to haggle like a grocer. "Very well," he replies. "You can have twenty now as surety for the rest."

It is Felix's turn to hesitate. Amara hopes he is not going to whip out a wax tablet, insist the men sign a promise for the extra cash in their own blood. Twenty is already more than she and Dido would earn overnight at the brothel. And surely, he must understand that men like this trade on their names all the time? Felix gives another bow. "For such honored customers, my pleasure."

Quintus snaps his fingers and several men in the crowd hurry over. Of course this pair wouldn't go anywhere without a retinue of slaves for protection. "Twenty for the *gentleman*," he says, nodding at Felix, and the oldest slave takes out a purse, well-hidden under his cloak. Thraso steps in beside the line of men, ensuring the trade is screened from view. Behind them, she can see the musician craning to get a look, no longer smiling at her. Gallus is at his elbow. They must have already cut a deal for the gift of his lyre. She hopes it was based on promises rather than threats.

"Quintus Fabius Proculus," says their temporary master, showing Felix his signet ring. "Where shall I send the payment?"

"To Gaius Terentius Felix Libertus at the establishment opposite the Elephant Inn."

"The Wolf Den?" Quintus begins laughing so hard, Amara thinks he will choke. "Marcus! We did a deal with the town brothel! *Wait* until I tell the others we brought Zoilus a pair of she-wolves!"

Felix does not defend his business, the promise of a small fortune no doubt providing enough balm to soothe his pride. Amara knows she should also say nothing but wants to reassert her presence. "I hope we will still be pleasing to you." She lowers her head, looking up at the men through dark eyelashes. "We only wish to serve."

"*Darlings.*" Marcus puts an arm around her and Dido, breathing wine in their faces. "You are *perfect.*"

14

"It was more like a musical comedy than a respectable dinner party."
—Petronius, *The Satyricon*: "Trimalchio's Feast"

Dusk has cast its haze over the streets as they walk to Zoilus's house, the stone buildings darkening into silhouettes against the orange sky. Amara had been surprised by just how many men in the crowd belonged to Marcus and Quintus. Six slaves now follow behind, a silent, protective troop, while two more go ahead with oil lamps. Quintus has her arm; Marcus has taken ownership of Dido.

"What are you doing working for that greasy little pimp?" Quintus asks, helping her over a stepping stone. "You're both so pretty. Lovely voices too."

"Thank you," Amara replies. His denigration of Felix gives her a strange feeling. For all her hatred, she realizes she must share some sense of identification with him. He does own her, after all. "I used to be free. In Attica. My father was a doctor in Aphidnai."

"Your old pa didn't teach you Sappho's songs though," he says, raising an eyebrow.

"No. I learned that as a concubine."

"Yes, I'm sure you know *plenty* of tricks." He stops to look at her more closely. The slaves in front also come to a halt, attuned to their master's movements. "Has anyone ever told you what beautiful lips you have? Red, like the heart of a pomegranate."

Amara understands the role he wants her to play. She smiles, dark eyes promising all he might wish to see.

"Hey!" Marcus complains, thumping his friend on the back to interrupt their kiss. "We're already late for Zoilus."

"Fuck's sake. Not like you've got an armful of one of the prettiest fucking whores I've *ever* seen," Quintus replies, as they start walking again. "You're lucky I took this one." He shrugs at Amara in apology. "No offence. She is more beautiful. You just have the sexier mouth. I like that."

Amara laughs. "And you're bold," she says. "I like that too." Quintus purses his own lips in pleasure. It always amazes her the way men accept flattery from a prostitute. Though in this case it's not a complete lie. She can see Marcus and Quintus are different from the rich men at the baths. No doubt, by the end of the night, they will expect the same service, but a whole evening of entertainment, conversation and singing is the prelude. Her heart beats faster, and she glances back anxiously at the slaves carrying her lyre. It's a long time since she has felt this alive.

They have walked down the length of the Via Veneria to the less fashionable end of town, not far from the Palaestra. The two lamp-bearing slaves stop outside a tall doorway, its massive wooden doors set ajar. Light from inside shines dimly on the marble doorstep.

"How are we going to do this?" Quintus asks Marcus. "The clothes are part of the joke, but it's almost funnier if he doesn't notice what they are."

"Isn't the old man's wife going to kick up a bit of a stink if we walk in with two naked girls though?" Marcus looks nervously at Dido. Amara wonders what they both talked about on the walk from the Forum.

"It's the Vinalia! Girls are meant to be naked!" Quintus protests. He turns to Amara. "What do *you* think?"

Both men are looking at her, waiting for an answer. Briefly, she considers the state of her and Dido's clothes. The colors are bright, but she knows the fabric marks them out instantly as cheap. There are few crimes as great in Pompeii as poverty. A naked entrance will trumpet their status as prostitutes, but perhaps not as objects of total contempt. She tilts her head toward Dido, a silent question, and gets a little shrug in answer. Amara smiles broadly at Quintus. "I say *naked*."

He whoops with delight, helping her out of her cloak and handing it to one of the long-suffering slaves in his retinue. Then he gets to work enthusiastically on her toga, removing it in a couple of tugs. Amara notices the clothes-bearer is the old man with the purse. He averts his eyes rather than look at her.

"Are you sure?" Marcus asks Dido, undoing her brooch, fingers fumbling from drunkenness. "You don't mind?"

"You're so kind to ask," Dido says, head down as she steps out of her toga.

"Perfect." Quintus turns from one woman to the other, both now standing naked and shivering on the threshold of Zoilus's house. "In we go."

They walk over a fine black-and-white mosaic of a snarling dog, elongated the length of the narrow hallway, and emerge into the biggest atrium Amara has ever seen. It is at least five times larger than the one at Chremes's house, her only real point of comparison. The mosaic from the entrance ripples outward in ever more intricate patterns, flowing into other darkened chambers that surround the hall. A table of solid silver stands beside a large pool to collect rainwater. Moonlight from the opening at the ceiling's center glows on its polished surface, and its pale reflection wavers in the water. Other precious objects—goblets, plates and lamps—are piled in a heap on top. Many look like gold. Put together, she knows it would cost several times the price Felix paid for her.

Behind her, their new masters' slaves negotiate with Zoilus's doorman, identifying the party as invited guests. The doorman doesn't sound happy about something, no doubt the presence of two naked women. She hears the word *actresses* repeated in the murmured discussion.

"This way," Quintus says, waving a hand airily, as if he were leading them into his own home. "The master will be in the dining room with his guests."

Amara resists the urge to skirt the edge of the atrium, following Quintus with a confidence she doesn't feel, clamping her teeth together to stop them chattering. When they reach the marble pool and the groaning table of silverware a ferocious barking rings out. She and Dido clutch each other, nearly stumbling into the water with fright. She looks back to see a dog straining against its chain on the far wall, a long way out of reach. The doorman shouts at it to be quiet.

Marcus and Quintus both laugh. "Perfect," Quintus says, slapping her hard on the backside, a gesture that reminds her of Felix. "You pair are absolutely fucking *perfect*." Amara likes him less this time. She stands straighter, still smiling, determined not to be the butt of jokes for the entire evening.

They pass through an enormous garden, walking round the painted colonnade. Scenes from the legends of Hercules flicker in and out of view. In the middle of the lawn, a fountain is illuminated by hanging lamps, its spray falling in the darkness like stars.

"This place," Dido whispers to her. "Where *are* we?"

"You like the house then, ladies?" Marcus asks.

"It's beautiful," Amara replies.

"Zoilus is a *freedman*," Quintus says, contempt apparent in the careful way he stresses the word. "Who knows. If you get your freedom one day, maybe *you* could have a house like this."

A house with money but no class. The sort of place a whore would find impressive. The meaning behind their visit, which Amara has resisted acknowledging, could not be clearer. She and Dido are intended as an insult to the host, a gift to represent his own low value. She can feel her cheeks burn in the shadows. Whoever Zoilus is, she will try not to disgrace him. Or herself.

They pass into a bigger walled garden, thick with plane trees. It is well lit and even without Quintus as a guide they would be drawn by the growing sound of laughter and conversation. The dining area is at the back, half in the garden, half in a room painted to look like a grotto. Two artificial streams cut through the area, diners sitting and reclining on couches set at the water's edge.

"Zoilus, my *dear fellow*," Quintus says, sounding like a parody of a man of his class, striding toward the host's couch. "I'm *so sorry* we are late. My father, *sadly*, could not come, but he *insisted* we bring along two of his treasured possessions for your entertainment. A pair of lovely little actresses. What could be more fitting to celebrate the Vinalia?" The background conversation quietens. Amara can hear titters and muttering from the other diners. She stands tall, looking straight ahead, ignoring the wild beating of her heart.

Amara had not formed a clear picture of Zoilus in her mind, but the man lying in front of her is nothing like what she would have imagined. The swathes of expensive fabric, yes, but not the nervous, darting eyes, the thin mouth twitching like a goat when it chews. Now he is staring at her and Dido, his face creased in confusion. Her sense of shame deepens. "Ah," he stutters at last. "How kind. How kind the young men are, aren't they, my love? Very modern, don't you think, Fortunata? To bring actresses."

Fortunata, who reclines next to Zoilus, has not missed the insult. She has a sharp, intelligent face, marred by thick makeup that sits caked over her forehead in lumps. Slave brands, Amara realizes. Fortunata must be disguising her former humiliation. "Yes, husband," she says in a loud voice. "Very *modern*."

Some of the company laugh. Fortunata smiles coldly at her two new guests, ignoring the naked girls entirely. Quintus smiles back, but Marcus has the decency to look uncomfortable. Zoilus swats at his wife in annoyance. "You'll have to forgive Fortunata," he says, the cringe of an apology in his voice. "She's rather old-fashioned. Please tell your father I am most honored. I hope he will visit soon, to receive my thanks in person."

"You must let them sing for you," Quintus presses. "That would please him most. To know they have pleased you."

"Very well, very well," Zoilus says, looking at Amara and Dido without huge enthusiasm. "But first, you must enjoy my new cook's speciality. We are just about to serve."

A slave in bright green silk hustles them away to a large empty couch. Amara sees with a pang that they are being placed at one of the most prestigious spots. Zoilus must have really wanted to impress Quintus's father. The two men recline, and she and Dido join them, draping themselves over the cushioned couch. She is conscious that nearby guests are staring. *I am not ashamed*, she tells herself as Quintus runs his hand across her breast and down her side. Another slave, dressed in the same lurid green as the first, appears with a silver platter, handing them all glasses of wine.

"Did you see Fortunata's face?" Quintus murmurs to Marcus, taking a sip. "Jumped up little bitch." Away from the full glare of his hostess's anger, Marcus laughs. Amara clutches her glass. Quintus kneads the flesh at her waist. "Drink up darling, this is the most expensive Falernian I've ever tasted."

"Two thousand sesterces a jar," says a red-faced man loudly from the couch beside them. "Only the best wine with Zoilus. Finest house in town. Bet you were pleased for an invite. Too bad your old dad couldn't make it." Quintus rolls his eyes and Marcus snorts into his glass. "So actresses are the thing now?" The older man continues, too drunk to notice their disdain. "Have to say I'm with Fortunata. That's all a bit modern for me, even for the Vinalia."

"Wasn't Fortunata once an actress herself?" Marcus asks.

"I don't know who told you that!" The old man is indignant. "She's a respectable freedwoman. The marks . . . I agree, they're . . . well, they're unfortunate. But that was from childhood. Before she was in the old master's household. Zoilus's master, I mean. Old Ampliatus."

Amara glances up at the couch where the hosts are reclining. A cascade falls into the waterway beneath them, decorated with carved dolphins. So Fortunata was branded as a child. She wonders what her young life must have been. She hopes the former slave is enjoying her wealth now.

"Really?" Quintus says. "How *fascinating*."

"He didn't have to marry her. Zoilus, I mean. But you know what he said to me"—the guest leans closer to them, almost toppling off the couch in his bleary state—"'Nicia, he said, I couldn't stand by and have men wipe their dirty hands on my Fortunata's front at dinner like she's a *fucking napkin*. Course I freed her, course I married her.'" Nicia raises his hand in a wobbly toast. "Too fucking right. That's love, that is."

"Beautiful," murmurs Marcus. Amara can feel Quintus shaking bodily with laughter beside her.

"I know many songs about love," she says. "Few reveal as much true devotion as Zoilus showed Fortunata."

Nicia nods vigorously. "You're right, that's true. That's true."

Marcus has to disguise his laughter as a coughing fit. Quintus leans closer, breathing into her ear. "Perfect girl."

Amara twists round and smiles at him. She understands, finally, how she can entertain all the audiences at this party. Quintus is far too ignorant to understand that she was sincere. She is safe to pay her respects to her host; the men who brought her will only imagine it's mockery. A little more at ease with herself, Amara taps Dido's arm. "Can you *believe* it here?" she whispers. She looks at the other guests, lounging on their couches beside the two streams. Dozens of oil lamps blaze with light and give off a heat that makes her nakedness easier to bear. Nobody else here is short of clothes. Some are sweating under the physical weight of their wealth. One woman wears a headband so heavy with jewels she is struggling to prop herself up on her elbow.

"We can't sing that old folk song at a party like this," Dido whispers back. "We *can't*."

"I think you'll find you can," Quintus says. "But first, here comes the old man's novelty dish." A troop of men in scarlet prance in, carrying an enormous platter on their shoulders, the way you would see slaves carry a litter in the streets. A huge pie sits on top, with a pastry lid crafted to look like a swan.

"Shame you were too late for the seafood." Nicia sniffs. "Those sea urchins were really something."

"How do you know Zoilus?" Dido asks him, unable to take her eyes from the monstrous pie.

"He's my dearest friend. The times we've had together!" Nicia sounds maudlin. "Our old masters loved each other as boys. And the pair of them did alright for Zoilus and me in the end. Mine left me my freedom in his will, though not a fortune *as well*." He swills his cup, holds it out for more wine. A boy in green scurries over with a large silver wine jug. "Not that old Ampliatus ever had all this. Zoilus can turn anything to gold. Always has done." Amara cannot imagine Felix leaving her so much as a tunic in his will, let alone her freedom. The thought of him making her his heir is almost comical. "You watch now," Nicia says to them, gesturing at the giant pie. "You'll like this."

The slaves guarding the pie stand aside as another man in red strides toward it brandishing an enormous knife. He bows to his master then skewers the pastry with a flourish, lifting the lid and standing back. He pauses. Something was evidently meant to emerge, but there's no movement. The cook leans over, poking at the inside with his knife. A handful of sparrows fly out, dazed and twittering. Two don't make it far from the platter before collapsing.

There's a mortified silence. "Bravo," Quintus yells, clapping from his couch. "*Bravo*!" Other guests join in, hesitantly at first, but then the applause builds to a crescendo. Amara glances over at Zoilus, sees the gratitude on his face. Fortunata looks furious.

"Shame," Nicia mutters. "It was meant to be a flock of sparrows, flying out for Venus. Must have smothered in the heat. That cook should have made bigger holes."

Quintus swings his legs from the couch and stands up. "My most esteemed host, while the dish is served, I insist you enjoy the sweet delights of a musical performance." He beckons over one of his own slaves who presents the lyre with a bow. Amara hopes the light is not strong enough to reveal what a cheap instrument it is. In this house of wrought silver and beaten gold it looks like a peasant's plaything.

"Yes, thank you," Zoilus says, nodding vigorously. "Delighted."

Amara takes the lyre and helps Dido off the couch. They pause a moment, taking strength from one another. "We'll sing Sappho's hymn first," Amara murmurs. "Aphrodite will smile on us; none of her worshippers are as beautiful as you."

Amara walks purposefully toward the stream then steps over it, avoiding the floating oil lamps. Dido follows so they are standing side by side between the waterways at the center of the gathering, light from the flames flickering on their skin. She feels grateful now that they left their togas at the door. She is not ashamed of her body the way she would have felt ashamed of her clothes. She whispers to Dido, and they both turn toward the host and bow.

Zoilus and Fortunata lie on their couch, watching. She knows she can neither speak to them with the crudeness of a whore nor the modesty of a doctor's daughter. There is no language from her past or her present. She will have to fashion a new one.

"Our names are Amara and Dido," she says, her voice cutting clearly through the tinkle of the water and murmur of the company. "We are your most grateful guests. We are here to celebrate Venus Pompeiiana. And in a garden of such beauty, the goddess of love would imagine herself in the groves of Olympus, should she choose to grace us here now with her presence." She nods toward Fortunata, who looks away. "We are, as you can see, the lowliest of her servants. But tonight, on the Vinalia, even worshippers like us have our place."

Amara takes the lyre, positions it in her arms, trying to ignore the plectrum trembling in her fingers. She strikes a chord. "And who better to praise Aphrodite, than the Tenth Muse, the Poetess of Lesbos?" She turns to smile at Quintus.

Amara and Dido begin Sappho's song, nervously at first, but with each line, as they sing the verses back and forth, they find their own joy in the music. They sway to the rhythm, copying one another's movements, just as they repeat each other's phrases. Dido guides Amara to turn as they sing, focusing on different guests, drawing them in. The crowd are not entirely won over—Amara has given Fortunata up as a lost cause—but many of the men are clearly enjoying the performance.

At the end of the song, they bow and Zoilus claps. He looks relieved. Perhaps he had been expecting something else. "Charming, charming," he says. "Very thoughtful of your father, Quintus."

"You must let them finish with a comic turn," Quintus replies. "All the best actresses do."

Amara glances at Dido, who raises her eyebrows. What choice do they have? Nothing for it but to belt out Salvius's folk number. Another flowery invocation to Venus feels excessive, so Amara begins strumming the strings of her lyre without explanation. Dido launches straight into the role of the shepherd, clasping her hands to her chest with a wail of mock despair. The guests look at each other, a little uncertain how to take the change in tone, but Amara beams round at them before ramping up the melodrama as the scornful mistress. Quintus and Marcus cheer loudly at each chorus, seeming to enjoy the performance even more than they did at the Forum. Other diners look less amused. But Dido's collapse at the end manages to raise a few laughs, and best of all, the arrival of the sweet dishes brings their performance to a close without the need for labored goodbyes.

Amara feels light-headed from nerves, excitement and lack of food as they make their way back to the couch. A third man is now sitting upright between their escorts, dressed in a cloak of midnight blue.

"This is Cornelius," Marcus says, slurring. He tries to slap his friend on the back and misses. Zoilus's wine has clearly gone to his head. "Cornelius! A lion in a herd of freedmen! He's in on our little joke."

Cornelius is older than Marcus and Quintus, and his stare, when he greets them, is harder and more knowing. He pulls Dido onto his knee, gesturing for Amara to sit beside him. "Aren't you both *lovely*," he says. "I could hardly tell from the first song. But that last number would have stretched the credulity of *anyone* but Zoilus." He laughs, resting his free hand on Amara's thigh, higher up her leg than she would like. "With a little more movement, a few more suitable songs, you could be quite delightful." He is looking at Dido as he says this, stroking her arm. Her face has taken on the blankness Amara recognizes whenever a man is mauling her. She wants to catch his wrist and stop him. Cornelius turns toward Amara, and she blinks. He smiles, as if he sees through her anger and is amused.

"How would you feel about performing at a *real* dinner party?"

15

"He who lies down with dogs will wake up with fleas."
—Traditional, attributed to Seneca

Amara's head throbs with tiredness and her cheeks ache from laughing. It is a happiness unlike any other, sitting with her fellow she-wolves in the Sparrow, recounting the pleasures of the night before. They have treated themselves to a larger meal than usual. Bowls of chickpeas, bean stew and olives clutter the table.

"The birds in the pie were *boiled* then?" Beronice shrieks, cackling with laughter. "After all that fuss?"

"Not so loud," Cressa murmurs, with one hand over her eyes. She is sipping her way through a small glass of wine, trying to recover from her hangover.

"That cook should have taken a few tips from my kitchen," Zoskales says from behind the bar. "And I could have supplied him with a much more reasonable wine than *two thousand* sesterces a jar." He snorts at the absurdity of the sum.

"This Cornelius," Nicandrus loiters at their table, "the one who liked your singing. He seemed like an honest man?"

Amara and Dido look at each other. "A bit early to tell," Dido replies, glancing up at him. She has one of the roses he gave her yesterday in her hair. It's the sole survivor from his garland which spent the night bundled up in her discarded toga.

"Come on!" Victoria says. "What about *afterward*?"

Nicandrus moves away, heading back to the kitchen. Amara shrugs. "Not that impressive. I preferred the party." It had been a strange end to the night. The four of them back at Quintus's house, all in the same bedroom, slaves wandering in and out to top up the wine, sex just another social exchange.

"You telling me they paid seventy denarii for no poking?" Victoria says. There's an edge to her voice. She has been laughing along with everyone else, but Amara knows she is devastated to have been excluded from such an exciting night. None of Felix's women have ever been paid to attend a private house party.

"They were quite drunk," Dido says.

Beronice and Zoskales laugh. "Money can't buy you everything," the landlord says. "Certainly not sense."

Victoria pulls a disgusted face. "Couldn't get it up then?"

Dido shakes her head. This isn't entirely true. Marcus had been unable to perform after the party but had more success in the morning. He had proved an exhausting lover, nagging Dido for constant approval, wanting to know if she was *really* enjoying herself, would she like it better from behind? Even Quintus had rolled his eyes. Amara guesses Dido would prefer Nicandrus to hear a less eventful version of her exploits whenever the evesdropping Zoskales fills him in.

"Yours was a flop too?" Victoria needles, jigging Amara's arm. "No action *at all?*"

She feels irritated at the focus on the least interesting part of the evening. "A few blow jobs," she replies with a shrug. "The *action* was the party." Amara turns back to Dido with a smile. "I still can't believe we sang that bar song. The look on their faces when you started!"

"And they didn't even want to swap girls? Having paid for *both* of you?"

Victoria's question is interrupted by the arrival of Felix sauntering into the bar, wearing a look of absolute self-satisfaction. "And how are my favorite whores this morning?" he demands, gesturing impatiently for Cressa to move along so he can squash in between Amara and Dido. He kisses them, one after the other, taking their faces in both his hands and squeezing hard. "Your boys paid their debt. Sent their slave round this morning." *He looks elated,* Amara thinks. She has never seen him in a mood like this. "Zoskales! Everything for the girls is on me today! Some wine for us all." He smiles at Beronice, Victoria and the drooping Cressa. "Even if you didn't all earn it."

"Poor Dido didn't even get a fuck out of them," Victoria sighs. "Her lover was limp as a cabbage."

"And they still paid!" Felix looks at Dido with renewed respect. "What a girl you are."

"It wasn't just about sex," Amara says. "You heard us sing. That's what they paid for, that's what they wanted. To be entertained."

"They could have dressed up as chickens and ordered a spanking for all I care," Felix says, taking the wine from

Zoskales as he brings it over. "As long as they paid." Beronice and Victoria snigger. Cressa buries her head in her hands, moaning at the noise. Felix tops up all their glasses. "So what was it like, this party?"

"The house was . . ." Dido hesitates, trying to find words that will conjure up the scale of the wealth. "Enormous. So much silver and gold! And fountains. And the world's *biggest* pie."

"Apparently the wine cost two thousand sesterces a jar." Zoskales sets one of his own amphora down behind the bar with a thump. "Madness."

"Almost everyone at the party was a freedman," Amara says. "Apart from the posh boys who bought us. And they did nothing but sneer." She remembers Fortunata and her branded forehead. "If *I* were rich, I wouldn't bother inviting men like that to share my wine. Why set yourself up to be laughed at?"

"Yes," Felix says with feeling. He glances at her then turns away. It is a rare moment of intimacy between them. "But the question *is*"—he stretches out his arms and puts them around her and Dido—"can you pull this trick off again?"

They both start answering at once, eager to tell him everything about Cornelius, from his blue robe to the songs he requested. "Too much, too much!" Felix points at Amara. "You can explain it upstairs." He keeps his hand on Dido's shoulder, pushing her downward as he rises. "You stay here. It's quite enough with *one* mouthy little whore."

Amara struggles from the bench after her master, looking back at her friends enjoying their free lunch. Beronice is digging into the food again, Cressa seems to have dozed off and Victoria is purposely avoiding her eye. Dido mouths *good luck*. She walks round the corner to Felix's flat, trailing behind him on the narrow pavement. Paris opens the door, and their boss shoves past him, pulling Amara up the stairs.

"In here," he ushers her into his study. The room, which always used to intimidate her, seems small after Zoilus's house. The painted bulls' skulls, usually so full of menace, look flat after the exquisite frescoes in Quintus's bedroom. She is already imagining herself elsewhere. Felix sits down, making himself comfortable. "So when can we expect more from our boys?"

"At the Festival of Flora," Amara replies, pulling up a stool without being invited. "But it's a different client. A man called Cornelius. This booking is a sort of . . . trial. He wants to see if we can do even better. Then he might have us more regularly."

"Do better?" Felix frowns. "He fucked you too but without paying?"

"No." Amara tries not to let her irritation show. "He wants us to do better at the singing and dancing. He's asked us to join him for the first night of the festival next month, for the Floralia, to perform at a private party. He didn't use either of us." She thinks of the way Cornelius gripped her thigh, his calculating stare. "Though I'm sure that would be part of the price. He said to tell you it would be seventy for the trial. Ninety for future bookings."

"All this money for *singing*," Felix says, taking his tablets out of a drawer to scribble down the sums she has promised.

"Well, whatever works. You and Dido had better practice. You can play up here, so I know what you're up to."

"There was something else," Amara says. She takes a silver coin from her purse, the one Nicia had pressed into her hand as she and Dido left. *For your sweet words,* he had said. *For Fortunata.* It is almost physically painful for her to place it on the desk in front of Felix and move her hand away. "A tip," she says, looking at him. "I would like to spend it on performance clothes for us both, maybe some music lessons."

"You expect me to be grateful for your honesty?"

"No. I expect you to understand a good investment. These men want a certain style. This"—Amara plucks at the worn material of her toga—"is not it. We performed naked last night. But you can't play the same trick every time."

He pushes the coin back toward her. "Take it then. But I want proof of how you spend it." Felix stretches his arms out behind his head, leaning back and grinning at her. "You're not the only one who had a successful night." Amara is slow to hide her surprise. She hadn't thought they were so intimate. "Not *that*, for fuck's sake," he says, laughing at her expression. "I wouldn't call a woman a *success*." He inclines his head. "Well, maybe if she earns me ninety denarii. No. I mean Simo has finally been taught a lesson." Amara feels the smile freeze on her face. "Some drunks trashed his bar late last night. Smashed the place up." He shrugs. "These things happen at the Vinalia. A lot of drunks around. Sadly, pretty little Drauca didn't move fast enough. Her face doesn't look so pretty now. Not after a glass took out her eye."

Amara stares at him, all the air crushed from her lungs. "No," she says, as if the word can wipe out what he's done.

"No." She thinks of Drauca at the baths, her perfect body and lovely face. She covers her own in horror. "*No!*"

"What's the problem? You were the one who suggested turning over his bar in the first place. You didn't even like the girl."

"But Drauca never did anything to you!" Amara shouts, torn between grief and rage. "She's just a woman! What will happen to her? How will she work? How will she eat? How will she *live*? Her poor face . . ." she breaks off, choked by tears. "Her poor beautiful face."

"She won't be competition for any of *my* girls, that's for sure," Felix says, completely unmoved by her distress. "Simo will have to spend a lot of money if he wants to invest in another whore like that. And I doubt he can afford to, not with the bar to repair."

"Was *Drauca* the real target?" Amara's sense of horror is growing. In her mind's eye she can see Drauca dancing with Victoria at the Vinalia last night, full of life, face lit with passion. She feels like she might pass out.

"Amara, come now." Felix's voice is soothing. He gets up from his desk and walks over to her, pulling her up from the stool. He holds her upright, gripping her shoulders, not quite in an embrace. "Don't pretend. You were the one who suggested biding my time, not striking straight after the baths. None of these men can be traced to me. Why do you think I keep so many of my clients private?" He draws her a little closer. "The thing about revenge," he says, his breath soft in her ear, "is that destroying your enemies is all that matters. Bragging about it, identifying yourself, that's for children." He stands back, releasing her slowly so she doesn't fall. "Now." He claps his hands as if to wake her from a trance. "Enough. You and Dido need to get yourselves some pretty clothes, start practicing your songs."

"Why tell me? If it's not bragging, why tell me?"

Felix perches on the edge of his desk, studying her. "Because you have even more to lose if this gets out than I do." He looks up at the bulls' skulls on the wall, as if suddenly noticing a new detail in the design. "Or maybe Simo would consider *Dido* more valuable than you. She is prettier after all."

Fear grips Amara. She feels it sink deep inside, like a hook piercing a fish, and understands it is a pain that will never let her go. Felix picks up Nicia's silver coin and uncurls her fingers, pressing it into her palm. She says nothing. He turns his back on her, settling himself behind the desk again.

"Drauca didn't do anything to you," Amara says. "She didn't deserve this."

Felix laughs. "Nobody gets what they *deserve*." He looks genuinely amused. "What do you think it takes to survive in Pompeii? It's not all sucking cocks and fine dresses. Now off you go, get a fucking move on."

Outside his flat, Amara leans against the wall of the brothel. She wants to scream, to smash her fists on the door, howl out her anguish. Instead, she stands silent, jaw clenched shut. The need to tell, to share the burden of knowledge, presses against the sides of her skull. She closes her eyes. Nothing will be gained by sharing this. Why should Dido walk in fear too? Every waking moment shadowed by the memory of what Felix has done. She doesn't consider trusting any of the others, not with a secret this lethal.

You were the one who suggested turning over his bar in the first place. Amara breathes in deeply, rubbing the silver coin between her fingers. There is nothing to be done but imagine it never happened, to try to pretend, even to herself, that she doesn't know.

The others put her silence down to Felix's usual tricks when she rejoins them at the Sparrow. Cressa has already left, gone to sleep off her hangover in her darkened cell.

"The man can never give it a rest," Beronice says, swiping the last of the chickpeas when it's clear Amara doesn't want them. "Sodding Felix. Always got to prove *his* cock's the biggest."

Dido squeezes Amara's hand under the table, and she feels a flood of guilt. Would her friend love her the same if she knew about Drauca? Was she really the one who gave Felix the idea?

"I don't think I'd be wearing a long face if he sent *me* out to buy new clothes," Victoria says. Amara knows what pains Victoria takes with her appearance, the hours she spends on her hair. She looks very upset, almost tearful, and Amara's sense of guilt deepens.

"If there's anything left over, we can buy something for everyone to share," she replies. Beronice and Victoria exchange a little look with each other, more sharp than grateful, and she understands that the sudden, unequal change in fortune is unlikely to bring them all closer together. "I guess we had better get going." Amara rises from the table again. Dido follows, eager to start shopping.

It's early afternoon, the sun baking the filth in the road, sharpening the smell of manure left by passing horses and pack mules. "Where should we go?" Dido says. Her face is bright with excitement as they head down the street, the back way that joins onto the Via Pompeiiana. "How many outfits can we buy?"

"I guess just one to start with, in case we don't get more bookings."

"Don't let Felix ruin this." Dido stops, her expression earnest. "Don't be unhappy. We have so little."

"You're right," Amara says, making an effort to smile. "Let's try Cominia's place. I've always wanted to go inside."

The dressmaker's is on the town's main shopping street, not far from Rusticus's lamp store. All the women like to visit from time to time, to loiter at the front billowing with fabrics, softer and finer than anything they can hope to wear. A small, round portrait of a younger Cominia, painted high up on the second storey, looks over her empire. Dido goes first, pushing through a tunnel of hanging material.

Inside, their eyes adjust to the dimmer light. Cominia herself is busy at the main counter with a customer, a matron whose slave lurks behind, ready to carry the load home. The two she-wolves stand, watching, unsure what to do.

"How can we help you, ladies?" A young assistant appears at Dido's elbow. She is thin, with a small, sharp-featured face. Her expression is polite but firm. If they cannot afford anything, they had better leave.

"We need clothes suitable for the Floralia," Amara says. "To entertain at a dinner party."

"You will be guests?"

"No," Dido says. "We will be . . . singing."

"I understand," the assistant says with a bow. "I am Gaia. Please come with me."

They follow Gaia, who parts some heavy gray linens hanging at the back of the shop, revealing another smaller room behind. It is much darker in here, and an oil lamp is burning. "I know exactly what you need." Gaia's tone is business-like. She has clearly decided these are not customers who need sweet-talking. "We supply a lot of actresses and concubines. This is by far the most popular fabric."

She is holding up a silvery material, so fine it is transparent. Gaia runs a hand gently underneath, demonstrating its translucence. "Assyrian silk," she says. "With a silver weave. You can see *everything* through it. If you want to tease, you can buy more fabric and fold it, making it opaque as required." She shows them, deftly manipulating the silk so that her skin is half-hidden in a glittery sheen.

"How do you fasten it?" Amara says, too nervous to touch the flimsy fabric. "Wouldn't a brooch tear it?"

"We sell special pins. I can show you how to fix it. But it doesn't tear that easily—the weave is tight." Gaia looks at them a little impatiently. "Are you going to try it on or not?"

Amara and Dido step out of their togas, letting Gaia dress them. They watch each other closely, trying to memorize how to fold the material when they are alone. Gaia gets out a tray of pins. "We go from the basic model"—her finger points at a round stud—"to something more delicate." Her hand travels to the other end of the tray, with its shaped birds and dragonflies.

"We could try the bird model for now," Amara says to Dido. "It fits with singing. Don't you think?"

Gaia pins the fabric in place for them both. They stand apart, looking each other up and down. "It's like wearing a cobweb!" Dido says.

"That's part of the magic," Gaia replies. "The men love it, trust me."

"Do that again," Amara says to Dido who has just moved nearer the light. She obeys. "It's lit you up! You've gone completely silver."

They both walk round the flame, admiring each other, moving to make the silk change color, feeling it rustle against their skin. "If you *really* want to make an impact," Gaia says, "we have this." She gets out a small jar from the cabinet, opens it for them both to see. Inside is a thick gold paste. "For the eyes," she says. "And also to gild the nipples."

There is very little left from Nicia's coin when Amara and Dido leave Cominia's shop. They buy the largest jar of gold paste on offer, planning to decant some into another pot for the others to use.

"We'll have to give the dresses to Felix," Dido says, holding her parcel close to her chest. "We can't risk leaving them lying round the brothel. One of the customers will steal them."

"He wanted proof of where we spent the money anyway," Amara replies. They are walking the main road home, and she knows they will soon be passing the lamp shop. She is desperate to stop.

"Isn't that where Menander works?" Dido says.

"Oh, yes."

"Give me that." Dido motions for Amara to hand over her new dress. "Why don't you go in?"

"I don't know, maybe we shouldn't." Amara hesitates, half-craning to get a view into the shop while they tussle with the fabric. Menander is inside. She gives up and lets Dido take her parcel. It takes him a while to see her loitering on the street. He is with a customer and gestures for her to wait.

"We were just passing," Amara says when he comes out, anxious to include Dido. "And we wanted to thank you."

"Thank me?"

"Yes. Because you got us to sing. Our master was listening, and he bought the lyre." Amara remembers the street musician's face and hopes Felix did really pay for it. "And now we are booked to sing at the Floralia. At a party."

None of it is quite what she wanted to say. But at least she is talking to him. "I'm glad he bought you the lyre," he says. "You played it so beautifully."

"*Menander!*"

"I can't stay now." He looks nervously over his shoulder. "Can I write to you? On the wall, outside the Sparrow?" He lowers his voice. "I will use Timarete and Kallias, so nobody knows."

"Yes," Amara says. "Yes."

Menander turns and hurries back inside without saying goodbye.

16

"I pawned earrings with Faustilla for 2 denarii.
She has deducted an ass a month in interest"
—Pompeii graffiti

The line at the well stretches along the street. Not that anyone is paying much attention to waiting their turn. Amara and Dido don't bother to shove ahead with the rest, loitering in the late morning sunshine instead. It's not the most restful place to stop. Hammering, banging and shouting rings out from one of the grander houses nearby. It has been dilapidated for as long as Amara can remember, the owners killed in a terrible earthquake, or so Victoria told her. Somebody new must have bought it, decided to spend their money on decking it out like a palace. One of the team of builders leans out from his ladder, whistling at her and Dido. They ignore him. He won't be buying a woman for hours. Barely worth their notice.

"Everyone liked the gold," Dido says, raising her voice to be heard. "They all used it last night, didn't they?"

"Beronice certainly did," Amara says, remembering the way Beronice had smeared it copiously around her eyes, and her fury when Victoria laughed at her. *That's what men in this stupid town expect Egyptian women to look like!* Beronice had insisted, face sparkling like a temple statue. Amara cannot imagine how small Pompeii must feel to Beronice after growing up in a great city like Alexandria, although as a slave, perhaps she never saw much more than the house where she worked. Victoria and Cressa had shared the new pot too, but Amara suspects it will take more than gold paste to smooth over the others' envy. The shift in power to the Wolf Den's newest women has unsettled everyone. "Felix will want us to practice for Cornelius today," she says. "We have to come up with some other songs."

"We could always ask Salvius for help," Dido says.

"I wouldn't know where to find him. Do you think Nicandrus might know?"

"He runs the ironmonger's, the one near Modestus's bakery. I think he owns it. I spent time with Priscus that night when you were talking to Menander. He told me where they both work."

Amara feels a sharp tap on her back and spins round, angry, expecting it to be the builder come down from the ladder to try his luck. A young girl steps back in alarm, clutching an enormous bucket to her hip.

"Sorry! I didn't mean to startle you," she says. "But aren't you from the Wolf Den? I'm sure I've seen you both at the Elephant before."

Amara looks at her. She sees eyes smudged with blue and shoulders stooped with exhaustion. A memory surfaces.

The same slight girl scurrying between customers at the Elephant, a nervous smile on her face. "Yes. You're the waitress, aren't you?"

"Pitane," says the girl. "I don't just wait tables though."

"No." Amara remembers Victoria's taunt to Drauca, about the customers she has to service as well as serve. She turns away, not wanting to think about her former rival or remember her suffering.

"It must be hard work," Dido says kindly. "The Elephant is always so busy. Have you got friends there?"

"Martha. She was my friend. But she died in childbirth. Hazard of the job, isn't it?" Pitane is staring at them both, desperation in her face, willing them to understand. "I guess you must both know all about that, about how to avoid it. Or how to . . ." She trails off.

End it, Amara thinks. "Is it *avoiding*, you want to ask about?" Pitane shakes her head. Amara glances down at the girl's waist, taking in her thin figure. "There's a woman you can see. But don't wait too long."

"You don't keep anything yourselves?"

"The herbs have to be fresh."

"*Amara*," Dido is shaking her head. "Not here."

"I don't have the money." Pitane looks disappointed. "I thought you might keep the herbs, that you might spare me some, let me pay you back over time."

"But why? Wouldn't your master be pleased?" Amara says. "They're usually happy to have home-grown slaves."

"Martha took three days to die," Pitane says. Amara and Dido exchange glances. Every woman understands the danger, the horror that childbirth can bring.

They have missed their place in the queue, but none of the three women rush to push back in. "If it's money you need," Amara says. "Then we might be able to help. But you have to be very sure you can pay it back."

On their walk to the ironmonger's Dido does not mention the deal Amara has just done, does not ask her whether Marcella has paid her debt yet, or when it's due. But Amara can feel her palms sweating at the thought. She tells herself that there's still time for Marcella to deliver, her debt isn't late yet. And perhaps finding Pitane will incline Felix to patience.

They pass the bakery and stop at the ironmonger's, listening to the clang of metalwork inside. "Do you think Salvius will even remember us?" Dido says.

"How many beautiful singers do you imagine he meets?" Amara replies, shifting the lyre higher in her arms, covering her nerves with bravado. It had been difficult to wrest the instrument from Paris. They had to pretend their music lesson was already arranged. No doubt he will drop them in it with Felix if the visit proves a failure. "*Of course* he will remember."

They walk past the front counter where a slave is busy with customers and head deeper inside. The flute player is at the back supervising an apprentice, helping him fashion a lamp stand, holding it steady while the boy hammers at the legs and giving the odd word of encouragement. He is as Amara remembers, the same kind manner and graying hair. The two women wait, not wanting to disturb him.

When Salvius looks up, she can see him take a moment to place them, but then he smiles. "This is unexpected," he says. "The lovely singing sparrows. What can I do for you?"

"We wanted to ask a favor." Amara holds up the lyre as an explanation, hoping to pique his curiosity.

Salvius walks over, wiping oil from his hands onto his leather apron. "If you're looking for an accompanist, I only play the flute."

"I would be playing," Amara says. "We were hoping you might teach us some tunes."

"We would pay for your time," Dido adds.

"Flavius," he calls to his apprentice. "Keep working on the feet, please. Just how I showed you." He turns back to the two women. "Let's talk."

They follow him, climbing the narrow wooden stairway to the floor above. "I'm not much of a musician," he says. "You might be disappointed. Where will you be playing?"

Salvius's living room is painted in warm shades of yellow. A procession of swans fly from panel to panel and tiny larks are painted around the skirting. He sits on a bench, inviting them to take the one opposite. "It's a party, much grander than anything at the Sparrow," Amara says. "On the first day of the Floralia. We were thinking of setting poetry to some popular tunes."

"Mixing high and low?" Salvius asks.

"Yes," Dido nods.

"Sounds fun. But what will you pay me? Or should I ask *how* will you pay me."

"That depends what you would prefer." Amara slips her toga off one shoulder, not far enough to show much but enough to make her point. She hopes he will take the bait. Salvius is not an unattractive man, but her reason for wanting him has little to do with desire and everything to do with saving money.

"Deferred payment would suit me best," Salvius replies. "An evening or two of your company, here, at my house." He nods at Dido. "I will invite Priscus."

Amara has no idea how Felix will react to this proposal, evenings are their most lucrative hours, but before she can suggest seeking their master's approval, Dido answers. "We would be delighted."

"I cannot spare too long today. Perhaps enough time to teach you a couple of tunes depending how quick you are." He rises, walking to a desk covered in clutter. His back is turned. They can hear him rifling through pots and boxes before he returns with the flute. "There are so many songs about spring," he says. "This one is Oscan. I don't suppose either of you speak the language?" Salvius looks hopeful, and Amara wonders if Campania's ancient tongue is also his own.

"No."

"Nevermind. You can adapt the tune as you wish."

Salvius begins piping. He is a more skilled musician than Amara remembers. She can hear the trill of birdsong in his tune, the sigh of the wind, and imagines Flora dancing, half glimpsed through the trees, in the repeated haunting melody. He stops, taking the flute from his lips. "Again? Or shall we go through it, line by line?"

Amara is nervous she will not match him. She picks up the lyre. "Let's go through it."

He is a patient teacher. He breaks the tune down for them, waiting for Amara to find the corresponding notes, nodding when she chooses chords that fit. Dido sings the melody note by note, committing it to memory. Their version is nothing like as lovely as his reed pipe solo, but it is enough to take away and polish.

"How about something a little more playful?" Salvius asks. They nod. He pauses, breathing in deeply, flute poised. Then he begins. This time he bobs and sways, closing his eyes at the higher notes. It is not beautiful like the first tune, but Amara can immediately see the potential. It is a tease of a song, perfect for her and Dido to play to one another. She takes up the lyre, daring to join Salvius as she anticipates the repeated melody. "I thought you might like that," he says, when they reach the end.

He begins again, not breaking it up this time, instead, letting them pick up the tune as he plays, as if they were back at the Sparrow. Amara throws herself into the music, even forgetting for a few moments that they are together for work rather than pleasure. She is expecting to perform it a third time, but Salvius stops a few notes in, almost as if he has forgotten what comes next. Dido's voice trails off into the silence.

"That should be enough for now." He turns his back to them, returning the flute to its box. Then he stands, resting his hands on the desk. "We can leave it there." His tone is not unfriendly, but something has shifted. Amara wonders if they offended him in some way, or if he has simply remembered his work.

He faces them again, making an effort to smile. "I hope that gives you something to work on."

Amara and Dido talk over each other in their effort to mollify him.

"It does! It was so helpful . . ."

"We're very grateful, I hope we didn't . . ."

Salvius waves away their thanks, ushering them both to the stairs. "I will send your master a message, to explain the arrangement." They wait, expecting him to go down first, but he holds out his arm as a gesture for them to leave. "I have some business up here. Be careful how you go."

At the brothel, Amara lets Dido do most of the talking. She watches Felix, his smile, the way he listens, his nods of encouragement. She sees Dido relax, lulled into thinking he is in a good mood, but all she can think about is Drauca. *Destroying your enemies is all that matters.* She stares at the bulls' skulls on the wall, the shadows of their empty sockets. It is not until Felix turns to her that she realizes Dido has just offered to perform for him, and they are both waiting for her to pick up the lyre. She finds she cannot move.

"No need to be shy," Felix says.

"We haven't chosen the words yet," she stammers. "Maybe we could practice a little first?"

"Music means nothing to me," Felix shrugs. "I just want to know you're working. Play next door if you like."

Dido helps her up. "Thank you," she says, answering for Amara who hasn't spoken. "We appreciate it." They walk out onto the balcony, and Dido slips an arm around her. "You shouldn't be so afraid. He wasn't angry today."

"I don't think you can ever know with Felix," she mutters as they head down the corridor.

"*Amara.*"

His voice stops them. Felix is standing in the doorway of his room. "A moment, before your singing. There is something I forgot to ask. No, not you," he says as Dido turns to go back with her. "Take the lyre for her."

Amara watches her own feet cross the painted wooden floor as she walks toward him. He takes her hand, guiding her over the threshold. "You didn't tell her," he says when they are inside. Amara says nothing. She knows it isn't a question. He takes her chin between his finger and thumb, forcing her to look up. "There are many ways to spill a secret. Especially if you sit there like a quivering sheep. Do you understand?"

"You are threatening me *not* to be frightened?"

"That's better. A bit of temper."

She isn't sure what she hates more, feeling afraid of him or sliding into familiarity. She pushes his hand away. "One of the waitresses at the Elephant wants a loan from you," she says. "Two denarii."

"*Two* denarii? Why chase small change like that when you will be making me seventy next week?"

"It's all money. Nobody got rich turning down a deal."

"What's the debt for?"

"An abortion."

"And she can afford it?"

"She says so."

"Like your fast-food seller." Felix crosses to the desk, looks through the drawers until he finds the agreement with Marcella. "We're still waiting for her. I didn't think you were meant to be taking on any more debtors until the first had paid up?"

"But her loan isn't due yet."

"Don't try it. You know her instalments have been too light. And I never accept late payments, particularly not from a *woman*." He smiles, as if suddenly remembering he is not meant to be threatening. "But then, of course, it's *you* who is collecting her payment, isn't it? So she is quite safe. Until the day it's late. Then the debt is mine."

17

*"Trickles of acacia pomade ran down his sweaty forehead and
there was so much powder in the wrinkles on his cheeks
he looked like a peeling wall in a thunderstorm."*
—Petronius, *The Satyricon*

The room still holds the heat of the spring day and is
much more crowded than Amara was expecting. A
troop of mime actresses, all of them naked save for garlands
of flowers, are practicing their routine. She and Dido look
overdressed in comparison, with their silvery robes and
gilded bodies. One of the actresses glances at them sidelong
then turns back to her friends, laughing through pretty
fingers.

"I didn't know there would be so many other performers,"
Dido whispers.

Amara's own fingers are sticky with paste. They had tried
to decorate the lyre, and although it now shines golden, so
do the palms of her hands. "It's as well we look different,"
she says, trying to convince herself as much as Dido. "We
couldn't *all* be naked."

"A few more flowers and you will be *perfect*." It is a deep boom of a voice. Egnatius, the self-declared master of Cornelius's entertainments. Amara is startled by his interruption; she didn't notice his return, but there is no sign he took their mutterings amiss. Instead, he is now fussing with Dido's hair, weaving the white roses he went to fetch between her curls. She has never seen a man wear so much makeup. His eyes are lined with kohl and the thick powder on his cheeks is cracked like badly dried plaster. The grooves cut deeper every time he smiles, which is often. "Such a pretty little thing," he says, standing back to admire Dido. "I never saw a face more exquisite." He turns to Amara, teasing his remaining flowers into her hair. "Except yours, *of course*, darling," he drawls, raising his eyebrows. She finds herself laughing. Egnatius purses his lips, pleased to have amused her. He is standing so close, his breath is warm on her cheek and the smell of acacia pomade in his hair is almost overpowering. He tweaks the last rose behind her ear. "Now!" He claps his hands together in a theatrical gesture of excitement. "What will you two nymphs be singing for us this evening?"

"Several verses from Sappho," Amara says. "A medley of songs about Flora and the spring and the tale of Crocus and Smilax."

Egnatius nods. "Very pretty. Perhaps you could sing me a line or two, so I know where to place you?"

Amara begins to play Salvius's Oscan song, which she and Dido have set to a well-known hymn to Flora. The mime actresses break off their own rehearsal out of curiosity, and Amara is gratified to see their expressions change from amusement to grudging recognition. She couldn't ask for a higher compliment.

"Delightful!" Egnatius beams. "Your voices are as sweet as flowers falling from the mouth of Flora herself! Have you read any Ovid? Oh, you must, you *must*," he declares when they both shake their heads. "I will write you out some of Cornelius's favorite verses for next time."

Amara wishes she had known Cornelius had a favorite poet before this evening but is touched by Egnatius's generosity. "Thank you," she says.

"You are too kind," Dido adds, laying her hand on his arm. Her sincerity is unmistakably genuine.

"You know," Egnatius continues, "my master is something of a poet himself. He has composed a few lines for the Floralia, if you could find some way of weaving them in . . ." He reaches inside the folds of his cloak and brings out a roll of parchment.

Amara restrains herself from seizing it. "We would be more than delighted."

Egnatius hands over the small scroll. Amara unrolls it, and she and Dido huddle round. For a moment, she cannot believe what she is reading. Then the words bring a stab of fear. She looks up sharply at Egnatius. "You are *certain* he will be pleased to hear this recited."

He meets her eyes, and the unspeakable truth passes between them. "I am certain." He bows. Then Egnatius gestures toward the mime actresses who are still busy with their rehearsal. "Ladies, goddesses and nymphs, I look forward to being entertained by you all. You will be sent for in the order you are required." He turns back to Amara and Dido. "I will make sure you have enough time to learn the verses."

"But it's *terrible*," Dido says, when he has gone. "How can we stand there and sing this stuff?"

Amara can feel herself sweating under her flimsy clothes. "We will just have to make it work. At least it's not very long. That last song Salvius taught us, could we sing it to this?"

"I suppose," Dido says, looking miserable. "But when?"

"At the end. When most of the guests are drunk."

The mime actresses are standing crowded together in their cloaks to escape the evening chill by the time Egnatius returns to call Amara and Dido in to dinner. There are not many oil lamps where they have been waiting, and Amara finds herself blinking as they pass into the brighter parts of the house.

"You look glorious," he says, leading them through a bewildering procession of rooms. The place is so large they did not even hear the guests arrive. Somewhere in this labyrinth, she knows Paris and Gallus are waiting out the long night to escort them safely home. Their value to Felix has gone up substantially. "Quite *ravishing*. Both as lovely as Flora herself."

Amara has the feeling Egnatius compliments everyone who comes to perform for Cornelius but is still grateful for his encouragement. They are walking too quickly for her to absorb all her surroundings. There is immense wealth here, but no table groaning with silver at the entrance as there was at Zoilus's house, instead when they reach the main hall, panel portraits of Cornelius's ancestors line the walls. She can hear laughter and snatches of song.

"Through to the garden," Egnatius murmurs, ushering them along. "I find it works best if you move between couches as you perform. And don't be afraid to involve the guests. Or to accept any *invitations*."

Dido looks at Amara. Neither of them are sure whether Egnatius means an invitation to share the wine or something else. The air is heavily scented with roses. Their branches have been trained around the walls in trellises, making a pattern of green splashed with color, reminding Amara of her mother's skill in weaving the threads on her loom. Cornelius's dining room is open to the garden on two sides, its walls and ceiling painted with the same flowering rose trees which grow in the front courtyard. The garden behind is so vast it is almost a meadow.

They draw closer. The guests' bright clothes blur and shimmer, seen through a screen of water. A fountain cascades from a giant conch shell held up by three marble nymphs. Amara realizes that the details on their naked bodies are gilded, not unlike the gold she and Dido have smeared on themselves.

Egnatius nods at the fountain. "I *told* you you were perfect," he says, raising his eyebrows. They walk past the nymphs and wait at the edge of the gathering. The atmosphere is more relaxed than their last party. There is also a clear imbalance toward men, with only four or five women present. Cornelius is laughing loudly at something his neighor has said, at ease with his role as host. She sees him flick his eyes in their direction, but he waits for another guest to finish his anecdote before acknowledging their presence.

"My dear friends," he says, raising his voice. "We have Marcus and Quintus to thank for finding us these two lovely musicians." Amara follows the direction of his finger as he points across the room. She sees their Vinalia lovers reclining on a couch, both looking rather less keen to be associated with the she-wolves now than they did at Zoilus's house. "Our boys were quite taken by these two songbirds." Cornelius beckons her and Dido over. "Or would that be nymphs of Flora?"

Egnatius has stepped back, melting into the other attendants serving the party. "Yes," Amara says, picking up on the host's playful tone. "We learned our songs from the goddess of spring herself." She glances back at the fountain. "In our former life as dryads."

"So many nymphs these days have a taste for gold," Cornelius replies. "Will you earn yours this evening?"

Both women bow. "Flora is a goddess of pure pleasure," Amara replies, striking her lyre with the plectrum. "And that is all we intend to give."

She and Dido slowly walk over to where their former lovers are reclining, while Amara plays the first notes of Salvius's spring tune. Amara sits on the edge of the couch, smiling coyly at the two men. They both laugh, less nervous now. Quintus rests one hand on her knee, pinching the silk between his fingers. Her closest neighbors are all listening, but she notices that some across the room are still chatting. She begins to play in earnest, and Dido takes up the melody.

Her voice rings out clear and sweet, silencing more of the company.

They arranged the Oscan song almost solely for Dido's voice. She weaves through the couches as she sings, plucking flowers from her hair and handing them to guests as she passes. For a moment, Amara worries she looks almost too pure and graceful—Flora is the goddess of sex, not poetry— but Dido has been working long enough for Felix to know how to behave. There is more than a hint of Victoria in the way she bends to drop a rose in Cornelius's lap.

"You should have given one to my wife," he says, pulling Dido closer to kiss her when the song is finished. "For all the children she's given me." It should be a compliment, but Amara can sense an unpleasant edge to his tone.

"You have a fine son," a woman replies from another couch, her voice querulous. She is younger than Cornelius and painfully thin. Even the brightly colored dress she wears, bunched in fat folds of expensive fabric, cannot hide how tiny she is underneath. Lying beside her is another woman, a little older, scowling ferociously. A friend, or perhaps even her mother. Amara still finds it difficult to understand the Roman custom of respectable women attending mixed dinner parties. Her own father would never have insulted his family by insisting they join him.

"Thank you, Calpurnia. Yes, *one son* after an abundance of girls."

"And delightful girls they are too," another man declares. "A credit to you both."

"Women have their uses," Cornelius replies, letting go of Dido. "Will you sing another song, little dryad?"

"Would you like a story?" Dido asks, glancing over her shoulder at him as she walks back toward Amara. "We can tell you the tale of Crocus and his love for Smilax."

"And we will sing of the goddess Flora who gave the unhappy lovers new life," Amara adds, finally breaking away from Quintus whose wandering hands have made her fearful for her expensive clothes.

Dido heads toward the fountain and Amara follows. In the lamplight, their figures must blend with the marble nymphs, she thinks, the hint of nakedness, the sparkle of gold on their bodies. She begins to play and, as always, watches Dido's transformation with wonder. The way she stands, so unlike herself, is both comic and somehow sinister. She could almost be one of their customers at the brothel, singing the role of the mortal Crocus in a parody of thwarted masculine lust.

Amara is Smilax, her voice deliberately shrill in rejection. Nobody is meant to have sympathy for the nymph, after all. She exaggerates the comedy, at times pausing her playing and holding up the lyre between them as a physical barrier. The guests laugh as Dido chases her, the song becoming more and more ridiculous, until they shift into another tune, allowing Flora to transform Crocus into a beautiful flower and Smilax into ugly bindweed. Dido sings the last notes, lifting her arms up like petals to the sun, until she stops, as still as the statues behind them.

The guests cheer, and Amara feels a flood of relief. She looks round at the unfamiliar faces, shining with wine and enjoyment. She smiles, bowing low. Egnatius is beside her when she straightens up, whispering that they must join the diners for a while. He leads them both, leaving Amara at one couch and taking Dido on to another.

"I always say Greek girls are the best," declares one of the two men she is now sitting between. He reminds her of an overfilled wineskin, not quite contained in the tight folds of his clothes.

"I like a bit of Gallic passion myself," replies the other, sipping his drink. His thick beard is curled, the black shot through with gray and ginger. "Though that was a lovely little number you sang just now. Not heard those words before."

"It's from a Greek poem," Amara replies. "The tune is local to Campania."

"Fuscus will like that," the first man says, nodding at his companion. "Always interested in poetry. More time to enjoy it now his stint as duumvir is finished." Amara turns to Fuscus and smiles, trying not to make her sudden interest in an influential man too obvious. The duoviri are the town's most powerful elected officials. Fuscus has a mildness to his face, she thinks. Perhaps he will be kind. Surely that's more important than the fact his hair is thinning? "Can't say I know so much poetry myself," the larger man continues. "I'm Umbricius," he adds, as if expecting her to be able to identify him by name alone.

"Forgive me," Amara replies in her thickest Greek accent. "I only just arrived in Pompeii."

"Oldest fish sauce business in town," Umbricius says. "And the best." He picks up a small jug from the side table and pours it liberally onto the plate of meat in front of them. Then he tears a strip off and holds it out for her on his knife. "Tell me what you think."

Amara takes it, eating the unknown food smothered in fish sauce as daintily as she can. It tastes like fermented anchovies left out too long in the sun. "Delicious!" she exclaims.

"What other Greek poems will you be singing?" Fuscus asks.

He is watching her lick the last of the sauce from her fingers. "Sappho," she says, leaning closer.

"Not very original." Fuscus stares through the transparent fabric of her dress. "But still a goddess among poets."

"What about some Latin?" Umbricius sniffs, clearly irritated at being overlooked.

"We will be performing a few lines by our host."

The two men laugh. "Oh, you poor girls," Fuscus says. "Do you have to?"

Amara knows it is one thing for Cornelius's friends to mock him, quite something else for her to join them. "It is always a pleasure to honor our host."

"Yes, yes, of course, *of course*," Fuscus says, rolling his eyes. "Well, I shall look forward to Sappho, at any rate." He takes her hand, rubbing his thumb over her fingers in an insistent, circular motion. "And perhaps you will join me again, afterward."

The atmosphere of the evening shifts as the hours pass and the wine flows. After every song, the guests become freer with her and Dido, their comments lewder. Fuscus exchanges words—or perhaps money—with Egnatius, who makes it clear that she is now the duumvir's special "guest." As the men become louder, the small group of wives play less and less of a role, retreating into their own self-contained gathering across two couches. Not that this assuages Cornelius's bitterness toward his wife. He contradicts everything she says—if she enjoys the honey-glazed dormouse, he finds it too sweet, her hopes of sunshine tomorrow are scorned. Even when she is silent, he cannot leave her alone, finding reason to mock her posture, her spinning, the way she holds her glass.

Already small, she seems to shrink further with every comment. Amara notices that her hand, when she raises the wine to her lips, is shaking. "I find I am exhausted," Calpurnia says at last. "I am sorry to leave you all."

Cornelius says nothing, as if she hasn't spoken. Thin and pale, his wife slips from her own dining room, looking more like a servant than the hostess.

"I don't know why he doesn't just divorce the poor girl," Fuscus says to Umbricius. "Put her out of her misery."

"Severus would ask for the whole dowry back if he had to take his daughter home. He's told me so himself." Changing his focus, Umbricius nods toward the older scowling woman who was sharing Calpurnia's couch and is now stabbing at the fruit on her plate with vicious determination. "My wife dotes on Calpurnia. I'll be getting a fucking earful after this, I can tell you. She'll be nagging me all night to talk to Cornelius. I've *told* her it makes him worse. But women never listen."

"That's why I left mine at home," Fuscus replies, his arm draped round Amara.

"You'll be staying then?" There's more than a hint of envy in Umbricius's voice.

"Oh, I think so, don't you?" Fuscus replies, drawing Amara a little closer. "I think so."

She smiles at him, hoping to convey how irresistible she finds the idea. Behind his head, she can see Dido sitting with Quintus and Marcus. The three of them are laughing together, like a pastoral scene of young lovers. She feels a pang of envy then reminds herself what a powerful friend Fuscus may prove to be. Neither of the Vinalia boys have shown much promise as regular patrons.

"Time for the mime, don't you think?" Cornelius's voice is loud over the hubbub. He is slurring badly.

"Not yet, not yet," Fuscus, shouts back. "I think the two little sparrows have a final present for you." He squeezes Amara's arm. "Sorry, darling," he whispers. "I couldn't resist."

"It's the parting I cannot forgive you for," Amara says as she gets up from the couch, letting go of his hand with a show of reluctance. She joins Dido back by the fountain, the blood beating loud in her ears. Neither of them have drunk much wine, but the same cannot be said for anyone else. Which is just as well. Cornelius's verses would be impossible to sit through sober.

"In honor of our gracious host," Amara says. "We have been bold enough to set your own hymn to music." She does not wait to hear the room's reaction but loudly strikes up on the lyre, at a much faster pace than when she played the same tune earlier. She and Dido sing in unison, as quickly as they can without gabbling.

Oh lovely Flora!
Goddess of flowers and fucking,

With your lovely toes and your dainty nose,
Your fanny like corn ripe for shucking,
Bless the spring with your lovely ring!

Oh lovely Flora!

Cornelius either does not care that everyone is laughing when they reach the final refrain or is too drunk to realize. He smiles as they all applaud, waving a hand as if to deprecate the admiration. "Just a trifle, a trifle," he says. "Though the girls sang it very prettily."

"Mime, mime, mime!" A number of people are stamping their feet, impatient for the final performance.

One of the nearby guests staggers up and takes hold of Dido, almost pulling her over in the effort to get her onto his couch. Amara hurries back to Fuscus.

"He must mean it as a parody, surely?" Umbricius is saying. "Fucking and shucking? It's parody."

Fuscus pulls her onto his knee. "Whatever it was, you looked adorable," he says, kissing her.

Egnatius leads in the eight mime actresses, two carrying long flutes which Amara had not seen them play in their rehearsal. She settles back against Fuscus, curious to watch them perform. "My wife won't like this," Umbricius mutters. "I'll never hear the end of it."

The two flautists let out piercing blasts and the actresses leap into action, more cavorting than dancing. What story there is to the play seems to revolve around some prank played by Flora on her nymphs, though the dialogue is thin and hard to follow. *Victoria would be better at this than any of them*, Amara thinks, watching the lead actress leap into the fountain like a frog and splash the others who shriek with pre-rehearsed alarm. An unwanted memory of Victoria dancing with Drauca slips into her mind, and she shrinks back instinctively against Fuscus.

He misunderstands her. "Soon, little one," he whispers in her ear.

By the end of the performance, the eight actresses have ended up sprawled over various men. Egnatius stands in the corner, taking stock of the room, sending a huddled group of slaves off to help where needed. It's the end of the dinner, but some guests show no signs of leaving, while others rise to say their goodbyes or collect their wives. Many are so drunk, their slaves have to act as human walking sticks. Umbricius stands up, groaning as he takes the weight on his knees. "Best get the old girl home," he says. "See you next week, Fuscus." Amara watches him stagger over to his wife whose face suggests she won't be waiting until they are home to share her thoughts about the evening.

Egnatius is hovering at the side of the couch. "Will you be joining the others?" he asks Fuscus.

"You know I never like to be watched." Fuscus is a little unsteady as he pushes himself upright.

"Of course." Egnatius helps Amara from the couch. He follows the direction of her anxious gaze. Quintus is arguing over Dido with the guest who claimed her at the end of their last song. "I will make sure she is safe," he murmurs. "Trust me."

"Thank you," she replies, her eyes meeting his as she stands. "For everything." Egnatius winks. He is as sober as she is.

"The boy will show you both somewhere more relaxing," he says, beckoning over one of the slaves.

Amara does not look back as the stranger leads her and Fuscus from the heaving dining room. They step into the cool night air, following their guide through the rose garden and into the darkened house.

18

"I hate and I love. How is this possible? Perhaps you ask.
I don't know. But I feel it, and I am tortured."
—Catullus, Poem 85

Amara wakes to the unfamiliar sensation of sunlight on her face. She is alone on the bed. For a moment, she cannot remember where she is, then memories from last night hit her in a rush. She sits upright, clasping the sheets to her chest.

There is no sign of Felix. He must have left for the Palaestra without waking her.

Amara breathes out. The sounds of the street outside the brothel are loud, carts rattling, the babble of conversations. She must have slept until the afternoon.

She follows her memories of the night, like a series of scenes painted round a room. It was Gallus who brought her back to the brothel by torchlight in the early hours, after Fuscus had finished. They came alone, as Dido was still busy entertaining. She had not been expecting Gallus to show her upstairs, but presumed Felix wanted to claim any tips. At that time, it was no surprise to find him in bed, more surprising that he had waited up.

Amara feels her cheeks grow hotter. It had been a pleasure to boast about the success of the night, Egnatius's promise to book them again, the tip Fuscus had given her. She had almost forgotten Drauca, sitting there with Felix, seeing his excitement at the money mirror her own. It was all the coins spread out on the bed that turned him on, she's sure of that, and the sex wasn't even that different from complying to his usual demands, though the lateness of the hour gave it an intimacy which was hard to ignore.

Even though she is alone, Amara covers her face with her hands in shame. When did she realize he wanted her to stay afterward? Did she want to stay? Did she linger too long? Remembering her feelings is like opening a door onto the darkest part of herself. Felix had held her hand so tightly, was still holding it, so far as she knows, after she fell asleep.

"I hate him," she tells the empty room. "I *hate* him."

She trawls through her memories, remembering every cruelty, the times he has raped her, his violence. *Drauca*. But other images push through like weeds. The figs he bought her and Dido, the laughter in his eyes when she met him at the Palaestra, his excitement at her stories last night. The fit of his fingers in hers. Amara flops back on the bed, flinging an arm over her eyes. "I hate him," she says again.

In the bright spots and blackness behind her eyelids, she conjures another memory, one that never existed, a vision brought to life solely by Felix's voice. *You could have been the goddess Diana, from the way you held yourself. As if you would call on your hunting dogs to tear apart every man who had* dared *to see you naked.*

Amara feels her breathing grow easier, soothed by more familiar feelings. The rage she had been searching for is still burning. Felix has seen her, seen all her loneliness and need, but she will not be torn apart by him. "I hate you," she says. "I will *always* hate you."

She swings her legs out over the bed, the wood cool beneath her feet as she stands. Her expensive silk clothes are still folded in a neat pile on a nearby chair. She cannot wear those; it will have to be nothing but her cloak. With the palms of her hands, she smooths out the bed, flattening it, hoping to wipe out all trace of her presence. Then she slips from the room.

Dido is alone in the brothel when she goes downstairs. At the sound of Amara's footsteps, she rushes into the corridor.

"*Are you alright?*" They ask one another the same question at the same time, then laugh.

"Did you spend the whole night with Fuscus then?" Dido says, leaning her back on the wall. She looks tired. "He seemed very keen."

"I had to see Felix afterward." Amara says, glad she doesn't have to meet Dido's eye as she changes into her toga. "But that was nothing; he was fine, pleased we had earned so much." She changes the subject. "I want to know what happened to you! Egnatius said he would look after you; I hope he did."

"He did," Dido says. "As much as he could. You wouldn't *believe* how odd that house is. Cornelius has a whole brothel at the end of his garden! A lot more luxurious than this place, and the paintings are better. But it's a corridor with cells, hidden behind the baths. And the finest room has a window looking into another cell." She makes a face. "He likes to *watch*."

"I should think he was too drunk to do anything *but* watch," Amara replies, grateful she only had Fuscus to entertain. He had been a dull lover but not a taxing one. Again, she can feel the warmth of Felix's body lying close to hers and pushes the memory aside.

"It's more than that," Dido says, with a certainty about men's tastes that would have been unthinkable a few months ago. "He's a watcher. I'm not sure he ever does anything else, drunk or not."

"Did you have to entertain a lot of customers?" Amara asks. "I hope they all tipped."

"It was mainly Quintus," Dido replies. "Cornelius wouldn't let that really drunk one in. I think he just wanted to watch the women with younger men."

"His poor wife," Amara says, imagining all Calpurnia must have endured with such a husband. "Did you hear the way he spoke to her?"

"She has a family, wealth, the respect of other women," Dido replies with surprising sharpness. "I wouldn't feel too sorry for her."

All the things Dido wants, Amara thinks. And the two she wants most, she will never have. Amara knows she herself would gladly settle for wealth at the expense of the rest. Respect and family did not, in the end, save her or her mother in Aphidnai.

The voices of the other three women float through the window moments before they step into the brothel.

"You won't believe the news!" Beronice exclaims as soon as she is inside. "Drauca is dead!"

"*Dead*?" Amara repeats with genuine surprise.

Life is cheap and a slave's life most of all. Dido, who didn't know about the fight, is curious but not shocked. "I didn't know she was ill," she says.

"She wasn't sick," Victoria says. "*Murdered*."

"No!" Dido grips Amara's arm. This hits closer to home. The threat of a violent customer always casts a long shadow.

"Some drunks turned over Simo's bar at the Vinalia," Victoria goes on, as all the others huddle round. "Drauca got caught up in it."

"She died on the Vinalia?" Dido asks.

"No, a couple of days ago," Cressa chips in. "She was in a bad way. Maria was at the baths today. She thinks Simo did it, though he denies it. He couldn't bear to look at her face anymore. It was all . . ." She trails off.

"She lost an eye," Victoria says. "Some cunt took out her *fucking eye*."

Amara understands the anger. Victoria didn't like Drauca, hated her even, but this is violence against one of their own. That a man held Drauca's life so cheap, reflects on all of them. "I imagine Felix would have done the same as Simo," she says. "If it had been one of us."

Victoria explodes. "Why do you have to make it about Felix?" she shouts. "Simo kills Drauca, and you turn it on Felix! Can't you give it a fucking rest for once?"

There are tears in Victoria's eyes. Her hands, as she pulls them through her hair, shake with agitation. *She knows it's true*, Amara thinks.

"We should go out," Cressa says, moving between them. "Amara, come with me."

Amara obeys, her own emotions too churned up to do anything but follow. They set off, passing the afternoon crowd at the fountain. Amara's heart feels heavier to drag along than an overflowing bucket.

"Where are we going?" she asks at last, as they cross the Via Veneria. It's a sweltering day, the afternoon sky almost white in the heat. They walk on the shady side of the road, hugging the walls of the buildings they pass.

"I don't know," Cressa says. "A bar, if you like? I could do with a drink."

"There's a fast-food place near the theater," Amara says. "I know the landlady."

"Fine," Cressa says. She takes Amara's hand and squeezes it. "Don't take it personally with Victoria, will you? She was just upset."

"She's upset because she knows it's true. Felix doesn't give a shit about any of us!" A respectable wife swerves out of their way, tutting. Amara has a sudden, vivid image of meeting her own mother on the pavement. What would she think of her daughter, swearing like a whore on a street corner? *I am a whore on a street corner*, Amara thinks. The absurdity almost makes her want to laugh.

"Can't you feel sorry for her then?" Cressa says. "Considering."

"I suppose," Amara replies, not sure why Victoria's anger is more deserving of sympathy than anyone else's. A sudden wrench of anxiety stops her, and she rests her hand against the wall to steady herself. Unless Victoria has guessed who is really responsible for trashing Simo's bar and blames Amara? *You were the one who suggested turning his bar over in the first place.* They were both with Felix when Amara hinted Simo should pay for the slight at the baths. Does Victoria remember what was said?

"She'll get over it," Cressa says, mistaking the drawn look on Amara's face. "Let's just have a drink. It will make you feel better."

Marcella's place makes the Sparrow look grand. It's nestled in a side street to catch passing trade from the theater, with very little room to do anything but stand and nurse a flask of wine or else take away one of the greasy-looking pies frying at the back. Cressa doesn't seem to care. She slumps at the counter. "A small wine. Whatever's cheapest."

The slave girl serving is red-cheeked and sweating, slowly roasting in the heat from the oven behind.

"Your mistress not here?" Amara says.

"Back in a minute," the girl replies. "What you having?"

"I'll wait until Marcella is back."

The girl shrugs and pours out Cressa's drink. She's careful not to overfill the measure. "Barely an acorn cup," Cressa complains, showing it to Amara. She takes a sip and pulls a face. "Strong enough to knock out a mule." She downs it and pushes the flask back toward the girl. "Another." The girl pours out more wine, and Amara is relieved to see

Cressa doesn't knock this one straight back too. "You know Drauca had a little girl?"

"No," Amara says, her heart sinking at the thought.

"Simo kept her. She's about five now, works doing odd jobs at the tavern in the day."

Amara knows Cressa never talks about the child she lost but, somehow, not mentioning him, not acknowledging her pain, feels even worse. "I'm so sorry about . . ."

"Don't," Cressa stops her. "Don't say it. I just can't." They sit in silence.

Amara fidgets. Cressa is shielding her eyes with her hand, as if to shade them from the sun, but really, Amara suspects, to hide her grief. It's uncomfortably hot, between the simmering pies and the sun. She feels strung out with nervous energy, waiting for her debtor, still not sure how she is going to persuade her to pay but knowing she must.

Marcella rounds the corner, and Amara darts forward, blocking her path. "There you are!" she exclaims, taking the other woman by surprise, not giving her a chance to escape. "What a day! The sun's scorching, isn't it?" She gestures at the bar. "Gellius still leaving it all to you?"

"What do you want?" Marcella asks, eyes flicking to her slave girl, well aware why Amara is there.

"Just to see how you are. I can't believe Gellius isn't here! You have to do all the work." Amara moves in closer as Marcella edges away. She lowers her voice, as if in sympathy, drawing on her memories of that first overheard conversation at the baths. "Does he even know what goes on at the bar? *This* bar, I mean. He probably wouldn't notice if half the stock went missing, would he?"

"Mind the store," Marcella says to the slave at the counter. "I'm just going to have a talk with . . . my friend."

"You're not having a drink?" Cressa asks, surprised at being abandoned.

"In a minute." Amara smiles, squeezing Cressa's shoulder as she passes. She follows Marcella up the narrow ladder to the rooms above the bar. It's even hotter here, a small airless space that adds to Amara's tension. It is hard to know who is more agitated, her or Marcella.

"You have to pay up," she says, anxiety making her voice sound harsh.

"No, *you* have to stop this," Marcella hisses back. "I've fiddled the takings as much as I can. Either take less or give me longer! Your master must understand. The rate was never reasonable."

"Then you shouldn't have signed for it." Amara gazes around the room. There is very little of value here, at least not on display. She wonders where the amber necklace came from. Perhaps the sisters' family fell on hard times, like she and her mother did. Anyone's fortune can turn on a knife edge.

"Keep the necklace then," Marcella says, her voice cracking. "I can't pay any faster."

"The necklace doesn't cover the interest."

Marcella looks at her, for a moment, too shocked to speak. "You can't be serious!"

Heat is radiating up through the floor, and Amara is now pouring with sweat. The smell of hot pies and the smothering sensation of guilt make her feel nauseous. She thinks of Drauca, of all Felix might do to the woman in front of her. She cannot leave without payment. "What about the ring?" she says, pointing to the cameo Marcella is unconsciously twisting round and round.

Marcella puts her hand behind her back like a child. "No."

"It would put an end to the payments. We could write off the whole loan today."

"It was my mother's. She's dead. I cannot give it to you."

Marcella looks fragile, standing alone in the shabby lodgings she shares with her drunken husband. Amara wonders how long it would take Felix to smash up the place, how much damage he could do. "Fires start easily in smoky little bars," she says. "You should be more careful with that oven downstairs." She leaves a moment of silence, allowing the threat to hang between them, then holds out her hand. "Give me the ring. If you don't, I cannot protect you."

Nobody has ever stared at her with more hatred than Marcella does as she turns the ring round and round her finger for the last time. It takes some time to pull it off— her fingers must be swollen in the heat, and she worries away at her hand, as if fighting with her own flesh over the parting. At last she drops it in Amara's palm. "Never come back here."

"Believe me," Amara says, "I just did you a favor." She knows it's true, that Marcella would have lost more than the cameo, but still, the words seem to come from someone else. She realizes she sounds just like Felix.

19

*"I like not joy bestowed in duty's fee,
I'll have no woman dutiful to me."*
—Ovid, *The Art of Love* II

"Those are the worst verses I have *ever* heard!" Priscus is laughing, almost overwhelmed with amusement after hearing the she-wolves sing Cornelius's hymn to Flora. Dido and Amara laugh too, while Salvius shakes his head. "If I had known what words you were setting to such a beautiful tune, I would never have taught it to you," he says, his voice grave, though his eyes are smiling.

It is the night of their repayment, but it feels more like a holiday. Salvius's small dining room twinkles with candles, and the cool of the evening air drifts through the open windows. It is nothing like as grand as the two parties they attended recently—there's bean stew, a small portion of roasted pigeon—but this feels the closest thing to a family meal that Amara has experienced since she left her father's house. She suspects it is the same for Dido.

Salvius pours them all more wine, handing the empty jug to his slave to refill. The young boy slips from the room. "So when is your next performance?"

"The last night of the Floralia!" Dido says. "Though we are reciting Ovid this time. Egnatius gave us some verses to learn."

"I will have to think of some more suitable tunes," Salvius says. "Unless you know any, Priscus?"

"There's that one your father always used to play. I love that song."

"Have you two known each other since childhood then?" Amara asks, dipping a piece of bread into her stew.

"Our fathers were in business together," Priscus says. "As we were too, until a decade or so ago. Responsible for some of the finest paintings in Pompeii, if I say so myself. My artists repainted half the Forum after the great earthquake. My father-in-law's men painted the other half," he gestures at Salvius. "That was after *his* wife persuaded him to desert us for metal work." The two men glance at each other, then away. "May she rest in peace."

Amara is not surprised their music teacher is a widower. It is stranger to think of Priscus with a wife waiting at home. No doubt she is the reason Salvius is the one hosting dinner. For a moment, the missing woman casts a shadow over the cosy pretence that this is an ordinary gathering of friends and equals. "And how did you two both come to Pompeii?" Salvius asks.

"Oh," Amara replies. "That's not a very happy story."

"Neither of you were born slaves, were you?" he says. Amara wonders how he guessed, then remembers Fabia's words: *You still act as if you matter*. She is not going to ask the same question again. "You are too educated," Salvius goes on. "I'm sorry; your current life must no doubt be painful for you both."

He means it kindly, but Amara wishes he hadn't said anything. She can sense Dido growing tense beside her. Can he not understand the need, sometimes, to forget?

"And *you* are far too modest," Priscus says to Dido, drawing a pointed distinction between them that makes Amara snort with laughter. "Sorry." He turns to her. "I didn't mean to offend."

"I'm not offended," Amara says. "And anyway, you are right. I was a concubine before this. She wasn't." *But I still hate it*, she wants to add.

Salvius senses the shift in mood. "I'm sorry. I shouldn't have said anything."

"Shall we sing?" Dido asks, in the bright, brittle manner Amara recognizes as her brave face. *At least she is learning to protect herself*, she thinks. *It's better than tears.*

"That would be wonderful!" Priscus exclaims.

Salvius fetches his pipe from the top of a chest, where he had obviously laid it ready for the evening. "Shall we start with our old favorite?" He doesn't wait for an answer but begins piping the tune of the shepherd and his love.

They all begin to sing, and after the first verse, the awkwardness and sadness begin to fall away. Amara looks at Dido, at the joy on her face, and realizes there is nobody she loves more. Warmth spreads through her. She has never had a friend like Dido. She is the light in the darkness of her life.

They sing song after song, learning new ones from Salvius and performing the tale of Crocus and Smilax for the two men. Aided by their high spirits, it's an even better performance than the one Cornelius paid for. Amara can feel her cheeks grow hotter, heat spreading through her limbs as she allows herself to drink too much. Is this what life might be like if she were a free woman in Pompeii?

The slave boy is almost falling asleep in the corner and the night sky bright with stars when Priscus finally says, "I should be going home soon." There is a pause, and the two men look at each other, the signal of a pre-agreed arrangement. Priscus turns to Dido. "Would you do me the honor . . . ? Would you be kind enough to join me for a little while?" *At least he has the decency to ask as if refusal might be an option*, Amara thinks.

"Of course," Dido says, taking his hand. He leads her from the room, leaving Salvius and Amara alone at the table.

"Would you like some more wine?"

She realizes he is nervous. "Only to join you. Otherwise, I am fine."

He pours them both a top-up. "I haven't been with a woman in two years. Since my wife died." He stops. Amara senses he is not waiting for a reply, only trying to find the right words, so she says nothing. "Sabina loved music," he says. "You remind me a little of her."

"I'm sorry. It is terrible to lose one you love."

Salvius waves a hand, as if to minimize his grief. "I am sure you have lost family too." She inclines her head, not wishing to speak of her parents, or Aphidnai. He drains his glass and stands. "Well then." Amara puts her own glass down, untouched, and rises. The slave boy jolts awake as they pass then gets up wearily to clear the table.

Salvius takes a candle to light the way to his bedroom. It's dark in the narrow corridor, and she picks her way carefully behind him. He pushes open the door. The room is gloomy after the well-lit dinner, but Amara's eyes adjust, and she makes out a woman's clothes spread over the bed. She does not ask who they belong to.

Salvius sets down the candle on a small table and picks up his wife's robe. "Would you perhaps mind . . .?"

She takes it from him. He turns away as she changes. It makes her shiver, wrapping herself in a dead woman's clothes. The sadness of her own loneliness, of Salvius's grief, brings a lump to her throat.

"That's her perfume over there." Amara picks up the bottle, dabs a little on her neck. Salvius stares at her. "You look so like her." He sighs. "Is there someone you would like me to . . . I mean, I can pretend to be someone else, if that's easier?"

Of all the things Amara expected him to say, this was perhaps the last. The wall outside the Sparrow blazes into her mind, the new graffiti she spotted there only this morning. *Kallias greets his Timarete*. "No," she says, emphatically. "That wouldn't help."

"I'm sorry," Salvius says. "But is there, perhaps, at least a memory of being with somebody you liked?"

"No."

"You have never been with a man by choice?"

"No." The simplicity of his question and the truth of her answer hits her with unexpected force. She turns her face away.

"I'm sorry," Salvius says. He sits down on the bed. Amara sits beside him, unsure what to say.

"It's not your fault," she says at last. "I am still happy to be here with you."

"You don't have to pretend," he says, taking her hand. "You must have to do a lot of pretending." She doesn't contradict him. "Have you ever . . . felt anything?"

Has she ever felt anything? What a question. A thousand answers crowd her mind. All the sensations of her life as a prostitute: disgust, panic, the obliterating blankness. An aversion to being touched so intense she is amazed she has got through a single night at the brothel without screaming, without fighting the men off. But she knows this is not what Salvius is asking. "No," she says quietly. "I never feel anything."

They sit together in silence. "Sabina was very afraid at first," he says. "It took her a long time to get used to being together." He puts his arms around her, drawing her closer. She wonders who he is seeing when he looks at her—the woman in front of him, or his dead wife. "Amara," he says, as if answering her question. "I will try and make this pleasant for you. All I ask is that you don't pretend." He brushes a strand of hair from her face, correcting himself. "Don't feel you have to pretend."

Victoria's singing wakes her in the morning. For a while, Amara lies in her cell, listening to the sound, the sweetness of the voice so at odds with the harsh reality of the singer's life. She knows almost nothing about Victoria's past. At least she and Dido were loved once, and she knows Beronice and Cressa spent the first few years of childhood with their mothers, but Victoria has never belonged to anyone but an owner. Yet every morning, she sings her heart out, filling this dark place with joy. Amara wonders where Victoria learned so many tunes. She realizes how much she has missed their friendship since her change of fortune at the Vinalia.

She gets out of bed, dressing herself quickly, and slips into the corridor. The compacted mud floor under her feet is hard and cool. She stands at Victoria's door a moment before drawing the curtain back. "Can I come in?"

Victoria's singing stops abruptly. "Suit yourself."

"What was last night like?"

"The usual. Have a nice *party*?"

"It was dinner above the ironmonger's. Not really a party."

"Still. *Dinner*, though," Victoria says, face turned aside as she does her hair. "In a house. With free wine. Better than one meal a day."

Amara pauses, wondering how much she owes Salvius for his kindness last night. "The customer got me to dress up as his dead wife. In this musty old robe." She sees Victoria hesitate, knows there's nothing she finds so irresistible as a ridiculous sex story. "Had the perfume out ready and everything."

Victoria gives in to curiosity, puts down the hairbrush. "You're *joking*."

"Asked who I wanted *him* to pretend to be."

Victoria laughs. "I hope you said Jupiter. In his form as a pile of fucking gold."

"What are you two sniggering about?" Beronice stands, bleary-eyed in the doorway.

"Just a customer," Victoria says. "Remember what they are? Before Gallus?"

"You know I had at least three last night," Beronice says, offended. "Including that really annoying idiot from the laundry. What's his name again?"

"Fabius," Victoria says. Amara wonders how she keeps track of all the names. "He's not so bad."

"She got drunk *again*," Beronice mutters, leaning out into the corridor and looking back at Cressa's cell. "I don't know where she finds the money. She'll drink every last penny she's ever saved at this rate."

"Wasn't Cosmus born about this time of year? She's probably missing him." Victoria goes back to brushing her hair. "Did Fabius have his usual cry afterward?"

Beronice sits down heavily on the bed. "So *boring*," she says.

"That's why you have to get them in the right mood!" Victoria says. "You can't blame him for crying, not if you're lying there with your sour I'd-rather-be-with-my-boyfriend face. At least make a bit of effort."

Beronice doesn't defend herself but lies in a slump. "He slapped me," she says.

"What? *Fabius?*" Victoria is shocked. "He's such a weed!"

"No. Gallus," Beronice looks miserable. "He says I enjoy it too much. The other men, I mean."

"What does he expect you to do? Wail and moan about your lost virtue all night? Prick."

"*Do* you enjoy it?" Amara blurts out. They both stare at her.

"What a question!" Victoria says. "You sound like a customer, Amara."

"But, I mean . . ." She stops, unsure what she wants to say. Last night with Salvius had hardly been a revelation. She didn't feel pleasure, in spite of his considerable efforts. But it hadn't been totally *un*pleasant either. For the first time, she had had an inkling that it might be different, if the man were different.

"Was there more to this dead-wife fuck than you're telling us?" Victoria asks.

"*Dead wife?*" Beronice says.

"You told them about Salvius then?" It's Dido leaning against the doorway. Victoria shoves Beronice along to make room for Dido to sit on the bed, leaving Amara the only one standing. All three of them are looking at her.

"Please don't tell us you're in love with a man who gets you to dress up as his dead wife," Victoria says.

"No!" Amara says. "Although, I do quite like him. As a friend."

"A *friend*?" Beronice repeats in disbelief.

"Would you marry him if he asked you to be wife number two?" Victoria is enjoying her role as prosecutor.

"Yes, but that's not *love*. I'd just rather be a freedwoman running an ironmonger's than a slave working for Felix. Wouldn't you?"

"Is he an amazing lay?"

Amara pauses.

"He *is* an amazing lay!" Victoria yells. The other two start laughing, and Amara finds herself laughing too.

"He just made an effort, that's all. Customers don't normally, do they?"

"That's why you steer them," Victoria says. "You can take some control of the situation."

"I'm not sure," Beronice says, frowning. "I know what she means."

"Nobody wants to hear what a great lover Gallus is," Victoria says, rolling her eyes. "Please spare us."

"Yes, but, it *is* different, if the man makes an effort. It just is," Beronice says. "Don't you think?"

"It's never any different," Dido says.

"You can't rely on the man to give you any pleasure," Victoria states, as if this were obvious. "You just have to do what you like and take them along."

"What if you don't like *any* of it?" Dido asks.

"Then," says Victoria, putting an arm round her like a conspirator, "you just have to hope, one day, if you are *really lucky*, an ironmonger asks you to dress up as his dead wife."

Amara looks at the three of them falling about on the bed, hooting with laughter, and smiles. Perhaps there are some pleasures in the life of a whore, after all.

"What's so fucking funny?" Paris glowers in the doorway. Ever since Victoria offered him the golden paste and asked if he wanted to gild his arsehole, he has been even less friendly than usual.

"Oh, is laughing forbidden now?" Victoria asks. "I didn't realize. But I'm afraid a scowl isn't going to scare the customers away. They can't see your face from behind."

Paris moves so fast none of the others have a chance to try and stop him. He punches Victoria hard in the face then swings back to hit her again. Beronice leaps, shrieking, onto his back, clawing at his arms, and he staggers, blow landing wide. Amara and Dido scramble in front of Victoria, holding their hands up, screaming at him to stop. Paris tries to dislodge Beronice, but she's clinging to his neck, putting pressure on his windpipe. Cressa runs into the room, tugging at Beronice, trying to stop her from strangling Paris, yelling at her to let go.

"*What the fuck is going on?*"

At the sound of Felix's voice, the screaming stops, and Beronice drops to the floor like a stone. Paris rubs his neck, gasping.

"I said what the fuck is this?"

"He hit her face!" Amara says, pointing at Victoria. "He hit her in the face!" It is the unbreakable rule at the Wolf Den. Neither Felix nor any of the other men are allowed to mark their faces.

Felix does not have to ask if it's true. Victoria is cradling her eye, the skin on her cheek bright red. "Let me see." He crosses swiftly to the bed. Amara and Dido scramble out of the way. Felix takes Victoria's hand from her face, examining the damage, pressing his finger against her cheekbone. She winces. "Nothing's broken," he says, standing up. "It will mend." He walks over to Paris, shoving him. "What the fuck were you thinking? Not such a big man now, are you? Get the fuck out of here."

Paris doesn't wait to be asked again; he lurches from the cell.

"And you," Felix says, turning back to Victoria who quails against the wall. "Mind your mouth. I know what will have happened. You provoked him. Didn't you?" She says nothing, and he grabs her by the shoulders, shaking her. "*Didn't you?*"

Amara looks at the pots of perfume lined up on Victoria's windowsill, imagines grabbing one, smashing it on Felix's head, pictures herself yelling at him to stop. But she does nothing. Just shrinks terrified against the wall, like all the other women.

Felix lets go of Victoria who pushes herself to safety, clambering away from him on the bed. The pain on her face grips Amara's heart, but Victoria's eyes are dry. Amara realizes she has never seen her friend cry.

"You watch your fucking mouths, all of you," Felix says. "I don't want a Drauca on my hands, with a useless, *ugly* face. Look at you." He spits the words at Victoria. "No man is going to want to touch you for days." He flings the curtain aside and storms out of the brothel.

"Don't," Victoria says, raising her hand to prevent Dido coming near. "Don't say anything. Just leave me."

All the women go back to their own cells, as if seeking comfort from one another would diminish Victoria's suffering. Amara sits alone on the bed, staring at her father's mouldy bag. She thinks of Felix upstairs, Marcella's cameo ring in his desk drawer, the smile on his face when she handed it over, and she closes her eyes.

JULIUS

20

"All the girls fancy Celadus the Thracian gladiator!"
—Pompeii graffiti

The sun overhead is so hot Amara feels she will faint, only the crush of the crowd and Victoria jabbing her excitedly in the ribs are keeping her upright. This is not how she would have chosen to spend her first proper day off in Pompeii. Up at dawn, trooping to the far end of town, standing out in the cool darkness, watching the sun rise and, later, wilting in the baking heat, all to get the best view of the gladiators' parade into the amphitheater. It is the first of July, the day the town's new elected officials take office and, more importantly, the day free games are held to celebrate it.

Amara wonders if Fuscus is already in the arena, sitting at the front, fretting about whether this extravaganza will overshadow the games he threw last year. He was quite peevish on the subject last time she saw him. Egnatius has done her many favors, but none perhaps as great as introducing her to the duumvir. She and Dido perform regularly at both his and Cornelius's houses, though Fuscus is a less demanding host. There, they are rarely expected to do much more than sing, mainly because Fuscus's wife holds greater sway over her husband. It feels strange, how intimate she is now with powerful men. At Cornelius's house, Fuscus will tell her little details about his life—the fountain he has ordered for his father-in-law, the books his two sons are reading—and of course, she knows exactly what he likes in bed. At his own home, he takes the role of a distant employer, bestowing her on his guests, part of the service to be enjoyed along with the fruit platter. In the street, should they bump into one another, she has no doubt he would ignore her. In that sense her life has not changed at all.

"There he is!" Victoria shrieks. "It's Celadus!"

Amara would never have heard her if Victoria were not yelling right beside ear. The blast of trumpets as the gladiators approach, the wall of sound from the crowd, makes her feel as if her skull might split open. But at last their long, tedious wait has paid off. They are rammed in, right at the front, just by the amphitheater entrance.

"Celadus!" Victoria screams. "Celadus!"

He cannot possibly have heard one scream above any other, and yet, at that moment, the Thracian giant turns, as if impelled by the force of Victoria's will. He takes two strides toward them, lifts Victoria off her feet in a single sweep, and kisses her. She is so astonished that, for once, she doesn't respond. The crowd around them erupts. Amara is smacked hard on the head by a girl wedged behind, thrusting her arms out, trying to grab at the gladiator's leather harness, touch his oiled chest.

"*Celadus! Celadus!*"

The gladiator sets Victoria down, says something in her ear then rejoins the procession, waving both arms at the crowd.

"He would have kissed *me*," Beronice shouts at Amara. "He would have kissed *me*, if I'd been at the front!" Her face is wild, almost unrecognizable in its rage and disappointment. Amara is glad Victoria cannot hear. Instead, she is standing uncharacteristically still, feet rooted exactly where Celadus placed her, buffeted by the passing flow of people now cramming to get into the arena.

"Come on!" Amara yells, grabbing her arm. "Or we won't get a seat!"

All five of them hold on to each other, clasping hands, grabbing one another's togas, anything to prevent themselves from being separated. They know their place at these games; they will have to climb all the way to the back row at the very top.

It's a long queue. They join a slow-moving column of women, all waiting to sit wedged into the worst seats in the arena. Amara's legs feel like they might give way by the time they get to the top. The back row is filling up fast and there's a lot of irritable shuffling around until Cressa spots a space where they might all be able to cram together. After a heated exchange with another group of women, they finally manage to sit down, though as the slightest out of the five, Dido is forced to sit half-perched on Amara's knee.

"You *have* to tell us what Celadus said," Amara says to Victoria, who has been resisting answering that question the whole way up the steps.

Victoria smiles, enjoying the secret. "Imagine what it would be like to have a man like that! Just *imagine*."

"Maybe he's nothing special," Beronice says. "Might be a rubbish lay."

"Oh, don't be so bitter!" Cressa laughs. "As if *you*'d turn him down."

"I *would*, I would turn him down!" Beronice insists. "I wouldn't do that to Gallus."

The rest of them laugh. "Even *I* might be tempted by Celadus," Dido says. "And that's saying something."

"The feel of his chest!" Victoria sighs. "Like being held by Apollo."

Amara shifts on her wooden seat. Even though Dido isn't very heavy, it's still uncomfortably hot having her on her knee. Awnings are stretched overhead to keep the sun off, but they also trap the rising heat. Not only will they have the worst view, it's also sweltering up here. The murmur of so many people talking, reverberating round the arena, makes it sound as if they are in a beehive.

"What time are you meeting Menander?" Dido asks her.

"After the first beast hunt."

"He must be something special, this boyfriend of yours, for you to miss the gladiators," Victoria says.

"He's not my boyfriend."

"Sorry, that's the ironmonger isn't it?"

Amara rolls her eyes as they all laugh. She and Dido have only had three nights with Salvius and Priscus, but from the way Victoria teases her, it's as if she's embroiled in a breathless love affair. It gives her an odd feeling to think of Salvius now, when she is about to see Menander.

Her intimacy with the widower has happened almost by accident, through the time they spend playing music together and his unexpected gentleness. But she never forgets that for all his kindness, he is a customer.

It's Menander she is attracted to—could imagine *loving* even—although their relationship has consisted of little more than a few snatched moments and graffiti exchanges outside the Sparrow. That's how she knows where to meet him. *I will wait for you by the second gate, Timarete. May fortune smile on us both!* She was the one who suggested the timing underneath. Then she spent hours agonizing over whether that looked too keen or too cool. Would it have been better to have suggested before the games started? Or later, after one of the gladiator fights?

"Salvius is just a friend," she says.

"If he's just a *friend*," Victoria says. "You wouldn't mind if he did a swap and had Dido next time, would you?"

Amara winces. "He wouldn't do that!"

"You don't like the idea though, do you?"

"I think of Priscus as *my* friend too," Dido says, coming to her rescue. "They're just not like that, either of them."

"You'll be saying they're better lovers than *Gallus* next!"

"Oh, fuck off!" Beronice rounds on Victoria. "Just because some gladiator kissed you, doesn't mean you get to lord it over the rest of us all day like fucking Venus!"

One or two of the more respectable women sitting on the row in front shuffle disapprovingly, though none is brave enough to risk a direct confrontation with a gang of rowing whores.

"Just leave it," Cressa says wearily. "She's only teasing."

The sound of trumpets rings out, and the murmuring hive subsides slightly, though not enough for the opening speeches to be heard clearly from the back. Amara thinks again of Fuscus, imagines how much he must have enjoyed his moment of glory last year. Perhaps he has brought his sons with him today, or would they be too young? She has never met them.

Cheering and yelling from the crowd alerts them to the beast hunters' entrance. The three men hold their arms up to the crowds, enjoying the glory before facing the danger.

"Will that be Celadus?" Amara asks, unable to tell one fighter from another at this distance.

"He wouldn't do a *beast* hunt!" Victoria is outraged. "He's a combat gladiator!"

There's more screaming, a mixture of fear and excitement, as the animals are released into the ring. The women jump to their feet to get a better view.

"What are they?" Cressa asks, standing on tiptoe. "I can't see."

"Tigers!" Dido says. "They've let loose tigers!"

Amara can see the beasts circling, lean and hungry, while the men stand with their backs together in the center of the arena. She has never seen a tiger before, but she's watched enough cats stalk their prey to recognize the low, slow prowl, muscles bunched, ready to spring. Beronice grabs her arm as the first attacks. It moves so fast, she cannot imagine how any of the hunters have time to react, but one catches it with his spear, and the animal sheers off, limping and wounded. Another tiger charges and, this time, lands a blow, knocking a man to the ground.

The yelling from the crowd is so intense, the action in the arena so frantic, she cannot work out what is happening. Beside her, Beronice is jumping up and down, Victoria is screaming and then she realizes she is too, though she's not sure who she is shouting for, the men or the beasts. Even Dido is caught up in the hysteria, punching the air when one man saves another, leaping on the back of the attacking tiger as if it were a horse.

The role of hunter and hunted switches back and forth, sometimes the beasts are in retreat, sometimes the men. The skill of the fighters, the grace of the tigers, all of it is punctuated by acts of savagery which make Amara gasp. She keeps watching, unable to look away, until the last tiger has been slaughtered. Their bodies are dragged from the arena, leaving thick red trails in the sand. One of the men is taken off too, his chest covered in blood from a shoulder wound. The remaining two hunters stand together, throwing their arms up to receive the adulation of the crowds.

"Doubt the injured one will make it," Victoria says, raising her voice above the din. "That tiger practically had his arm off!"

"Will they replace him?" Dido asks. "Or will the next fight just have two hunters?"

"They usually replace them if it's this early, otherwise the hunt doesn't last long enough," Cressa says.

A few women are getting up, making use of the break to go to the latrine. "I think I had better go," Amara says.

"Don't break the ironmonger's heart," Victoria says.

Dido squeezes her arm. "Good luck."

Amara's own heart is thumping with nerves as she makes her way down the outside steps of the arena. What if Menander misunderstood and thought she meant the end of all the beast hunts? What if he doesn't come? She walks quickly to the gate where they have arranged to meet and can see, even from a distance, that he is already waiting for her.

Then they are standing together, and nothing else matters.

"I can't believe you're really here," he says, taking hold of her hand.

"You too."

Neither seem able to do anything but stare at one another, until Menander laughs and breaks the moment. "Shall we get a drink?"

They walk out into the square. It's dotted with stalls selling food, drink and souvenirs. Amara no longer minds the heat or notices the noise. Her cheeks hurt from smiling, and they both laugh over nothing, amused by everything. They wander aimlessly for a while, before remembering why they went for a walk and buy a glass of wine to share, and some bread, and head off to sit in the shade under the plane trees beside the Palaestra. The rarity of a day off means they are not the only slave couple taking advantage of the time, though the baying of the crowd as the next hunt starts draws some of the loiterers back into the arena. Menander has still not let go of her hand, and when they sit down, he puts his arm round her. Amara rests her head on his shoulder and can feel his heartbeat, as fast and nervous as her own.

"Would your father have liked me?" he asks.

"I don't know," she says, surprised into honesty by his question.

Menander laughs. "That's better than a *no*, I guess."

"What about yours?"

"I think he'd have been quite happy with a doctor's daughter."

"My parents wouldn't have been too pleased by this sort of behavior."

"No, I suppose not," Menander replies, holding her tighter, in case she is minded to honor the dead by sitting further apart. There's a pause, and she suspects he is thinking, like she is, of all they have lost.

"And now I have nothing to offer you," he says. "No shop to inherit, no freedom."

"I think we can agree I have even *less* to offer you," Amara replies. She says it as a joke, but it hurts, the distance between her old self and her life now.

"Oh, I don't know," he says, smiling. "You would fetch at least five times as much as me at the market."

"But nobody's buying anyone, not today."

"No," he says. Then he bends to kiss her, quickly, as if he might otherwise lose his nerve. *This is what it's supposed to feel like*, Amara thinks, holding him. *When you want someone. It's meant to feel like happiness.*

"Are you alright?" Menander breaks off, looking anxiously into her face. "I hope I didn't upset you?"

Amara realizes she is shaking. "No, you didn't upset me!" she says, holding him closer to reassure him. "I just feel . . ." She stops, unable to find words for the mixture of happiness and pain. He is looking at her, waiting, still worried. She tries again. "You get used to having nothing, don't you? And then suddenly to have something, to *feel* something, it's . . ." She trails off.

"It's happy–sad?"

"Yes, because nothing belongs to you, not even the happiness."

"Timarete, even slaves own their happiness. Feelings are the only things we *do* own." He passes the small flask of wine to her, and she takes a sip. "And I know that this afternoon is short, but we have it, we own it."

"Are you going to tell me not to waste it?"

"No, because talking isn't wasting it," he says, taking the wine back from her. "Nobody is telling us what to do today. Just feel whatever you want to feel." He pauses. "Although I'm hoping that means you might feel like kissing me again."

She laughs. "Might do."

"I want to know all about your singing too," he says, brushing the hair from her shoulders. "I half thought you might be too grand to see me now, after all the parties you and Dido go to."

"Never," she says. "And anyway, there wouldn't be any singing if you hadn't got the lyre for me."

"It was entirely selfish. I just wanted to hear you play," he says, drawing her closer. His intensity is familiar, pulling on a dark undertow in her body. She has seen desire in so many men and almost every association is painful. *But this is Menander!* She puts her hand out to touch his face, cupping it in her fingers, to remind herself who he is, remind herself that she has chosen to be with him.

"I wish I had known you in our other life."

"I know."

"You try to keep it inside, don't you, all the different parts of yourself, but they don't exist anymore. I thought of my mother the other day, what she would think of me, who she would see. If we met now. But she wouldn't know me. I wouldn't know me." Amara is talking fast, trying to rush the words out, hoping she makes sense, not sure why she is even telling him this, aside from the longing she feels to be understood. "Sometimes I think it must be harder for you. Because my life is just completely different, there's nothing left of the past. But for you, it must be like living on the wrong side of the mirror."

"To be the potter's slave, rather than the potter's son?"

"Yes."

"It is hard. But I know it's not harder than your life." He takes her hand and places it against his cheek again, covering her fingers with his. "You are the same person though. I still see you as the same person."

"I miss so many things." She sighs then smiles, trying to lighten the mood. "The food for a start."

Menander makes a face. "Italian cheese! What do they feed their goats?"

"And that horrible fish sauce on everything!"

"No beans so bland they can't be spiced up by rotten anchovies."

"And the bread here tastes like somebody tipped grit in it."

"It does, doesn't it!" Menander says wonderingly. "What *do* they put in the flour?"

"I miss my mother's stew."

"Me too." He shoots her a sly look. "Bet mine's was better."

"Nobody makes better stew than the women in Aphidnai."

"Is that a promise?"

"Might be."

Menander kisses her again, and this time, the darkness stays at the edges, unable to break through.

The afternoon, which always drags so painfully in the brothel, seems to end moments after she has sat down with Menander, even though hours have passed.

"Amara! There you are! You were meant to meet us after the second gladiator fight! We've been wandering round and round for ages!"

She has never been sorry to see Dido's face before, but now, the sight makes her heart drop through her stomach. She stares up at her four friends, ranged round, and instinctively grips Menander's hand. "It can't be time to head back, not yet!"

"You don't have to tell me," Victoria says, looking furious. "Celadus hasn't even been on yet!"

Felix had ordered them all to leave in good time, to make sure they missed the crowds and were back at the brothel to pick up the inevitable surge in trade after the event. As the most famous gladiator, Celadus's duel must have been left until the end.

Menander rests his hand on her arm. "We'll see each other soon," he says gently.

"But we won't! You know we won't!"

He hugs her, crushing her against him. "We will have another whole day, just for ourselves. I promise. Even if we have to wait until the Saturnalia."

"*Amara*," Cressa says. "We can't be late."

She doesn't say goodbye and neither does he. Letting go of Menander, standing up, walking away from him, knowing what she will now have to face instead, almost stops her breath. The pain is physical in its ferocity. She cannot bear to look back. She tells herself it is easier not to want, not to feel. When you cannot make your own choices, what good is wanting anything, or anyone?

Dido takes her hand. "I'm here," she says, squeezing Amara's fingers.

21

"For assuredly to live is to be awake."
—Pliny the Elder, *Natural History*

The stall selling flowers and garlands is on the shady side of the street, but the heat of the late afternoon has still caused many of the blooms to wilt. Amara and Dido whisper together, trying to pick out the freshest stems from buckets of water, watched by the hovering shop assistant.

"Can we afford lilies?"

"We should probably make the effort, if we want Aurelius to book us again."

It's only the second time they have been to the wine seller's house. Aurelius is a friend of Fuscus, but not Cornelius, and his tastes seem more decorous. A secret brothel at the end of his garden is an unthinkable idea.

They buy the lilies and wander slowly back. The streets are less crowded than usual, nobody who doesn't have to be out is braving the heat, and if last night at the brothel is any indication, half Pompeii has a hangover. Amara rubs her arm where she knows a bruise marks the skin, a gift from a particularly aggressive customer last night. It will be a nuisance to hide the blemish tonight.

"Are you feeling better?" Dido looks anxiously at her arm. "I know last night was difficult."

"I almost wish I hadn't seen him now," Amara says, and they both know she isn't referring to the customer. But it hurts too much to talk about Menander directly. "It makes everything feel so much worse."

"I told Nicandrus this."

"Were you meant to see him yesterday too?" Amara is surprised Dido didn't tell her.

Dido nods, then they pause their conversation to let a cart pass, standing close against the wall to avoid the dust. "What can we give each other?" Dido asks, as they start walking again. "Apart from a moment's kindness. When you cannot be with someone, is it worth the pain, pretending it's any different? I'm sorry," she says, seeing Amara's stricken face. "But I'm not sure what loving Menander gives you? If it were Salvius even, I would understand. Might he not buy you one day? At least it's possible. Another slave . . . there's nothing he can give any woman, however much he might want to."

"I know," Amara says, trying not to think of the feel of Menander's arm around her or the laughter in his eyes. "I know he can't."

"Do you think Salvius *would* ever buy you?"

"No. I mean, I have wondered about it," she admits. "But you should hear him talk about Sabina, her extraordinary virtue, her shyness. He's not the type to keep me as a concubine, and it's obvious I'm not someone he might think of as a wife." She hesitates. "What about Priscus?"

"No chance!" Dido laughs. "What would he do? Keep me at Salvius's house as a secret lover? He has that already."

They reach the brothel and knock at the door to Felix's flat. Paris answers.

"Master's busy," he says, scowling at them both.

"Doesn't matter," Amara answers, giving the door an impatient shove. "We're here to practice for this evening. He knows about it."

"No need to be a bitch and kick the door down!" Paris snaps, stepping aside to let them enter.

"Doesn't he ever get lonely?" Dido whispers, after they've climbed the stairs. "I don't think he has any friends."

"Not surprising, with that attitude," Amara replies, not bothering to lower her voice.

The lyre is kept in the small living area off Felix's bedroom. As soon as they walk in, they realize he has company next door. It's Victoria. Amara would recognize her ecstatic moaning anywhere, although it sounds like she is putting in an extra effort for the boss.

Dido grabs her arm, stopping her from walking further in. "Should we be here?" she whispers.

"Not like we don't hear her every night."

"Yes, but that's different; she doesn't know we're here now!"

Their deliberations are interrupted by a sound neither have ever heard before. "Is that Felix?" Amara asks, incredulous. They forget their scruples and listen, looking at each other in astonishment. It's unquestionably Felix groaning in pleasure.

"I can't believe it!" Dido says. "This is the face I normally get." She stands, imitating Felix's swagger, and pulls a look of pompous disdain, as if staring down at the top of an imaginary woman's head.

Amara snorts with laughter then claps a hand over her mouth to cover the noise. They both try to suppress their giggles, but the effort not to laugh only makes it worse, and soon, they are shaking with silent hysteria.

"*I love you; I would die for you. I love you. I love you . . .*"

"She's really overdoing it now!" Amara says. "He'll never fall for *that*, surely?" From the sounds next door however, it seems she has overestimated Felix's powers of discernment.

She and Dido wait. The shrieking and moaning finally comes to an end, but still, Victoria doesn't stop with her protestations of devotion.

"*I love you so much; you're everything to me. I love you. I love you . . .*"

There is a pleading, debased sound to her voice that Amara can barely recognise. It almost sounds as if she is crying. Felix's voice is soothing in answer but too low to make out the words.

"She's some actress," Amara whispers. "He seems to have bought it all!"

"We really shouldn't be hearing this." Dido looks uncomfortable. She tiptoes to the corridor door and slams it open as if they have just come in. "Shall we get dressed first, or do you want to play?" she demands loudly.

Instantly, the voices next door fall silent. Amara and Dido tramp about, getting their clothes out of the chest, running through their first song. Felix opens the door, stripped to the waist, unconcerned to see them both. "You can go now," he says, calling back into the room.

Victoria hurries past, clothes disheveled, her face damp, perhaps with sweat. Amara tries to catch her eye and wink, but she avoids looking at her, instead stepping into the corridor and softly closing the door.

Reclining modestly on Aurelius's amply upholstered couch, Amara is grateful she and Dido decided to wear their gauzy dresses folded, making the fabric as opaque as possible. She is not sitting with Fuscus tonight. Instead, in what she suspects is a touch of teasing mischief by the host, Aurelius has placed her on a couch with one of his oldest friends: Pliny, the Admiral of the Fleet.

He is an austere-looking man, with dark gray hair and a hard-set jaw. Aurelius tries to draw him out with anecdotes of military life, but Pliny seems to be that rare person who prefers to observe rather than talk about himself. "I would be delighted," he says to Aurelius, who offers to take him on a pleasure tour of his vineyards. "But you might find me rather dull. I'm hoping to travel a little further inland toward Vesuvius, to see some of the rarer plants. Though of course, my research touches on wine as well."

"Wine is for drinking, not researching!" Aurelius laughs. "But we can venture further inland if you wish."

Pliny has said nothing to Amara all evening, save a brief compliment on her and Dido's presentation of Sappho, and so it is a surprise when he addresses her directly. "You don't share our host's view?"

"I'm sorry . . . ?" Amara is bewildered by the question.

"Your wine. You've barely touched it all night."

Amara looks at her glass. It stands beside her companion's which is equally full. "Ah," she says. "Well, I find drinking too much is akin to falling asleep, and I prefer to be awake to whatever life offers."

He stares at her. "Interesting," he says. "We are of the same view."

Having caught his attention, she is quick to press further. "Are you studying the medicinal quality of plants?"

Pliny's mouth twitches, a dismissive look she does not like. "Are you going to tell me all the special properties they have for women?"

"I wasn't talking about love potions," Amara says, her cheeks flushing. "My father was a disciple of Herophilos."

"*Herophilos*? Is he a favorite of yours? Perhaps you could set him to music."

There is laughter from the guests, who have been listening to their conversation with amusement. Amara has endured so many insults, usually dressed as compliments, from the men at these dinners. She knows it is irrational, as well as foolish, for this one man to provoke her above any other, but her heart is racing, and she cannot stop herself from retaliating. "*When health is absent*," she says, raising her voice and switching to Greek, "*wisdom cannot reveal itself, art cannot become manifest, strength cannot be exerted, wealth is useless and reason is powerless. I would not set Herophilus to music, sir, but I would live my life by his wisdom.*"

"I have offended you." There is surprise, not anger on Pliny's face. He looks at her, almost as if she were a dog that had started talking. "Forgive me. There is no reason why you should not have read Herophilos. What did your father teach you about him?"

His question snuffs out the flame of Amara's anger. She feels afraid of having exposed herself. "I should not have presumed . . ." she murmurs.

"Of course you should have presumed! Why should you let me be pompous?" Pliny sounds irritated. "Enough with the false modesty. Just answer my question."

"My father, Timaios, was a doctor in Aphidnai," she says. "He had no son, and he wanted a companion to read to him. Which I did." Pliny is silent, so she continues. "He was particularly interested in Herophilos's theory of the circulation of the blood." Amara pauses. "May I?" She motions permission to take Pliny's hand. She takes his wrist, feeling for the pulse, senses it quicken at the light touch of her fingers. "That is your blood's rhythm, driven by your heart," she says. "Or at least, that is what Herophilos believed."

"Careful! Don't let her bleed you!" one of the guests jokes.

Amara lets go of Pliny's wrist, and they both laugh. The conversation moves on, she and Dido get up to perform another song. Pliny says nothing when she rejoins him on the couch. But even though he does not speak, she can sense his intense awareness of her.

She is not surprised that he chooses to leave early, but before he rises, he addresses her again. "Would your master spare you for a week? I should like to take you home."

He makes his request so casually, no more than if he were asking to borrow a coat, that it takes her a moment to understand. "I'm certain he could spare me," she says.

"Good."

Across the room, she can see Dido staring at her. Amara's eyes dart to Pliny and then back to Dido again. *Explain to Felix.* Dido nods.

There is a great deal of smirking between guests as she follows Pliny from the room, though none are quite bold enough to tease the admiral outright. Aurelius comes closest. "I hope you have a delightful night, my dear friend," he says, with a pointed look at Amara. "I'm glad the dinner pleased you."

Pliny thanks him serenely, choosing to ignore or, perhaps, oblivious to his hint. They walk through to the atrium, Amara following at a distance, joining his silent retinue of slaves. One of them has picked up her lyre. The porter helps her on with her cloak. Then she steps out into the moonlit street.

22

"I pursue my research in odd hours, that is at night—just in case any of you think I pack up work then!"
—Pliny the Elder, *Natural History*

The house Pliny takes her to is near the Forum, only a short walk from the brothel, but stepping over its threshold is like entering another world. A delicate fountain of a faun greets them as they enter the atrium, starlight reflected on its waters. The air is heavy with the smell of jasmine.

"My friends were kind enough to let me have the run of the house while they are in Rome," Pliny says, taking a lamp from a slave and leading her across the darkened hall. "It's this way." They climb the stairs, walking along an interior balcony, until he pushes open a door. The smell of jasmine is particularly intense here, and she can hear the splash of another fountain. Amara guesses the room must overlook the garden.

"Here we are." He gestures for her to enter. She had expected him to be attended by slaves so is a little nervous to step into the room alone. The walls are painted with maritime scenes, tiny boats in picturesque battles, plumes of smoke rising from the defeated enemy fleet. She wonders if Pliny visits regularly, if this room was painted specially for him. Traveling cases overflowing with scrolls and wax tablets trail across the floor. Another pile sits on the large bed. Pliny lifts them off carefully.

"If you could get undressed," he says, turning to fuss over his tablets while she does so.

There's no point doing a seductive striptease if he's not even watching. She removes the cloak, carefully folds up the silk dress and undoes her hair. Then she arranges it artfully over one shoulder and perches at the end of the bed.

Pliny is a while flipping through his notes but eventually turns back to her, a wax booklet and stylus in hand. They look at each other. "Could I get a better view?" he says.

Amara is nonplussed. Is her pose not sexy enough? What is it he wants to see? She arches her back, pouting.

"No, no," he says. "Not that. Just lie down or something, so I can take a better look. See more of you."

She lies back on the bed, feeling more nervous by the minute. Pliny looks her over, scratching away at his tablets. *He is taking notes*, she realizes. The thought is so funny, she has to cough to hide the laugh that rises up her throat.

"May I?" he asks, putting down the tablets, gesturing he would like to touch her. He runs his hands over her whole body, frowning with concentration, tutting slightly to himself when he gets to the bruise on her arm. She flinches when he touches her between her legs, not sure what to expect, but he doesn't linger any longer than he did on her elbow or her chin. "I'm glad to see you don't remove all the hair," he says, approvingly. "Disgusting habit." He pats her calf. "Though that's all nice and smooth, as it should be. Thank you," he says, sitting down on the bed. "You can sit up now."

Amara does as he asks, not sitting too close to him. She is not sure that even Victoria is going to believe her when she recounts this night.

"I've talked to a number of courtesans for my research," he says, dignifying her with a more illustrious title than they both know she deserves. "I would be interested to know about your herbal knowledge. I wasn't, in fact, scoffing about love potions earlier."

"What would you like to know," she says.

He is poised with his tablets. "Do you do anything to prevent pregnancy?"

"I insert a sponge. Soaked with honey when I can afford it. I use it as a barrier. My father let me read all of Herophilos, including his book on midwifery. He thought it would be useful to me when I married."

Pliny nods. "Very sensible. So you don't use any charms?"

"No, though some of the others at my establishment do. Another washes herself out with wine and vinegar. The companion I sang with this evening also uses a sponge, like me."

He scratches away on the wax. "How did you become a . . . courtesan?"

"Which part of the story do you want?"

"Well," he says, frowning. "All of it. You started out reading Herophilos to your father in Attica, and now, here you are in Pompeii. I should like to hear everything."

He is asking for nothing other than her entire life laid bare. Amara isn't sure whether sex might have been easier. "My father was a doctor in Aphidnai," she says. "I was his only child. He died when I was fifteen. A disease he caught from one of his patients. My mother tried to support us for a number of years, and when this was no longer possible, she sold me as a house slave to one of my father's former patrons."

"Wait a moment." Pliny holds up his hand. "This makes no sense at all. Why did your mother not simply marry you off as quickly as possible? They must have been expecting you would marry soon anyway, at that age. You were an only child, what about the dowry?"

He has managed, inevitably, to hit on one of the most shameful parts of her story. "My father did not always charge his patients as he should have," she says, feeling the need even now to defend him for his neglect. "The debts we expected to call in were never paid. And he had significant debts of his own. What dowry there was, my mother spent to provide for us both."

Pliny is outraged. "But this was the most terrible negligence! From both of them!" He sees the distress on her face. "No, I am sorry, go on. You were sold as a house slave. What then."

"My mother left the money she was paid for my sale with my possessions," Amara says, wanting at least to clear her mother of greed. "But my new master took it, and he did not use me as a house slave, as *promised*, but as a concubine." Pliny rolls his eyes, as if amazed anyone could have been duped into imagining otherwise. "I was there perhaps a year, but his wife became jealous and sold me as a whore. I was taken to Puteoli and sold there at the market to the pimp who runs the town brothel. That is how I am here."

"The journey of the mind is always stranger than that of the body," Pliny says, cryptically. "How have you adjusted? You must have spent your early life imagining becoming . . . what? A respected wife? A mother?"

"I knew that was my duty."

"What did you want then, if not that?"

"What I wanted was idle daydreaming," she says. Pliny huffs, impatient at her quibbling. Amara gives up. "I wanted to be a doctor," she says. "Like my father. I just assumed this was going to happen because of all the hours he had me spend reading his texts. I had not understood. Then when I mentioned it one day, he explained that, of course, this was not possible."

"That isn't strictly true," Pliny replies. "Certainly, you could not have *practiced* medicine like your father, but there have always been women scholars, philosophers, living modest enough lives. Especially in Attica. But I understand his concern at the irregularity. Though," he mutters, clearly still irritated by her parents, "that was all the *more* reason to have saved up the dowry." He puts down the tablets, glancing round at his books. "Do you have a good reading voice?"

"I suppose I must have."

"Excellent. You can help me a little, while you are here." He switches to Greek. "We can even read Herophilos, if you wish. I'm minded to include him in my *Natural History*."

Pliny's accent is appalling, but his Greek is perfectly fluent. "I should like that so much," she says, smiling at him. "It would be a pleasure for me."

He smiles too, evidently satisfied with how the evening has gone. "Now, I will be up reading for a few hours," he says, getting off the bed. "But please don't let that disturb you. Feel free to sleep while I work."

"Where would you like me to . . . sleep?"

"On the *bed*, of course," Pliny says, exasperation creeping into his voice. He sits at his desk. It's angled so that he can still see her. Amara makes a show of getting under the covers and half closes her eyes, watching him from under lowered eyelashes. Pleased to see her settled, Pliny turns back to his scrolls and ignores her. She fully intends to stay awake, but the rustle of parchment, the sound of the fountain and the smell of jasmine are all so soothing, she has soon drifted off.

She is still half asleep when she feels his fingers run through her hair. "You've not left me much room," he whispers.

Instantly, she is alert. "Oh!" she exclaims, realizing she must have sprawled across the entire bed in her sleep. "Sorry," she scrambles to the other side.

Pliny slips in beside her. "It's a gift, to sleep well," is all he says.

They lie next to each other in the dark. Amara has no idea what time of night, or perhaps morning, it is. She can sense from his extreme stillness and shallow breathing that Pliny is also fully awake. It is difficult to know what he might want, but Amara feels she had better suspect the obvious rather than offend him. She shuffles over, placing her hand gently on his arm. "I'm so grateful you invited me," she says.

"You are a delightful girl," he replies. Amara knows he is looking at her, but his face is obscured in the darkness.

She leans over and kisses him. He has dry, papery lips. Pliny doesn't respond to her kiss, but he doesn't shove her off either. She relaxes, letting her body rest on his, while her hand travels across his thigh. Immediately, he stops her, catching her by the wrist. "There's . . . no need."

"I only want to please you," she says, moving away, so she is no longer lying against him. "I didn't mean to presume."

"I understand," he says, kissing her hand with his dry lips and releasing her wrist. "But there's no need. It's a pleasure for me simply to have you here." He stretches out his own hand and rests it on her waist. It's the only part of their bodies that is touching, though he is so close she can see the dark of his eyes and feel the warmth of his breath. "What lovely soft skin you have," he says.

Amara remains braced in the same position, expecting that perhaps *he* wanted to be the one doing the seducing, until she realizes, as his hand grows heavier and his breathing deeper, that he is asleep.

She gently lifts his arm, moving his hand from her body and placing it on the bed, then shuffles away slightly, not wanting to roll into him later by mistake. Amara closes her eyes. She thinks this is going to be a very pleasant week.

23

"No other part of the body supplies more evidence of the state of mind. This is the same with all animals, but especially with man; that is, the eyes show signs of self-restraint, mercy, pity, hatred, love, sorrow, joy; in fact, the eyes are the windows of the soul."

—Pliny the Elder, *Natural History*

Pliny is stroking his fingers through her hair. The sensation wakes her. She opens her eyes to see him staring down at her. Daylight is less forgiving of his age. There is gray hair on his bare chest and an oddly intent expression on his face. She wonders how long he has been watching her.

"I'm so glad you don't dye your hair like so many silly women," he says, by way of greeting. "Yours is such a lovely natural shade. Soft like a squirrel." He leans over and gives her a dry kiss on the nose.

He is such a bewildering mixture of affectionate and creepy, Amara isn't sure what to say. "Thank you," she manages, hoping he will stop looming over her soon, so she can sit upright and move away.

He leans down again, this time kissing her on the forehead. Then he sits up, swinging his legs over his side of the bed.

"I need to write this morning," he says. "But I should like you to read to me in the afternoon. In the meantime, take a scroll or two and enjoy the gardens. Secundus will bring you anything you might need; he knows you are staying for the week." Pliny has been dressing himself as he talks—again she is surprised by the absence of slaves in his private room —but when he sees her pick up the transparent silk robe, he stops. "You're not wearing that, are you?"

"I don't have anything else," she replies, amazed such a clever man is capable of being so obtuse.

"I suppose not." He looks round absently, as if expecting sensible women's clothes to sprout from one of the travel cases. "It will have to do for now. Maybe . . ." He frowns, watching her. "Maybe fold it a few more times?"

Amara doesn't trust herself to reply. When she is dressed, he fusses round her while she chooses a scroll or rather accepts the bundle he gives her, then he escorts her to the door, seemingly now anxious for her to leave so he can work. She steps out onto the interior balcony, the glorious sweep of the gardens below. "Just take the stairs," he says with a vague gesture before disappearing back into his study.

She walks slowly down into the garden with a sense of total enchantment. It is the cool of early morning but already the sky is blue, a promise of the blazing day ahead. The scent of flowers she cannot name is sweet in the air, and the fountain sparkles as it falls, the gentle rhythm of its splash like light footsteps. The balcony of the upper floor forms part of the shaded colonnade, and there are a number of benches, already strewn with cushions for whoever might wish to rest. Amara stands and stares, unable to believe what she sees. All this is hers for the day. She has nothing else to do than sit and read and look at this beautiful garden.

"Would you like some refreshment, mistress?"

A man, who may or may not be the Secundus Pliny mentioned, is standing a polite distance away.

Amara is embarrassed by the formality of his address. She clutches the scrolls to her chest, hoping to cover the thin fabric. "That would be very kind, thank you."

The man leaves, and she sits down on one of the benches, facing the fountain. It's a little chilly in the shade. She inspects the scrolls Pliny has given her. Both are Greek. Homer, she is familiar with, even though her family only owned a copy of two sections of *The Odyssey*, but she has never seen Apollonius's *The Argonautica*. She unravels the top carefully and starts to read, when the same man comes back with a tray and a blanket.

"I thought you might be cold," he says.

"That's very thoughtful, thank you," Amara replies, wrapping the throw round her shoulders. "Are you Secundus?"

"Yes."

"I am Amara. It is very nice to meet you."

His mouth twitches slightly in amusement, but he remains studiously polite. "Nice to meet you too, Mistress Amara."

"Thank you," she says again, as he sets down his tray on a small table beside the bench. "Do you know what music the admiral likes? I am hoping to play for him later; he has been so kind to me. I should very much like to sing something he might enjoy?"

"I am certain the admiral would be delighted to hear whatever you might wish to sing," Secundus says, gravely. "Given he has been pleased to invite you here as his guest." He bows and leaves her.

When he's safely out of sight, Amara eagerly inspects the tray. It contains a piece of soft crumbling bread with honey spread on top, a glass of water and a plate of fruit—apricots and damsons. She tries not to eat it all too fast or too greedily then gets up to dip her fingers in the fountain. She is certain Pliny would not like honey or damson stains on his parchment. Then she settles back to the cushions with a sigh and begins *The Argonautica*.

It is a morning unlike any other in Amara's life. Even at her father's house she never knew such leisure and luxury. Secundus appears with another light tray of food—cheese, olives and more bread, a small glass of sweet wine—but otherwise, she is left completely undisturbed. She reads, she strolls round the garden inspecting the flowers, admiring the jasmine that she knows will smell even sweeter in the evening. She looks at the paintings around the colonnade—exquisite garden scenes, wild birds in flight, a dove resting at a fountain that mirrors the real one which splashes gently through the day. She knows she is near the hustle of the street, but very little of its noise disturbs her tranquility.

By late afternoon, the sun's heat has warmed every corner of the garden, and she has discarded the blanket Secundus brought her. She is beginning to feel a little anxious that Pliny has forgotten her, when he arrives, followed by a slave carrying a trunk. "How have you enjoyed the gardens?" he asks, joining her in the shaded colonnade.

"They are wonderful," she says. "I've never known such happiness."

He nods, looking pleased. "If you would read a little to me now," he says; "I will be able to tell if I find your voice easy to listen to or not." The slave hands her a scroll. "I brought Herophilos's *On Pulses*; I need to study him in any case, and it helps if you are familiar with the text."

The scroll in Amara's hands is a thousand times finer than the one from her father's house, but she feels a flood of emotion unrolling it. "Is there a section you would prefer?" she asks.

"Start from the beginning," Pliny says wryly. "I generally find that helps."

Amara begins to read. The text is more complete than the one her father owned, but the phrases and cadences are still familiar. It is like recounting a prayer, an incantation to all she used to hold dear. She has been reading for some minutes, with Pliny scribbling notes, when he stops her. "Go back a little," he says. "Just a couple of lines." She obliges, and he nods, satisfied. She continues, reading solidly for several hours, helped by the odd glass of water brought by the ever diligent Secundus. Eventually, they break for dinner.

"You have a musical voice," Pliny says. "Not too cloying. I can see why your father found you so useful. I find many women's voices hard to listen to for long periods, but yours has just the right quality."

"Will you let me sing for you?" she asks.

"I'm not sure I'm really a man to be serenaded with Sappho," he says, sounding amused rather than unkind.

"I wasn't going to," she replies. "I used to sing a version of Nausicaa's meeting with Odysseus for my parents. I thought you might find it pleasant."

"By all means then," he says, though his tone suggests he has agreed more through politeness than eagerness.

Amara and Pliny have dinner in the garden. With only the two of them present, there is no question of the dining room. He asks her about *The Argonautica*, about her views of Apollonius's depiction of the love between Jason and Medea. She is grateful to have read enough to discuss it. After they have eaten, one of the slaves brings her the lyre, and she plays for him, a tune that takes her back to her childhood and the affectionate gaze of her parents.

She looks at him expectantly when she finishes, hoping he has enjoyed it. But the expression she sees on his face is one of immense sadness.

"Your parents did not serve you well, Amara," he says at last. "You are a lovely girl. They should have ensured you had a dowry."

"Please," she says. "They are both dead. I cannot think badly of them."

Pliny inclines his head in acknowledgement. "I understand. Forgive me."

When it is too dark and chill to stay longer in the garden, they walk back up to Pliny's room. There are even more scrolls scattered about than she remembers. "Ah, I forgot," he says, pointing to a pile of women's clothes. "I had them find you some more suitable things."

"Thank you," she says, resisting the urge to pick them up and see what he has given her. "I will wear them tomorrow. You are so kind to me."

He watches her get undressed, with the same intent expression that she remembers from the morning. Amara hopes that he wants her, that this evening he will not move away. She knows that it is not *him* she has fallen in love with—it is the gardens, the beauty of the life he possesses —but there is no focus for her desire other than the man in front of her. In spite of her efforts undressing, he does not join her on the bed, instead sitting down at his desk to work.

"Could I not read for you?" she asks

"You must be tired," he answers. "I would not expect you to sit up reading all night."

"Please," she says. "I would like to."

He hesitates then passes her the scroll he is studying. "From there," he says, indicating the point in the text with his thumb.

This time there is no Secundus to bring her discreet glasses of water and the treatise on plants is unfamiliar and even worse, the scribe's handwriting is cramped and hard to decipher. More than once, she hears Pliny wince or tut impatiently as she stumbles over a phrase, but still, Amara reads on and on, until she thinks she'll lose her voice or fall asleep exhausted over the parchment. Finally, he has had enough and gets ready for bed. "I see we are alike in our avoidance of sleep," he says. "It always seems a kind of death to me."

She lies closer to him as he gets in beside her, hoping he will put an arm round her. He doesn't. "Amara is not a name

I have heard before," he says, when they are lying facing one another in the dark. "I take it it is not your real name."

"My master gave it to me," she says, and the mention of Felix is like the cold of a knife laid flat against her heart. "He told me it is halfway between love and bitterness."

"Yes, *amare, amarum*," he says. "A bit poetic for a pimp."

Pliny rests his hand in the hollow of her waist, the same as he did last night, and she is afraid he is going to fall asleep. She leans toward him, so that his hand slides into the small of her back and kisses him. His lips are as dry and unmoving as before. She kisses him again, trying to imagine he is Menander, that he will respond to her like Menander, but instead, he pushes her gently away.

"I just want to please you." It's a line that she has repeated endlessly to so many customers without a trace of sincerity. This time she wishes the need wasn't so abject in her voice.

"You do please me," he says, as if humoring a child. "I like looking at you; you are very lovely." He runs his fingers slowly through her hair, the same way he did when he woke her in the morning. "I don't feel the need for more."

He must be impotent, she thinks, and finds the idea neither disturbs nor reassures her. She is too exhausted and the bed is too comfortable for her to mind anymore about the puzzle of Pliny. She falls asleep, lulled by the sensation of him still stroking her head.

Time passes like a silk ribbon through her fingers. Every hour spent as Pliny's guest sees her fall more deeply in love with his life, her days an endless procession of pleasures. She bathes alone in the private bath suite, has her hair dressed each morning, eats freely without considering the price of the food. Slowly, she feels her own body return to her. Nobody touches her without permission, still less with violence. In the beautiful garden, the brothel's ugliness starts to take on a sense of unreality. But she still knows it is there, like the fading bruise on her arm.

Pliny becomes the obsessive focus of her hopes. She never spends as much time with him as she did on her first day—he is often busy receiving guests or dining out—but every night, she reads to him and falls asleep under the weight of his hand. She sits in the shadow of the colonnade, watching silently when guests call on him in the garden, trying to learn more about his habits, his views, anything that might allow her to make herself indispensable to him. He would be a good master, she tells herself, imagining her life as his secretary. Even if he lost interest in her, if she became a half-forgotten beautiful object in his home, something to set alongside the flowers or the fountains, her voice would still be useful to him, he would still treat her with kindness. Sometimes, alone in the garden, she thinks of the other women, of Dido most of all, and she longs to talk to her. Then she is flooded by guilt at her planned abandonment. She tells herself elaborate lies: that if Pliny bought her, she would persuade him to buy Dido too, that her own good fortune could be shared. She tries not to think of Menander, the memories are as painful to hold as burning firewood.

On her sixth day at Pliny's house, her fear of being sent back to the brothel is so intense, she cannot read. He's said nothing about her leaving but has not mentioned extending her stay either. She is sitting silently in the garden, hidden in the shadows, when two of Pliny's acquaintances visit.

They stand gossiping by the fountain as they wait for him. It is a while before she realizes what they are talking about.

". . . I don't know why he picked her up. Only Pliny could be so eccentric, taking home some funny little Greek girl who sang at a party."

Startled, she turns her attention to the speaker. He is much younger than Pliny, with an arrogant, self-satisfied air. He reminds her of Quintus.

His companion has his back to her, but she can hear the amusement in his voice. "Caecilius saw her when he dropped in this week. Quite pretty, he said, but perfectly ridiculous. So lovelorn she was practically quivering, gazing at the admiral with tragic dormouse eyes. And Pliny paid her no mind at all!"

The first man snorts with stifled laugher. "Well, you have to hand it to him. I'll be quite happy if I can fuck a whore into a state of devotion at that age."

"The old boy's put a bit of weight on. Let's hope she doesn't give him a heart attack."

The men's mockery doesn't hurt Amara, but her powerlessness does. Across the garden, standing silently in the colonnade, she realizes Secundus is also listening. His exact role in Pliny's life is unclear to her, but she soon guessed that he is more than a steward—he is his master's eyes and ears. She can see from his face, usually so inscrutable, that he is angry. The two men carry on chatting idly at the fountain, oblivious to the two slaves listening. Secundus looks at her. He has always known she was there. He smiles, inclining his head slightly toward the men. She knows then that whatever favor the pair came to seek from the admiral today will not be granted.

It is Secundus who tells her later that Pliny will dine alone with her that night.

"Do you think he would like me to sing for him?" she asks.

"I think he enjoys your reading voice most," Secundus replies, tactfully. "He has told me how helpful you have been, reading to him for hours, long into the night without any complaint."

"It has only been a pleasure for me."

The look Secundus gives her has more than a little pity in it. Her sense of foreboding grows.

Pliny is in a good mood at dinner, more than usually solicitous about what she has been reading, complimenting her, even, at one point, kissing her hand, the only sign of physical affection he has ever shown her outside his bedroom.

He is saying goodbye to me, she thinks. She watches Pliny's mouth move as he talks. There is no cruelty in his face. The merry splash of the fountain mingles with his well-considered words, the air is scented with jasmine. She cannot imagine going back to Felix, back to the brothel with all its darkness, its daily violence. It will kill her.

"I shall miss you," Pliny says at last, when one of the slaves brings out a large bowl of fruit. He takes an apple. "It has been a pleasure to have you here."

"Don't send me back," Amara says, the words coming unprepared and unbidden. "I beg you, please, *please* don't." He looks at her in surprise, and her sense of desperation grows. She clasps his hand, pressing it against her heart. "I would be loyal to you; I would give my life to your service, I would be the most devoted secretary you could ever wish. I would be anything you wanted, go anywhere you asked."

"My dear girl," Pliny says, "there is no need for this . . ."

"Please don't send me away from you," Amara says, losing all sense of dignity, falling to her knees and weeping into the palms of his hands. "*Please*. You could buy me from my master. I would read to you every night, dedicate every hour to your work. I would never sleep in your service."

"You do have the most beautiful voice," Pliny says. She looks up at him and sees that for a moment he is wavering, considering her offer. Then he looks down. "But I already have a number of secretaries. I don't know what place there would be for you. I have already asked you everything I need to know for my work. And you know I'm not a man to keep a concubine, enchanting as you are." He helps her to her feet, seats her beside him. "It is very sweet of you to make such an offer. I am touched by your loyalty. But I cannot accept."

She collapses, weeping, onto the couch beside him. He rests a hand on her shoulder. "Amara, *please*, control yourself. There is no sense to this at all."

But she cannot control herself, and the beautiful garden is filled with the ugly sound of her hysterical crying. Eventually, when she is completely exhausted and her eyes too swollen for more tears, he suggests retiring to bed. He seems weary, irritated even, by her emotion.

"It's a shame to have wasted your last evening," he says, watching her undress. "I've already explained it to you. It's not that I don't find you delightful, but there's just *no place* for you in my household. And really, I'm an old man. You must want something else, surely? Plenty of courtesans end up married, or settled in some way, in the end."

"I don't want anything else," Amara says, lying down heavily on the bed, her limbs weighted with misery. She can already feel the walls of the brothel closing in on her.

For once, he does not head straight to his books but lies down beside her. He props himself on one elbow, leaning over her, and runs a hand through her hair. "You're an intelligent girl. You *must* understand."

Amara closes her eyes, tears leaking from beneath the lashes. She feels the warmth of him as he comes closer, his papery lips planting a kiss on her forehead. She turns away, curling into a ball, hiding her face in her hands. He sighs loudly with annoyance and thumps off the bed.

She hears him mutter the word *ridiculous* as he sits down at his desk. Amara is exhausted by unhappiness. She falls asleep, as she did on the first night, to the sound of Pliny working, the splash of the fountain in the garden below.

24

*"Perfumes are the most pointless of all luxuries. . . . Their
highest attraction is that, as a woman goes by, their use
may attract even those who are otherwise occupied."*
—Pliny the Elder, *Natural History*

When Amara wakes, Pliny is already sitting at his desk,
watching her. From his expression, she knows there
is no point in repeating her humiliation from last night.

"I'm sorry for my behavior," she says, sitting up, holding
the covers to her chest. "I did not mean to repay your kindness
in such a way. I hope you are not offended."

Pliny relaxes, obviously relieved to find her calm. He walks
over, takes her hand and pats it. "I know women are naturally
emotional creatures," he says. "There was nothing offensive
about your offer. I'm only glad you understand. Now,"ewline
he ushers her out of bed and shoos her toward her clothes,
perhaps nervous she might become tearful again. "I have been
thinking this morning about a favor you may be able to do
for me. The nephew of a dear friend is calling on me shortly.
If you are willing, I should like you to be a friend to him."

Amara pauses in her dressing. "A friend?"

"All young men need some experience with a woman before they marry," he says, with a shrug. "A father can only hope his boy doesn't land on some coarse, unintelligent whore who runs through the family money. Of course, Rufus is rather romantic, a little naive I suspect. I am trusting you to be a loyal, *helpful* friend to him. One who always understands her place. No hysterics. Can I rely on you to do that?"

Amara nods. "I would perform any service for you," she says.

"I hope not too onerous a service," he says. "Rufus is a pleasant enough boy." Pliny peers at her face. "Perhaps it might be wise to see the maid this morning. I will meet you in the garden."

Amara walks out onto the interior balcony, heading to the small room at the front of the house where Sarah, a maid belonging to Pliny's hosts, has dressed her hair each day. She takes in Amara's reddened eyes and, without asking any questions, soaks a scrap of cloth in cold water. She motions for her to sit down at the dressing table. "Hold this against your eyelids," she says. "It will help."

Amara wonders what Sarah thinks of Pliny sending her a prostitute to look after. She has never been anything but polite. Amara sits obediently in the darkness, the cloth pressed to her closed eyes, while Sarah does her hair. When she has finished, Sarah takes Amara's hands from her face. "Better," she says. "Now dry them."

Sarah picks up the kohl and a slender brush, drawing delicate lines around Amara's eyes with swift, deft movements, and then dabs a dark gray powder on her eyelids. A glass vial sits on the dresser, jasmine distilled from the garden. She passes it to Amara who unstoppers the lid and rubs the scent along her neck. Sarah takes it back, hands her the small silver mirror, the final rite in their ritual. Amara looks at her reflection. In the respectable clothes Pliny has given her—no doubt also chosen by Sarah—she does not look like a young woman who works in a brothel.

"Thank you," Amara says. "For everything." Sarah nods, polite but not inclined to talk. Whatever she really thinks of Pliny's guest, it is impossible to guess.

Pliny himself is reading a scroll when she joins him in the garden. She sits down silently, trying not to think about how soon she has to leave this place. She wonders what Rufus will be like, tries to summon the energy to charm him, muster the will to seize the opportunity Pliny has laid out for her. Secundus arrives with bread and fruit. He has not served food since the first day of her visit, when she suspects his real purpose was to examine her, so she is surprised to see him with the tray.

Secundus looks at Amara, as if appraising what is wrong with the scene. "Shall I bring you your lyre, mistress?"

"Thank you," she says, grateful to be given something to do.

She has breakfast—Pliny is still too engrossed in his scroll to talk to her—then begins to play. The feel of the strings beneath her fingers, the chance to lose herself in singing, is a relief. An hour passes, the sun warming the garden, the flowers opening their faces to its light.

She plays tirelessly to Pliny as he reads, as if she were his devoted daughter.

"Rufus is here." Secundus is standing by his master. As always, she did not hear his approach.

Amara deliberately carries on playing, only glancing up briefly to see a young man hovering by the fountain. He is gazing at her, clearly not expecting to see anyone but the admiral.

Pliny beckons him over. "Rufus! How is Julius? I was sorry to miss him in Misenum."

"He sends you his warmest greetings," Rufus says. "As do my parents. They are spending the summer at Baiae, or else they would have called on you while you are staying in Pompeii."

"Be sure to send them my best regards," Pliny says. "Baiae is delightful at this time of year." He glances over at Amara. "Your uncle told me you are very fond of the theater these days. This is Amara, a little guest of mine; she is a gifted musician."

It is the first time Pliny has expressed any interest in her music. Amara stops playing, bowing her head modestly to Rufus. The young man looks a little uncertain, perhaps having heard the jokes about Pliny and his new Greek girl. "Lovely to meet you," he says.

The two men chat for a while, but it is clear that, aside from a shared affection for Rufus's uncle, Julius, who served with Pliny in the army, they have little in common. Secundus appears again, murmuring something in his master's ear. Pliny excuses himself, asking Rufus to wait a moment while he sees a client.

Rufus and Amara sit in silence, both at a loss over how to navigate this particular social circumstance.

"That was a pretty tune," Rufus finally says to her. "Might you sing something else?"

Amara obliges, playing one of the more haunting melodies Salvius taught her. She has never performed it in public—she and Dido decided it was too melancholy—but Rufus is enchanted.

"What a lovely voice you have!" he exclaims, like a delighted child. He seems so much younger than her, she thinks, even though he is almost certainly older. He is not exactly handsome, his nose is too big and his face too broad, but he is tall, and his smile is so open and friendly she finds it hard not to smile back. He does not have the careless arrogance of a Quintus or Marcus.

"Thank you."

"How did you . . . er . . . *meet* the admiral?" Clearly, he has heard the rumors.

"I was performing at a dinner," she says. "The admiral was interested in the work of my late father, who was a doctor, and asked me to assist him for a few days with his work on natural history."

"Right," says Rufus, looking dumbfounded.

"The admiral is a man who is interested in the pursuit of knowledge above all else," she continues. "He does not have the prejudices or assumptions of lesser men. Meaning," she looks directly at Rufus, "he does not pick up whores at parties for the purposes others might imagine."

He blushes deep red. "No! Of course! I mean, I didn't think . . ."

She quickly interrupts to save his embarrassment. "Forgive me," she says. "The admiral's respect means a great deal to me, and he has been so very kind." She looks down, as if ashamed. "I should not have spoken so bluntly."

Rufus looks even more discombobulated by the switch back to virtue than he did at the mention of whores. "How long are you staying to . . . help him with his studies?"

"I am leaving today," Amara says, and this time there is nothing artful to her sadness.

"That's a shame!" he exclaims. "Will you be leaving Pompeii altogether?"

"No, I live in the town." She can see Rufus is intrigued. She needs to press his interest past the tipping point. "I was interested to hear you enjoy the theater. Which plays do you like?"

His face lights up. "There's nothing more truthful than a play, is there? I love them all, but do you know, I think comedies are braver somehow. All of life up there on the stage, and actors have the courage to say what one cannot say elsewhere." He stops, looking a little embarrassed for gushing. "But you must know all this already, doing what you do. I must say, I rather envy you for being a performer."

The thought that this wealthy young man, with the entire world at his feet, might envy a penniless slave who sings to lecherous punters at parties is so absurd Amara cannot, at first, think of a reply. But he is gazing at her earnestly without any idea how ridiculous he sounds. "That's so sweet of you," she says. "I particularly enjoy arranging the words to music, finding ways to tell the story."

"What fun you must have," Rufus says, disarming her with his infectious smile. "Do you get the chance to go to the theater much yourself?"

"No, sadly," Amara says. "Though I should like to. It has been such happiness for me here, having time to read. But losing yourself in the story of a play is another pleasure entirely."

"You must let me take you one night," Rufus says. "That is, if you are really sure it wouldn't be stepping on Pliny's toes."

For the first time since they began talking, Amara sees a degree of calculation in the way Rufus is looking at her. He still thinks Pliny had her, she realizes. "I used to live a very different life," she says carefully. "I was a doctor's daughter. The admiral is the first man to have treated me as if my past were still my present. At no time has he shown me anything other than a fatherly kindness." It is a lie, and yet, as she says it, she knows there is also truth in it. None of the usual rules quite apply to her relationship with Pliny. Amara remembers last night, the humiliation of begging, his uncomprehending rejection and, for a moment, fears she might cry again.

Rufus mistakes her sudden emotion and rushes to sit beside her. "I'm sorry," he says, clasping her hand. "What an oaf I am. I didn't mean to upset you." He gazes into her eyes. His own are hazel, wide now with concern. "What a tragic life you must have! And how insensitive I have been, asking you such things."

He wants a sob story, Amara thinks, *so he can rescue me*. She has acted many parts, she tells herself. At least this one has the virtue of mirroring real life. "No, you are very kind." She looks down in what she hopes is a show of shyness. "I am only sad because I must return to my master today and leave the admiral's protection."

"Where is your master's house?"

Amara hesitates, wondering if it is too soon to relay the crucial information. "The Wolf Den."

"The town brothel?" Rufus recoils.

Amara hides her face in her hands, defeated. Reality has proved a plot twist too far.

"You poor girl," Rufus says. "How utterly tragic." He takes her hands from her face. "Please don't cry. I won't think any less of you, I promise. I will call at . . . I will call and take you to the theater. It would be a pleasure to know you better."

Amara is in danger of crying genuine tears of relief. "I should like that so much," she says.

He leans closer, his hand resting on the bench, close to her knee. There is a more familiar look on his face. "Might I kiss you?"

She feels a flash of annoyance. After everything she has told him about her past, about the way Pliny has treated her, he still wants to own her after five minutes' conversation. She lifts her hand for him to kiss.

"Of course," he says, taking it. "Of course, not in the admiral's house."

"Thank you," she says, giving him what she hopes is an adoring smile. "It means everything to be treated with kindness."

"You deserve nothing less," he says, gallantly. They sit awkwardly for a moment. "I'm going to have to leave now though." He stands up. "Perhaps you could pass on my goodbyes to Pliny. I promise I will call on you this week."

"Thank you," Amara replies. "Don't leave it too long."

When he has left, Amara sits in the garden, lifted by a current of hope. She is looking forward to thanking Pliny for the introduction. Then she sees Secundus step from the shadow of the colonnade. He is carrying a small bundle. Her things. Instantly, she understands. Pliny will not be coming back to say goodbye.

Secundus walks over and sits next to her on the bench, putting her clothes down between them. "When he brought you here," he says, looking straight ahead to the fountain, "I told him he would be lucky if you didn't demand your weight's worth in gifts every day. At the very least you would leave here with one priceless jewel. He wagered me a denarius I was wrong." He smiles at her. "So you cost me a denarius."

She smiles back at him. "Sorry." The thought of asking Pliny for gifts had in fact crossed her mind. But she knew Felix would only have taken them all. "Did he tell you what I did ask from him?"

"Your undying service. That's a gift though. Not a demand." He turns away from her. "We both know what service costs."

They sit, united briefly by the unspoken understanding one slave has for another. "I also heard you crying last night. I think the whole house heard you." He looks at her, not unkindly but with determination. "That *cannot* happen today."

She blushes. "It won't." Secundus nods, satisfied. "You know, it wasn't just for the life," she says, gesturing at the fountain, the garden. "I mean, of course it was for that. But I believe I love him too."

Secundus does not immediately reply. Then he stands, and she knows he is going to leave, that she will have to leave. Amara bites her lip, determined not to embarrass herself with more tears.

"You didn't ask for a gift," he says. "But he has chosen a gift for you, nonetheless. I have put it with your clothes." He pauses. "I will give you a moment, so you can have the privacy of your thoughts before you leave. But it can only be a few minutes."

"Thank you," she says.

Secundus bows and walks away.

Amara picks up the bundle of clothes, expecting to find coins slipped between her robes. But whatever it is, it is much heavier. She draws out the scroll Pliny has left her. *On Pulses* by Herophilos.

25

"They must conquer or fall. Such was the settled purpose
of a woman—the men might live and be slaves!"
—Tacitus on Boudicca, Queen of the Icenii, *Annals* 14

"Look who it is! Look who it is!" Beronice screams as Amara steps into the brothel. "We thought you were never coming home!"

Victoria and Dido rush out into the corridor to join her. "I'm so happy you're back; I'm so happy to see you," Dido flings her arms round her, crying into her neck. "I thought I was never going to see you again."

"It was only a week!" Amara says, torn between happiness at seeing Dido and guilt from knowing she spent yesterday begging never to return here.

"What was he like then?" Victoria also looks very pleased to see Amara but would never be so soft as to say so. "Bet he was a total pervert; the old ones always are."

Amara hesitates. She had so looked forward to laughing with Victoria about that first, ridiculous night with Pliny, but now it feels too private. The thought of mocking him only makes her sad. "He was the kindest man I've ever met," she replies, her voice quavering.

"Oh, look at her!" Victoria laughs. "You're all welling up. We've had the weird ironmonger, and now you're in love with some doddery old granddad. You have the worst taste in men I have ever known!"

"That guy she met at the games was alright," Beronice says, defending her. "He wasn't bad at all."

"Say that louder, and Gallus might hear you," Victoria whispers, and they all laugh as Beronice whips round.

"Fuck you," Beronice says to Victoria, but she is laughing too.

"And what's all this?" Victoria gestures at her to hand over the clothes. "How many new outfits did he give you?"

"Three," Amara says, passing them round. "I guess I'll have to give them all to Felix."

"Lovely material," Victoria says, stroking one of the dresses. "But you do look a bit matronly." She squints at the respectable clothes Amara is wearing. "I shouldn't think anyone would dare ask for a shag if you swanned around in that." An idea strikes her. "Please don't tell me the old man wanted you to dress up as *his* dead wife too!"

"No." Amara laughs. "Nothing like that."

"What then?" Beronice says. "Must have been something special to buy you for a week."

"He wanted me to read to him."

"Sexy books?" Victoria is too shocked to make a joke out of it. "Is that it?"

"No! I mean we went to bed together," Amara says defensively, thinking of the nights she spent lying naked beside Pliny, his hand resting on her while they both slept. "Just that . . ." She trails off, not knowing how to explain what happened or how she feels about it.

"It's alright," Dido says, hugging her again. "You don't have to say anything."

"*Went to bed together*," Victoria says, copying her coy phrase. "I've heard it all now."

Amara feels suddenly exhausted. After so much time alone, it is going to be a strain returning to the total lack of privacy. "I might just have a rest so I'm not too tired tonight."

"Oh, you can't go in there . . ." Victoria says as Amara draws the curtain to her own cell.

"Who's this?" Amara asks in surprise. An unfamiliar woman is sitting on her bed. She is shockingly pale and has a tangled mass of long red hair. At the sight of the others, she springs up, towering over them, babbling urgently in a strange, guttural language. Amara cannot tell if she is furious or terrified. She steps back into the corridor in alarm.

"Sit!" Victoria shouts, pointing at the bed. "Sit!"

The stranger goes back into the cell, still talking in her incomprehensible tongue, gesturing at them.

"Felix bought her with your old man's money," Victoria says. "He told us it's because you and Dido are out so much, we need more bodies in the brothel."

"Where am I sleeping then?"

"You can come in with me," Dido says. "Makes sense."

"Doesn't speak a word of Latin," Victoria says. "We've called her Britannica, because that's where she's from.

Cressa's the only one she seems to like. She's off buying more food for the greedy thing now."

"I thought all the Britons had blue faces," Beronice says, looking at Britannica with disappointment. "That's what everyone says, isn't it? Blue-faced Britons."

"She's certainly a savage," Victoria says. "She just screams all night, scratching the men, *biting*. She punched one yesterday! Like some sort of animal!"

Amara doesn't like the way Victoria is talking about Britannica, even if the other woman doesn't understand. She glances at her again. The Briton is silent now. She certainly looks like a wildcat, with her mane of red hair and green eyes. But the emotion in them is all too human. Rage at her confinement.

"Are you all just standing there talking about her again?"

It's Cressa, carrying a lump of bread. She shoves them out of the way so she can get in the cell. "You might have a little compassion."

Britannica's face lights up at the sight of Cressa, and she begins gabbling. Cressa sits beside her, talking soothingly to her as if she were a small child, stroking her hair. She gives the bread to Britannica who wolfs it down. "Sorry, Amara, I didn't realize you were back," she says, finally noticing her.

"That's alright," she replies. "I remember my father telling me about the women in Britain. A lot of them are warriors. Maybe Britannica was a soldier."

"The women go to war?" Dido says.

"Not all of them. My father told me they had a famous queen; I don't know her name. But she destroyed a Roman army."

Beronice makes the sign of the evil eye. "Women aren't meant to rule. It's unnatural."

"Britannica's hardly a warrior queen! She can't even defeat a drunken sailor," Victoria says, though Amara notices that she eyes the stranger with a new, wary respect.

"Were you a warrior?" Cressa asks Britannica gently. "Is that why you hate it here so much?" Britannica smiles at her, not understanding the words, only the kindness behind them.

"Amara!" Thraso is shouting from the doorway of the brothel. "Are you still in there? I told you to go up to Felix."

"I'm just coming," she calls back.

"No, you're not," he snaps, barging inside and grabbing her hard by the arm. She cries out in pain. "You're a fucking timewaster. Move it." He lets go of her and stomps off again.

"He's just annoyed Balbus gave him a black eye yesterday," Victoria whispers. "Some stupid fight about Drauca."

"What about her?" Amara asks, suddenly anxious.

"Who knows," Victoria shrugs. "Thraso would start a fight about anything."

It is a room she had hoped never to see again. The red glow, the bulls' skulls. She stands, saying nothing, as Felix goes through her new clothes.

"Is this all he gave you? After a week?"

"There was this as well," she says, holding up the scroll but not handing it over.

Felix gestures impatiently, and she gives it to him. He unravels it clumsily, looking for hidden coins or jewelry. "Anatomy?"

He frowns, looking more closely at one of the illustrations. Amara doesn't answer. If Felix understands her attachment to Pliny's gift, he will only use it against her. He hands it back, and she takes it, rolling it up again, trying not to let the relief show on her face. "Not much after such a long stay."

"He introduced me to a new client though. So those dresses will come in useful."

"What new client?"

"A man called Rufus. He will be calling on you to buy me for an evening." She hesitates, knowing how much Felix hates being given advice. "I'm hoping that he is a long-term investment, so I think we might be better not charging too much at first, so that he continues paying."

"You're running the business now, are you?"

"No," she says. "I didn't mean . . ."

"Amara," Felix says, grinning. "I was *joking*. You've done well. The old man paid a fair price." He picks up one of the dresses. "If this new one turns into a regular client, you can keep these to wear out with him. If not, I will sell them." He waves a hand at the clothes she still has on. "But you certainly don't need to be wearing them now."

Amara had guessed he might make her change and has brought her old gaudy toga up from downstairs. She strips off, handing him the new clothes.

"You've put weight on," he says, looking her over as she dresses. "It suits you."

"You'll have to feed me more then," she says, risking a joke, "if you like it so much." Felix shakes his head but looks amused. A memory of the night they spent together comes back to her. The way he rested his head on her shoulder, looked up with the same flash of humor in his eyes. And she had smiled back.

Amara doesn't like remembering. "Thraso looked worse for wear," she says. "Why were he and Balbus fighting?"

She knows, as soon as she has asked, that it was a mistake. Any hint of playfulness has gone from his face. "I thought the old man was going to buy you," Felix says, ignoring her question. "The Admiral of the Fleet! What a change that would have been. But here you are, back at the brothel." She says nothing. "What did he do with you all week?"

"Just the usual," she says, her mouth feeling dry.

"I doubt that," Felix says. He puts his arms round her in an exaggerated parody of affection. "Did he tell you how lovely you were? Gaze into your eyes? Was he *gentle*?"

"No."

"He *wasn't* gentle?" Felix pretends to be shocked. "What a shit! He certainly fed you well. But I'm not sure I believe you. I think he spoiled you, that old man. Made you forget who you are."

His fingers are digging painfully into her upper arms, but she doesn't flinch. Amara has belonged to Felix so long, she knows that he is going to rape her, to humiliate her, to try and destroy the last traces of the happiness she has brought back, now fading like the scent of jasmine on her skin. She grips the scroll Pliny gave her. There are parts of herself Felix cannot know or touch.

"I never forget," she says.

"Good," Felix lets go of her. "You should get back to work then."

She is almost over the threshold of the doorway, giddy with relief, when he stops her. "Did I say you could take that?" Amara waits as he walks up to her, lets him take Pliny's gift from her hands. "I might be able to sell it." He turns the scroll over, a dismissive look on his face. "You never know what someone else will value."

26

"Thais: Me not speaking from my heart?
That's not fair! What have you ever wanted from me,
even in fun, that you didn't get?"
—Terence, *The Eunuch*

The theater's stage is blazing with torches, even though dusk has not yet fallen. The brightly painted columns and statues, the flamboyance of the actors, the laughter, reminds her of the atmosphere at the Vinalia. Amara has never been to see a play before and is enjoying the luxury of watching rather than being watched. Let someone else have the hard work of entertaining for a while. Beside her, Rufus has taken her hand, and his look of utter delight at the unfolding scene endears him to her. *He really is like a child*, she thinks.

She finds the play easy to follow. It is *The Eunuch* by Terence who, Rufus eagerly assures her, is a greater master than Virgil. She would certainly like to borrow the luck of the play's courtesan, Thais, who seems to rule the men through charm alone. Amara suspects Thais never encountered a pimp like Felix.

She finds herself laughing at this world where the slaves are cleverer than their masters, and the men love women to distraction. She remembers Rufus telling her he admired the theater for telling the truth—can he really think the world is like this? On stage, she watches as an actor disguises himself as a eunuch in order to rape the slave girl he fancies. He is a tall man, lisping and mincing to convince everyone he is safe to leave with the young virgin. Laughter ripples round the theater at the absurdity and audacity of the joke.

"The comic timing!" Rufus whispers to her. "It's perfect."

The girl's exaggerated screams off stage cause further titters of amusement. Rufus laughs with the rest. Amara sits listening to the actress's cries, a fixed smile on her face. Perhaps comedy is a mirror after all.

The sky turns a deeper blue, and the shadows on stage lengthen. Rufus is caressing her hand, teasing out the shape of her fingers with his own. She had worried, before this evening, about being out of place in a respectable crowd. Victoria had insisted she let her make some changes to the white robe Pliny gave her—"You don't want Rufus thinking he's taken his mother! At least show a *bit* of shoulder."—and now she is grateful to her friend. Many of the women here are obviously courtesans, out with wealthy lovers. Her eye is drawn to one woman, sitting with the poise of a queen, her robes elegantly dipped at the back to show the line of her dark brown shoulder blades. Amara shuffles on her seat, trying to pull her own dress a little further down her arm.

The play's end surprises her. Thais gets to keep both her lovers—the one she likes and the one who pays. She looks at Rufus who is cheering enthusiastically. Perhaps her life will disturb him less than she feared. He turns to her, face lit with excitement. "Did you like it?"

"It was *wonderful*!" she exclaims. "I cannot think of a happier evening!"

"I'm so glad," he says, kissing her hand. "I hoped you would."

They spill back out onto the streets with the rest of the audience. Laughter and conversation warm the evening air. Amara can see a small crowd pressed around Marcella's bar and instinctively turns away.

"Is there somewhere to entertain privately at your place?" Rufus asks. He has not yet been to the brothel—one of his slaves was sent to collect her.

"Oh!" Amara says, looking horrified. "We couldn't go there!" She imagines Rufus stepping into the narrow, sooty corridor, greeted by some vomiting laundryman, embracing her to the sound of Victoria's moaning, the air stagnant with the smell from the latrine. She would never see him again. "It's a *terrible* place!"

"But you seem so . . . lovely," Rufus replies, looking at the nearly respectable white dress, her carefully dressed hair.

Amara knows she cannot tell him she is ashamed of the squalor; she must invent a more poetic reason to stay away. "My master is unbelievably cruel," she replies. "If he thought there was a chance I might be happy with you, even for an hour, he would never let me see you again."

"Really?" Rufus looks alarmed.

Amara glances at him sidelong, as if too shy to be direct. "If he thought I might care for anyone, he would punish me dreadfully." Even as she says it, she can imagine Felix laughing. As if he would care about *anything* other than the money.

Rufus squeezes her hand. "I will take you to my home. My parents are away for the summer."

They walk to his house, accompanied by a small retinue of slaves who must have had to hang around outside the theater during the performance. Rufus is still enjoying talking about the play, and together, they amuse themselves imagining what mischief Thais and her lover might make after the action has ended. "And even our eunuch married his girl in the end," he says about the rapist, "so no harm done."

The porter lets them in, and Amara feels a flood of relief that they did not go to the brothel. It is a wealthy home, not far from Zoilus's house, and as Rufus leads her across the atrium, a beautiful marine mosaic beneath their feet, she imagines his horror at the Wolf Den's baked mud floor. They pass through the courtyard, and he stops to break off a sprig of jasmine.

"This scent always makes me think of you," he says, giving it to her. "The way you were sitting in that garden! Surrounded by a thousand white stars. I was just thinking to myself I had no idea the admiral had a daughter and then I remembered . . ." He stops abruptly.

And then you remembered Pliny had hired a whore, Amara thinks. "That's such a beautiful thing to say," she whispers, inhaling the flower's scent before tucking the stem behind her ear. "Thank you." She doesn't stop him when he kisses her this time. Why else, after all, is she here?

"A little further," he says, letting go of her. "My rooms are this way." One of the slaves has accompanied them, and Rufus turns to him before leading her off. "Some refreshments please, Vitalio."

Rufus's rooms are set off the large garden. She smiles to herself to see the paintings on the walls: theater masks and actors on stage. Rufus offers her a couch, reclining beside her. Vitalio brings them wine and sets down a light supper on a small table by the couch: bread, cheese, dried figs. Then he leaves.

It is clear Rufus has no intention of eating yet. No sooner is Vitalio gone, than he is all over her. Amara finds herself unexpectedly afraid. This feels too familiar, too like the brothel. So much rests on him liking her, and she has no idea how a courtesan might be expected to behave. Should she acquiesce or will he want to chase her?

"Stop!" she says, pushing him off and sitting up. She rearranges her dress to cover herself. Her heart is pounding with anxiety. "Just a moment."

Rufus is looking at her in surprise. He had not, after all, been violent. And what else is a man meant to do when he has hired a woman for the night?

She thinks of Thais, of the illusion of power she wielded. Rufus believes that is what life is really like. He has all the power, and she has none, but he does not know this. And she cannot let him realize.

She turns to him in anger. "You presume too much."

They stare at one another in mutual astonishment. The words seemed to come from someone else. It is a part Amara is playing, yet somehow, she just found her own voice. She takes the jasmine flower from her hair, allowing the real anger she always carries inside to catch fire. "So you thought I was the admiral's daughter," she says. "And then, because I am not, you decide to treat me as a whore. I told you that this has not always been my life, that I value kindness and respect and you show me *none*."

Amara is ready for him to argue, ready to leave him, to blaze out into the night in rage, but Rufus immediately surrenders.

"I'm sorry," he says, brow creased with remorse. "I didn't mean to upset you."

Amara finds, having lit the spark, it is not so easy to extinguish it. "Is that what you think? That you can take without asking?" she demands.

"No! Not at all, I . . ."

"What about all these plays that mean so much to you? What about love?" Her voice is scathing. "I have enough clients," she lies. "I thought you were different; I thought you wanted something else." The anger is starting to take on a momentum beyond Rufus, and she knows she has to stop. She takes a breath, turning her face aside, as if to hide emotion. "I thought you might *care* for me." She falls silent, waiting to see if he will accept the role she is offering.

He touches her arm, tentatively at first, then more confidently when she doesn't move away. "Please," he says, laying his hand over hers. "I'm very sorry. Let me make it up to you."

Amara slowly allows herself to be won round. It isn't a difficult part for her to play. Nobody has ever made such an effort to charm her. Rufus teases her, playfully trying to serve her food, turning all his humor against himself. He smiles and his cheeks dimple like Cupid. Amara accepts the glass of wine he offers, smiles back when he compares himself unfavorably to the "eunuch" in the play they have just seen and, when he finally jokes about the terrifying effect that her anger had on him, widening his eyes in a ridiculous parody of surprise, she finds her laughter is genuine.

"I do so wish *I* could write for the theater," he tells her, once they are clearly friends again. He gestures at her to take a handful of dried figs then, when she has, helps himself. "But I don't have any talent."

"I can't believe that's true."

"No, it is. I might be an idiot, but at least I know that I am," he says. "And besides, my father would hate it. He wants me to run for aedile next year." He pulls a face. "Can you imagine? All that endless smarming, getting people to vote for you, followed by a year of total tedium listening to everyone drone on about grain distribution. I'd be hopeless at it."

"Couldn't you choose the celebrations you threw though?" she says, thinking of Fuscus. "Maybe a free performance at the theater rather than the usual games at the arena?"

"Yes, I had been thinking that." His look of surprise reminds her of Pliny when she quoted Herophilos. "Might make the whole thing more bearable." They smile at each other. He holds her gaze and leans closer, then, when she doesn't move away, kisses her. There is more sensitivity to him this time; she can tell he is trying not to rush her. "I have to ask you something," he says, stroking her arm.

"I know you are trapped by your life at the . . . where you live. I know you don't have a choice. But is your heart free?"

Amara thinks immediately of Menander. "Yes," she lies.

"And at the admiral's house, you two didn't . . . I mean, you and Pliny . . ."

"No. He never touched me. Not like that."

"Right," Rufus says in relief. "You just seemed so *fond* of the old man. I had to wonder. He must have a will of iron, keeping his hands to himself with you round."

"He knew about my past," she says. "He felt my life had not taken its right path."

Rufus nods. "Terence writes about that, the mistakes that are made. When a girl isn't *meant* to be a slave. Were you kidnapped?" He asks, an idea suddenly striking him. "Then you might not *really* be a slave at all. If one could prove it."

For a moment, Amara thinks of borrowing Dido's life story, taking it as her own. But she has already told Pliny the truth and cannot risk discovery. "No. I lost my father and everything else with him."

"My poor darling," Rufus says, kissing her again. He is a little bolder this time, easing her back on the couch, his hand creeping up her leg. She stops him.

"You can take what you want," she says. "We both know it. But wouldn't you rather it was given?" She kisses him to soften the rejection. "Wouldn't you rather wait? If it was given along with my heart?"

Amara knows she is gambling, and the dice are not weighted in her favor. Rufus has every reason to feel irritated. He has paid Felix for her; he was promised sex, and now she is asking him to treat her like a virginal heroine in a play. But her lies have the intensity of truth. She gazes at him with wide, dark eyes.

"Yes," Rufus says, touching his fingers to her lips. "I would like to win your heart."

Four of Rufus's slaves, including Vitalio, escort her back to the brothel. She feels the irony in knowing that the place they are taking her is not much safer than the darkened streets. The five of them walk quickly, the slaves' torches throwing out fingers of light, brushing the houses as they pass by. Nobody speaks.

She thinks of Rufus, feels a sense of elation shot through with anxiety at the memory of his kiss goodbye. The tender way he tucked the jasmine back behind her ear before she left, his wholehearted acceptance of the part she offered him. She could almost love him for the gift he has given her: granting her the illusion of being a person and not a slave. But she knows it is an illusion, and the fantasy they have created together is fragile. It would be so easy to care for him, to forget how little she really has. Now begins the painstaking journey of discovering how he might help her escape. It's not a journey on which she can afford to have feelings.

27

"Pythias: I don't know who he was, but the facts speak for themselves about what he did. The girl herself is in tears and when you ask her she can't bring herself to say what's up."
—Terence, *The Eunuch*

The screaming is like nothing she has ever heard. Fear grips Amara, and she runs to the door, terrified one of her friends is being murdered, but Thraso looks perfectly calm.

"Just the new girl," he says, with a shrug.

She pushes past him, finds Victoria, Dido and Cressa huddled in the corridor.

"It's Britannica," Cressa says, her face wet with tears. "I can't bear it."

"What are they doing to her? What's happening?"

"Nothing!" Victoria snaps. "Nothing that the rest of us don't have to put up with. She's fucking crazy!" Britannica is shouting, screaming in her own language, calling Cressa's name. Even though none of them understand her words, they know she is begging for help. Victoria grabs Cressa's arm to stop her responding. "You *can't*," she says. "What are you going to do? Tell them to stop and Felix will pay their money back?"

Dido bursts into tears. "We can't just *leave* her. There are two of them in there!"

"Two men?" Amara is appalled.

"She was fighting so much," Victoria says, not meeting her eye. "The other one went in to hold her down."

Amara looks desperately at Dido, then Cressa. It seems impossible that none of them are helping, that they are all standing by uselessly, letting her suffer. Britannica's screaming cuts through her, visceral because it is familiar. It shocks her that she has never shouted her own anguish like that, that she has been silent instead. She presses her hands over her ears, wanting to stop the horror, stop the ear-splitting sound.

"Why can't she just *shut up*!" Victoria shouts, suddenly angry. "Why can't she fucking *understand*? It gets the men in the wrong mood; they're going to be violent with all of us soon if she keeps this up. Stupid fucking bitch."

"They're hurting her!" Cressa shouts back, distraught. "*They* need to stop. Not *her*."

Britannica's screaming subsides into sobs. "It's nearly over then," Victoria mutters, not wanting to confront Cressa. "She always fights right to the end. So that means they've finished. She'll be alright soon."

The curtain scrapes back, and the two men step out into the corridor. The women instinctively draw back, clinging together. One man gives them a contemptuous stare, spits on the floor. They swagger off. Cressa breaks from the others and rushes into Amara's old cell. Britannica is quiet; the only crying they can hear now is from Cressa.

Another man steps into the brothel. His shape, his walk, is familiar to Amara. It is Menander.

The shock sends the blood rushing to her heart. She stares at him, unable to speak.

"I came to see you. Thraso said you were free."

He is standing where Britannica's tormentor spat on the floor, and it is as if the last piece of her innocence is ripped from her.

She says nothing but walks to Dido's cell, barely waiting for him to follow, then draws the curtain behind them both. She cannot bear to look at him, to see his beautiful face, so she stands gripping the material, her back to the room.

"What do you want?"

"Timarete . . ."

"What service do you want?"

"Service?"

"Yes, you paid for it," she swings round, torn between rage and heartbreak. "So what service do you want? What fuck did you pay for?"

"I didn't."

"Why are you here then?"

"To see you. To talk with you."

"You wanted to *talk* in *here*?" Amara replies, her voice rising with hysteria. Even with the curtain closed, they can still hear Cressa weeping, the sound of Beronice with a customer next door, and Victoria, now rowing with Thraso, yelling at him not to let thugs into the brothel.

"Where else do we have?"

She sees the quiet sadness in his face and knows, without question, that he is telling the truth. Her relief is almost more painful than the shock before. She walks to him, puts her arms round his neck and rests the side of her face against his. "You paid to talk to me."

"I didn't want to wait until December," he says, holding her tightly. "I've been saving for a while. Rusticus is in favor of his slaves getting some pleasure; he thinks it keeps us all more obedient."

"But you mustn't spend your money like that!" she says. "You need it. You need to save it."

"I needed to see you."

She thinks of Rufus, of all the ridiculous things she said that evening about love, of all the lies she told. "I can't give you anything; I have nothing," she spreads her arms out to illustrate the empty cell. "I don't even own myself, my own body, my own life."

"Neither do I."

"Then what are we doing?" She sits down on the bed. "What are we doing here talking."

"I know that you're lonely," he says, sitting beside her. "I'm lonely too. But I don't feel it when I'm with you."

"It hurts so much afterward though," she says, leaning her head on his shoulder, letting him hold her again. "It just hurts."

"Because it makes you think of home, and all we lost before."

"Not just that," she says. "Do you know how many men I've been with? I didn't want any of them, but it happened anyway, and it's my life now, and I have to accept it. And then I see you, the only one I actually *have* wanted, and even though we are alone together now, and there's nothing to stop us, even though you paid my fucking pimp for me . . . I just can't. Not in this place. I can't."

"I know," he says. "I won't ask it of you. Not here." He leans over to kiss her on the temple. "But we can belong to many places. Don't you ever think of yourself as being somewhere else?"

Amara thinks of Pliny's garden, the smell of jasmine and the splash of the fountain. "Yes," she says.

Menander helps her sit further back on the bed, so that he is leaning against the wall and she is against him, his arms all the way round her. "At night, sometimes, when I'm sleeping on the floor above the shop," he says. "I imagine I am back in Athens. I picture walking through the street in the evening, back to my old home, the shop my father used to own. But it's not my parents or my sisters waiting there for me, it's you. I can see you in the hall, though you've never been there, and we talk, we have all the time we need."

"I think of you in Aphidnai, sometimes too," she admits. "But mainly I imagine us being somewhere else altogether. Somewhere we don't even know yet." Amara stops. What can she tell him really? That she thought of him when Rufus kissed her, that she wished it was him instead? Or that she told Rufus her heart was free because she cannot afford for it to be otherwise.

"Might it not be possible?" he asks, holding her even closer. "Slaves do marry, don't they? Or Rusticus might grant me my freedom one day; he has no heir, nobody to take over his business."

Amara cannot even begin to imagine Felix's reaction to the first idea, and she doesn't have the heart to tell Menander that every unscrupulous owner since the dawn of time has duped a talented apprentice into working harder with the vague promise of freedom one day. She can't bear to destroy the fantasy. "If I had the choice, it would only be you," she says.

They talk together through the night, and Amara can feel her loneliness ebb with every moment in his company. The brothel even starts to feel like a less terrible place, simply because he is there. She tells him about Pliny, about how she felt having those few brief days of freedom, and he tells her about the way he feels in the shop, the moments he forgets he is a slave, caught up in the business of creating a new lamp, a new object, just as he did in his life before.

They are lost to everything but each other, until it is time for lock-up, and Thraso arrives to throw any lingering customers out.

"Fuck off now," he says, barging into the cell. "You've more than had your money's worth."

Amara tries to kiss Menander goodbye, but Thraso comes between them, shoving her hard. She sees Menander react instinctively to step in.

"No!" she shouts. Amara looks at Menander, shaking her head. "Please." She cannot bear the self-loathing on his face, their shared understanding that he is powerless to protect her from Thraso, or from anything else.

When he has gone, Amara does not cry. She stands with the palms of her hands flat against the wall of her cell. She wants to scream her rage into the night like Britannica. Her anger is rising like the sea, drowning her. She has to get out.

28

"Poems are praised, but it's for cash they itch;
A savage even is welcomed if he's rich."
—Ovid, *The Art of Love* II

It's hot in the Sparrow, even though it's not yet midday. Cressa has stayed in the brothel to look after Britannica, and Amara and the others sit at a table, sharing some bread and cheese, a small pot of cold vegetable stew. Amara can already feel her clothes sticking to her skin with sweat.

"So the boyfriend turned up then?" Victoria asks. There is none of the usual spark to her question.

Amara nods, not wanting to talk about Menander, and Victoria doesn't press her. "Sorry you two had to share together," Amara says.

"We thought you might want some space," Dido replies.

"Thanks."

They lapse back into silence. "What are we going to do about her?" Beronice says. Nobody has to ask who she means. "When is she going to stop with the fighting and screaming?"

An old man is mumbling at the table next to them, either drunk or unwell. He reaches out a shaky hand. It's not clear if he is trying to reach for their bread or grope Beronice. "Not today, Grandad!" Victoria snaps, her voice loud. "Can't get any fucking peace anywhere," she mutters, turning back to the table.

"It's not right," Beronice continues. "It put my customer off his stride. Then he was in a bad mood and rough with it."

"I think she's brave," Dido says.

"Brave?" Victoria says. "She's a savage."

"I wish you wouldn't call her that," Amara says. "Just because she doesn't speak Latin. And I agree with Dido. She's only doing what the rest of us would, if we had the guts."

"If you think she's so fucking fabulous, why don't you teach her some Latin then?" Victoria says. "And it's not brave. It's stupid. Have you seen the bruises on her? Who fights a battle they're never going to win?"

"That's what courage means."

"Oh, get lost, seriously," Victoria says. "If you can't see what a problem she is, maybe it's because you spend all your time at fancy fucking parties. You won't be around when the rest of us get attacked, will you? What do you care?"

Amara gets up from the table, taking a piece of bread and cheese with her. She was already in a terrible mood before this and doesn't trust herself not to lose her temper.

"Where are you going?" Victoria asks, halfway between conciliatory and cross.

"To try and teach Britannica some Latin."

Amara stomps back toward the brothel, almost barging into Nicandrus walking along the pavement to the Sparrow with a bucket of water. "Careful!" he says.

She holds her hands up in apology but doesn't stop to chat. Seeing him makes her think of Menander, of the choice Dido made not to let her feelings for Nicandrus take root when there is nowhere for love to grow. Perhaps she was wise.

Thraso is still on the door, exhausted from guarding the brothel all night. He barely steps aside to let her in, making her squeeze past him.

"Cressa?"

"She's not well," Fabia says, not looking up as she sweeps the corridor. "She's feeling sick." There's a sound of retching from the latrine.

Amara hurries to the end of the corridor. "Cressa! Are you alright?"

Cressa comes out, holding onto the wall. She is pale, her eyes dark with misery. Amara feels sick herself, guessing what Cressa is facing.

"You should eat something," she says quietly. "It will help. The others are still in the Sparrow."

Cressa shakes her head. "Nothing will help."

"At least eat something, *please*. You will feel less nauseous."

"What about Britannica?"

"I can look after her."

"Are you sure?" Cressa looks relieved. "Be kind to her, won't you? You promise?" Amara nods, touched that

Cressa's first thought is always for someone else. "She's in my cell. I was just about to help her wash." Cressa starts to head past Amara who stops her, catching hold of her arm.

"Can't I help you too?" she says, her voice low.

Cressa looks down, as if unable to bear Amara's kindness. "Nobody can help me."

She hurries from the brothel, stepping aside to avoid Fabia. When she has gone, the old woman turns to Amara, shaking her head.

Britannica startles when she sees Amara, drawing her legs up toward herself on the bed. She seems wary rather than afraid. There are bruises on her pale arms, including vivid fingerprints where she must have been held down. Dried blood is smeared on her face. *Cowards*, Amara thinks.

She smiles at Britannica, pointing to herself. "Amara. I am Amara. Friend of Cressa."

"Cressa?" Britannica looks past Amara, clearly hoping the other woman will appear.

Amara leans over and puts the bread and cheese on the bed. "For you. Cressa will be back soon."

Britannica takes the food without acknowledging Amara or gesturing thanks. Amara waits for her to finish eating then goes through a painstaking performance, naming objects in the cell, asking Britannica if she can wash her face.

"Water," she says, pointing to the jug. She dips her hand in it, showing Britannica the drops falling from her fingers. "Water. Now you say it. Water."

In answer, Britannica releases a torrent of words in her own harsh language. Her gestures are violent, her expression intense, but although the incomprehensible tirade makes Amara feel uncomfortable, she guesses the anger is not directed at her. Amara reaches for the jug again, and Britannica grabs her arm. Her grip is as strong as a man's. Britannica repeats the same strange word over and over, staring intently, willing Amara to understand. Then she lets go of her with a cry of exasperation, flinging herself back on the bed.

"I know. I want to kill them too," Amara says. "But it doesn't work that way. We don't get a choice."

Britannica has turned her face to the wall, ignoring her. She doesn't resist as Amara splashes water on her skin but does nothing to help either.

"Your hair is a mess," Amara says. "Can I brush it?" She takes the silence as agreement, picking up the brush from Cressa's shelf. "Red," she says, trying to tease out the knots. "Your hair is *red*." Amara has never seen anything like it. She can imagine it glowing like fire in the July sun when Britannica stood naked in the slave market, her skin unnaturally white. It's obvious Felix wanted something exotic and didn't bother about the fact she couldn't speak. "Fucking idiot," she mutters to herself.

Britannica doesn't make a fuss, though it must be painful having so many knots untangled. Amara lets her mind go blank, concentrating on nothing but combing out the mass of hair, until she hears Felix's voice, talking to Thraso at the door. All her senses are instantly alert.

Someone steps over the threshold of the brothel. Britannica whips round, shouting at Amara. It sounds more like a command than a warning, but she has no idea what it might be.

"Making friends?"

Felix stands at the doorway, looking in. Britannica bunches up, reminding Amara of the tigers in the arena. She bares her teeth at Felix and hisses. Victoria's insult comes into her mind, unbidden. *Savage.*

Their master is unconcerned. He draws a small knife from his tunic. Examines it, as if it needs a clean. Britannica stops hissing, watching him, eyes so wide the whites are showing. Felix gestures with the blade, casual rather than threatening. "You don't like this, do you?"

"She doesn't understand any Latin," Amara says.

"Oh, she understands me," he replies. "We understand each other perfectly well. Don't we?" As if in answer, Britannica shrinks back. "You see," he says to Amara, tucking the knife away. "She speaks my language."

"She doesn't understand life here," Amara says. "She screams all night; it's not good for business."

"She'll get used to it. And if not." He shrugs. "Some customers like that. Not that you have to worry, not after I got this letter from your posh boy," Felix holds up a note, a look of amusement on his face. "He is demanding you have lodgings outside the brothel."

"*Rufus?*" Amara is stunned.

"How many posh boys do you have? Yes, Rufus. I've sent a reply back with Gallus. He's not offering enough for every night. But I've agreed you will only spend two nights a week here, as long as he pays the retainer."

Amara thinks of Rufus at the theater, the way he gave her the jasmine, his acceptance of her anger. She feels touched in ways she cannot express, certainly not to Felix.

"Don't just sit there!" Felix says, irritated by her lack of reaction. "Pack your things up."

"But where am I going?"

"You can sleep upstairs. In the storeroom with Paris."

"I can't leave Britannica alone; I promised Cressa."

Felix draws the knife again, crosses to Britannica, points it at her face. She flinches, but Amara is surprised she doesn't show greater physical fear. "*You. Stay. Here. Not. Move.*" He leans forward, gripping her thigh with his free hand, in an unmistakable gesture of sexual aggression. This time Britannica looks more afraid. Felix stays where he is, until she cowers, no longer meeting his eye. Amara has never despised him more.

He stands up. "You just need to be firm with her," he says, heading for the door. "Now get your things."

Amara follows him, looking back briefly at Britannica before leaving the cell. She hopes the hate on her face is meant for Felix alone.

Paris is as delighted by the new living arrangements as Amara imagined he might be. Felix's slave boy doesn't dare express his discontent in front of their master, especially after the boss makes it clear he doesn't want any squabbling, but as soon as Felix has left Amara in the storeroom—one more piece of property to be added to the pile—Paris turns on her.

"You can sleep over there," he says, pointing to some empty sacks in the far corner. "*Right* over there. I don't want your smelly cunt anywhere near me."

"Oh, piss off," Amara replies, dropping her father's bag on the sacks. She isn't going to argue for a space closer to Paris; the further away they are from each other, the better. "As if you don't have to rent your arse out too. And I bet you don't just get down on your knees to scrub floors up here."

"Fuck you," Paris says, clenching his fist. His face is red with fury.

"No fighting, remember," Amara says, plonking herself down on the floor by her bag, making it clear she is here to stay. "You heard what Felix just said. If you give me a black eye, just think what he'll do to you in return." Amara sees Paris flinch, a look of fear on his face. She presses home her advantage. "He fucks you too, doesn't he? Just like all the rest of us."

In that moment, for the first time, Amara sees something of Fabia in her son. It's there in the cowed stoop of his shoulders, in his wounded expression. She knows he is not much younger than she is, but with his skinny legs and thin frame, he looks like a beaten child. Guilt pricks her. She is about to say something kinder when he speaks.

"You *disgust* me," he says, his face screwed up with malice. "All of you. Dirty fucking whores. And if I find you've touched any of my things with your nasty, grubby fingers when I'm out, I'll kill you!"

Paris stomps from the room, leaving Amara to wonder if Rufus did her such a favor after all. She shifts on the hot, dusty sacks. They are not going to be much more comfortable than the stone bed in Dido's cell, but at least she will be able to sleep, not work all night. It feels strange being in the quiet of the storeroom, knowing the brothel is downstairs. Cressa's cell must be right below her, or maybe Beronice's. She looks up at the shelves in the narrow room, stacked with jars and bundles of cloth. On the floor beside her, there's a half-empty bag of beans she might be able to use as a pillow. A few spill out from a small hole in the corner as she moves it. She hopes there aren't too many mice. Or rats.

Amara gets up and creeps to the door. She doesn't know much about what goes on in Felix's flat. She supposes the room next door must be where Gallus and Thraso sleep. She regrets not being friendlier with Paris, if only to try and get more information out of him.

Already Amara misses her friends downstairs, and it has only been a few minutes. She wonders if Thraso will even tell them what's happened, why Felix has moved her. For a moment, the strangeness of being alone makes her feel emotional. She leans her head against the wooden door jamb, trying to clear her thoughts. There's no point being miserable and wasting her time up here; it's impossible to say how long Rufus will keep her, whether his interest will ever pay off. But she could use this time to learn more about how Felix runs his loans, see if she can convince him to use her that way, rather than selling her. It would at least be a better life than the one in the brothel. She sets off down the corridor.

His study door is ajar, to let in a breeze in the summer heat. He must have spotted her shadow, because he calls out before she even has a chance to knock.

"What do you want?" His tone is not inviting.

Amara steps into the room but doesn't approach too close to his desk. "That girl from the Elephant who paid off her loan. Pitane. She mentioned to me that she might have another customer for you. I thought I could use this time to do some business."

"I can't spare anyone to go with you."

"Couldn't I go on my own?" Amara asks. "It's only to the Elephant. I could make a note and see if you like the terms."

She waits for Felix to answer, palms sweating. "It's like a never-ending itch for you, isn't it?" he says. "Making money."

If Felix were a different man, if she thought he would be pleased by the comparison, she would say: *As it is for you.* Instead, she shrugs. "Everyone wants to make money. Though in this case I'm making it for you."

"Go then," he says, turning back to his accounts, dismissing her with a wave of his hand.

The Elephant is a grander bar than the Sparrow, attached as it is to a large inn. A copper lantern shaped like an elephant hangs over the doorway, dangling with chiming bells, and the walls inside are lined with pictures of the giant beasts pitted against gladiators in the arena.

There is a fair exchange in trade between the brothel and the inn, and Sittius, the landlord, gives Amara a nod of recognition when she leans against the bar.

"Not many customers in for you today," he says.

"I wondered if Pitane might be free for a moment," she answers.

"She's in the courtyard," he replies. "But if you're going to keep her chatting, best get a drink."

Amara buys the smallest wine she can, missing the easy charm of Zoskales at the Sparrow. Sittius is notoriously tight. She walks through to the small courtyard behind the bar. It is partly shaded by a vine growing over a trellis and dotted with outdoor tables. A couple of guests sit drinking in a corner. Pitane is busy sweeping the flagstones. She brightens as soon as she sees Amara.

Amara did not just get the waitress a loan but her undying gratitude along with it. The abortion worked, and Amara paid off the last few pennies of the interest when it looked like Pitane wouldn't manage it. Without telling Felix. It is not only that she couldn't bear to endure another Marcella; she guessed it would be worth the money to build up a few favors. Felix might be able to rely on brute force, but she needs a different model, if she is going to win any clients.

"You look very well," Amara says to her.

"I am!" Pitane replies, then lowers her voice. "And I've been using that sponge just as you suggested," she whispers, with a sidelong look at the drinkers in the corner.

"You said there was another woman who might need help." Amara perches on the edge of a table in the shade, sipping her wine. She makes a face. Sittius has given her the cheapest vintage. It tastes like vinegar. She is becoming spoiled by all the Falernian the rich men drink.

Pitane nods, clearly delighted to be called on. "It's Terentia. You know, who runs the fruit stall, the last one on the corner before the Forum? Well," she lowers her voice again, enjoying the chance to gossip. "She made a loss last month—some bastard sold her a rotten batch. She was telling me when I got our supplies for the inn, and I said

I knew someone who could get her a loan, so she can get more stock in, make it back sooner."

"Fancy selling rotten fruit! What a crook." Amara tuts. "How much does she want?"

"Ten denarii."

Amara calculates Felix's extortionate rate of interest in her head. She hopes Terentia will be able to pay up—her own savings would never stretch that far. "I think I can help," Amara replies. "I will call on her this week."

"Beronice was telling me you and Dido go to so many parties these days!" Pitane says, clearly reluctant to let Amara go. "It must be exciting."

"It makes a change.' Amara smiles. She spends some more time chatting with Pitane, enjoying being out in the sunny courtyard rather than cooped up in the dusty storeroom. The guests in the corner fall silent and watch them, curious. Amara's toga makes her low status obvious, and Pitane has no doubt had to serve them already, yet here the two women are, ignoring the chance of picking up an extra tip.

"Hey ladies," one calls. "What does a man need to do around here to get a bit of attention?"

Amara thinks of Rufus's retainer and feels warm with gratitude. She doesn't have to entertain any idiots today. "I'd better let you get back to work," she says to Pitane, giving the two men behind her an unfriendly stare.

"Oh," Pitane is crestfallen. "I suppose so, yes. See you around." She heads over to the guests, narrow shoulders drooping, her fun over for the morning.

29

*"Vouchsafe no easy promise to his prayer
Nor yet reject it with a ruthless air;
Blend hopes with fears; but hopes must grow more bright."*
—Ovid, *The Art of Love* III

Amara's life above the brothel takes on its own disjointed rhythm. It is a huge relief to spend her nights unmolested, something she has not enjoyed since her stay with Pliny. Not that she sleeps as well as she did under the admiral's protection. The sacks are scratchy and uncomfortable, the mice scrabble, and she can hear the sounds of her friends working below, which fills her with both guilt and relief.

Some nights she dreams of Menander, and when she wakes, his absence is like a weight on her chest. In the dark of the storeroom, she relives every moment she has spent with him, finds herself turning the memories over in her mind like precious stones, until they start to lose their sharpness and she cannot be sure where fantasy and reality meet. Then she will remember Dido's warning about wasted love and forces herself to relive the last time she saw him, when he was powerless to protect her, or himself.

Paris is a largely silent companion, often ignoring Amara if she tries to speak with him. She suspects their master has warned him off, not wanting a repeat of the black eye he gave Victoria. Even so, she is never sorry to have the storeroom to herself when he has to work in the brothel. Worse are the nights when Felix lends him to Thraso. Paris is completely unresisting, as if Thraso were having sex with a corpse. Amara curls up as small as possible, facing the wall, trying to give Paris some dignity. She finds his total silence almost as disturbing as Britannica's screaming. The first time it happens, after Thraso has left, she risks asking Paris if he is alright. "It should have been you," is all he says.

She tries to meet her friends at the Sparrow as before, but apart from Dido, conversation is strained. Victoria has barely spoken to her since their row over Britannica. Returning to the brothel to work, she finds the Briton's resistance has permanently changed the atmosphere. Everyone is on edge, trying to shield her from customers, for their own sake as much as hers. The rare times anyone shares a joke, Amara no longer feels part of the banter. On the evening she and Dido are sent to entertain at Cornelius's house, Amara is so happy to see Egnatius, with his absurd compliments and eternal good temper, she almost kisses him.

And then there is Rufus. He has not called for her quite as often as she would have hoped—no more than twice a week—but every time she sees him, she feels a little more confident in his attachment. Her own feelings are growing like bindweed, tangling her thoughts, threatening to choke her scheming. He makes such an effort to be charming, his manner is so gentle, it is hard not to care too much. But she is always aware of the imbalance in power, and fear is her affection's shadow. She lives with the knowledge that he could tear her life apart on a whim, while she could do him no more damage than a pebble dropped in a pond.

It is her third week living above the brothel when Rufus's slave Philos calls round on the Thursday morning, warning her to be ready for his master in the evening. She hears Felix take the message—and the money—then the creak of his footsteps as he approaches the storeroom. Amara scrambles to her feet, dusting off her toga.

"I take it you heard that?" Felix says, sticking his head around the door. "You can at least make yourself useful until then."

"Of course," she replies, following him out into the corridor and walking to his study.

This is the strangest part of her new life, all the hours she spends with her master. She takes her customary seat near the doorway, tucked in beside a small table. Felix has never asked her to share his bed again, but eventually, he relented and let her help with his accounts. It started with Terentia's loan, when he got her to draw up the contract and write the records. Now he has her working on a number of files. She wonders how he ever managed to do it all himself.

Amara has always thought of her master as a thug, but she is forced to acknowledge the charm, as well as the threats, he deploys in his money lending. Clients visit, not noticing the small bent figure in the corner recording their conversations, and Felix treats the men to wine, using jokes and flattery, drawing out their hopes and their secrets. "There's no such thing as useless information," he tells her, after one client leaves having lamented about his mother-in-law for half an hour.

He is meticulous with his accounts, all the prostitution money gets ploughed into the loan-sharking, and he takes very little out for pleasure. In fact, pleasure seems to rank low in his life altogether. He hangs out with cronies in bars some evenings, probably the same men she saw that day at the Palaestra, but she is unsure how much he likes anyone, or if he has any real friends.

She tries to let go of her hatred for a while, to study him the way she has watched him study other people. If he were a stranger what would she notice? His love of money, his determination, his cruelty, his surprising fascination with the thoughts and feelings of others. His total lack of compassion. The last, she almost cannot admit to herself: his loneliness.

She is trying to work out the interest payments on a loan, setting it against the information Felix has gleaned about the debtor's assets, when she realizes he is looking at her.

"Have you still not fucked the posh boy yet?"

"No."

"Cold-hearted bitch." There is laughter in his voice, and she knows the insult is meant as a compliment. "I wouldn't leave it too long. The novelty of rejection wears off after a while. And you're a whore, not a wife."

He has read her own anxieties as if they were branded on her body. "I'm afraid of him," Amara lies. "I think he might enjoy violence."

"You'll manage," Felix says, going back to his accounts. "Not like you haven't had plenty of practice. And I can charge more if it's anything extreme, so make sure you tell me."

"Now who's cold-hearted?" Amara asks, raising her eyebrows. "What if he killed me?"

"I'd be sorry to lose such a valuable whore."

"How sorry?"

"Don't beg for crumbs," he says with a look of distaste. "It doesn't suit you."

His words bring back painful memories of Pliny, of her abject pleading with him to buy her. That has surely cured her of ever being tempted to beg again. She steals a look at Felix's desk. The scroll of Herophilos is still sitting on it, no doubt left there deliberately to torment her. She has never given him the satisfaction of asking if she can read it.

"I think you could charge this one a little more," she says, referring to the account she's been looking over. "When you think about his business, Manlius definitely has other assets he could draw on. You've noted here that the brooch on his cloak was bronze."

"It's his third loan," Felix says. "And he's never late. He's too safe a bet to squeeze too hard. Only go for blood if you think they can't afford to come back again."

Amara thinks of Marcella, wonders if he has sold her cameo yet. She remembers the other woman's finger, the pale circle where her mother's ring had sat, the way Marcella struggled to get it off. "I ought to go to the baths today," she says. "You're right, I can't keep Rufus waiting forever. Would you allow me the money to get my hair done? I could do with it being styled."

Felix squints, looking at her hair, clearly debating whether it's a necessary expense. Then he takes some coins from a drawer. "You can go in a couple of hours," he says. "After you've been through the rest of those files."

Amara steps onto the street, relieved to have some space from Felix. His clients' accounts make her wonder what notes he might have made on his women, what observations he has stored away about her. She hesitates as she walks past the back door of the brothel, torn between the desire to see if Dido is in, to ask her to come too, and worry that it will look like she's lording it over everyone by getting her hair done. Gallus is on the front door.

"Is anyone in?" she asks him.

"Just Victoria," he says. "Can't you hear?" Amara realizes she can indeed hear Victoria's voice, talking to a customer, cooing over his virility. "The others are out fishing. Apart from the savage."

"Thanks. Give Beronice my love."

"I'm not some girls' fucking messenger slave." Gallus scowls. "Tell her yourself."

Going to the baths by herself is another new experience since she moved upstairs. Amara stores her cheap toga in one of the cubby holes in the changing room, pressing past a couple of gossiping friends who are still loitering after packing their own clothes away. The stone walls echo to the chatter of women's voices and the shriek and splash of some bathers cooling off in the small plunge pool in the corner. She finds a beauty attendant touting for business and goes through to the hot room, strapping on wooden clogs to protect her feet from the scalding floor.

The attendant is Greek but seems in no mood to swap tales of the home country. She is brisk with Amara's body, tweezering out the hair under her arms, slathering her legs with waxy resin then scraping them until they are smooth. Amara winces at the pain. All around her, other women are being similarly pruned and primped, though some have opted for the relaxation of a massage instead, and she can hear the slap of hands on bare skin. Her attendant fetches a small tub of water, and Amara cleans herself, washing away the last of the resin and the dirt of the storeroom. She feels scoured from the heat and all the scraping.

Having her hair done is a more restful experience. Dressed again, she goes with another attendant to a small room and sits down. It's cooler here. The hairdresser places the tongs in a brazier. "That's enough," Amara says, watching the glowing heat. "My hair's already curly, I just need it styled." *And I don't need you singeing it,* she thinks.

"How do you want it?"

"To impress a man."

"Not a husband?"

"No."

The hairdresser smirks. As if she didn't already know from Amara's toga. While the other woman piles up her hair in a cascade of curls, she thinks of Rufus. It is so hard to know exactly what he would like. Would he prefer her as she really is, to see that she is feeling nervous, even shy, or is he expecting to be lavished with pleasure and treated to all the expertise of a courtesan? She wishes she could ask Victoria's advice.

"Fit to fuck an emperor," the hairdresser says when she's finished. "If you'll pardon the expression."

Amara laughs and thanks her. She walks out onto the street, ignoring the whistles of a couple of men hanging around the entrance to the baths. It's a notorious spot for picking up customers. She wonders if any of her friends have been this way today.

The smell of frying food tempts her on the way home, but she walks past. She will be eating for free this evening, and it's better to save her money. Paris lets her back into the flat, and his expression when he sees her hair is pure malevolence.

"Master wants you," he says, turning on his heel as soon as Amara is inside.

She walks up the stairs, wondering what Felix needs, but when she enters his study, he doesn't speak, just gestures impatiently at a pile of tablets on her table. She sits down to work. Shortly afterward, one of his clients, Cedrus, arrives. They discuss the loan, chat about business, the scorching summer heat. Felix offers him a discount at the brothel if he ups the amount he is borrowing, something Amara has noticed he does fairly often. Cedrus swivels round to look at her.

"Is she . . . ?" he asks.

"Yes, but she's usually booked. Costs a little extra."

"Wise man," he says. "I'd keep that one to myself as well."

"If you're choosing downstairs, I recommend Victoria," Felix replies.

"Do all your whores do accounts?" Cedrus asks, amused.

"Just that one. A doctor's daughter."

Cedrus is impressed. "You invested in quality stock then. Not got any virgins, I suppose?"

Amara thinks of Dido, of the pain she endured losing her innocence in this place, and almost snaps her stylus from pressing it so hard into the wax.

Felix shakes his head. The men move on to other matters and when Cedrus leaves, he doesn't so much as glance at her, as if he has forgotten her existence.

"Don't do that again," Felix says when they are alone.

"Do what?"

"Listen."

Amara is about to protest but thinks better of it. "I don't remember telling you my father was a doctor."

"It was after I bought you," he replies. "I gave you and Dido some figs, and you told me they were your father's favorite. I asked what he did."

The memory comes back to Amara, so vivid it is searing, like the scalding floor of the baths. The way Felix smiled, touched her gently on the arm, offering her the fruit. Almost with tenderness. And her own foolish relief. *This one is kind.*

She shrugs. "I don't remember that."

Amara works silently the rest of the afternoon, keeping her head down as a procession of clients come in. She does not seem to pay attention, not even when one weeps, begging Felix for more time, but all the while, she disobeys her master, listening intently, hatred coiled in the pit of her stomach. At last, Paris comes to tell them Rufus's slave Philos is waiting. Felix dismisses him then walks over, watching her pile up the tablets.

When she has finished, he hands her one of Pliny's dresses, not moving aside as she changes. His presence makes her nervous, and she fumbles with the brooch. Felix helps her, and the sensation of him holding up the fabric, his frown of concentration as he fixes the pin, makes her think of a husband's familiarity with his wife. When she is dressed, she turns to go, but he catches hold of her wrist, pulling her closer. It is not a moment of intimacy.

"Remember what happens to people who betray me," he says. Then he lets her arm drop, walking back to his desk without watching her leave.

30

*"If anyone has not seen Venus painted by Appelles,
he should look at my girlfriend; she shines just as bright"*
—Pompeii graffiti

The restaurant is a step up for Amara, a step down for Rufus. She imagines it must give him a thrill, dining out somewhere not quite respectable. Anybody who is worth anything eats in, safe in the knowledge that luxury lies closer to home. For her, the experience is a delight. They are served on a terrace, and the red glow of dusk gives them a view over the terracotta rooftops, the sharp-peaked mountain a darkening shadow beyond. Lamps hang from the trellis above, a far more elaborate affair than at the Elephant, woven with vines and heavy with ripening grapes.

Rufus orders, and she has the anxiety of trying to eat the sea urchins without making a mess. "I thought we could go to the theater again next week," he says, sloshing fish sauce everywhere. "One of my favorite plays is on. And it's an excellent company too, touring all the way from Rome. I'm very interested to see how they stage it."

"That would be wonderful," she says, as always relieved that he is thinking ahead to another meeting. "Have you ever been to Rome?"

"No. The furthest I've traveled is Misenum. Stayed with the admiral, as it happens. He has a beautiful place out there."

Amara smiles, not wanting to think about how she once aimed to make the admiral's villa her home.

"I'd love to see Greece," he continues. "So many of our plays are based on ones your poets had already written. Did you ever spend time in Athens?"

She cannot tell him that her abiding memory of the city was passing through it to the slave docks. "Not really, no. The only place I know is my hometown, Aphidnai. I think you would like our statue of Helen of Troy."

Rufus takes her hand and kisses it. "I'm sure she is not as beautiful as you."

They stare at each other, and she can read the question he is asking with his eyes. *Have I waited long enough?*

"Rufus!" They are interrupted by a familiar voice. Amara looks up to see Quintus standing by their table. He is accompanied by a beautiful woman. Amara realizes she has seen her before. It is the courtesan she noticed at the theater, with the dress dipped at her back. She is even more striking close up, hair circling her head in elaborate plaits and her skin unusually dark, like Zoskales. A gold bracelet shines on her upper arm. "I think you know Drusilla?"

"Of course," Rufus says. "Always a pleasure." He turns to his own girlfriend with unmistakable pride. "And this is Amara."

"Indeed!" Quintus says, pursing his lips. "Lucky man. I've heard her pretty voice before." Amara feels a stab of alarm. There is no mistaking the smirk on his face.

"Oh, do you sing?" Drusilla exclaims. "How delightful! I adore music. You must both join us one evening at my home." She smiles warmly at Amara who smiles back, grateful for the distraction.

"Loves entertaining, this one." Quintus rolls his eyes. "I can barely set foot in the house; it's always stuffed full of gossiping girls."

Drusilla makes a playful show of being affronted. "As if I ever deny you *anything*." She flounces off to their table, and Quintus follows with an apologetic shrug.

Amara turns back to Rufus, still smiling, but his expression chills her. "So you already know Quintus?" he says.

"He has attended parties where I was performing," she replies, with a toss of her head, determined not to show her fear, still less any guilt. "My singing partner Dido knows him better."

"He's got a reputation." Amara cannot tell whether the anger in his voice is for her or Quintus. "I hope you never got too close to him."

"Do you think I ever had a choice about such things?" she says sharply.

"Forget it." He waves his hand to dismiss the conversation.

"No," she says, her voice icy. "I won't. If you will hold the most painful parts of my life against me, I cannot be your friend."

"I didn't mean anything bad by it . . ." Rufus looks more like himself again, startled into his familiar frown of anxiety at displeasing her.

"I hope not," she says. "Just because you have been generous enough to allow me a choice, doesn't mean anyone else has." Amara feels a sudden weariness. The exhaustion of holding his interest, of trying to explain herself, all the while knowing he is incapable of understanding. A memory of Menander comes to her, of their afternoon outside the arena, talking about the past. *You are the same person. I still see you as the same person.*

Rufus recognizes her sadness, even though he has no way of guessing the cause. "I'm an idiot, sorry. I know you have . . . sung at a lot of parties." He pulls a rueful face, to show the euphemism is mocking him rather than her. "It's ridiculous of me to be jealous. You're just so lovely. I know you could have anyone." He reaches for her hand. "Friends again?"

"The ridiculous thing is imagining I could ever prefer Quintus to you," she replies, squeezing his fingers. It sounds like a line, but she means it. "Drusilla seems very pleasant." She lets go again.

"Oh, she's great fun," Rufus exclaims, then stops, horrified at himself. "Not that I've ever . . ." he stutters. Amara laughs, and he joins her, relieved. "Well, anyway. She throws the most wonderful dinners. Her old master left her her freedom and, clearly, a fair bit of cash too. Though I think her *friends* also support her."

Amara glances over at Drusilla with even greater interest. She has the same poise that she remembers from the theater. Even the arrogant Quintus seems to be making some effort to impress her.

"We should certainly accept her invitation," Rufus says, following the direction of her gaze. "If you would like to."

"I would. Very much." Amara looks down, her nerves perhaps easy to mistake for shyness. "But then I think I should enjoy being anywhere with you." She looks up and can see Rufus has understood her meaning.

The rest of their dinner passes without much attention to the food. Both are on a high of anticipation, every small touch of the hand, even when passing the wine, is heightened. It almost feels like love.

It's dark when they walk the short distance back to Rufus's house. Philos and another slave accompany them, lighting their path. The house is familiar to her now. The jasmine has faded in the garden, instead, the air is scented with myrtle. She remembers her offering to Venus at the Vinalia, the favor she asked. It helps her make her decision about how to behave. Tonight will be all about performance.

She is grateful when Rufus dismisses the other slaves; she prefers to be alone with him. Philos has left the lamps burning, and wherever their glow touches the walls, they illuminate scenes from the stage, though much of the room is draped in shadow. Amara realizes she has never been inside Rufus's home in daylight.

She had half expected him to leap on her, the way he did on their first evening together, but instead, she finds he is reticent. Amara steps out of her clothes—slowly, so that he misses nothing—and steps into the role she has chosen for herself: the courtesan in love. It sits halfway between truth and lie. Every trick she has ever learned, every means of giving pleasure, she gives to Rufus. She even finds her nights with Salvius useful, not for herself, but because he taught her about delay, in his own unfulfilled quest to please her.

None of it is unpleasant. She even finds, for the first time, a certain enjoyment in making a man happy, because this particular man is one she likes. But it is impossible to separate her affection from her need to make him want her, not just for the one night, but to want what she can give like this, over and over.

Afterward they lie together, covered in sweat, his skin warm against hers. "I love you," he says, kissing her. "I love you."

"I love you too," she replies, holding him tighter.

"I've never known a woman like you. You never ask for presents. The only thing you've ever asked is that I give you time."

Amara thinks of her friends, of Dido and Victoria. She knows there are many women like her, but they are rarely afforded the compassion Rufus gives her. "You have already been generous to me," she says. "You listen. You protect me, even when we are not together."

"This is why I love you," he says, kissing her again. Then he props himself up on an elbow, and leans over his side of the cushions, searching for something underneath the couch. He hands her a wooden box, his face expectant like a small boy.

"What's this?"

"Open it, open it!"

Amara does as she is told. Inside is a silver necklace with an amber pendant. For a moment, she is too stunned to speak. "It's beautiful!"

Rufus helps her fasten the clasp. "It does look very lovely on you, I must say." He is extremely pleased with his choice.

"It's from my family's own business. I got one of our best craftsmen to work on it."

Amara has seen the jewelry store and gem-cutting workshops that surround Rufus's house; she sneaked past one morning with Dido to have a look. She touches the smooth drop of resin at her neck. Amber makes her think of Marcella, of the necklace she and Fulvia brought to the Forum, but she pushes the unhappy women from her mind. "It's the most beautiful gift anyone has ever given me," she says. "But my darling, I cannot take it with me. My master would never let me keep it."

"But this is a personal gift!" Rufus says, outraged. "He would have no right."

"I will wear it whenever we are together," she replies, putting her hand over his to reassure him. "You can keep it safe for me, here. It will remind you that I am always waiting for you."

"But what about you? What will you have to make you think of *me*."

Amara looks at him, her lover with all his wealth, his endlessly sociable life, and she can see that he is genuinely worried she might forget him, as if she could do anything other than count the hours in Felix's storeroom until she sees him again. "I know!" she says. "You can buy me some cheap glass beads, wooden even, that I will wear as a bracelet. Felix would never bother with that, but it would remind me of your love whenever I saw it."

"It is romantic," Rufus says, somewhat mollified. "Though it will make me look abominably tight if you go around telling your friends that's all your boyfriend has given you. Particularly if they know about my family's business!"

"I promise I won't," Amara says, amused that he might fear a poor reputation among the whores of the town brothel. Unless he imagines she has other, classier friends.

"Will he try to stop you seeing me," Rufus asks her. "Your master? If he thinks you care for me?"

At first, Amara cannot understand what he means, then she remembers the lie she told to ensure he didn't come to the brothel—that Felix is monstrously jealous of her happiness. "Oh," she says. "I hope you don't mind. I told him I was afraid of you. He was pleased by the thought you might be cruel to me." No need to add that it was the prospect of charging extra for violence that Felix liked.

"He sounds appalling!" Rufus says. "My poor, darling girl." He squashes her in a hug so tight, the pendant digs into her skin. "I was hoping you would stay all night. But will that make your life more difficult?"

He is clinging on to her, clearly willing her to stay, and Amara herself is longing to accept. But she knows that if she gives in to every desire, fulfils every passion, she risks his infatuation burning itself out too quickly. Better to deny him from time to time. "I think that might be safer," she says in a small voice. "Next time, I will stay."

He lets go of her, cupping her face in his hands, kisses her tenderly on the forehead. "Whatever you think is best," he says.

His sincerity hurts her heart.

31

"I see that it's brothels and greasy bars that
stir your desire for the town."
—Horace, *Satires* 1.14

Felix is alarmed to see her before daybreak. He is waiting in the corridor as she comes up the stairs, obviously having heard Philos drop her at the door.

"Don't tell me you didn't do what he wanted."

"I did everything," Amara says. "I just didn't want to stay the whole night. I told you, he scares me. And besides"— she meets his cold stare with one of her own—"it keeps him keener that way. We want to string this out as long as possible, don't we?"

"Little bitch," Felix says. She starts unfastening her cloak, expecting to be dismissed, but he gestures at her to stop. "Don't take that off. I'm heading out. You can come with me."

"Why?" Amara asks, unable to hide her astonishment.

"Doesn't hurt to show off the wares," Felix says. He puts an arm around her, and for a bewildering moment, she thinks it is a gesture of affection. Then she feels his fingers, hard and pinching at her waist, like a baker checking the quality of his dough. "Just don't open that big fucking mouth of yours."

The bar is in an unfamiliar part of town. It is low and cramped, barely more than a hole in the wall, and reeks of pipe smoke. Amara is the only woman present; she sits wedged against the wall, Felix between her and the men he is there to meet. Most of the others are drunk when they arrive, but even though he makes a show of ordering wine, she notices Felix stays sober. His hand is on her thigh, and she understands he is giving a signal to the other men: Don't touch.

She is not the only one to express surprise at Felix bringing a woman along.

"What did this one do?" asks a man, gesturing at her with his wine. Some slops on the table. She recognizes him from the Palaestra, by the white scar across his face, but he doesn't recognize her. "Something special, is she? Or is she bored of your cock and here to try some of ours?"

Others join in, but although they're all talking about her, they're only talking to Felix, as if she isn't really there. She says nothing through it all, just looks down at his hand on her leg.

"Plenty more cunt where she comes from," Felix says. "You can try some later."

They lose interest in Amara and move on to business. She is so exhausted she could almost rest her head against the wall and fall asleep; it must be the early hours of the morning.

"I think the cobbler's getting jumpy about paying," says one man. He is thin and shifty as a weasel. "All the work we do, keeping the streets safe. Not very grateful, is it?"

The man with the white scar laughs, but Felix looks unimpressed. "Maybe he needs a little reminder. Nothing too drastic." Amara realizes they are not talking about loans. "Best it's someone he's not seen before."

"I know who," says Weasel, nodding.

The conversation flits back and forth between business and banter: who is paying, who needs persuading, the latest games at the arena, the best whore by the docks. Amara is not surprised Felix is involved in a protection racket but is uneasy that he would take the risk. Doesn't he earn enough already? What if someone retaliated? Can everyone at this bar be trusted? She hopes any trail to the brothel is well hidden.

Time drags, and she feels like a ghost, only Felix's hand physically anchors her to the present. She remembers what he said about showing off his wares and doesn't dare doze off. Instead, she makes occasional eye contact with the men then looks suggestively at Felix, ensuring they remember her role, what they might be getting.

When Felix finally gets up, hauling her to her feet, she could almost cry with relief. A couple of the men walk back with them to the brothel, somehow still awake enough to take Felix up on his offer of a discount. She feels sorry for whoever has to entertain them. Watching them step into the darkened corridor of the brothel, knowing they won't be arriving at her cell, she realizes exhaustion has sapped her sense of guilt. She follows Felix into the relative safety of his flat.

At the top of the stairs, he takes hold of her wrist, leaning back to look at her, as if weighing up the possibility she represents. Then he lets her go. "Send Paris to me," he says, walking off.

She hurries to the storeroom, nudging the sleeping Paris with her foot. "Get up. Master wants you."

Paris springs awake like a cat, scrabbling the blankets off himself. "Now?" he gasps. "He wants me now?"

"I'm sorry," she replies, heading to her corner. "That's what he said." Paris gives a stifled sob, a sound of utter wretchedness. Amara watches him creep from the room, unable to feel anything but gratitude that he is the one being tormented instead of her. She is asleep moments after her head rests on the lumpy sack of beans.

When she wakes, she is aware of someone leaning over her. She opens her eyes. It is Paris, his face so close, their noses are almost touching. "Brothel day for you, bitch," he whispers.

"Get away from me!" Amara shoves him, and he lands on his backside with a thud. "What is it with you?"

Paris dusts himself off, angry at being made to look foolish. "Last night was *your* fault," he snarls. "Why couldn't *you* have fucked Felix? You were awake anyway. And it's *nothing* to you. Nothing." His voice grows shriller. "It's what you're there for; it's the whole point of you!"

Paris stops. He is on the verge of tears, his thin chest rising and falling with the effort of controlling his emotions. Amara thinks about all the cruelties Paris must have endured: the confusion of growing up in the brothel, watching the way his mother was treated, his fear when he became a target himself. And then having to suffer the contempt of other men, even ones like Gallus who he is so desperate to impress. "I'm sorry he hurt you," Amara replies, keeping her voice steady, not wanting to humiliate him further by a show of sympathy. "But you know it wasn't because of me. Nobody tells Felix what to do."

"He doesn't even screw you, does he, when he has you in the study?" Paris takes her silence as his answer, kicking at the wall in frustration. "All these years I've wanted him to trust me with the business, and then he chooses *you* instead. As if I were the woman." Paris spits out the last word like a curse that might defile his mouth by speaking it.

Amara does not point out to Paris that he would not be much use to Felix with his accounts, since he cannot even read. "It won't be forever," she says. "He won't treat you like this forever. I'm sure he does trust you."

Paris looks at her, biting his lip. She can see he wants to talk, all his loneliness pent up inside him like a cranked-up well before the water falls. But pride gets the better of him. He shrugs, as if physically shaking her off. "Nobody's paying for you to stay up here today, are they? So why don't you fuck off back to where you belong and leave me in peace."

Amara gets wearily to her feet. It feels like she only slept a couple of hours. Paris obviously woke her as early as possible. "Behaving like a shit isn't going to make your life any easier," she says. She walks past him, closing the storeroom door behind her.

It's barely light out on the street. Everyone in the brothel is likely to be asleep. The back door is ajar, and Amara creeps in, resigned to sleeping in the corridor rather than waking Dido. She sinks down, her back to the wall, then hears the sound of muffled weeping. Britannica never makes an effort to be quiet, so at first, she assumes it must be Dido, but after getting to her feet and tiptoeing the length of the corridor, she realizes it is Victoria.

It takes her a while to trust her own ears. Victoria never cries. Amara hesitates before drawing the curtain. It has been weeks since they have spoken properly to each other. But she cannot bear the thought of her friend suffering.

She sticks her head around the curtain. "Are you alright?" she asks, her voice low so as not to wake the others.

She expects Victoria to stop crying or tell her to go away, but instead, she remains curled up on the bed, sobbing into her blankets. Amara hurries over, afraid. She sits down on the bed, touching Victoria's shoulder.

"What's wrong?"

Victoria pushes herself upright, furiously wiping her face. "What's wrong? *What's wrong?*" She stares at Amara, her eyes red-rimmed, her hair wild. "Like you don't know!"

Amara stares back bewildered. "Know what?"

Victoria slaps her across the face. Amara gasps, clasping a hand to her stinging cheek, too shocked to retaliate. "Don't pretend to be such a fucking *idiot*," Victoria shouts at her. "Rich old men and fancy boyfriends aren't enough for you, you have to have Felix as well? You don't even *like* him, still less want him! What are you doing? Rubbing everyone else's nose in it, making us all feel worthless?"

"Like I have any choice!" Amara shouts back. "You think I *enjoy* being around Felix? And anyway, why do you care? You hate him as much as I do!" As soon as she has said it, she remembers the afternoon she and Dido overheard Victoria panting out her devotion. *I love you; I would die for you.* Amara looks at her anguished face and understands what she should have realized long ago. Victoria wasn't pretending. "But you *can't*; you can't love him," she says. "He's a fucking monster! He doesn't care about any of us."

"Can you keep it down?" Beronice is standing in the doorway, looking haggard with exhaustion. "Or else take it outside. Some of us are trying to sleep." She flings the curtain back across with a swish.

The interruption startles Amara and Victoria out of their anger. "I know he's a shit; I know it," Victoria says, lowering her voice. "You don't have to tell me. But you don't understand what he can be like sometimes. You've never seen it." Her eyes are shining with tears, and she tumbles over her words, tripped up by all the feelings she keeps buried. "He can be so loving and gentle. And he's always really sorry when he's hurt me. He begs me to forgive him; he really *begs*. I see a side of him the rest of you don't." Victoria is unrecognizable in her desperation; Amara almost cannot bear to be near her. "He's lonely, like I am. I love him so much."

Amara thinks of the way Felix spoke to Victoria after Paris punched her, the many times she's seen him hurt her, the way—only yesterday—he offered her body to Cedrus as if she were nothing. She feels sick to her stomach. She takes Victoria's hand, squeezing it. "I just think you deserve so much more," she says.

"What more is there?"

"Somebody who wouldn't hit you," Amara says. "A man who didn't sell you."

"What do you think we are? Where do you think we are living?" Victoria asks, incredulous, gesturing at the soot-stained walls. "This isn't a fucking play. We're not goddesses. How high are you aiming? The emperor?"

There is a sound of violent retching. They look at each other in alarm. "Cressa!"

Beronice has reached the latrine before them, craning over the low wall. "Are you alright in there?"

"No, I'm not alright," Cressa's voice comes back, before she vomits again.

The three women wait, helpless, while Cressa is sick. There's a pause, then Cressa comes out, leaning on the wall to steady herself as if she is on the roiling deck of a ship.

"Do you think you should eat something?" Victoria says.

Cressa nods wearily. "But not the Sparrow."

"It's too early anyway," Beronice says, shooting a look at Amara and Victoria, still annoyed they woke her up. "They won't be open yet."

"We can go to a bakery. Get some bread in you," Amara says.

They leave Dido and Britannica to sleep. Outside the sky is turning blue, and the streets are starting to get busy.

Gallus is surprised to see them all out so early. He glances furtively up and down the road, checking for Felix, then kisses Beronice. "Couldn't you leave them to it?" he says, sneaking his hand inside her cloak, fondling her.

Beronice looks at her friends, torn, while Gallus breathes into her neck. "I'll catch you up," she says, letting him lead her back inside.

Amara watches her go, disappointed. "She doesn't know where we're headed."

"Leave her," Victoria replies, striding off down the street. "She lets that shit walk all over her."

Amara thinks of Victoria's own hopeless devotion to Felix, but says nothing.

"Not too fast," Cressa says, holding Amara's arm. She looks even worse in the daylight, her skin covered in a film of sweat. "And let's not walk for miles."

A few cafés near the baths are open. They pick one and claim a table rather than stand at the counter. The bread is hard and stale. Amara thinks she will cut her cheeks to shreds by chewing it. Cressa orders a sweet wine to settle her stomach. She sits in silence, not looking up, dipping her bread in the wine to soften the crust.

"You can't keep ignoring the obvious," Victoria says to her quietly, in case anyone is listening. "We all know you're pregnant. Just tell us what we can do to help."

Cressa pauses in her dipping. "Nothing," she says, her voice flat. "There's nothing anyone can do."

"Pitane from the Elephant had an abortion recently," Amara says. "And it worked really well. Shall I ask her where she got the herbs?"

"No," Cressa says, still not looking up. "I tried that last time, with Cosmus, and it didn't work. Just cost a fortune and made me really ill."

Victoria rubs Cressa's arm, as if she can rub away her pain. "Perhaps Felix will let you keep the baby this time?" she says, her voice unnaturally cheerful. "Isn't it at least worth asking?"

Cressa's shoulders start to shake, and Amara knows she is crying, even though she doesn't make a sound. "What good would that do?" she whispers, pressing the palms of her hands against her eyes to stem the tears. "What life can I give a child? Another Paris? A little girl sold as a whore before she's even grown? It would kill me to watch that; I would rather die." She takes a deep breath, trying to control herself. "And besides," she says, her voice flat again, "he already told me. Any more babies are going straight on the town's rubbish heap. He doesn't make enough from selling a child."

"Maybe that would be best," Victoria says. "And it doesn't mean the baby would die. Look at me. I survived."

"You don't understand," Cressa says. "You have no idea. Do you think because I never talk about Cosmus, that I never think of him? Every second of every day I miss him, want him. Just to see his face. All the time, every waking moment." She holds her hand to her heart, as if to staunch a wound. "It's a constant pain, like nothing else. I *cannot* give another child away."

Amara and Victoria look at each other, unable to think of any words of comfort. "Maybe the pregnancy won't work out," Victoria says in a small voice.

"Maybe," Cressa replies, drinking her wine. "Maybe."

On the way back to the brothel, Cressa shakes them both off, choosing to walk alone instead. Victoria takes Amara's hand, gripping her fingers, like a woman afraid of drowning.

SEPTEMBER

32

"Take me to Pompeii where love is sweet!"
—Pompeii graffiti

Amara takes one of the figs from Drusilla's table, peeling it, savoring the soft sweetness on her tongue. It is nearly October. Rufus is reclining beside her, his body warm at her back. They have been spending more time at Drusilla's house, ever since Rufus's parents returned from their summer at Baiae. His parents do know about her, Rufus has assured her, it's quite proper for him to have a girlfriend, but it's probably better neither of them bump into her in the atrium. His mother has funny notions. She thinks a household slave is enough for such things; she doesn't understand what it means to be *in love*.

Amara would have been desperate if it were not for Drusilla's generosity in letting them stay over at her house. Rufus pays her, of course. Amara thinks it must be nice to rent out rooms, rather than your own body. She takes another fig from the table. Tonight is the first time Dido has joined them, and this feels as close to happiness as life can get.

"So you are both Punic?" Drusilla says, addressing Dido and Lucius, the wealthy young man she invited for Dido to entertain. Amara suspects he may be one of Drusilla's former lovers, but she cannot be sure.

Lucius raises an eyebrow at the question, turns to Dido and says something in a language nobody else understands. It is clearly a joke, and Dido laughs, delighted, replying to him in the same tongue. He smiles at her, pleased by whatever it is she has said. He turns back to Drusilla. "It seems so."

"But that's wonderful!" Drusilla claps her hands. "Such a coincidence." Quintus who is sitting beside her, sighs and rolls his eyes. Amara would like to throw a fig at his head. She still cannot imagine why Drusilla, the most glamorous woman she has ever met, would have such an *ordinary* boyfriend. He must be a lot richer than she realized.

"My family are all from Carthage," Lucius says. His accent is similar to Dido's but not identical. Amara supposes he must be several thousand leagues above her on the social scale. "I've been banished to Italy to look after the business. We have a number of bases here in Campania."

"You must miss it, being so far away," Dido says, her expression wistful.

Lucius replies to her in Punic, and she smiles again then looks down. Amara guesses he just paid her a compliment.

"Weren't you kidnapped?" Rufus asks Dido. "That means your sale wasn't legal! I'm *convinced* yours wasn't either," he says to Amara. "Convinced. It's not possible to go from being a doctor's daughter to a slave, is it?" He looks round at everyone else. "Don't you think?"

Amara could wince with embarrassment. Rufus is determined to turn their lives into the plot of a Plautus play, where she is, in fact, a freeborn, marriageable girl. A world where tragedy, not snobbery, is what holds them apart.

Lucius coughs politely. "Perhaps not."

"It's completely possible," Quintus says lazily. "I mean all sorts of people end up as slaves, if they aren't Roman citizens."

Drusilla changes the subject before Rufus can object. "Would you both sing for us? Amara told me what a delightful voice you have, Dido."

"But only if you play the harp," Amara says.

"Oh, *please* do," Dido exclaims. "I've been longing to hear you play."

The three women go through a show of false modesty and reluctance, paying each other little compliments, flirting with the men, while Drusilla's maids bring out her harp. Dido and Amara drape themselves nearby. It's meant to look artless, even though they have been practicing all afternoon. Then it was a much brisker scene, all three concentrating on the music, trying out different sets, with the odd joke from the hostess, invariably aimed at one of her lovers. Amara had wondered at first why Drusilla was so kind, but now she understands. A steady stream of female guests allows her to rent rooms and entertain, supporting her reputation as one of Pompeii's most sought-after courtesans.

Drusilla has no reason to fear being upstaged by Amara or Dido. She is a skilled harpist, showing off her graceful arms and slender fingers, while her voice vibrates with emotion, elevating the other women's singing as they try to compete. The men lounge on the couches, drinking wine and laughing with one another, looking entirely satisfied to be the recipients of so much devoted labor. Amara is touched that Rufus rarely looks at her companions. The other two are quite shameless in eyeing up one another's girlfriends.

The evening rolls on pleasantly. The food is good, if not lavish, and there's plenty of wine. The men have a mock wrestling session—which Rufus finds amusing and Quintus takes too seriously—and quote poetry at one another, making up their own rhymes as they get increasingly drunk. Amara is gratified to see how much Lucius has taken to Dido, though she suspects he may not be a man who is looking for love in the way Rufus was when she met him. She touches the new earrings he has given her, feeling the light swing of them against her fingertips. There is an ever-growing hoard of gifts in the wooden box in his room, all hers. She slips her hand into his, stroking his palm, while he smiles, good-natured, at one of Quintus's jokes.

Amara suspects she should try and share her good fortune with more of her friends, but she struggles to imagine Beronice or Victoria carrying off an evening like this. The thought makes her feel guilty. Victoria would probably be all too popular; she can just imagine her dancing like she did at the Vinalia, doing a striptease, but that, in itself, would tip the balance, tearing the veil that hides the real intentions behind these dinners.

"I think it might be time for bed," Quintus says, stretching out luxuriously as if he were the host and not Drusilla. "Otherwise, I will be fit for nothing but sleeping."

"I hope you wouldn't dare, not under my roof," Drusilla replies. "I cannot think of a worse insult."

Everyone laughs, and the men bid each other goodnight, retiring with the women as their spoils for the night. Drusilla's house is nothing like as grand or large as her clients' homes, but it is elegant and comfortable. Every room Amara has seen is painted with scenes of mythical lovers, the one she usually stays in has a painting of Leda and the Swan. It is up the stairs, above the small courtyard and dining room.

She and Rufus follow Drusilla's maid to the bedroom. He starts undressing her before the girl has even finished lighting all the lamps. It is something she has noticed about Rufus, the way he doesn't seem to see many of the slaves who serve him. At his own house, Vitalio would come in unannounced to set out wine or fruit, even when they were in bed together, until Amara asked that he stop.

"He doesn't think anything of it!" Rufus had protested, but Amara was not so sure. It was the way Vitalio had looked at her once, one slave to another, while Rufus waxed on about a play. She knew then that he disliked her, that serving her made him angry, even though she still doesn't understand why.

Tonight, she is relieved that they have not progressed beyond nakedness before the maid leaves. It is an effort now, always remembering to perform with Rufus. His affection for her seems so genuine; she wonders what would happen if she tried to pursue her own pleasure, or suggest what she might like. But it is easier just to please him and fake it. She knows her inability to enjoy Salvius's efforts was what cooled his interest in the end, for all he asked her not to pretend.

It is afterward that she enjoys most, hearing Rufus tell her he loves her, holding her as if he will never let her go. She doesn't really believe him; she knows he cannot love her, not truly, not the way she loved her family or loves Dido, as someone you consider of equal value to yourself. Still, she never tires of hearing him say the words.

After Rufus has kissed her goodbye and crept from the room, she hears him in the courtyard below, laughing with the other two men. He rarely stays the whole night at Drusilla's, but Amara has no intention of ever telling Felix this. It is one of the perks, staying over like a guest, not a slave, in the house of a friend. She smiles to herself, imagining Dido safe nearby, stretching out on the sheets, just as she is, a night of blissful, undisturbed sleep ahead.

The cool morning air has the scent of autumn. Amara and Dido wait for their host in the small courtyard, enjoying the tranquility. Drusilla has made clever use of space, the fountain is against the wall rather than taking up too much room in the center. It falls in a cascade over a mosaic of blue tiles, water splashing against a statue of Venus who stands naked at the edge of the pool beneath, as if poised to bathe.

"It's so pretty," Dido says, looking around.

"The fountain is perfect," Amara agrees.

"I'm glad you ladies approve." They turn to see Drusilla watching them. She is in a light tunic, the gold band on her arm. Her head is dressed in a silk wrap that Amara instantly wants for herself. It's the perfect way to disguise undressed hair, if there was ever anyone she needed to impress in the morning. "Why don't you take some refreshment with me before you leave?"

They are only too eager to agree, following her to the dining room. It has been cleared since last night, and a plate of figs, pears and bread is waiting on a side table.

"So how was Lucius?" Drusilla asks, tucking herself up on a couch and gesturing at the others to take the one opposite. "He seemed quite taken."

"He is going to try and find my family," Dido says, looking from Drusilla to Amara, clearly excited to share the news. "He thinks it might be possible, through the census."

"But that's wonderful!" Amara exclaims.

"Did he tell you this before, or after?" Drusilla asks.

"After," Dido says. "As he was leaving."

"That's a good sign." Drusilla nods. "That means he was serious. Though you may still need to remind him. Lucius is not used to thinking of other people." She pushes the platter toward them, waiting until they have taken some food before helping herself. "And if he finds them? What then?"

"I don't know," Dido says, looking more uncertain. "It would mean so much just to know they were alive."

"Would they not buy you back?" Drusilla takes a bite of pear.

Amara looks at Dido, anxious for her. They have discussed this many times. "No," Dido says. "I don't believe so. Not when . . . not after what I've been. There would be no place for me at home now. If I were free, if I had some money saved, then they could overlook it. Save face and pretend. But not when I'm . . . like this."

"Does Lucius know?"

"Yes. I told him there was no way back for me."

"Perhaps it's as well. Less work for him, and he might actually do you the favor if there's no chance of drama. Unless he has finally found his romantic side."

"Were you and Lucius once . . .?"

"We were lovers once, yes." Drusilla nods. "For some months. And he sometimes still visits. I have a certain fondness for him. Though I have to be careful with Quintus; he has more pride than you might imagine." She looks at Amara, raising an eyebrow. "Though not as careful as you. Rufus would not take well to a rival *at all*."

"No," she replies. "But there's no danger of that." She looks down, peeling her fig, thinking of Menander. It had been Dido who insisted she stop communicating with him, even through graffiti. She had not had the strength to tell him herself that she now had a "patron" and so took the coward's way out, letting Dido visit the potter's shop instead. It hurts even thinking of him. She stops peeling. The fruit lies pale and naked in her hands. She glances up at Drusilla. "Have you and Rufus ever been lovers?"

"Would the answer to that matter to you, one way or the other?"

"No," Amara replies. "My feelings aren't . . ." She pauses, not sure how to explain the way she feels. She shrugs instead.

"Only very briefly," Drusilla answers. She watches Amara's reaction. "I see I have upset you."

"No, not at all," Amara says, surprised to feel as shaken as she does. "Or rather I'm not jealous. It's just he told me you hadn't. He was quite convincing."

Drusilla laughs. "All men are born liars. You should take it as a compliment. He didn't want to hurt your feelings. At least he realizes you have some."

"Does Quintus not?" Dido asks.

"Well," Drusilla says drily, breaking off a piece of bread and leaning back on her cushions. "I don't even have to ask if either of you have fucked Quintus. I know you must have. Otherwise, he would be pestering me to try you out." They all laugh. "He is just as he appears," she continues. "But it is strange how men can grow on you, even Quintus."

"Some men never do," Amara says.

"Your master?" Drusilla asks. Amara nods, not wanting to say his name.

"I don't know," Dido teases her. "You and Felix sitting together, going over the accounts. Surely you've seen his softer side?"

"He's a *shit*," Amara snaps. The ugliness of the word slams into their pleasant morning, bringing the shadow of the brothel with it. "I'm sorry," she says to Drusilla, flushing with embarrassment. "I didn't mean to be crude."

"I'm sure nobody here is shocked by swearing." Drusilla laughs. "Quintus is also a shit, though I cannot imagine him making me angry enough to say so." She looks more serious. "But then he is the one paying the money, and believe me, I understand the difference."

Because she is free, and we are enslaved, Amara thinks. It is easy to forget with Drusilla—she is so welcoming, so friendly, and yet, she is almost as distant as Rufus in the privilege she holds as a freedwoman. Even if she does have to earn her bread the same way they do.

The thought of Felix brings a strain to the gathering where before there was only playfulness. "I suppose we had better head back," Dido murmurs, after the second awkward pause in conversation.

Drusilla does not press them to stay, though she is gracious in her insistence that they visit again, as if they were real guests rather than ones paid for by the men they accompany. On the threshold of the house, Dido and Amara stand together for a moment, watching life on the street flow past. Then Dido steps down onto the pavement, and Amara follows.

33

"I don't care about your pregnancy Salvilla;
I scorn it"
—Pompeii graffiti

The brothel feels even less like home now Felix has crammed in yet more women. Only Beronice and Victoria have a cell to themselves, after two Spanish dancers moved into Cressa's cell a week ago. Cressa is sharing with Britannica, and the pair of them see far fewer customers than anyone else. Felix cannot admit it, but Britannica was a terrible investment.

Ipstilla and Telethusa either speak little Latin, or perhaps they simply prefer not to mix. When Amara and Dido walk in, they are laughing loudly, shouting at one another in Spanish, taking up the entire corridor. Fabia tries to sweep the floor around them, but they ignore her, refusing to move their feet.

"Thank goodness you're back," Victoria says, beckoning them into her cell. Amara and Dido sit down on the bed. "Felix wants us to take the new girls out, teach them how to fish."

"Can't they go out together?" Amara asks. "I'm sure they'd prefer that anyway."

"No, he wants us to keep an eye on them. And somebody has to take Britannica out. He's fed up with her doing nothing." Amara suspects Victoria is too. She has never warmed to the Briton. "If Dido and I take the Spanish girls, can you have Britannica?"

"Why me?"

"We can't ask Cressa, can we? And Beronice isn't too well. Rough customer last night. Besides, I thought you *liked* her."

"Fine then," Amara sighs. "I'll take her."

She leaves Dido and Victoria to their noisy negotiations with the Spaniards and trudges to her old cell. Inside, Cressa is lying on the bed, eyes closed, though Amara suspects she is not asleep. Britannica sits on a stool, watching over her like a pale guard dog.

"Britannica." Amara holds out her hand. "Come with me. Come." The Briton looks back at Cressa, uncertain. "Come," Amara repeats more firmly. "We go look for men."

Britannica stands up, immediately towering over her, and strides to the door, her face grim. Amara is not sure how much Latin she understands now. She suspects a lot more than she lets on, though she has yet to speak a word other than Cressa's name. They leave by the back door since the shouting and gesticulating is still in full flow in the corridor.

"Baths," Amara says, shepherding her strapping companion onto the pavement. Walking out with Britannica, they are scarcely short of attention, but none of it is the sort Amara wants. Britannica stalks along, her movements unfeminine, more prizefighter than prostitute. She makes eye contact with all the men, her gaze angry and challenging. If any return the look, she bares her teeth and hisses. They have only walked one street, and Amara begins to feel afraid they will be beaten up before they even make it to the corner.

"That's enough," she says, exasperated. "You win. We go back."

Britannica turns on her heel, striding along the pavement, and Amara scurries after her. The corridor is finally empty, but Amara knows she cannot give up and stay in; she will have to go out fishing with someone. She follows Britannica into the cell where Cressa is still lying, prostrated in misery.

"Cressa? I know you're awake," Amara says. "Why don't you come out with me? The air would do you good."

"I don't feel like it," Cressa says.

"I know, but you can't stay in all day," Amara pleads. Britannica is following the discussion anxiously, but Amara ignores her. "We could walk to the harbor. I'll buy you a wine."

Slowly, Cressa pushes herself up. Her stomach has filled out, but her face looks hollowed and empty. "Alright," she says wearily. "I'll come."

"Cressa!" Britannica says, her voice urgent. "Cressa!"

"I will be back soon," Cressa says soothingly, patting the tall woman's arm as if she were a child. "You rest."

Amara knows Britannica will not be resting. She's spied on her alone in here before, watched her throw endless punches and kicks at imaginary men's heads. She shoots her a warning look as they leave. *No trouble.*

The walk to the harbor is slow and labored. It is hard to believe Cressa once made the same effort with her appearance as the rest of them. Now, she is grubby and disheveled, her hair unkempt. *Whores age in double time*, Amara thinks, and the idea chills her.

"I don't know why everyone is so unkind to Britannica," Cressa says, looking back over her shoulder, as if somehow, the Briton might be visible behind them. "What did she ever do but hate being trapped here? She has a good heart, you know that? I'd put her loyalty above anyone else's. And she's smart. I know nobody else sees it, but she is."

"She's not easy though," Amara says.

"Why should she be easy? Is her life *easy*?" Cressa's voice is quavering, and Amara is afraid she might cry.

"I know," she says, her tone apologetic. The last thing she wants is to upset her already anxious friend. "I know. I'll try and make more effort, I promise."

They carry on at their painfully slow pace, until Cressa stops altogether. Amara realizes she is gazing at a small child, perhaps aged three or four. The child's piping chatter carries, and his mother smiles, indulgent, before noticing the strange, bedraggled woman fixated on her treasure. She puts an arm around her son, nervously steering him out of sight.

"Cressa," Amara says, trying to usher her along. But Cressa is crying.

"Don't," Cressa says, shaking Amara off when she tries to comfort her.

Amara sighs. She almost regrets asking her to come out.

They walk under the marine gate, passing Vibo's baths where none of them have worked for some months since

Felix decided the tips weren't worth it. Further down the hill, the sea sparkles into view. The air is fresh, the salt sharp. Cressa seems a little calmer now they have reached the harbor. At the docks, several boats are unloading. Men scurry and shout, busy as ants moving crumbs to their nest. Amara offers her arm, nervous after the last rejection, but this time, Cressa accepts. "Shall we have a walk, before fishing?"

Cressa nods, and they head to the colonnade that circles the port. Amara feels her spirits rise. Sunlight, reflected from the sea, ripples over the pillars and painted statues, and the call of the gulls, the sing-song shouts of the sailors sound almost musical. She helps Cressa sit down in a patch of sun by the water's edge. Below their swinging feet, she can see gray fish darting in the clear water.

"Felix never told me where he sold Cosmus," Cressa says. The mention of her son is so unexpected Amara does not know what to say. She looks at Cressa but cannot read her expression as her face is turned to the sea. "Fabia tried to find out for me, but we never managed it."

"Fabia?" Amara asks in surprise. She cannot imagine Paris's mother having the necessary bravery, or cunning, to make such an attempt.

"Why not Fabia? She sees more than you think. And everyone overlooks her. That's what happens when you get old." There is no mistaking the bitterness in Cressa's voice.

"Even though it was so hard for you," Amara says, desperate to try and make Cressa feel better. "Do you think maybe it might have been for the best? So that Cosmus wasn't trapped at the brothel?"

Cressa turns to her, and Amara is shocked by how old and tired her face is in the full glare of the light. "I know that none of you understand," she says. "That you think it's something I should just get over," Amara starts to protest, but Cressa raises a hand to stop her. "If you ever have a child, Amara, you will understand what I feel."

She says nothing, aware of Cressa's swelling belly, of the new baby she is carrying. They sit in silence, until Cressa starts to heave herself to her feet. Amara tries to help, but Cressa motions for her to stay where she is.

"Do you mind if I have a few moments to myself?" Cressa says. "You can wait here. I won't be long."

Amara is not keen on the idea. It's never too safe at the harbor. But Cressa is looking down at her, eyes pleading, and she cannot refuse. "Alright," she says. "But not far. I don't want to be by myself out here for ages."

Cressa sets off at a swift pace. She looks stronger and more determined than she has done for a while. The sea air was a good idea, after all. Amara holds onto the base of a pillar and cranes her neck round so she can see where Cressa is going. She watches her approach the docks then come to a stop by some amphora that are being unloaded from a boat. Cressa leans against one of the large jars, perhaps taking the weight off her swollen feet. She is looking out to sea, at the heave and swell of the water. Amara does too. The light is dancing on the waves. She looks further out, to where Venus Pompeiiana stands, the water breaking against the heavy stone base of her column. The goddess of love, Amara's new mistress. She has more respect for her since the Vinalia. It was after her prayers to the goddess that her fortunes began to change. *Don't forget me, Aphrodite,* she thinks, staring at the statue. *Show me a way out, and the rest of my life is yours.*

She glances back to where Cressa was standing and gasps, scrambling to her feet in alarm. A man is remonstrating with her, trying to stop Cressa leaning on his goods, but she is stubbornly clinging on. Amara breaks into a run. The man is shouting; it looks as if he is about to grab hold of her. Amara yells at her to let go, and to her relief, Cressa steps away, but then, in a violent movement, she pushes an amphora over the edge of the harbor wall. Cressa goes with it, pulled so fast over the side, she is almost a blur. She must have tied her cloak to the handle.

Amara cries out in shock. She hurtles past people, knocking them aside in her desperation to reach the water's edge, oblivious to their anger. At the docks, she flings herself onto her knees. "Cressa!" she screams, leaning over the side of the jetty. "Cressa!" Her heart is pounding, her mind unable to take in what she has seen. She stares at the waves, but there's no sign of her friend, just foam and a slight disturbance of the water where she broke its surface.

Amara stands up, distraught, looking for help. The man who shouted at Cressa is standing beside her, staring at the water, as dumbstruck as she is. She grabs his arm. "Can you swim? Can you jump in and save her?" She is sobbing, hysterical, almost pushing him in the water in her urgency. "Please, do something! *Please*! She's going to die!"

The man shakes her off, furious. "That fucking bitch just stole some of my best olive oil! Do you think I'm going to risk drowning for some filthy, thieving whore?" He looks more closely at Amara, taking in her toga. "Were you with her? Do you have the same master?"

Amara looks again at the water. Its surface is almost calm now, as if Cressa never jumped in, as if she never even existed. Amara cannot swim. With every moment that passes, the chance of Cressa surviving recedes. If she's not already dead. She realizes other sailors and merchants are starting to gather behind them, exclaiming to one another, excited by the commotion. Fear grips her.

"No," she says, trying to hide her distress, to control her trembling. "I don't know her. I've just seen her around." Amara turns and walks as fast as she can without running, back toward the marine gate.

34

"When you are dead, you are nothing"
—Pompeii graffiti

She can barely get through the words, she is crying so much. Amara pours it all out to Felix. They are alone, and he is standing close to her, grasping her arms to keep her steady. She wants him to hold her, to comfort her, to share her grief. Instead, he listens to the whole story without interrupting, his face impassive.

"You did well not to tell them you shared a master," he says, when she has finished. "They would have made me pay for the oil. And Cressa had cost me enough already. Barely earned a penny in months."

Amara is shocked out of her sobbing. Felix is looking at her, completely unmoved by her distress. His coldness should not be a surprise, but it still hurts, and with the pain comes the anger. She shoves him, blinded by rage. He steps back, and she hits him again, not a slap, but a punch. He is too quick for her, and she misses his face, catching his shoulder instead. "I hate you!" she screams. "You don't give a shit about anybody! She died because of you, and you don't care. You don't feel anything. I hate you!" He dodges all her blows; she is too upset to aim straight. "I wish you were dead!" Amara shouts, catching hold of his clothes, trying to shake him. "I wish you were dead!" He grabs her right arm, twisting it behind her back. She cries out and drops instantly to her knees.

"You don't get to tell me what I feel," Felix shouts, his mouth so close to her ear it deafens her. He releases her with a shove, and she cradles her arm. "Stupid fucking bitch. Do you think I chose this life? *Do you?*"

Amara says nothing. She has never questioned how Felix came to run the brothel. He seems made for it. He crouches beside her, agitated, and she shrinks away. "I was born here. Not here." He gestures at the study, as if impatient with its existence. "Downstairs. You think I don't know what it's like? That I don't understand?" His face is unrecognizable with anguish. "My mother wasn't as brave as Cressa. Too much of a fucking coward to kill herself and spare her son."

Amara doesn't move, doesn't dare say anything. She cannot imagine Felix will forgive her for seeing him like this, not when he realizes what he has just said. He is hunched over, and for the first time since she has known him, he looks defeated. She understands, watching him then, that however much she hates him, Felix will always loathe himself more. "My father, or the man my whore of a mother insisted was my father, ran this place," he says. "He gave me my freedom, so I suppose he must have believed her. But not until I had served a *long* apprenticeship." He is staring at the desk—presumably his father's—when he says this. Amara thinks of his meticulous bookkeeping, imagines him sitting there as a child, watched over by an older, nastier version of himself. Learning his trade. But then she remembers the graffiti on her cell wall.

Amara looks away from Felix, her breathing shallow. Is it possible her master was once a prostitute? That he lived the same life as Paris? She is afraid to speak, to remind him of her presence, but the growing silence is frightening too. "What happened to your mother?" she says, her voice small.

"She died when I was ten." He is staring at the red wall, his eyes glazed. His grief is so palpable that Amara forgets herself. In that moment all she can see is the frightened boy who lost his mother, who was tormented by his father, and her heart aches for him. She touches his arm, her fingers gentle.

"I'm sorry," she says.

Felix is startled out of his own thoughts. "Don't touch me," he snarls, getting to his feet. Amara scrambles out of the way, afraid he will kick her where she sits. He stares at her, and they both know she can see the tears in his eyes. "Get out."

She runs from the room.

Amara closes the door of the flat behind her, stands on the pavement, her back to the wood. She feels torn apart, almost as much by her confusion over Felix, as her grief for Cressa. She cannot bear to go into the brothel, to face Britannica, to make Cressa's death real, to see her fall in the water again as she tells the others what happened. She lurches off down the street, walking quickly but without aim. Rufus comes into her mind, the way he holds her, tells her he loves her. But it would be unthinkable to disturb him at his own house, in the daytime, with her ugly whore's tale of pregnancy and death. She almost takes the street that will lead to Drusilla's house, sensing the courtesan would not turn her away, and yet, she doesn't really know her. Amara's feet know where they are taking her before she realizes it herself. The potter's shop on the Via Pompeiana. To Menander.

She stands outside the shop, watching. He is there, laughing with another slave. A young woman. There is no sign of Rusticus. Amara feels a pang. Perhaps this is his girlfriend now. She has no right to mind what he does; she was wrong to come here and impose her grief on him. Menander sees her just as she is turning away, and he rushes from the shop.

"Timarete!" he calls, stopping her. He catches up, sees her face wet with tears. "I can't talk outside the shop," he says. "Wait here. We can walk to the fountain."

Before she has time to protest, he has run back. Amara sees him talk to the slave girl at the counter who stares at her, curious, then fetches him a bucket.

"Come on," Menander says, rejoining her. "This way."

They walk quickly down the street. "I'm sorry," Amara says. "I'm sorry for what happened between us." They reach the fountain, where a small gathering of gossips is already milling about. It's a favorite haunt for loitering slaves.

"Never mind that now," he says, pulling her to the side to let an impatient man pass. "Tell me what's wrong. Has somebody hurt you?" His concern for her is so obvious, it makes her want to cry all over again.

"Cressa is dead," she says. "She was pregnant. We went to the harbor together." Amara stops, not wanting to describe Cressa's final moments, the flash of her cloak, the foam on the water. "She drowned herself."

"It was just the two of you? You were left alone there? At the docks?"

Amara nods. "Nobody would help. Nobody. And when this man asked me why I was upset, I said I didn't know her." She covers her face with her hands, overwhelmed by her final act of betrayal. Menander puts down his bucket and embraces her. She clings to him, crying into his shoulder.

"You didn't do anything wrong," Menander says. "It's alright. It's not your fault."

"Nobody helped, nobody cared," Amara says. "They were just angry she pushed an amphora of oil in the water. She didn't matter. And now she's gone, and it's like she never lived at all. Like she was nothing."

"She wasn't though," he says. "You loved her, didn't you? She mattered; she mattered to you, to her friends."

"I didn't help her; I let her drown."

"You *couldn't* help her," he says. "And she *chose* to drown."

Amara lets Menander hold her, until she becomes suddenly aware that they have attracted a number of gawpers, no doubt listening to every word. She straightens up, wiping her face. Menander confronts the small crowd, hovering with their buckets. "Just leave us alone, will you?"

"Fuck you," one of the other slaves mutters, but the gossips still turn round to give them some privacy. Nobody here wants a fight, not when they all have masters waiting.

"You did nothing wrong," Menander repeats, holding her shoulders, making her look at him. "You hear me? Nothing at all."

Amara looks at his kind face, at the dark eyes she has tried so hard to forget, and knows that she will never love Rufus, not how she loves this man. "I'm sorry I sent Dido," she says. "I'm so sorry. I should have told you myself." As soon as she says the words, she can see how she hurt him. "I don't love him," she says. "But I owe him."

"He bought you," Menander says, letting go of her. "I understand."

It isn't only money that Amara meant. She owes Rufus for more than that. She owes him some semblance of loyalty, not to make every word she says a lie. But she doesn't want to hurt Menander even more than she already has. He bends to fill the bucket with water he doesn't need, except as an excuse for Rusticus. "I didn't want you wasting your feelings on me," Amara says, as he works the pump. "Not when I can't give you anything." *Even though I want to*, she thinks. "And I'm sorry I came here, dragging you out, burdening you. I just couldn't bear what happened to Cressa, and I forgot. I forgot I shouldn't have been speaking to you. That I should have left you alone."

"You can always speak to me." Menander lifts the bucket down, moving away from the well. "Always. And I know you have to look after yourself. I understand that."

Amara looks down. It feels as if he is letting her go, and she doesn't want him to. "There is nobody like you," she says, unable to tell him she loves him. "There is nobody else like you in my life."

"Or mine, Timarete." He leans forward, kissing her quickly on the forehead. Then he picks up the bucket, turning to go. "Please be careful. And don't blame yourself."

Britannica understands, as soon as she sees Amara, that something is wrong. "Cressa?" she demands, her voice high with anxiety. "Cressa?"

Amara cannot bear to tell her Cressa is dead while they are alone; she isn't even sure Britannica will understand. All the other women are out, even Beronice, and she has to wait while Britannica paces the corridor, muttering to herself, sometimes turning to shout at Amara who only shakes her head.

When Dido and Beronice return, they are both with customers. She knows her stricken face will have told them there is bad news as soon as they step over the threshold, but they are still obliged to pleasure the men first. Amara sits in her old cell, waiting for them to finish.

"Where is she?" Beronice says, rushing in as soon as she is free. "Where's Cressa? What's happened to her?" Britannica hovers by the bed, looking from Beronice to Amara, her eyes wide with fear.

"I'm sorry," Amara says. "I'm so sorry."

"No," Beronice shakes her head, understanding. "No, she isn't. She can't be."

"She jumped into the sea at the harbor," Amara says, trying to keep her voice steady. "She tied herself to an amphora to make sure she drowned. I couldn't get there in time to save her. I didn't realize."

"No!" Beronice wails. "No!"

It had been Britannica's grief Amara feared, but instead, it is Beronice who loses all control. She beats her fists on the walls of the cell, tearing at her hair, at her face, screaming and crying. "I loved her!" she sobs. "I loved her! She can't be dead!"

Amara doesn't dare touch her; Beronice is like a mad woman. Britannica curls up in a ball on the floor, covering her ears. Dido walks in. She has no need to ask what has happened. She throws herself at Amara, and they hold one another, rocking back and forth.

They are all still crying and keening when Amara hears Victoria, her patter cutting across the noise. "*Oh! I can feel it! How big you are!*" There is shrieking and giggling from the Spanish girls, and the deeper tones of male voices. Amara disentangles herself from Dido and steps out into the corridor. She stands in silence, her shadow reaching out across the floor.

A man is draped over Victoria, but her attention is only half on him. She has heard the wailing. "Who?" she says to Amara. "Who is it?"

"Cressa."

"Out!" Victoria shakes the man's arm from her shoulders. He looks at her, bewildered by this whore who moments before was panting after him. Victoria shoves him hard. "Get out!" she yells, her face red with fury. "All of you! Out! I don't want any fucking men in here!"

Ipstilla and Telethusa stand frozen with fear and surprise. One of their customers gives a nervous laugh. "What the fuck is this?"

"I said, all of you, out!" Victoria screams, wrenching his arm from around Ipstilla's waist. He steps back, too shocked to hit her. His companion makes the sign of the evil eye.

"You heard what she said!" Amara shouts. "We don't want you in here. Get out!"

Beronice rushes from the cell behind her. She looks unhinged with her scratched face and wild hair. "Bastards!" she shrieks. "She's dead, can't you leave us in peace?"

The men need no more urging. They don't even take the time to hurl insults back. Instead, they hurry from the house of angry women, almost tripping over the doorstep on their way to the street.

35

*"You may look perhaps for a troop of Spanish maidens
to win applause by immodest dance and song,
sinking down with quivering thighs to the floor."*
—Juvenal, *Satire* 11.162

On any other morning, Felix would have been down to rage at the takings, but their wild grief has made the women untouchable, for one day at least. Amara wonders if he too might be grieving but crushes her sense of sympathy. Whatever happened to Felix as a child does not change who he is now. Fabia dresses their hair, her own face red from crying. Amara remembers what Cressa said about the old woman trying to find Cosmus, wonders what else the two women talked about, what secrets Fabia might know about their master.

When everyone is ready, they leave Ipstilla and Telethusa at the brothel and walk in a silent line to the Sparrow. The Spanish girls passed a miserable night, quiet for once, cowed by the frenzy of mourning for a woman they barely knew.

As soon as they walk in, it's clear Zoskales has already heard the news. Amara suspects half the neighborhood must know by now, after they threw their own customers out. The landlord orders them wine and food on the house. He brings it to their table himself. "For the memory of your friend," he says, pressing each of their hands in turn, his voice deep with sincerity. "For Cressa. May her shade rest easier in the other world."

They thank him, Beronice weeping, but Amara fears Cressa will not rest, wherever her spirit is now. They cannot even bury her; there is nothing they can do to ease her passing.

"To Cressa," Victoria says, knocking back the wine. The others follow. Amara tries to give Britannica a flask, but she turns her head. The Briton has not made a sound since she learned her only friend had died. Her silence disturbs Amara far more than the wild grief she expected. She feels an even greater sense of responsibility for Britannica now. It was, after all, the last request Cressa ever made, that they should care for her.

"Her pain is over," Victoria says. "It was her choice. We should respect that."

"Hardly a choice," Amara replies, remembering Cressa's face turned to hers in the harsh light of the harbor, and the misery in her eyes. "She didn't want to lose her baby. Whose fault was that?"

"Don't," Dido says, shaking her head. "Please don't. It doesn't help."

"It could have been any of us," Amara continues, ignoring her. "Any of us. We don't matter to anyone." Beronice starts crying again, slumping down on the table, her shoulders shaking.

"Just *stop*," Dido says.

"Sorry," Amara replies. She looks guiltily at Beronice, who is wiping her eyes, trying to control herself, while Dido puts an arm round her.

"We should mark a spot for Cressa," Victoria says. "Use her savings for some offerings, have the rites performed. All pay toward it if we need to."

The others nod. "And we need to look after Britannica," Amara adds. "It was the last thing Cressa asked me. She wanted us to be kinder to her." This proposal is met with less enthusiasm. Paying respects to a shade is an easier task than caring for a large, angry Briton.

"I hope Ipstilla and Telethusa are alright," Dido says. "They seemed very quiet this morning. It must be strange for them."

"Pair of complete bitches," Victoria replies. "I doubt they have any feelings at all. You should have seen them outside the baths yesterday. Shameless! I thought they were going to start screwing a man against the wall, in broad daylight." She looks at Amara, her expression not entirely kind. "*You*'re in for a fun night tonight."

Amara and Dido are due to perform at Cornelius's house, but they won't be going alone. Ipstilla and Telethusa have also been booked to dance.

"They can't be that bad," Amara says.

"Well," Victoria says, "you'll just have to tell us all about the party tomorrow. I'm sure none of us can wait."

Amara knows it is grief making Victoria lash out, but the look she exchanges with Beronice suggests the bitterness the two women feel runs deep. She understands, watching them both, that there will have been many other conversations like this when they vented their jealousy in her and Dido's absence. Perhaps Cressa joined in too. Amara knocks back her wine, wanting to blot out the thought.

Amara has never seen Egnatius make a scene like the one he puts on for Ipstilla and Telethusa. He bursts into the chilly waiting room, unable to contain his excitement at meeting the new girls. They all gabble in Spanish together, and Amara can see what an unfeigned joy it is for him to speak his native language. She knows that feeling, remembers what it was like the first time she spoke with Menander, the sense of instant recognition and understanding.

She and Dido practice quietly in the corner. It's more Ovid tonight; they have set some of his *Art of Love* to music. Verses about dancing, to blend with the Spaniards' performance. Egnatius pays them very little attention, and she remembers the first time she came here. Then the fuss was all for her and Dido, and the mime actresses were largely expected to fend for themselves. There is nothing like the lure of the new.

Eventually, Egnatius remembers them. He heads over, semi-apologetic, to dress their hair with garlands. "They're quite perfect!" he gushes, tucking some leaves behind Dido's ear. "Your master bought exactly the type of girls I requested."

"That *you* requested?" Amara is stunned.

"Slave girls trained in Cadiz." He nods. "Oh! I remember seeing them in my youth. No other dancing like it in the world. It takes years to learn the skill." He raises an eyebrow, sly with innuendo. "Trained in other arts too, of course."

Amara and Dido exchange a horrified look. Who is going to be interested in a pair of sparrows when there are two phoenixes in the room? Egnatius picks up on their alarm, perhaps realizing his lack of tact. "But nothing like your *enchanting* performance!" he exclaims, without a trace of sincerity. "My fair, innocent little nymphs!"

He prances off, exchanging what is clearly a filthy joke with the Spanish girls as he leaves. All three of them cackle.

"Shit," Amara says.

"We haven't even got any new tunes tonight," Dido whispers. It's true. Salvius has given them all the songs he knows, or perhaps all the songs he wants to share, and now, they have to spice up their routine with fresh words, but familiar music.

"It will be alright," Amara says, convincing neither of them. "We're just different from each other. It's fine."

"Did you know Felix was speaking directly to Egnatius?"

Amara shakes her head. All those days she has spent with him, working on his accounts, and he has never mentioned it. "No," she says.

At first, Amara thinks it will be alright. She is soothed that Fuscus is there, that he has still requested her to lie on his couch for at least part of the meal. It has been many, many weeks since he paid for her company for the entire dinner. They chat about his sons, his business, even his wife, and he caresses her in a lazy, familiar way. But isn't that how it should be? There's not the same urgency when you've known a lover for a while.

Amara has a niggling sense of unease that there are fewer guests than usual, and no wives are present, not even their hostess, Calpurnia. Even so, much of the dinner feels reassuringly predictable. She and Dido perform, everyone seems to enjoy their singing, and Egnatius graciously steers them around the room. But Ipstilla and Telethusa are not left until the end of the meal like the mime actresses. Instead, Egnatius brings them in as the high point, just when everyone's spirits have built to an especially convivial pitch.

Amara is reclining on a couch with a man she doesn't know when they enter. He hasn't spoken to her directly, but she thinks he might be called Trebius. He runs a tannery and is droning on about leather to his equally dull companion when Cornelius starts talking, his voice loud over the murmur of his guests.

"My friends," he exclaims, "I think you may enjoy the next course. A Spanish dish with extra spice."

There is expectant laughter, and Amara realizes that everyone has been *waiting* for this. She and Dido were only here to whet the guests' appetites. The entire evening has been based on the new women's performance.

Ipstilla and Telethusa whirl their way past the fountain of nymphs, clacking their red castanets. Even the tedious Trebius has stopped talking, suddenly interested and alert. The two dancers are naked, though Amara realizes they have made liberal use of the gold paste she and Dido unwisely left unattended in the waiting room.

Their initial flourish over, the two women begin grinding in earnest. Amara stares. She has never seen dancing like this. It makes Victoria's performance at the Vinalia look matronly. She is not even sure how they manage all that shaking and quivering, lowering themselves to the floor but not quite touching it, without toppling over. And the singing is worse. It's a medley of wordless wailing and moaning, the least subtle imitation of sex she's ever heard.

Trebius grabs her leg, and she flinches. She turns to look up at him, but he is not looking back at her, does not even seem conscious of her; his hand is grasping the flesh of her thigh purely because he wants to touch a female body while he watches the dancing. She resists an overwhelming instinct to pry his fingers from her skin, preferably bending them back until the bones snap, and instead glances round desperately for Fuscus. He too is mesmerized by the dancing. She keeps her eyes focused on him, willing him to notice her, sending out a silent plea. Eventually, he glances over. She locks eyes with him, determined that he should understand. He motions to Egnatius, pointing toward the couch where she is trapped with Trebius.

Amara has rarely felt more grateful to see Egnatius sidle over. "Please forgive me," he murmurs to Trebius. "a most *terrible* oversight, this one is booked elsewhere . . ." Trebius looks at Amara, almost surprised to see his own hand touching her. "Take it," he says impatiently, almost shoving her off the couch. "You're blocking my view."

Amara reclines next to Fuscus whose expression is smug. "Did the dancing put you in the mood for *me*, little sparrow?" he asks, hoicking her closer to him, breathing heavily in her ear.

"I couldn't be with anyone else!" She sighs. Let the foolish man imagine she was longing for his body rather than his protection. At least she knows him. Even if he has no real affection for her, he won't hurt her, he won't use her body without any thought there might be a living woman attached to it.

She looks round for Dido, ashamed that she has only just remembered her friend. She spots her near the fountain with a man she does not recognize. At least he seems to be leaving her largely alone, too caught up in the women dancing to notice the one next to him.

Dinner is, unsurprisingly, a shorter affair than usual. It is less of a saunter to Cornelius's brothel, more a stampede. Other hired women are already waiting, no doubt booked by Egnatius to make sure none of the guests go short. Amara is disappointed Fuscus does not take her to a private room; she supposes he has made an exception to his usual preference not to be watched, confident that the other men, like him, will be more interested in watching the dancers than each other. Ipstilla and Telethusa flit between the lavish cells, putting on a performance for the men while they have sex, but not, Amara thinks bitterly, having to endure being used themselves.

She is not afraid of Fuscus, but when he maneuvers her into a painfully awkward position, purely to get a better view of Telethusa, she realizes the distance between him and Trebius is not as great as she imagined. Her body, which is too familiar to be exciting on its own, is a means to heighten his pleasure in the dancers. She is trapped by him, his weight like the waves of the sea, pushing her under. She thinks of Cressa, lost beneath the water, and turns her face to the side, gripping the expensive fabric on the bed. At the edge of her vision, she can see the flash of Telethusa's legs as she dances. *Felix put this woman here*, she thinks. All the gold she has earned him, and he spent it on diminishing her value. He destroys everything in the end.

36

"Suns when they sink can rise again,
But we, when our brief light has shone
Must sleep the long night on and on."
—Catullus, Poem 5

Amara can hear Thraso before she sees him. Gallus is leading them back home in the dark, although this street, with its bars and brothel, is never so dark as the others. A small crowd is gathered around the foot of a ladder. It stands propped against the wall, just round the corner from their own front door, and a shrieking woman is trying to shake it, stopped only by drunken bystanders. At the top, Thraso bellows down at her, clinging onto a rung with one hand and waving a hammer with the other.

"What the fuck?" Gallus says, raising his lamp to illuminate the scene.

Amara takes Dido's hand, and they draw closer together, but Ipstilla and Telethusa seem excited at the prospect of a row, bouncing up and down to get a better view. Both are still ecstatic over their success at Cornelius's house. Even

Egnatius tipped them for their performance, something Amara has never seen him do before.

"What's this?" Gallus yells, barging into the crowd. He grabs the shrieking woman's shoulder. "Are you trying to fucking kill him?"

The woman turns round, still screaming, and Amara recognizes her. It's Maria, Simo's least valuable woman. She stops yelling when she sees Amara and Dido, then screws her face up, spitting at their feet. "For Drauca," she says, her eyes bright with hatred. She turns back to Gallus, flinging her arm up with anger. "Get him to stop! Look at him! He's destroying my master's property!"

Thraso is swinging his hammer at a stone cock that has sprouted high up on the wall. Amara hadn't noticed it before, but then there are so many in Pompeii. Maria takes advantage of everyone staring upward to give the ladder a violent shake. Thraso clings on, swearing at her. "You've no right!" she shrieks. "Stop it!"

"Bitch," Thraso yells back, brandishing the hammer. "Mind I don't drop this on your fucking head!"

Ipstilla steps forward, yanking at Maria's toga to move her out of danger, shouting at her in Spanish. The two women grapple with one another, and the crowd cheer, delighted by the night's unexpected entertainment.

"Get Felix," Gallus says to Amara and Dido. "Now."

They run back to the brothel. It's no distance away, but the carousing outside the Elephant is so raucous that the noise of the row, just a few houses down, is lost in the chaos. Paris is on the door and is startled to see them charging up the street on their own.

"You need to get Felix," Amara says. "There's trouble with one of Simo's whores. He'll know what I mean."

Paris hurries to the flat, banging on the door and yelling. The door opens, and he disappears inside. A few moments later, Felix comes out armed with a metal rod. Paris slinks out behind, obviously being sent back to guard the brothel rather than join in the action.

"Where are the dancers?" Felix asks, surprised to see them on their own.

"They stayed with Gallus," Dido replies, as they trot behind him.

Felix shakes his head, irritated. "Better take them back with you."

They reach the ladder, and the crowd parts, more out of respect for the weaponry than the man carrying it. Maria and Ipstilla are still scrapping, Gallus trying to get between them, but at the sight of Felix, they all pull apart. Gallus bundles Ipstilla out of the way. "Fucking women," he mutters.

"What's this?" Felix asks. He sounds casual, almost bored, leaning on the metal rod as if it were a staff.

Maria squares up to him, shoulders heaving from her recent exertion. "You tell me!" she shouts. "Your thug's smashing up my master's business! Simo rents this room; it's his. You have no right."

"This room?" Felix says, swinging the rod toward the small darkened cell that opens directly onto the street. He wrinkles his nose, as if he can smell its stale odor. "Simo rents this room?"

Maria steps protectively in front of the doorway. Amara cannot help admiring her courage. "You know he does. That's why that bastard's been trying to smash the sign."

Felix smiles at Thraso, who has just descended the ladder. "I think we can leave the lady her sign," he says. "Though that's a big fucking cock for a very small brothel, isn't it? What's your master hoping? Some of the dregs from my business will swill down the road?" Felix turns round to the watching drunks. "Which women would you rather fuck? That fat one there"—he points at Maria—"or my girls here." Some of the crowd laugh, and Ipstilla with them, but Telethusa looks less impressed. Amara suspects she doesn't fancy a night with any of the drunks on display. At least there they can agree.

"You can mouth off all you like," Maria says, jutting out her chin. "You don't impress me. Think I've never been called fat before? Well, my *big, fat arse* is staying right here."

This time it's Maria who raises the laugh. Felix nods, and Amara recognizes his smiling expression as one of pure cruelty. "No doorman though, is there?" he says, looking theatrically up and down the road for her nonexistent protector. "Simo can't think much of you if he's selling cunt straight on the street. Anything could happen. You leave your goods for a moment and"—he snaps his fingers—"somebody's stolen them. Or smashed them." He is staring at Maria as he says this, so that she cannot mistake his meaning.

For the first time, Amara can see that Maria is afraid, but she chooses to cover it with bravado. "If I'm so fucking ugly, not worth your while to threaten me, is it?"

Felix bows. "I'm sure, for your performance tonight, you will have the pick of all the men here." In answer, a couple of the drunken bystanders jostle toward Maria's small, dark cell, and Felix watches her discomfort as she realizes she will have no means of limiting or controlling her customers. *He must really hate her*, Amara thinks, *to frighten her at the expense of making Simo some money.* She thinks of Drauca and feels afraid of what might happen to Maria. Felix turns to the remaining men. "If you prefer wine to water, the brothel's this way."

Most were only there for the spectacle and slope off, not willing to pay for their fun, but a couple tag along. They walk along the narrow pavement in a gaggle. Ipstilla and Telethusa exchange anxious glances. Surely, the master doesn't expect them to entertain drunks like this, not after their performance at the grand house? Ipstilla catches his arm. "Why does she go upstairs?" She points at Amara. "She is better in brothel. We make you much more money tonight."

Felix slaps Ipstilla hard across the back of the head, and she yelps. She stares at Felix, bewildered, obviously not used to a master with no favorites and no loyalty. "*She* didn't brawl in the street like a rabid bitch either," he says. "Don't fucking question me again." They arrive back at the brothel, and Felix greets Paris at the door. "Make sure you take the clothes from them first," he says, pointing at the women who have returned from the party. "I don't want them torn." He clicks his fingers at Amara, and she follows him. She cannot bear to look back at Dido, left behind with the rabble.

"Little dog," Ipstilla hisses as she passes. "He will tire of you."

Felix says nothing to her as they walk up the stairs, but before she can head to the storeroom he stops her. "Did the dancers earn more than you tonight?" It is the first time they have spoken alone since he told her about his mother.

"Yes," Amara says, not wanting to betray any emotion in her answer.

He leans on the wall, looking her over. She can tell from the hatred in his eyes that he will never forgive her for seeing him as she did, that he will always need to diminish her. "Posh boy today, isn't it? You'd better get some sleep. You look tired. Like Cressa." He presses his finger to her cheek, testing its softness, as if she were fruit at the market. "Pretty face. Nobody ages faster than a whore."

Drusilla's dressing table reminds her of the luxurious mornings she spent with Sarah, at Pliny's house. Amara is conscious of the favor the courtesan is showing her, allowing her into her intimate space. Drusilla's favorite maid, Thalia, is dressing Amara's hair. She has dark brown skin like her mistress, and deft, clever fingers. Drusilla has already explained Thalia's worth, how expensive it was to find a woman who would know the best styles for her own hair. Thalia listened to it all in silence, without betraying how she might feel, or what it meant to her, being shipped all the way from Axum to Pompeii to make a stranger look beautiful.

"I was only a small child when I came here," Drusilla says. "I remember almost nothing of my family. My master

Veranius became everything to me." She fingers the gold bracelet on her upper arm. It is the most Amara has ever heard her speak about herself.

"Was that his gift to you?" she asks.

In answer, Drusilla slips the bracelet down her arm and hands it to Amara. It is heavier than she expects, shaped like a snake, its eyes glittering gemstones. Inside is an inscription. *From the master to his slave girl*. Amara admires it then gives it back. "He must have loved you dearly to have made you such a beautiful bracelet," she says.

Drusilla slides it back on. "I was the fifth woman in his life to wear it," she says. "I knew some of those who wore it before me." She smiles at Amara, seeing the expression on her face. "An early lesson in men. The fourth was Procris, his wife's maid. She raised me. When I was a grown woman, she had to give this up to me, along with all the favor that went with it. He broke her heart."

Amara does not know what to say. Drusilla just told her Veranius meant everything to her, yet the man sounds as monstrous as Felix. "I loved him," Drusilla says, as if guessing her thoughts. "And I despised him. What else is possible toward the man who gives everything and takes everything?"

"He must have favored you the most," Amara says. "As you kept it, and he freed you."

Drusilla laughs. "You can be as naïve as Rufus!" she says. "I survived him, that's all. Nothing more to it than luck. If he had died when Procris was wearing this, no doubt she would be free, and I would be dressing his widow's hair."

Thalia stands back from Amara, offering her the mirror to see her work. Amara turns her face, admiring her curls. "It's lovely, thank you," she says, carefully laying the silver disc on the table. Drusilla nods at Thalia who leaves the room. "Thank you for letting me come here," Amara says, when the maid has gone. "I could not continue to see Rufus otherwise."

"He will never love you more than he does now," Drusilla replies. Amara puts her hand to her neck, upset because she knows it is true. "I don't say it to be cruel," Drusilla continues. "But you need to think carefully about what you want from him. There will never be a better time to ask."

"He is always saying he will marry me," Amara admits. "But it's impossible! I would be arrested, the marriage dissolved. Roman citizens don't marry brothel whores. Life isn't one of his plays."

"I didn't mean marriage!" Drusilla is amused. "Perhaps aim a *little* lower."

Amara laughs with her, embarrassed to have exposed the heights of her own ambition. "Can I ask you something?" she says, feeling a little shy. "Why did it not work out between Rufus and you?"

"Rufus wants to give everything to a woman. You could almost say he wants to make her." Drusilla cups her hands, as if sheltering something precious. "What he wants is a little wounded bird he can hold, feel its wings flutter against his fingers." Her voice is low and crooning. Amara can almost imagine holding the bird herself, its tiny, frightened heart beating beneath soft feathers. "I was not fragile enough for him. You are." Amara stares at Drusilla, still sitting with her hands cupped together. There are no words for the pain she feels, knowing it is true. "I have been you," Drusilla says. "Veranius would never have let me go, only his death did that. But Rufus might be different. You might persuade him that there would be no greater pleasure than opening his fingers, watching the bird fly, knowing every beat of its wings, every breath it takes, it owes to him." Drusilla opens her hands, and they both stare at the empty air. Then she drops her arms, sadness in her eyes. "At least, you have to try."

Amara dines alone with Rufus, served a private dinner in the room with Leda and the Swan. Amara knows Drusilla is entertaining Quintus elsewhere in the house. She feels reassured that Rufus wants to lie with her before eating, at least making love to her is still more exciting than food, but she no longer feels the same comfort when he caresses her afterward. She keeps thinking of the bird, of what it feels like for him, holding his fragile, tragic little whore.

"I wish I could spend every evening with you," he says, tucking into Drusilla's grilled fish and beans. "If I had my way, we would spend every waking moment together." He takes her hand and kisses it, looking sentimental. "You know that, don't you, my darling?"

Amara's heart is beating so fast, and her nerves are pulled so tight, she cannot touch her own meal. She won't beg, not after Pliny, and in any case, she does not want to swap one enslavement for another. "If only I had a home, like

Drusilla," she sighs. "You could visit me whenever you wanted."

Rufus kisses her, but she can tell he hasn't taken her seriously. She tries again. "You are more generous than any man I've ever met," she says. "I cry sometimes, when I'm alone, thinking about how you would marry me, because I know you meant it sincerely when you asked. Even though I could never accept. I would never dishonor your family that way."

Rufus kisses her again, more passionately this time, distracted from eating by her adoration. "How I love you!" he murmurs.

"But if you set me up in a home like this, I could be a second wife for you," she says. "As your freedwoman." Amara sees a flash of alarm in Rufus's eyes, but she has rolled the dice and has to play her hand. "I would exist only for you, never taking from your family. Not now, or in the future. I would need nothing other than to be allowed to love you."

"Is that really what you want?"

"More than anything in the world," she replies. Her lip is trembling from fear, not love, but Rufus cannot tell the difference.

"Perhaps it might be possible," he says, turning from her. He looks distracted, rather than excited by the idea. "It would need some work. This isn't a small thing, what you're asking."

"I know. But ours isn't a small love," Amara says. "And although I cannot bring myself to dishonor you by allowing you to have me as a wife, I could love you as a mistress without bringing shame to anyone."

"It would be wonderful," Rufus agrees, beginning to warm to the idea of a constant well of devotion. "And then, even when I marry, if my wife isn't . . ." He stops, perhaps realizing that speculating on the desirability of his future wife isn't very romantic. "Anyway, whatever she were like, I could always spend time with you, whenever we wanted."

"Yes," Amara says. "I would *always* be waiting for you."

"Maybe Drusilla could teach you the harp?" Rufus replies, his face hopeful, like a child. "You two like each other, don't you? And you've no idea how happy it makes me, seeing you lost in your music. I think you would look even lovelier playing the harp than you do with the lyre."

Amara smiles, relieved he has so easily succumbed to the image of her as the mistress singing in her gilded cage. But his words set off an unwelcome echo, and without wanting to remember, Menander's rival fantasy plays through her mind. She sees herself as he did, waiting for him in his father's house. The shared life they will never have together in Attica.

She leans over and kisses Rufus gently on the lips then gazes up at him, not as Timarete, the woman he will never know, but as Amara, the woman she is now. "Whatever you want."

"I'll do it." He sounds more determined. "There must be a way of managing it. And I wouldn't have to pay for you all the time then, not after the initial outlay." He stops, wincing with embarrassment. "I'm sorry, my darling, that sounded unforgivably crude. What I *meant* was, if it makes financial sense, even my father might see it's a good idea."

"You are the best man in the world," Amara says, clasping her hands.

He smiles at her, but she can see the same distracted look on his face. She leans her head against his shoulder, the blood pounding in her ears, hoping that he means what he says and that she has not just sped up her descent and exit from his life.

DECEMBER

37

"Now, my little love, entrust your happiness to the wind
Trust me, the nature of men is fickle"
—Pompeii graffiti

It is cold in Balbina's small atrium. A film of ice covers the rainwater in the central pool. Amara and the other two women huddle together in their woolen cloaks, trying to come to an agreement. It cost her dearly, paying off some of Terentia's interest to Felix, but now it may finally be worth it. The fruit seller has introduced her to another client.

"I will keep the contract safe for you both," Terentia is saying. "I found her fair, more than fair."

Balbina has run up a dicing debt and doesn't want her husband to know. Perfect, as far as Amara is concerned, provided Balbina can hand over enough surety.

"Let me see the necklace," she says, softening her command with a smile. The chain slips through her fingers, light and supple. She lacks the expertise to know whether it is worth the same amount as the loan, but she suspects the cameo pendant, at least, would fetch something. Amara loops the chain around her own neck, tucking it under the woolen cloak, then hands Balbina a purse. "You may want to check it's the agreed amount," she says.

Balbina counts the coins out twice, while Terentia and Amara watch. Then Terentia holds out the tablets for them both to sign. "*Much* better rate of interest than I got." Terentia sighs.

"I know," Amara says. "But this is much riskier for me." What she has just done is worse than risky, and she knows it. Should Felix ever discover the betrayal, the consequences are unimaginable. She tells herself that brokering this loan is a safety net, a means of earning extra cash if Rufus disappoints her. But she knows this is only partly why she has taken such a terrible risk. The real reason is the pleasure she gets from cheating Felix, the fierce joy of outwitting him. Ever since Cressa died, the hostility between them has been relentless, a battle of wits she is determined to win. *I am better at this than he is*, she thinks.

Amara turns to Terentia. "We are both trusting you with the contract," she says. "So please keep it safe." She has sweetened that trust by five asses though no need to tell Balbina that. If the gambling wife is wise, she will have given the fruit seller her own bribe. "When the interest is paid," she says to Balbina, who has already tucked the purse out of sight. "I will return the necklace."

"I'll pay it in no time," Balbina says, sounding tetchy. "I just got unlucky, that's all."

Nobody wants to linger, so after a curt goodbye, Amara and Terentia step out onto the street. "Good job you have the necklace," Terentia says. "She'll have to get very lucky at dice to pay that off in one go."

"Thank you for arranging it," Amara replies.

"I'll expect the same interest myself next time," Terentia says, hurrying off down the street. "Your master's a skinflint."

Dido is standing across the street, loitering outside a bakery, pretending to form part of the queue. "Thanks for waiting," Amara says, joining her, stamping her feet on the cold pavement. "I guess we should get something to eat."

"I don't know how you do it," Dido replies. "How your nerves can stand it."

It's true that Dido looks more anxious than Amara. The risk she is running is so great, she has moved beyond fear. Instead, she is high on the sense of betrayal. Deceiving Felix is even more satisfying than she anticipated. "It should be fine," she says. "Rufus will keep the surety safe for me." He had also provided her with the purse full of cash, yet another test of his love. She told him it was for a friend who had got into debt, and he did not question her. He has no need to know about this side of her life. When she is installed in their love nest, she doesn't want to rely on him for everything; it's better if she has some means to support herself.

Dido is looking at her strangely. "What is it?" Amara asks, putting her hand to her neck, worried the chain might be showing. "What's wrong?"

Dido shakes her head, embarrassed. "Nothing, it's just . . ." She pauses, obviously not wanting to say.

"What?" They have reached the front of the line, and it will be their turn at the counter soon. Amara is impatient to know.

"I know how much you feel things, because I know you. But you look so cold sometimes. You look like . . ." Dido falters again.

Amara is annoyed by her dithering. "Like what?" she snaps.

"You look like Felix," Dido blurts out. "I'm sorry. But you do."

The words sting, but she doesn't want to show it. "I suppose slaves get like their masters," she says, tossing her head as if she doesn't care. "At least he's good at business."

"I didn't mean to upset you," Dido says, knowing her too well not to notice Amara is offended. "You could never be cruel like him—that's not what I meant."

They are interrupted by their arrival at the counter. Dido orders the bread, buying a little extra for Fabia and Britannica who cannot afford their own. Amara says nothing, still upset by the comparison with Felix. She thinks back to her dealings with Balbina, how different it felt to that first loan with Marcella, how much less she cared this time. *I don't have a choice*, she tells herself. *He is free, and I am not.*

It is starting to sleet when they step back on the street. They pull their cloaks up, trying to protect themselves from the wet and the cold, hurrying along the slippery pavement. Amara takes Dido's arm to show she's forgiven her. "I don't know how we're meant to pick anyone up in this," she grumbles.

"Aren't you seeing Rufus tonight?"

"Doesn't matter. Felix says I have to start earning something on these days too, or he will charge Rufus double. I can't risk costing him yet more money." She feels a sense of weariness, the exhilaration of the loan already fading. Rufus has promised he will buy her, but there always seems to be some excuse to delay. Now he says it will be the Saturnalia, that it will soften the blow for his parents if his indiscretion is lost in the celebrations. She hopes he means it. Every day she spends in Felix's service is like another stone added to the growing pile that weighs down her heart. However clever she is, however often she outwits him, he still holds all the power.

"The baths might be our best chance. At least the customers won't have to walk far." Dido looks tired too. Guilt pricks Amara. Whatever anxieties she has, Dido's worries are surely worse. Egnatius is booking them less frequently, Aurelius and Fuscus were only ever occasional clients, and Drusilla's friend and former lover Lucius has largely proved a disappointment. He does still pay for Dido's company at Drusilla's house, but nothing like as often as Rufus does. And he has never said anything more about finding her family. "If Rufus doesn't let me down," Amara says, taking her arm, "I promise I won't leave you there. I will get you out too." It is a promise she has made a thousand times before.

"If Felix lets you," Dido says, looking depressed. They both know buying her freedom is likely to be out of Amara's gift, unless Rufus showers her with gold.

The square outside the baths is much less busy than usual, nobody caring to linger in the sleet. They press close to the men's entrance, sheltering under a wine shop's balcony. As the men come out, still red-faced from the heat of the steam room, they wish them good day, trying to make eye contact. Dido has been in Pompeii over a year now, and almost no trace of the shy girl from Carthage remains, or at least not now, when she is focused on picking up clients. *It is a brutal waste of her acting talents*, Amara thinks, remembering the way Dido dances, the sweetness of her singing voice, her ability to inhabit a character. All that skill used to play a street whore.

Most of the men push past without responding to their greeting, others stop to trade insults, or try to steal a kiss. Dido is the first to secure a serious customer. She hesitates before leading him home. It's not how they like to work, splitting up like this, but the brothel is near enough for them to take the risk. Amara nods at her, the signal that she is fine. She doesn't wait to watch Dido hurry off with her catch, a portly older man. She cannot afford to slacken her own sales pitch—a rival prostitute is at the doorway now. The other woman is much more poorly dressed, her cheeks hollowed out by hunger. *Nothing like being undercut*, Amara thinks bitterly. Anyone looking at the scrawny creature will know she's unlikely to charge much.

Sure enough, the starving woman is picked up in no time, no doubt leading her suitor off somewhere no more salubrious than a back alley. Amara calls out more loudly, increasingly aggressive in her approach. She interrupts men's conversations, pressing her body too close to them.

Two young men stop to return her greeting, taking their time in spite of the cold, their cheeks pink and sweaty.

"Need heating up do you?" one says, looking her up and down.

She laughs, pretending to be amused. "Not just me," she says, stepping back, beckoning them toward her. "Lots of lonely girls."

"Told you the brothel was just round the corner," the other man says to his companion. "It's by a bar too. I remember it from my last time here. We could have a drink afterward."

Amara walks swiftly, and they hurry to keep up with her. *Not much further*, she tells herself. *Just get it over with.* She passes Simo's single-cell brothel on the way, its door ajar. The sight of it always gives her an uneasy feeling, but so far, Felix seems to have decided to ignore the insult. Maria is still alive.

Felix didn't specify how many men she needed to find today. But if she can bring two past the door, surely that should be enough? Gallus is on sentry duty, looking wet and miserable. He shows Amara three fingers. Three women in. "Make sure he knows I brought them," Amara murmurs, as she passes.

Beronice is waiting in the corridor, bored and chilly in her cloak. One of the men saunters over to claim her. Dido must still be busy. Amara doesn't even have to ask herself who the third woman is. It will inevitably be Britannica.

Victoria's room is free, so Amara leads her man in there. Since Felix bought so many women, they have all had to be less particular about where they entertain. *I don't want to do this*, Amara thinks, as she draws the curtain. She has lost the sense of horror, the terrible panic that used to overwhelm her. Instead, what she feels is a wordless aversion, a feeling that she has been pushed too far, beyond what she can physically stomach. *Think of the money.*

She turns and smiles at the man. He is already half-undressed.

"Against the wall," he says.

Amara waits for Philos to collect her. She sits alone on the hard sack of beans in the storeroom, her head resting on the wall, eyes closed. She tries to imagine herself back in Pliny's garden, tries to recreate the sense of tranquility, the sound of the fountain. It has been hours since the man from the baths touched her, but she can still feel him. Afterward, she walked to the well in the rain, struggled back with a bucket of icy water, stripped herself off. She tried to scrub away every trace, the water so cold on her skin it was painful. Perhaps when Rufus tells her he loves her later, the feeling might start to fade.

"I hope you don't show the posh boy such a fucking miserable face."

She opens her eyes. Felix is standing in the doorway, watching. She didn't hear him approach. She resists the urge to put her hand to her neck, to check Balbina's chain is still hidden. "I told you he's violent," she says, not bothering to stand up. "A miserable face makes him happy."

"As long as he keeps paying," Felix answers. She looks at him, standing there, an ugly sneer on his face, as if he can still pretend that he is any better than she is. *Your mother was a whore and so were you.* The words are too potent to risk saying aloud, but just knowing his secret makes her feel stronger.

Amara has tried to find out more from Fabia, ingratiating herself with presents of food, asking what the old woman remembers of their master's childhood. Fabia had opened her mouth, pinching her own tongue between her fingers. "*He told me he would cut it out himself,*" is all she said.

"Gallus let you know I brought in two customers today?" Amara says.

Felix nods. "I'll let it pass this time. Next time I want at least three." She says nothing, not letting her anger show. She hopes now he has thrown his taunt he will leave, but he doesn't. "Posh boy never leaves any marks. A violent lover usually does."

"You don't."

They stare at each other. Their silence is like that of two tigers, circling one another. Her hatred for this man is more ferocious than desire could ever be.

A loud rapping announces Philos's arrival on the street below. Felix stands aside to let her pass, but she can feel his animosity follow her, even when she is out of sight and heading down the stairs. She opens the door. Philos, with his cheerful smile and friendly greeting, is like a visitor from another world.

Philos never speaks until they are walking side by side down the street, well out of earshot of the brothel. He turns to her when they are at a safe distance, and she can see the smile in his eyes, even though his face is solemn. "We're going somewhere new tonight."

"Not the theater?"

"It's a surprise." He laughs at her curious expression. "More than my life is worth to spoil it."

Amara feels her pulse quicken with hope. "Is it . . . ?"

"I've said too much already!" Philos exclaims, but his broad smile is surely her answer. "Just make sure you look *astounded*, that's all I'm saying."

Amara laughs too. She likes Philos; he has a kind, easy manner. Rufus relies on him for everything, in the way she remembers Pliny relied on Secundus. She suspects Philos is considerably smarter than his master, but far too discreet to show it. "Did you have anything to do with it?" she asks.

"Possibly."

"Then I know it will be wonderful." Philos looks pleased by the compliment. Amara knows only too well how little thanks any slave gets for his labor. They walk to the cheaper part of town, and she feels her excitement growing.

"Here we are," Philos says, stopping at a darkened doorway. She stands close to him, eager to see everything, and he pushes her away slightly, as if they were children jostling over a toy. He gives her the lamp to hold and fishes out some heavy keys, deliberately taking his time with the lock, until she hits him playfully on the arm. Philos turns the key, cranking open the wooden door. They step inside. The small atrium is cold, with a few oil lamps set on the floor, their flickering light dimmed by the moonlight from the opening in the ceiling. She turns to ask Philos where they are, but he has already melted into the shadows.

"Welcome home, darling."

Rufus is standing in the archway to the garden, his figure cutting a deeper shade of black in the darkness.

Amara flings herself at him with a cry. She can scarcely get the words out, all her love and relief and fear are jumbled together, the threads too tangled to unwind.

"You're shaking!" Rufus exclaims. He sweeps her up into his arms, relishing the theatricality of the gesture. Amara is perhaps a little heavier than he was expecting, as he stumbles on the first step, but then he regains his footing and strides toward one of the darkened rooms. It is cold and barely furnished. A couch and a burning lamp stand in the corner. More than enough.

There is no pretence to Amara's happiness. That side of her performance, at least, is genuine. And after she has given him every pleasure his body can bear, Rufus hardly has the chance to tell her he loves her. She has already said the words herself, over and over again.

The chill is too sharp to lie together on the bed for long. "I'm afraid the house is only rented at the moment," Rufus says, hurrying to get dressed. "But perhaps we can buy the place if we like it enough." A sliver of fear prickles Amara, as cold as the sweat drying on her skin. She shivers. Surely this house is more than proof that he will free her? Rufus leans toward her, kissing her again. Slowly, she relaxes. He cups her face in his hands. "We can decide when you belong to nobody but me."

38

*"A common night awaits us,
we all must walk death's path."*
—Horace, *The Odes* 1.28

Amara stands alone in the brothel corridor. Nobody else is awake yet. She looks at the familiar space, the sooty walls, the paintings above the doorways. A woman on top for Victoria. A man with two cocks for Beronice. All those women on the walls, never taking a break from getting fucked, even when the real whores are sleeping. She wonders how many more nights she will have to spend in this place and hugs herself, thinking of the empty house. Waiting for her.

She is sure Rufus will free her soon, he must do. But even if he doesn't, if he only buys her, it will still be a thousand times better to be his slave than belong to Felix. The prickle of fear returns, but she rubs her arms angrily, as if she can physically brush off her anxiety. A bang from Cressa's old cell distracts her. Britannica.

The cell's curtain is moving slightly, swayed by the movement behind it. She bunches the fabric in her hands.

It stinks. "It's Amara," she says in a low voice, announcing herself before she enters.

Britannica does not look over. Not for the first time, Amara is struck by her strangeness. She is far too tall for a woman, and now her red hair is too short. It grew so matted they had no choice but to cut it. She is almost ugly in her disregard for herself, yet Amara still feels a sense of admiration for Britannica's body, for its undoubted strength. All the effort the rest of them put into looking desirable seems feeble in comparison.

Amara watches the pale arms, jabbing the air. She wonders when Britannica last left her cell, when she last saw daylight. She thinks of the promise she made Cressa. "You should get out for a while," Amara says. "Come to the well with me."

At first, the other woman gives no sign of having heard, but Amara waits. She has learned that Britannica will always respond eventually. She watches her aiming punches that fall just short of the wall. If she misjudged, she would surely break her hand. Then, without warning, she suddenly stops. Britannica rifles through the blankets on her bed, finds her cloak and flings it on, before picking up a jug on the floor. She tilts her head to one side, looking at Amara, impatient. *What are you waiting for?*

Amara collects the brothel's communal bucket from its place by the back door. They walk together down the street. The silence is anything but companionable. Britannica radiates aggression, staring down anyone foolish enough to look at her. Amara wonders if she would actually be *glad* should one of the men approach—Britannica seems even more eager for a brawl than Paris.

They reach the well. Two men are already there, perhaps slaves from different households, grabbing the chance to chat. Amara waits patiently, even though they are doing nothing more than blocking the way, neither showing any inclination to fill a bucket. Eventually, they deign to notice the women and step aside, but there's no mistaking the way they stare at her body. She wouldn't be surprised if they have kept her waiting on purpose.

Amara says nothing but walks forward, swinging her bucket into the well. It clanks onto the stone. She starts working the pump, aware the men are standing too close. One places his hand on her backside, pushing her. "Need some help?"

Before she has time to turn round and tell him to back off, Britannica has seized him. Amara drops the bucket, splashing herself. The man is almost off his feet, Britannica has lifted him by his scruff like a dog. He takes a swing at her, but she blocks it, grabbing his arm, twisting it hard. He cries out, and Britannica smiles. One of her front teeth is missing, a memento from a violent customer.

"Alright, no need to overreact!" the second man shouts, darting over. "Look," he points at Amara. "Nobody is touching her!"

Britannica does not respond. She stares at the man she is holding, still smiling her unfriendly smile. Then she lowers him. She waits a moment, like a cat toying with a mouse, before finally letting go. The two men look at her, then each other. It's clear neither of them has the stomach for a fight with this unnerving stranger. They hurry off down the street.

Britannica watches them go. "Savage," she says. Her voice is harsh and rasping from lack of use.

"What?" Amara gasps. "What did you say?"

"Sav-Age," Britannica repeats the Latin word slowly, as if savoring its hard edges. She smiles again, her fierce gap-toothed grin.

"You speak Latin?" Amara exclaims. "You can speak!"

Britannica inclines her head. The barest acknowledgement. It is the closest she and Amara have ever come to genuine communication.

"I knew you could understand! I *knew*!" Britannica does not look entirely pleased by this effusiveness. She walks past, starts filling up the abandoned bucket. Amara follows, unable to restrain her eagerness. "Please, talk to me. You can trust me. *Please*." Britannica does not answer, just gestures impatiently for the jug she left on the ground. Amara hands it to her. "I promised Cressa I would be your friend. I promised her."

Britannica stiffens at Cressa's name. She yanks the bucket from the well, dumping it in Amara's arms with such force that she staggers and almost drops it. Then Britannica picks up the jug and strides back to the brothel. Amara has no choice but to totter after her. The bucket is too full and heavy for her to have any hope of catching the other woman up. By the time she gets back, Britannica has disappeared into her cell.

"Making yourself useful?" Victoria steps out from the latrine. She leans against the small wall, rubbing her abdomen. "Only good thing about a period is it means you're not pregnant."

"Britannica just spoke to me!" Amara says, dumping the bucket. "She just spoke Latin!"

Victoria is surprised. "Really? What did she say?"

"Savage!"

"*Savage?*" Victoria wrinkles her nose. "Nothing else?"

"No, that was it."

"That's not talking then. She's just repeating sounds she's heard."

"She understands though." Amara looks over at Cressa's old cell and lowers her voice. "She got upset when I mentioned Cressa."

The dead woman's name has a dampening effect on them both. "We should visit her grave," Victoria says, easing herself down from the steps into the corridor. "None of us have been in ages."

"Do you want to go now?"

Victoria glances down the corridor, with all its closed curtains. "I suppose so. Why not? We can stop by the Sparrow. Get some wine to offer her." She goes into her cell, comes out in her cloak, holding a small clay pot. It's an old one of Cressa's. "Come on."

They walk the short distance to the tavern on the square. Amara tries to ignore the wall with its tapestry of graffiti. It pains her to remember Menander writing to her on it; she doesn't want to see the traces of his last message. Nicandrus is busy at the bar, setting up for the day's business. He greets them with a smile. "How's Dido?"

"Fine," Amara says, feeling awkward.

"You never give up, do you?" Victoria sighs.

"I would if there were another man," he says. "But there isn't." He looks at them nervously. "Is there?"

"No," Amara replies.

"We wanted to buy some wine for Cressa." Victoria hands over the pot. "How much?"

Nicandrus fills it then looks over his shoulder, checking Zoskales is out of sight. He shakes his head, the meaning plain. *No charge.*

"Thank you." Amara is touched by his gesture.

"Cressa was a good woman," he says. "We all miss her."

They leave the bar and walk down the street, bunched close together so they are side by side. "I don't understand Dido," Victoria says, gripping the pot. "He's a sweetheart. Imagine the *effort* he would make! She might finally have a decent time."

"She doesn't want to break her heart loving a man she can never have," Amara replies. Victoria says nothing. She knows they are both thinking of Felix.

The streets fill up as they wander toward the gate that leads to the town of Nola. Most of the traffic is going in the opposite direction, traders arriving to sell at the Forum or deliver stock to the shops. Those lucky enough to have a cart make a racket over the stones, others trudge along with goods piled up in baskets on their backs. A gaggle of squealing hogs run by, darting between the rolling wheels of their owner's wagon. Amara watches them scurry off up the street, tails frisking, as if eager for their own slaughter. Victoria nudges her, pointing at a mule cart rumbling up from the other direction. She holds Amara's arm and stands on tiptoe to get a better look, admiring its rolls of brightly colored fabric. The muleteer sees them and cracks his whip, laughing as they both jump.

Amara feels less safe here at the edge of town. There are so many strangers drifting into Pompeii only to vanish again like smoke. They wait for a line of wagons to pass, piled up with blocks of masonry, no doubt part of the town's never-ending building work, then walk under the high stone arch, crossing from the city of the living into the city of the dead. The road here is lined with enormous colorful tombs, some almost as big as the brothel where they work. Only the rich can afford to be remembered this close to the gate. In the doorways of their own graves, the once powerful dead stare out, their brightly painted statues watching the living pass by.

The she-wolves could never have bought Cressa a memorial here; even the smallest would be unimaginably expensive. Instead, Victoria and Amara walk further and further out of town, until the road widens and the crowds thin. They pass a group of mourners gathered round a marble urn in their finest clothes, burning offerings to appease the dead. Amara thinks of her own parents, of all she owes their shades but cannot give, and looks away.

It is Victoria who remembers the turning. A narrow road cutting through a gap between two monuments. The tombs become smaller the further they get from the main highway. They pass a large vineyard, its branches bare above the stone walls. Amara wonders if it might be one of the vineyards Pliny visited on his tour but supposes it isn't grand enough. She turns and looks toward Vesuvius, the mountain whose plants he wanted to study. Its sharp peak is shrouded in cloud.

Eventually, they reach the place they came for. The paupers' field. It stretches out in an ugly jumble of mounds and piles of rock and broken amphora necks. The last stick out from the earth like gaping mouths. There is a foul smell from the nearby dump, and Amara wonders, but does not ask, if that is where Victoria was found as a baby.

"How will we know where it is again?" Amara whispers, as if the unhappy dead might hear her. The only other mourner she can see is an old man, crying over a heap of freshly dug earth.

"I know the spot," Victoria says, picking her way confidently through the jagged field. She stops by a small tomb, barely more than a slab, though still grander than anything else nearby. At its base is a pile of stones. All that is left to remember Cressa. There had been no point in burying an amphora jar; they had no ashes to put in the bottom, no human remains to receive their gifts of wine. Victoria takes the flask Nicandrus gave her and pours the Sparrow's cheapest vintage over Cressa's stones. "She always did like a drink," she says.

They stand, staring at the spattered pile, remembering the dead woman. Amara thinks the stones look like all the kindnesses Cressa heaped up in her life, insignificant, yet touching the people closest to her. She tries not to remember Cressa's last day, the sight of her standing at the water's edge, watching the waves.

"How much?"

It's a thin, wheedling voice, right behind them. Both women jump. A man is hunched in a craven position, like a beggar, but something about his eyes frightens Amara.

"We don't have any wine to sell you," she says, pulling her cloak around herself.

"How much to suck me?" He paws at his crotch.

"Have some respect!" Victoria snaps, shooing him away. "Can't you see we're mourning?"

The man reaches out to her. "Take pity!" he whines.

Amara can feel Victoria's fear in the way she snatches her arm. They hurry over the field of ashes, back toward the narrow road. The man is too quick, darting in front. "Why won't you fuck me?" he pleads. "*Please* fuck me!"

They walk even faster, stepping over the amphoras' dead lips. The beggar keeps pressing closer, and his voice is getting deeper, losing its thin whine. Amara calls out to the old mourner, still stooped over his mound, but he ignores her. He must have heard the other man pleading for sex and has no interest in helping a couple of whores fend off a customer.

The beggar starts to run, and at first, Amara thinks her cries for help might have scared him off, but then she realizes he has only gone ahead to block the road. The stone walls of the vineyard are on one side of him, a large tomb on the other, making it almost impossible to get past. They edge closer, trying to decide on which side to break through.

"Come with me," he says, staring straight into Amara's eyes. He is like a snake, poised to strike. She stares back, too frightened to look away. He lunges forward, grabbing for her arm, but she anticipates his move. Victoria seizes her hand, and they run back to the field, heading for the old man. The beggar skirts round again, forcing them toward the tombs, toward the opening of another, unfamiliar path. There is nowhere else for them to go.

They flee, their pursuer close behind, driving them on through the necropolis. Amara trips, looks down and realizes grass is growing through the paving stones. With a flash of fear, she understands that this is not only a quiet road but a deserted one. He has trapped them. She gasps, lurching forward in panic and stumbles again, only just catching her footing.

"Keep going," Victoria yells.

Amara has no idea where they are. The tombs are getting closer together, harder to run between. She looks back and screams. The man is on her, catching her round the waist, dragging her over. She hits the ground hard. He straddles her body, a knife in his hand. Victoria grabs his arm, shouting, but he throws her wide. Amara sees her strike her head on the side of the tomb and fall, dazed, on the ground.

"Your master thinks he can do anything." The man has her by the throat, his ragged breathing hot in her face. She is so terrified she cannot move. "Covering his fucking tracks. As if Simo wouldn't find out in the end." He brings the knife closer, pointing it toward her eye. "This is for Drauca."

The sound of smashing pottery startles them both. Her attacker turns, just as Victoria plunges a shard deep into his neck. He claws at it, his hands drenched in blood, but Amara knows whatever he does, he is already dead. She stares at the clay buried in his throat then scrambles out from underneath, not wanting to be stained in the spatter. She stands back, watching, Victoria beside her, the remnants of Cressa's clay pot on the ground at their feet.

The man is shuddering where he lies. Death only takes a moment. Amara grabs Victoria's hand and they run.

39

"He who does not know how to protect himself does not know how to live"
—Herculaneum graffiti

They cower together behind a tomb, trying to get their breath back, to collect their thoughts, to make sense of what has happened. Victoria is in shock, shaking so badly Amara is afraid her friend's teeth will break from chattering. She holds her close to keep her warm.

"He was going to kill me," she whispers, rubbing Victoria's shoulders. "You saved my life. You saved me."

"I killed a man," Victoria whispers, the horror of it slowly sinking in. "I killed him! I'm a murderer!"

"Nobody is ever going to know," Amara replies. "Nobody will find out. You're safe. We're both safe." She thinks of the man's body lying on the ground and feels a sense of calm. He is dead. All that matters now is avoiding suspicion. She inspects their clothes, peers at Victoria's face, wipes a hand on her own cheeks, then checks her fingers. They are both lucky not to have more blood on them. She gathers mud in her hands, rubbing it over any red spots she can see on their cloaks. "Is there anything on me?" She turns her face, as if asking her friend to check her make-up. Victoria shakes her head. "Good. Then we should head back."

"We have to tell Felix." Victoria is still trembling. "Did you hear what he said?"

"That Felix killed Drauca."

"Do you think he did?" There is desperation in Victoria's eyes. It is one thing to suspect the man you love might be capable of murder, another to know it for sure.

"I think so," Amara says. Victoria turns away, too upset to speak. "I owe you everything," she says, taking Victoria's hand. Her skin is icy cold. "And so does Felix. Without you, he would have no warning of what is coming."

"How are we going to get home? What if somebody remembers us?"

"Nobody will. We are nobody. We'll just head back into town slowly, keep our heads down. It will be days before the body is discovered. If it ever is."

Victoria stands up, gripping the tomb to steady herself. "Some benefits to being worthless, I guess."

They pick their way slowly through the necropolis, not walking back the way they came. It takes a long time to find the road again, and when they do, it's an even longer trudge. Victoria is jumpy, but Amara grips her hand, stops her walking too fast. They pull their hoods up, as if to keep out the cold, half hiding their faces. Neither of them says a word.

By the time they reach the brothel, after what has felt like the longest walk of their lives, both women are ready to drop from exhaustion. Amara raps on Felix's door.

"What?" Paris glowers at them both through the crack.

Amara slams her hand on the wood. "Don't mess me around today. This is important."

He stands back to let them in. "But Felix is with a client!"

"Then tell him we're waiting for him in the bedroom."

Amara feels as if she is standing outside herself, watching Victoria recount what has happened. She has never seen anyone cry so much. Victoria sobs her way through the murder, and all the while, Felix is holding her, kissing her face, pressing her hands to warm them. There is a tenderness to him Amara could never have imagined. She watches, a pain in her chest that she cannot name. He has never been like that with her, not even when she told him about Cressa, when she would have done anything to be comforted. Nobody but Menander has ever held her the way Felix is holding Victoria. The thought upsets her. She is not sure whether it makes Felix worse, if he is capable of love.

He looks up at her over Victoria's bent head, the familiar coldness in his eyes. It is as if he has stepped outside himself too, in order to talk to her. "Tell me again what he said about Simo."

"He said you won't get away with it. You didn't cover your tracks. Simo discovered what happened." She pauses, remembering, as if the violence happened to somebody else. "Then he held a knife to my eye and said, *This is for Drauca.*"

"And nobody saw?"

"No. The body is in a deserted place. There was only one old man at the pauper's field, and we didn't even go back that way. I covered any trace of blood on us that I could see." She shrugs. "Who would notice a couple of women?"

"You don't seem too disturbed by watching a man die. Are you very sure he is dead?"

"She hit him here." Amara gestures at her own neck. "Nobody survives a blow like that. Even if I had never read a book on anatomy, I would know he's dead." Victoria cries out again, weeping against Felix. He holds her head to his chest, rocking her back and forth. Amara stares at them both, unable to understand Victoria's sense of guilt, irritated that she is still crying over such a worthless man. "He tried to kill me, and now he's dead. There's nothing to be upset about."

"You will feel it later," Felix says. "Everyone does, the first time. Even if you're a bitch with stone for a heart."

"What are you going to do?" Amara asks. "We're all at risk now. All of us." She is still too afraid of Felix to express her anger, but she feels it. *Because of you*, she wants to add. *We're at risk because of you.*

"First, you don't tell anyone. Not even Dido. And if you value her life"—he strokes the sobbing Victoria—"you will never mention it again, even to each other." Amara nods. She knows the killing ties all three of them together, her blood debt to Victoria, the secret they now share. It is not a bond she wants to have. "As for Simo, I can take care of him."

"We can't afford to leave it."

"No," he says. "We can't."

"I didn't mean to *kill* him." Victoria looks round, desperation on her face. "I just wanted him to stop. I didn't want anyone to die."

"I know," Felix says, rocking her again. He kisses Victoria's forehead, whispering into her hair. "You were very brave."

Amara looks at her friend, twined around their master like a needy child, unrecognizable from the strong woman she knows. Is this who Victoria really is? The thought makes Amara angry. "It's nothing to *cry* about," she says, her voice loud. "He fucking *deserved* it."

"Shut your mouth!" Felix shouts. She sees Victoria shrink from his anger, even though it is not directed at her. He strides over to Amara, taking hold of her shoulders, shoving his face into hers. "She just saved your life. Have some fucking gratitude. Not every woman is a heartless *bitch* like you." He lets go of her then scoops Victoria up again, as if protecting her from Amara.

She does not wait to be thrown out but walks from the room. In the corridor, her legs are unsteady. She manages to make it to the storeroom, collapses on her bed of sacks in the corner. Her sense of calm is fracturing. She thinks of Cressa's pot, all those pieces on the ground. The shard in the man's neck, the blood. Feelings are returning to Amara, coming back like the incoming tide, bringing terror with them.

She grips the sacks, feels the rough fabric against her fingers, tries to imagine burying her fear, shoving it under. She doesn't want to feel afraid; she doesn't want to feel anything. Tomorrow, she will see Rufus, sit with him in Drusilla's lovely home, laugh, chatter about the house they will share. She will not be a woman who nearly died, who was held powerless with a knife to her eye. It will be as if it never happened.

Calm begins to settle back over her heart, like the ice on Balbina's pool. Amara exhales, relaxing her fingers, letting go of the fabric. Nobody has their arms around her, but it does not matter. She does not need Felix, or anyone else, to comfort her. Every fear can be overcome if she only tries hard enough.

Amara does not move from the storeroom for the rest of the day. She is supposed to earn extra money on the days when Rufus pays for her, but Felix does not insist she go out. Night falls, and she is still sitting curled up in the same spot. Paris tries to goad her, imagining she must be jealous at Victoria staying the night, at the huge favor their master is showing a rival, but Amara stares ahead, as if she hasn't heard him. Somehow, she sleeps.

The next morning feels as if she is still dreaming. She forces herself to go downstairs, spends time with Dido at the baths, listens to her as she pours out her fears about Ipstilla and Telethusa. It is the second time the Spanish girls have been booked by Egnatius while she and Amara are left behind. Amara can see how upset Dido is but somehow cannot reach her. Even though they are sitting side by side, it feels like she is a long distance away.

"Are you alright?" Dido asks. "Was it Felix?"

"Yes," Amara says. Dido looks so worried that Amara wants to tell her what really happened, wants to warn her to be careful, but she cannot betray Victoria. Besides, it is not a lie. Felix is the cause. If he had not killed Drauca, she would never have been attacked. She begs Dido to stay close to Britannica, pretending it is for Cressa, but in reality, because she hopes the Briton will keep them both safe.

When her friends go fishing, she goes back to hide in the storeroom. Even if Felix charges Rufus double today, she cannot bring herself to pick up any men. The thought of approaching strangers takes her back to the necropolis, the knife, the man's hands at her throat. How would she know if any of her customers wanted to kill her?

The effort of getting through the day is such a strain, Philos notices her distress when he collects her. At a safe distance from the brothel, he offers his arm.

"Do you need a moment?" he asks. "Just to collect yourself?" She nods. They cross over to a less crowded patch of the pavement, and she rests her back against the wall. "You're alright," he says to her. "I know it's not easy."

"Thank you," she says, breathing out slowly, trying to let go of the fear. She turns to Philos. There is nothing but kindness in his gray eyes. The warmth of him, standing close to her, is comforting. "I'm so grateful to Rufus."

"I know," he says. "And I know how hard it all is. I've been there myself." He glances back along the street where they came from. "I don't mean I worked in a brothel," he adds, lowering his voice. "But I don't think I felt safe for a minute when I was younger."

Amara tightens her grip on his arm. "You don't have to tell me," she says. "I understand."

"Who'd be a slave, eh? When you're young, they fuck you, and when you're old, they fuck you over."

"Rufus values you though."

"Yes, he does," Philos looks away. "I can't complain now."

"The man who . . ." Amara stops, not wanting to say the word, not wanting to humiliate Philos. "It wasn't Rufus's father, was it?"

"Not Hortensius, no. He's not interested in boys. *His* father, on the other hand, was very interested."

Amara wonders how old Philos is, perhaps ten years older than her, maybe a little more. He is nice looking, she realizes, though she has never really noticed him that way. When he was young, he must have been striking. The thought of him ever living in fear, unable to defend himself, makes her angry. That Rufus's grandfather was responsible is even worse. "What's Hortensius like?" Philos says nothing, and she realizes he doesn't want to be disloyal. "You can trust me," she says. "But I'm also not offended if you don't."

"I wish you had asked me earlier," Philos says, rubbing a hand over his face. He looks at her, obviously torn. "I'm not meant to tell you, but Rufus is bringing him along tonight. To meet you. It was supposed to be a surprise. Hortensius insisted Rufus keep it quiet; he wants to see you 'as you really are,' catch you on the hop, so to speak."

"Oh," Amara replies, not liking the sound of him. "I suppose he wants to look after his son."

"If you were *my* wife," Philos says, surprising her that he would refer to her in such a way. "I wouldn't leave you alone with him. Not if I could help it."

"I'll be careful," Amara says, conscious that she is still holding his arm, that perhaps she should let go. "Thank you."

Hortensius looks so like his son, Amara has to stop herself from staring. Even the mannerisms, the exaggerated hand gestures so particular to Rufus, have their double in his father. She is grateful Drusilla is part of the gathering, that she can, at times, take away the heat of his attention. It is the only obvious difference between father and son. Where Rufus is kind and lacking in guile, Hortensius seems shrewd and calculating.

"Rufus tells me you helped the admiral with his research," he says to her. "You must be highly educated. Was it your first master who taught you?"

"It was my father," Amara says. "When I was free. He was a physician in Attica."

"I *told* you all this," Rufus says, looking flustered.

Hortensius throws his hands up, inviting her to laugh with him at his son. "You told me she was a concubine in Aphidnai!"

"That was later," Rufus insists.

"Nothing wrong with being a concubine," Hortensius says, turning to Drusilla and kissing her hand. Drusilla smiles at him, as if charmed. But Amara knows Drusilla is so skilled at hiding her feelings, she could wish Hortensius dead, and he would never know it. "So your father was a doctor. Then you were *hurled* into tragedy and ended up a heartbroken whore. Is this right?" Amara inclines her head, not liking his sarcasm, even though it is delivered with a smile. "You seem rather young for your master to have become bored."

"His wife was not happy."

"If the fool couldn't control his women, it's as well you left," Hortensius says, as if she had any choice in the matter. "Do you dance? Play music? Sing?"

"I told you . . ." Rufus begins.

"But I'm asking *her*."

"My father taught me . . ."

"Oh, come now!" Hortensius interrupts her, laughing. "You know that's not what I meant. I'm sure your father didn't teach you how to perform in male company. Not if he really *was* a doctor. What did your first master teach you?"

"I learned the lyre at my father's house," Amara says, ignoring the insinuation she is a liar. "Then as a concubine I learned a number of songs by Sappho and other Greek poets. I have continued my musical education in Pompeii."

"Musical education!" Hortensius raises his eyebrows, amused. "At least you have some wit."

"Perhaps you would allow us to play for you?" Drusilla says, her silk tunic rustling as she rises. She looks at Hortensius sidelong, as if she finds him irresistible.

"Why not." Hortensius leans back on the couch, gazing at her.

Amara does not have her lyre, but Drusilla beckons her over to the harp. "I will play Sappho's 'Hymn to Aphrodite,'" she murmurs. "But you sing it alone."

"Thank you," Amara whispers, grateful she will not have to compete with Drusilla's superior voice. She sways to the music, using the graceful hand gestures she learned at Chremes's house, pouring her heart into the song. Seeing Hortensius watch her, appraising her, it is almost like being back before Chremes, as if all the many changes in her life as a slave have brought her full circle to the point where she started. She thinks of Philos. *If you were my wife, I wouldn't leave you alone with him.* Rufus is also watching, beaming with pride. It does not reassure her. How long before he starts to see her through his father's eyes?

"Very well," Hortensius says to Rufus, when she has finished singing. "She is delightful. You win." He turns back to Amara. "But I really don't understand all this nonsense about renting a place. When he's bought you, you can just join the family household."

"Really father, not now." Rufus is crimson, looking anxiously at Amara.

"Fine, fine. Have your little romance." Hortensius sighs. He shakes his head at Drusilla and Amara. "Boys. I cannot *imagine* how you pair put up with them."

"Rufus is the kindest man I have ever met," Amara replies.

"I've no doubt he is," Hortensius says with a snort. "Well, I suppose I should let you all enjoy your night of young love." Everyone rises with him. Hortensius goes to Drusilla, kissing her. "Delighted, as ever." He turns to Amara but rather than kiss her too, he runs his hands down the length of her body, as if they were in the slave market. She is so shocked she cannot speak. "Very fine." He smiles at her, though there is no warmth in his eyes. "Not a bad investment at all." Nobody fills the silence. "Aren't you going to show me out, boy?" Rufus hurries over and leads his father from the room. He doesn't look at Amara.

When the men have left, Drusilla makes the sign of the evil eye. "What did he mean?" she hisses. "You told me Rufus was going to free you!"

"That's what he said!" Amara is shaking.

Drusilla pinches her arm. "Don't get upset! Don't! This is too important. Use your head. Make it as hard as possible for Rufus not to do what he promised, use his guilt, whatever you can. You cannot let him believe you will be satisfied as a slave!" She steps back as Rufus returns, smiling serenely, as if she and Amara have been exchanging pleasantries. "I find I am a little tired," she says, yawning. "I hope you don't mind if I abandon you both?"

They watch Drusilla leave, her walk effortlessly languid, even though Amara knows she isn't tired at all. "That went rather well, I thought," Rufus says. He leans in to kiss her.

Amara pushes him off. "What did he mean, that I could join your *family household*?"

"That's just what he's like," Rufus says. "He knows about the place I've rented. He'll come round."

"Does he know you will free me?"

Rufus doesn't look at her, but she can see the blush creep up to his hairline. "Would it be so terrible if I didn't?" He takes both her hands, pulling her closer. "We'd still be together. You wouldn't be at the brothel, that's the important part, isn't it?"

"I cannot believe that you don't understand the difference," Amara says, withdrawing her hands from his.

"How often have you told me you can see how hard it was for me, to lose everything in Aphidnai. I lost *my self* when I was sold. Why would you keep me a slave, if it is in your power to set me free? Why?"

"It's not so simple. My father isn't keen on the idea. I don't know that I can defy him on this." Rufus sits down heavily on the couch. "Freeing you . . . I would have to give you the family name. It doesn't just belong to me."

Amara sits beside him. She can still feel Hortensius's hands on her body. She thinks of Philos, of Chremes, of all that happens to slaves who become familiar objects in their masters' houses. Rufus puts his arms around her, kissing her softly on the forehead, the cheek, her lips.

"I promise you, if you belong to me, I will never let anyone hurt you. I promise."

40

"He who hates life easily scorns god"
—Pompeii graffiti

Victoria and Amara wait in Felix's bedroom. Neither imagine they have been summoned for sex. Victoria sits cross-legged on the bed, as if she belongs there, but Amara doesn't want to touch it, doesn't want to remember the night she spent there with Felix. She perches on a stool instead.

"It's about Simo, isn't it?" Victoria whispers. "It must be."

"I thought he was going to take care of that himself," Amara says. "I don't see why he needs either of us."

"He told me I saved *his* life, as well as yours," Victoria replies. "He's never been like that with me before." She looks drunk on love, completely unaware that Felix's sudden devotion is likely to be as much manipulation as genuine. A warm-up act for whatever horrible job he has lined up for them both now. "He said no woman has ever shown him greater loyalty than me."

Amara thinks about her own deception, the secret loan with Balbina, her plotting with Rufus. It's impossible to imagine why anyone would want to be loyal to a master, still less to Felix. She tries not to let Victoria's stupidity make her angry. "He *should* be grateful to you," she says. "If he had any decency, he would free you for what you've done." Victoria's face falls and she almost regrets her spitefulness. They both know that's not going to happen.

Felix opens the door. Amara flinches, hoping he wasn't listening, but he looks distracted. He doesn't waste time with greetings. "We can't wait any longer," he says, sitting down on the bed next to Victoria. "Simo will have given up waiting for his man. We need to strike now, before he does. Make sure he's finished."

"What do you need us to do?" Victoria asks, as if she *wants* to be asked to put herself in danger.

"Some friends of mine will take care of the bar. And of Simo. I need you two to act as a distraction and keep watch."

"Keep watch on what?" Amara asks.

"Paris will be keeping watch too," Felix says, ignoring her question. "He's not as recognizable to Simo as Thraso or Gallus."

"Does Paris know about the necropolis?"

"No. Nobody knows," Felix says. "Safer that way." Victoria looks at him gratefully, and he rests a hand on her knee. "You will have to be veiled. Pick up a few men opposite the bar, that should distract some attention."

"You want us to fuck men in the street?" Amara says. "On our own? No protection?"

"Paris will be around."

"But he's not there to look after us though, is he!" Amara protests. "He'll be watching the bar."

"There will be two of you," Felix says. "I don't see the problem."

"What are you going to do to the bar? I don't want to go if we don't know."

Felix loses his temper. "Nobody is offering you a choice," he shouts at her. "Since when did you tell me what to do? If I want to sell you on the fucking street, or in the brothel, it's not for you to argue."

"Please," Victoria says, looking imploringly at her. "Please, we have to. What if Simo attacks us again?"

Amara looks at the pair of them, sitting together like a married couple, united against her. She thinks of all she owes Victoria and knows there is no way out, even if she weren't bound to Felix. She nods.

"Better if you both stay upstairs until tonight," he says. He looks from one woman to the other, his expression sly. "You can go to the storeroom now," he says to Amara. "Leave us."

She hurries out, not wanting to see Felix push Victoria back on the bed, and closes the door. Paris is outside on the balcony, scrubbing the floor with noticeably more vigor than usual. She tries to step clear of the suds and give him space, but he stops her, his thin face eager. "Did Felix tell you?" he says, getting to his feet and glancing up and down the corridor. "Did he tell you he's sending *me* on a job? Not Thraso. Not Gallus. Me."

Amara nods. She thinks about Felix's reasoning, that Paris is less noticeable. No doubt he is also more expendable. She has little affection for her roommate but also knows that Fabia's unhappy son is going to be solely responsible for her safety tonight. "I told you he would start to use you more," she says, flattering him. "It's a big job he's given you."

"You'll both have to do as I say," he says, not sure if she is mocking him. "I'm the man; I'll be in charge."

"Of course." Amara bows her head slightly to show him she understands. Paris swallows, flicking his eyes to Felix's room, and she can see that for all his bravado he is also afraid. "You don't have to do anything you will regret though," she says, thinking again of Fabia, of all that the young man means to his mother. "You don't have to put yourself in danger."

Paris draws himself up to stand even taller, throwing his shoulders back like Gallus. "It's what I was born for," he says. "You wouldn't understand. You're just a woman."

The day drags, but Amara still wants it to go on longer, doesn't want darkness to come. She is not sure exactly what Felix has planned for Simo but knows he must intend to kill him. How else is he going to end the feud? Amara thinks about how close she is to leaving this place, the Saturnalia is only a few days away. She cannot die *now*, not when her escape is all but guaranteed. She thinks about trying to smuggle out a message to Rufus, or even Philos, begging one of them to come and get her. But who could she possibly trust to deliver it? Paris would see her if she tried to sneak out. And Felix's rage would be terrible.

It is Victoria who finally comes to collect her from the storeroom. She is swathed in a veil, like a married woman.

Though it looks more like a shroud. Amara's heart starts to race with fear.

"I don't think we should do this," she says, not wanting to touch the veil Victoria is holding out to her. "What if somebody from Simo's bar recognizes us? What if Maria or Attice come out?"

"He promised me we would be safe," Victoria says, throwing the material over Amara's head. "And anyway, what choice do we have? Let's just get it over with."

"But won't Simo be watching the brothel? Won't one of his spies see us leaving like this?"

"Paris is outside the door," Victoria replies, fussing with the cloth, making sure Amara is covered properly. "He will check it's clear and then open it. Felix said when that happens, we walk as quick as we can, up toward the well on the corner then round the back way to Simo's bar."

Amara wonders if Victoria is enjoying being in Felix's confidence. The thought makes her bitter. She has to remind herself that she owes her friend her life, even if Victoria is now making her risk it all over again.

It is dark on the street, made worse by the material over her face that obscures what little light remains. They shuffle along, their hands to the wall, feeling their way. Paris is supposed to be following, but there's no sign of him or his lamp to light the path. They skirt a small group at the well, somehow avoiding attention, and head further into a less familiar part of town.

"I don't even know where the bar is," Amara whispers. "I don't know where we're going!"

"Felix told me the way several times," Victoria replies. "I'm sure I can get us there. And we don't really have to keep watch; we're more of a distraction."

"Isn't that worse?" Amara asks. Victoria doesn't answer.

Simo's bar is sitting in a pool of lamplight. A hanging bronze Priapus casts its sickly glow over the door. Simo must have repaired the place since Felix's earlier attack. It seems full, several drinkers standing on the street in spite of the cold. Amara finds she is too scared to walk any closer. "Come *on*," Victoria hisses, pulling at her arm. "Let's just do this and get home."

They stand together, sheltering in a small archway across the road. From the smell, Amara suspects they are not the first whores to work this spot. Victoria hitches her cloak and toga up, showing her bare legs, and after a pause, Amara does the same. At first, nobody notices, then a couple of the drinkers spot them. They point and laugh. A couple of men walk across.

"What's with the covered faces?" one asks. "Too ugly to see?" Amara takes a step back. Both men reek of alcohol.

"We're married," Victoria says, her voice a plaintive whine. "We need to feed the children."

"That's what every woman says," the man replies, hitching her cloak up further.

A third man passes by, stopping to see what's going on. "Leave some cunt for me."

Amara recognizes the voice. She squints through the weave of her veil. It's the man with the white scar, the one she saw at the Palaestra with Felix, and again at the bar. He turns and saunters across the street, chatting with the remaining men outside, pointing at the women, urging them on. There's laughter. The drinkers head over and then they are surrounding her and Victoria, jeering, yelling encouragement. Amara begins to panic.

One of the men already has her backed against the wall, pulling at her clothes. She looks over his shoulder, trying to see between the faces of the baying onlookers. Everything is gray and distorted through the fabric. The man with the white scar is standing alone outside Simo's bar. She sees him reach up, take down the fiery hanging Priapus, swiftly light a torch from its flame. He starts setting fire to the timber frame of the building, waiting a moment until it starts to take hold. Then he flings the lamp through the door and runs off down the street.

At first, the men surrounding her aren't distracted by the noise. Then customers pour out of the bar, yelling, pointing up at the burning building. The drunks finally start to realize what is happening. The man crushing her against the stone is dragged off by a friend, his anger at being interrupted quickly turning to alarm. Victoria and Amara are left alone as their tormentors scatter, adding to the chaos.

"We should leave now," Amara says. "Quickly!"

"Felix asked me to make sure Paris finished the job," Victoria says, grabbing her arm to stop her escaping. "Simo can't leave here alive."

Amara feels caught, too afraid to run back blindly on her own, even more terrified to stay. She clings on to Victoria. They huddle back into the hollow of the arch, watching. In the light of the flames, the gaggle of shouting men are more hindrance than help. Some rush back with water fetched from a nearby well, but a few buckets are not going to save the bar. She notices another familiar figure, the weaselly man from Felix's protection racket. And Paris is there. She would recognize his scrawny form anywhere, even though his hood is up. They are both hanging around the doorway, looking like idle gawpers but, no doubt, checking who is coming out. It must be almost empty inside, the roar from the flames is getting louder, the heat oppressive even from the opposite side of the road.

Amara has never seen Simo before, but she knows it must be him from the way Paris and the other man take a step forward. He is coughing, almost bent double from the smoke. Paris grabs him, as if to help, but shortly afterward, Simo collapses in his arms. Paris lays him gently on the ground. Others rush forward. Paris edges back, until he's at the fringes of the crowd. Then he turns and walks quickly in the direction of the well.

"We have to leave now," Amara says. "He must have stabbed him. It's going to get worse."

They don't run but walk as fast as they dare. By now, people from the neighboring buildings have spilled out onto the street, trying to stop the spread of the fire. A woman is screaming from an upstairs room. Sparks swirl in the heat, Amara is afraid their cloaks might catch fire. Then there's a noise like thunder, a terrible crack as the roof of the bar collapses, the upward rush of the flames. She looks back at the inferno in horror. Anybody still inside will not have survived.

Victoria tugs her arm, and they keep walking, leaving the light and the noise, slipping back into the darkness.

41

"The pair of us were here, dear friends forever"
—Pompeii graffiti

Felix keeps Victoria upstairs with him after the fire, moving her into his room. A reward for helping him kill Simo. He barely acknowledges Amara's role. She tells herself it doesn't matter, that his coldness cannot hurt her if she hates him. It's harder to watch Victoria, to see the way she opens up like a flower that has finally found the sun. In the mornings, Amara can hear her singing for Felix, imagines how she must be lying in his arms, gazing at him, pouring out all the love in her heart. The thought makes her furious.

Amara finds it easier than she imagined to say nothing to the other women about what happened. When they go to the baths together, she makes up a lie about her and Victoria being used to entertain clients at a bar, surprised at how quickly the tale trips from her tongue. Even if she didn't find lying so easy, the bar story is soon forgotten, buried by the far more interesting gossip that Felix seems to have chosen Victoria as some sort of *wife*.

When news of Simo's death finally reaches them through Gallus, Amara still gives nothing away, feigning shock to match the rest. But although she can bury her feelings in the daytime, at night she struggles to sleep, her heart racing, every fibre taut with fear. Her body relives the terror her mind cannot. She knows that Paris is suffering too, hears him weeping in the dark. But in the morning, he always refuses to speak to her. Whatever guilt he might be feeling, he is clearly determined to bury it.

On the third day after the fire, Felix sends for her. She follows Paris to their master's study, waits while he pushes open the door. Inside, Victoria is perched on Felix's lap, sitting with him behind the desk, her arms around his neck. She drops them as soon as Amara walks in, embarrassed, and Amara loves her for that, knowing Victoria doesn't want to make her feel small.

"Time for you to go back to the brothel," Felix says. Amara bows her head, goes to walk back out again, but he stops her. "Not you," he says. "Time for *you* to go." He tips Victoria from his knee. She grabs the desk, only just managing to save herself from falling flat on the floor. For a moment, both women think he is joking. Then they realize he isn't.

Amara knows something has broken in Victoria then; she sees it in her face. Victoria does not beg or even say goodbye. She turns and walks out of the room, her eyes dry, not acknowledging either of them.

When she has gone, Amara and Felix are left looking at one another. "I missed you," he says. She cannot reply. For the first time since she has known him, Amara senses that Felix does not know what he wants to say. He gestures at the pile of tablets heaped up on her old table. "Who else do I have to do my accounts?"

She sits down, still without speaking, and opens the first tablet.

By the eve of the Saturnalia, Rufus has still not told her when he will buy her. The strain of waiting and worrying is so great she is afraid she will break down and beg the next time she sees him. She knows there are no depths she would not sink to, not if it means escaping from Felix. Even a lifetime under the same roof as Hortensius.

She sits at a table in the Sparrow, drinking with her friends, while they discuss what presents they can afford. The whole town is heaving, and street sellers ram the pavements, trying to shift a few more trinkets before the festival starts.

"I can't wait to see what Gallus has bought me!" Beronice cries, giving Dido a smacking kiss on the cheek. She has had a lot more wine than usual. "Three whole days with him! Oh! Just think of it!"

"One more night, then we get a rest from customers," Dido says with a sigh. "Are we buying something for Britannica? We ought to."

"She do nothing," Ipstilla huffs.

"That's not really the spirit of the Saturnalia," Beronice says, frowning. "I don't mind chipping in. Though I don't know what she'd like."

A knife, probably, Amara thinks. But she doesn't suggest it.

"Getting *me* anything, girls?" Zoskales calls from the bar. He is in an excellent mood, no doubt looking forward to a day off from his customers too.

"A kiss if you're lucky!" Beronice shrieks. Everyone laughs, apart from Victoria. Beronice notices her silence. "Maybe Felix will get you something," she says kindly. Even though Victoria has teased her relentlessly about Gallus for the past year, Beronice has been nothing but supportive over her friend's heartbreak. *Can you imagine*, she had said to Amara after Victoria returned to the brothel, *the pain of thinking a man's going to marry you and then he sends you packing! What a shit!*

"He always gives us a denarius each," Victoria replies. "I don't care anyway. Fuck him."

"How should we do this?" Amara says to Beronice. "Maybe Dido and I can buy for you, Britannica and Victoria, then you and Victoria buy for Dido and me." She turns to the Spanish girls. "And do you two want to buy for each other, or do you want a surprise?"

"We buy," Telethusa says emphatically, looking askance at Amara's cheap wooden beads, her token present from Rufus. Clearly, she doesn't trust the other women's taste.

"No more than five asses each," Beronice says. "Let's not go mad. Then we'll split the costs of it all afterward."

They finish the last of their wine, taking their time, then part ways to go shopping. Amara and Dido stroll toward the Forum. "What *would* Britannica like?" Dido says. "She's not going to want beads or anything pretty."

"I can think of something," Amara replies. "There was a hawker selling amulets of gladiators' blood. To pass on their courage."

It takes them a while to find the seller; he must have moved since the last time Amara saw him. It's hard to walk in the crush; everywhere, people are jostling at stalls, haggling loudly to get a better price. It seems most of Pompeii has left their gift buying until the last moment. Eventually, Amara spots the man with his gruesome trophies, a range of goods soaked in the blood of gladiators killed in the arena. They range in price, depending on the fame of the dead. The women can only afford an unknown fighter, killed on his first appearance, though Amara tries to haggle for something better. There is nothing pretty about the leather amulet they choose, engraved with a roughly drawn sword. Amara suspects Britannica will like it.

Their enthusiasm for shopping has been exhausted from walking round and round searching for the amulet seller, but at least the other women are easier to buy for. A cheap hair clip for Victoria, some ankle beads for Beronice.

"I'm so happy that Rufus is buying you," Dido says, as they start walking back home. "But I'm going to miss you so much."

"I don't know for sure that he will," Amara says. "He hasn't given me a day. I don't understand why he hasn't done it already, if he really means to."

"Perhaps he wants to make a grand gesture during the festival," Dido says, taking her arm. "That would be very like him."

Dido is so kind, wanting to reassure her, but Amara can tell she is upset. She hates herself for not being more considerate; she should have paid greater attention to Dido's feelings over the past few days. She would be desperate if their roles were reversed. "I will do everything I can to get you out," she says. "Everything. I promise. I love you. You are everything to me."

"I love you too," Dido replies. She is on the verge of tears.

Dido is the only person Amara has told about her plans, but even she doesn't know where the new house is. Amara had worried about the risk of them being followed, but now she realizes this will leave Dido with no way of finding her, no way of leaving a message. "Do you want to know where it is? The house, I mean," she says, her voice quiet, even though it's unlikely anyone is listening. "Then if Rufus keeps his word, you can visit." Dido nods.

They walk single file, Amara leading the way across town. She remembers the first time Philos brought her to the house. She has never been down the road in daylight. Even on the eve of the Saturnalia it is relatively quiet. Living here will mark a big change from the brothel's noisy crossroads. The thought of escaping brings her a rush of excitement, and when they stand outside the tall building with its golden doorframe, she finds herself believing that life might be kind after all. She raps on the wood, not expecting anyone to answer, but Philos opens it. He is astonished to see her.

"Come in!" he exclaims, hurrying them both inside. He shuts the door behind them. "Is anything wrong? Are you alright?"

"I wanted Dido to know where to find me," Amara says. "If Rufus really does mean for me to stay here."

Philos gestures at the atrium behind him. Vitalio is staggering past with a table. "I think you can see that he does. Has he not said anything?"

Amara shakes her head. "I didn't like to presume."

"You've no need to worry," Philos replies. "He has every intention of buying you. Don't distress yourself."

"I told you it was fine," Dido says, smiling at her. "And what a beautiful place this is!"

Vitalio walks back into the atrium, now relieved of his burden. He scowls at Amara. "Let's see how long *this one* lasts," he shouts, stomping up the stairs.

Amara stares after him. "What did he mean by that?"

"Oh, nothing. You know Vitalio; he's always bad-tempered." Philos smiles, but he looks uncomfortable. Vitalio's outburst was too extreme for this to be a reasonable explanation, and they all know it.

"No," Amara says, feeling nervous. "He meant something in particular. What did he mean? Please tell me. Please."

Philos does not look at her. "Rufus was fond of Vitalio's daughter for a while."

"His *daughter*? Is she part of the family household?" Dido takes Amara's hand, trying to lead her away, to calm her down, but Amara shakes her off. "*Tell me.*" She stares at Philos, willing him to obey, and the sadness in his gray eyes strikes her with fear.

"You've met her a few times," he says. "It's Faustilla, the serving girl."

At first, Amara cannot imagine who he means, the only maid she can remember is a shy young thing who never spoke. "But it can't be the girl I met; she's so *young*," she says. "And Rufus never seemed to notice her. A few times she was even there when . . ." Amara puts her hand over her mouth, too shocked to continue. Dido puts an arm round her, and this time, she doesn't push her away.

"Rufus is no different to any young man of his class," Philos says, sounding a little defensive of his master. "You know they *all* sleep with their slaves. Whatever happened between them was never any reflection on his feelings for you."

"That's not what I'm upset about!" Amara says, although it's a lie, because she had believed Rufus was different. She thinks of his disarming smile, the way he has always seemed so beguilingly sincere. The way he tells her he loves her. "I'm upset about the girl," she insists. "No wonder Vitalio hates me. His daughter having to serve the woman who took her place. Did she love him?" Philos does not reply, but he doesn't need to. "*Of course* she loved him. She must have thought he was the kindest man she'd ever met." Amara thinks of the way Felix treats Victoria, his deliberate cruelty. But Rufus is no less cruel to Faustilla, even if he doesn't mean to be. "Had it even finished between them when Rufus met me?"

"Amara," Philos says, his voice low, "just remember you have to live with my answers. And so do I."

"He's still sleeping with her," she says, understanding him. "Of course he is. You must think I'm an idiot."

"I don't think that at all." Philos has the studiously blank expression of the slave who is habituated to hiding his feelings. She remembers what he said to her when they were alone. *When you're young, they fuck you; when you're old, they fuck you over.*

"Well," she says to Dido, with false cheer. "He didn't rent her a house. So hopefully, I have a *little* time before I'm serving wine to his next mistress."

"Just think of Felix," Dido says. "Think how much safer you will be here. It's paradise in comparison."

"She's right," Philos agrees, eager to repair the damage. "And I truly believe he loves you. I've *never* seen him do this much for any other woman. Not even close."

Amara thinks of Hortensius, how he hurt her, insulted her, and yet Rufus said nothing. "The love a master has for his slave," she says, looking at Philos who quails at the bitterness in her voice. "I suppose it's as much as any of us can hope to build a life on."

42

"The Saturnalia, the best of days!"
—Catullus, Poem 14

Felix's study is crammed, his entire motley household of whores and thugs spread around on various stools and blankets like Pompeii's most peculiar family. Felix himself sits on his desk, an unlikely paterfamilias, while Thraso and Gallus serve Paris and the women with sweet buns and wine. According to the true Saturnalian spirit, it should be Felix serving everyone, but nobody questions this departure from tradition.

"I'll have another, maybe two more!" Fabia declares, ransacking Gallus's basket for a bigger helping. He sighs but doesn't push her scrawny arms away.

"That's enough!" Paris snaps. Fabia recoils from her son, dropping the fifth bun back into the basket.

"Be nice to your fucking mother," Felix says. "Surely you can manage not to be a complete shit for *one day*?"

Paris hands the bun back to Fabia, his cheeks flaming. Then he gets up and goes to sit on the opposite side of the room.

"Presents!" Ipstilla says, clapping her hands together. "Is time for presents, yes?"

They all go through the performance of Felix's gift giving, passing round a purse, taking out a denarius each. He quickly gets bored of all the thanks, waving it away. By the time it is Amara's turn to take the money, he isn't even looking. She is sitting in the corner with Dido, her stomach too churned up to eat the sweet pastry. They told Philos the whole brothel would be heading to the Forum in the late afternoon. She cannot relax, wondering if today is the day Rufus will buy her. Every moment, she is expecting a knock at the door, dreading the thought it won't come.

"Now for the rest of them!" Beronice gets out the small bundle of gifts, all wrapped in a blanket. Her cheeks are shining from the wine, and she looks by far the happiest person in the room. Gallus sits down beside her, getting as close as possible, childlike in his eagerness. *Perhaps he does love her after all*, Amara thinks. Or maybe he just wants a present. "Not yet! Don't be greedy," Beronice says, kissing him.

Amara glances over at Felix, but he seems completely unconcerned by this outburst of affection. She remembers what Cressa said at the Vinalia, that a master never minds a love which keeps his servants obedient. The thought of her dead friend, and her short brutal life, hurts Amara's heart.

"Right, this one's yours Fabia," Beronice says, handing her some coins wrapped in a piece of cloth. They had decided the penniless old woman would prefer five asses in cash rather than some overpriced trinket. "This is yours, this is for you . . ." Beronice hands out all the other gifts, enjoying her role.

Amara unwraps her gift from its scrap of cloth. It's a cheap hair clip, not unlike the one she and Dido bought for Victoria. Dido has been given the same. Britannica is staring at her pendant with a frown, dangling it between her fingers. "It's been dipped in the blood of a gladiator, of a fighter, to give you strength," Amara explains. She knows Britannica has understood even though she does not thank or even look at her. The Briton slips it on, tucking it under her toga, and rests her hand on her chest. Then her eyes flick over to Amara and Dido. She gives them the briefest nod of acknowledgment.

The men have all bought each other extra wine, more expensive than the sweetened variety the women have been served. Thraso pours it out, tipping an especially generous portion into his own flask. With a stab of remorse, Amara realizes everyone has forgotten Paris. He is sitting slightly away from the gathering, holding his thin knees in his arms, face pinched with disappointment. Fabia is waving at him from across the room, motioning that he can have her five asses. Paris ignores her. As ever, it's not his mother's attention that he wants. Gallus nudges Thraso's elbow as he pours out more wine, gesturing at the forgotten slave.

"Is he really a *man* though?" Thraso says. "Couldn't one of the girls have given him a hair clip or something?" He laughs at Paris's expense, clearly expecting Felix to join in. Their boss doesn't smile at the joke.

"Give the boy some wine," he says. "He earned it this year."

Gallus sits down again beside Beronice. He gives her a quick kiss. "This is for you," he says, handing over a parcel.

She takes it, and he looms over her, getting in the way, almost unwrapping it himself in his excitement to see her reaction.

Beronice gasps. "But it's beautiful!" She holds it up for everyone to see. It is a cameo pendant, a tiny one, but still by far the most expensive gift anyone has produced. "Oh, I love you!" Beronice exclaims, flinging her arms around him. Then she pulls back. "And I only got you some pomade!"

Victoria is stuck, sitting beside the lovers who are now kissing noisily. She looks down, her shoulders hunched over. All that mockery, and Gallus has done more for Beronice than anyone could ever have imagined. Felix slips off the desk, crouching on the floor beside her. "For my favorite whore," he says, handing Victoria a packet. She glances at him, eyes full of hope, then slips the contents out into her fingers. It is a string of wooden beads. Victoria gazes up at Felix, the love on her face painful to witness. She beams round at everyone, proud to have been singled out in front of them all. Amara smiles back, not wanting to ruin her happiness. Beronice catches Amara's eye. Victoria has no idea that her friends pity her, that where she imagines love, they only see cruelty.

The day rolls on, everyone getting increasingly drunk. Everyone, that is, except Amara and Felix. It seems neither is prepared to relinquish control of themselves, not even on the Saturnalia. She is aware of him watching her and wonders if he suspects something, though he surely cannot know about Rufus or Balbina's loan. She's been so careful. If he were any other man, she would have said he was looking at her with lust, but she knows this is impossible.

The men insist on trying to cook the bean stew, declaring it a day off for the girls, but they make such a mess, slopping the food over the brazier, almost putting the fire out, that Telethusa shoves them aside and takes over. They laugh at her, still interfering while she tries to cook. "You ruin it!" she shrieks in annoyance. "Go away! Shoo!"

Fabia offers to help, but Telethusa gestures at her to stay sitting. "No reason we all suffer," she says, with a pointed look at Thraso.

"I'm so happy for Beronice," Dido says to Amara. "Gallus must really love her after all!" Amara smiles in reply, almost too tense to speak. "He won't forget," Dido says to her. "I know he won't."

Amara is aware that Felix is watching them again. She takes Dido's hand. "I love you," she whispers back. "I meant everything I promised."

After their burnt, mushy stew, Felix declares it a good time to head outside and walk to the Forum. Beronice and Gallus disentangle themselves with reluctance. They have been sitting huddled in a corner, long since abandoning any pretence of joining in with the party.

"Why don't you just stay behind and fuck her?" Felix says to Gallus in exasperation. "Join us when you've got it out of your system."

They pile onto the streets, muffled up in their cloaks. The shops are shuttered for the festival, but a number of other households are out for a stroll, taking the chance to get some air before the afternoon grows too dark. Amara takes Dido's arm as they all amble to the Forum. Everyone on the street seems in high spirits, and even Paris is escorting his mother, who looks as if this was the present she has been waiting for the entire Saturnalia. Amara remembers the way Paris carried Simo from the burning bar, as if he were helping him, all the better to slip in the knife. She shudders.

Dido squeezes her arm. "Are you cold?"

Amara shakes her head.

Crowds are milling around the Forum, drinking and laughing, watching street performers and musicians. They stop near a man juggling torches. Amara watches the flames as they rise and fall, the man catching them in his gloved hands.

"I hoped to see you today."

His voice is a memory from home. Amara has not met Menander in months, but hearing him, it feels like yesterday since she held him. She turns. For once, he doesn't look entirely sure of himself.

"We said we would meet at the Saturnalia. I know that was some time ago," he adds, seeing the flustered look on her face. "I'm only here as a friend. I brought you a gift."

He holds out an object wrapped in cloth. She takes it, unwraps it. Inside is a beautiful clay lamp with a green glaze. The figure on it is familiar. It is a likeness of Aphidnai's Helen of Troy, the statue from her hometown, the one she loved to look at as a child, when her father pointed it out to her with such pride. Menander made this for her. She stares at the lamp, unable to speak. Then she flings her arms around his neck. "It's beautiful," she says. "It's the most beautiful present anyone has ever given me."

Dido yanks hard at her arm, and she lets go, but Menander catches hold of her hand. "I know you have a patron,

Timarete, I know this," he says. "But if I were free, if I gained my freedom, would you feel differently?"

Amara withdraws her hand, at last understanding what Dido saw behind him.

"What's this?"

She has never known Rufus so angry. Terror almost stops her heart. She pushes Menander aside to reach her boyfriend, but he blocks her embrace. "*Who is this?*" For a moment she is almost afraid he will hit her.

Amara hesitates. There is no question in her mind what she should do, only whether she has the courage. "This?" She turns round to look at Menander as if she has only just noticed him. "He's nobody! Some boy who wanted to give me a gift on the Saturnalia, because he said I had a pretty face. I don't even know his name." She laughs. "Why are you so angry?" she exclaims, taking Rufus's hand. "Don't be ridiculous! You cannot *possibly* imagine you have anything to be jealous about. He's just some slave boy." Amara is aware of Philos, standing beside his master, but she ignores him. It's not Philos she needs to convince. "Look, I'll prove it to you," she says, as if humoring a child. "I can just give it back to him, let him give it to some other girl," she inclines her head, teasing, looking at him from under lowered eyelashes. "Though I'm sorry if you think I'm *not* the prettiest girl at the Saturnalia, because that's who he wanted to give it to."

Amara is almost carried along by her own performance until she turns to face Menander again. He is staring at her as if she were a stranger. She holds the lamp out, looking into his eyes, willing him to understand. "I'm sorry but I cannot take this." He does not move. She forces herself to take a step toward him, still holding his gift, offering it to him. Amara's hand is trembling, and the glaze slips through her fingers. The lamp smashes at Menander's feet.

The shock of it makes her gasp. She and Menander stare at one another. She understands, seeing his face then, that whatever affection was once between them has ended. Amara looks down at the ground. Shards of glazed clay are scattered at her feet. All that work, engraved with such love, marked with memories of home and who she used to be, gone. She remembers Cressa's smashed pot at the necropolis, the man dying, the sacrifice Victoria made to save her life. The only choice she can ever make is to survive. "Oops, silly me," she says, turning to Rufus, biting her lip as if it were a joke. "I seem to have broken it!"

It is perhaps her callous disregard which finally convinces him. He strides over, puts an arm around her. "Sorry, boy," Rufus says to Menander, reaching into his purse for some coins. "My girlfriend didn't mean to be clumsy. I hope this compensates you."

Menander takes the money, not looking at Amara. "You're very generous, sir," he says.

Rufus physically turns her, back toward where Philos and Dido are standing, obviously eager to forget the whole incident. "How ridiculous I am," he says, kissing her. "I'm sorry to have been jealous."

"I'm flattered you were," she replies, gazing up at him. She is conscious of Menander walking away, even though she does not see him leave.

They reach Philos, and Amara realizes that Quintus and Lucius are also there, together with a retinue of their slaves.

They make quite an audience. "But I do at least have a small present for you myself, my darling," Rufus says. His tone is theatrical, aimed as much at his friends as at her. Hope makes her heart beat faster. Rufus lowers his voice. "Where's your wretched pimp?"

Amara knows Felix will not be far away, spots him almost immediately. He must have watched the whole scene unfold, seen how she treated Menander. She hears his voice in her head. *Not every woman is a heartless bitch like you.* Felix walks over as soon as she catches his eye.

"Honored," he says, bowing to Rufus, who recoils.

"I want to make you an offer," he says, loud enough that the rest of the brothel gather round to listen. "I would like to buy this woman on behalf of a friend."

Amara looks at him in bewilderment. "A friend?"

Rufus holds up a hand to silence her. "I would like to buy this woman on behalf of Gaius Plinius Secundus, the Admiral of the Roman Fleet."

Amara gasps at Pliny's name, but Rufus does not notice. He is caught up in the drama, relishing his role as hero in front of the crowd. "The admiral has considered her price and is prepared to offer you more than she is worth. There can be no haggling, he will not stoop to it. You must take his offer or leave it." Rufus gestures at Philos, who produces a seal. "This is his pledge, which you may keep if you agree the sale, as a guarantee you will be paid. He is offering you six thousand sesterces for the slave known as Amara."

It is two thousand more than Felix paid for her. Amara can see Dido and Victoria clutching one another, open-mouthed, staring at Rufus. She looks at Felix, but his face is inscrutable. Surely, he cannot refuse?

Felix bows. All this time, he has not acknowledged her. "I will accept the admiral's offer."

Amara says nothing while her master signs the agreement, transferring ownership. Everyone watches in silence, unable to believe what they have just seen. Shock has almost emptied her of feeling. Rufus hands Felix the seal and turns to her, radiant with his own power. "Amara. On behalf of the admiral and in the presence of witnesses and in the sight of the gods, I grant you your freedom. You are now Gaia Plinia Amara, Liberta."

Amara stares at him, speechless. Then she bursts into tears.

43

"Many who Fortuna has raised high, she suddenly throws down, and hurls them headlong"
—Pompeii graffiti

Amara cannot stop crying. Rufus has to restrain her from flinging herself at his feet, as she sobs out her undying love and gratitude. He kisses away her tears, clearly enjoying the adoration. She embraces Dido and Victoria over and over again, weeping onto both their shoulders, holding their faces in her hands, unable to express all the love she feels. The pain of what she has done to Menander, the ecstasy of freedom, is unlike anything she has ever felt. She laughs with Quintus and Lucius, professes her devoted friendship to Ipstilla and Telethusa—who look less than delighted by her good fortune—and startles Paris into giving her a bony hug. When it is Fabia's turn, the old woman clings to her, weeping, and Amara finds herself promising to help if she is ever in need. Thraso however, is a step too far. She nods at him, the way a queen might acknowledge a peasant. More than he deserves.

It is the only time she has ever seen Felix look truly surprised. He must have realized that all her tales about Rufus and violence were lies. Perhaps he is wondering what else she has lied about. She turns her back. *Let him wonder,* she thinks. He cannot hurt her now.

Amara wants to wait for Beronice, desperate to share the news, but Rufus is less keen. "My darling," he says. "I think I may have had enough of whores and pimps for one night. *Delightful* as I'm sure this other girl is." He looks at her companions from the brothel, both friends and enemies, and wrinkles his nose in distaste. Quintus and Lucius laugh, obviously eager to return home too.

Amara feels a jolt. Of course, this is the other side of the deal. A Saturnalia spent without Dido, without any of the women she loves. She wants to go back, to hug them one last time, but Rufus is leading her firmly away. She catches Dido's eye, hopes she understands it as a reminder of the promise she made.

Leaving is not easy in the press of the crowd. Philos and the other slaves try to go ahead first, clear the path, but nobody is inclined toward deference on the Saturnalia. While they are fighting their way through, a heavy-set man carrying bells dances between them, dressed as the Lord of Misrule. He is wearing a horned satyr mask, dressed all in red. He capers closer, brandishing the bells in Amara's face. Rufus draws her away, putting his arm around her. For a moment, it looks like the masked man is going to be a nuisance, but Quintus, Lucius and the rich men's phalanx of slaves are too formidable a barrier.

The satyr dances off. People cheer him and nudge one another to make space. Amara watches. She realizes, as the satyr prances about, stopping now and then to make people laugh, that he is not moving at random. He is slowly heading toward Felix. Her feeling of unease curdles into fear.

She yanks at Rufus, forcing him to stop. Victoria is standing near her boss. Amara shouts at her, but her voice is swallowed by the noise of the crowd. Felix is already aware of the danger. As the red satyr comes toward him, he draws his knife. The red satyr draws too. He is twice Felix's size, but Amara suspects he has none of her former master's speed or agility. The satyr lunges at Felix, but he feints, and the blow falls wide, narrowly missing Victoria. She scrambles back, disappearing into the safety of the crowd.

The two men are swiping at each other, and it could almost look as if they are dancing, if it weren't for the deadly flash of silver. The crowd don't seem to realize what's going on, or perhaps mistake the fight for a staged part of the misrule celebrations. They have cleared a small space and are all wedged together, cheering the pair on.

"We should leave," Rufus says. "He's nothing to you now."

"Where's Dido?" Amara says. "I can't see her! Where is she?"

"The others will look after her," Rufus says, losing patience. "This is no place for you."

She turns back to look again, too afraid to obey him. She can see Ipstilla and Telethusa, arms locked, managing to make a break for it.

"There she is," Amara cries. "Over there!"

Dido is clearly trapped, alone, unable to scramble her way back into the crowd like Victoria, forced to watch as Felix and the satyr swipe at one another, sickeningly close.

A drunk has hold of her arm and is trying to kiss her, unaware of the danger they are both in. Thraso is hovering near Felix, not wanting to get his boss killed by intervening. She spots Britannica on the other side of the circle, close by, avidly watching the fight, unaware of Dido's distress. Paris and Fabia are nowhere to be seen.

Amara looks desperately at Lucius, the man who promised to find Dido's family, who has spent so many nights with her at Drusilla's house. "Can't you help her? Please!"

Lucius looks uncomfortable but doesn't answer. Amara feels a surge of anger at his cowardice. She tears her arm from Rufus, shoving her way back toward the fight. "Britannica!" she screams. "Britannica, help me!"

For a moment, Amara thinks she is going to drown in a sea of arms and elbows, crushed in the chaos, then the tall woman is reaching down, grabbing her by the scruff of her cloak, pulling her to safety.

"Dido!" Amara screams, pointing at where she is trapped. Britannica's eyes widen. She drops Amara and shoves a man aside, punching him in the throat when he doesn't get out of her way quick enough.

Britannica tries to charge through the crowd, but her strength is no match for so many people. Amara can see her struggling, surrounded. The space for the fight is getting smaller and smaller, pushing Dido ever closer toward the violence. More and more people must be pouring into the Forum, packing everyone together. Amara tries to push toward Dido herself, but people are too drunk or disinterested to let her pass. She drops to her knees, crawling her way through, almost stifled by her fear of being trampled. She reaches the edge of the crowd. The fight is on top of her, and the satyr nearly stamps on her fingers, but she is too low down to be in range. She can see Britannica yelling, held back by a group of drunken, angry men. Just a short distance away, Dido is scrambling, not facing Amara, instead, trying to claw past the crowd, away from the knives, the drunkard still holding her around the waist.

The men have almost run out of room to fight. Felix is so close, she could almost reach out and touch him. There is no fear on his face, but he looks vulnerable, his body more exposed than the satyr's in his heavy, protective costume. Amara watches, willing Felix to kill his rival, willing him to end it. Instead, Felix swings round and stumbles over someone's foot, almost crashing into Dido. The red satyr sees his chance, swiping the knife toward his opponent while he is off balance. Felix dives out of the way. The satyr stabs Dido in the back, burying the knife between her shoulder blades. The drunk holding her lets go in shock. Now, when it is too late, people draw back, letting Dido pass. She takes two steps forward and collapses.

Somebody in the crowd screams, then another. Finally, it is dawning on the gathering that this is not a performance. A group of men rush forward, seizing the red stayr, tearing off his mask. His face is familiar. It is Balbus, Simo's freedman. He disappears into the mob, mouth open in terror, buried in a frenzy of kicks and punches. The crowd is clearing, some pushing forward to watch Balbus die, others fleeing from the violence. Amara reaches Dido. Britannica is already holding her, cradling her in her arms.

"I'm here!" Amara cries, dropping down beside her. She takes Dido's hand. "We're all here. You're safe now."

Dido does not answer. Blood is coming from her mouth. She looks at Amara, pain and terror in her eyes.

All the times they have exchanged messages without words, only with glances, and Amara knows she cannot hide her own anguish. She kisses Dido on the forehead. In her head, she hears her father's voice. *Nobody should die in fear.*

"I've seen people recover from worse than this," she says. "All those patients my father treated. You'll get better; I know you will." Dido's hand is cold, so she holds it against her own body to warm it. "You're going to be alright, I promise." Victoria arrives, breathless, and sits down beside her. "And Victoria's here now too. When Beronice comes, she can get Gallus to fetch a doctor."

"We're here with you," Victoria says. "You're not on your own. We're here."

Dido closes her eyes. "You can have a rest," Amara says. "It's alright to have a rest." She lies the palm of her hand against Dido's cheek so her friend can feel her, even though she cannot see her. She is still cupping Dido's face in her fingers, long after she knows she has died.

"She is gone," Britannica says. Nobody remarks on the fact that she can speak.

Amara shushes her. "Just a moment," she says, not wanting to let go of Dido. "Not yet. She's not gone yet."

"She's dead, my love," Victoria says, putting her hand on Amara's knee. "She's gone now." Amara cannot see, tears are blinding her. Victoria drags Amara's arm around her own shoulders, pulling her upright. Amara realizes a man is watching them. Felix.

"You did this!" she screams. In her grief and rage she knows she could kill him, tear him apart where he stands, but Victoria is holding her, preventing her. "That knife was meant for you. You killed her! You did this!" Felix is silent as Amara shouts at him, threatening him, screaming out her hatred until her voice breaks.

Then a man is picking her up, lifting her over his shoulder, taking her away. She thinks it is Rufus, beats her fists against his back, sobbing, ordering him to put her down, to let her go back. Eventually, she gives up, collapsing against him. It is only when they reach the edge of the Forum and she sees Rufus standing, waiting for her, that she realizes who is carrying her. It is Philos.

44

*"We thus began to imprison animals to which
nature had assigned the heavens as their element."*
—Pliny the Elder, *Natural History*, on the caging of birds

The Saturnalia is over. Amara sits at her desk, dressed in black. The sound of the fountain does not reach this room, but she knows it is there, murmuring gently in the garden below. She is safe in the house with the golden door. She has her freedom. And her heart is broken.

The wooden box is no longer under Rufus's bed; it sits in front of her. She opens it. Folded above the jewelry is a letter from Pliny to Rufus. She picks it up. Words jump out at her ". . . *the attagen, also of Iona is a famous bird; but although it has a voice, at other times, it is mute in captivity* . . ." And so it goes on. There is almost no mention of Amara in the letter. Pliny built his case for her freedom by calling on a multitude of birds, perhaps feeling more comfortable making his argument in abstract terms. But she knows what a gift it is. Not only that he paid toward her freedom, but that he gave her his name.

It was the name, not the money, that mattered in the end. Caught between his father's refusal, and Amara's desperation to be free, Rufus had written to the admiral, asking his advice about what he should do. It was Pliny who had introduced him to Amara in the first place, so surely, he would know. Pliny responded with unimaginable generosity. "I never *asked* him for the money," Rufus has told her, over and over again. "And I did pay half, so it's not like you didn't cost me *anything*." Amara is beginning to suspect that, for Rufus, the pleasure of opening his hands to see the bird fly will never be quite as satisfying as feeling its fragile form beneath his fingers.

He did not enjoy her grief after Dido's death. It wasn't a pretty flurry of tears he could kiss away, but a frenzy of pain and hysteria that swamped her gratitude and his glory. He let Philos take her back here to recover herself. She spent the first two days of the Saturnalia alone, save for a handful of slaves. Rufus has 'lent' them all to her. Philos is the only one she knows.

She cannot remember much of that first night, other than the agony, but the following day is stamped on her memory. She was huddled here, in this study, wrapped in a pile of blankets, when Philos brought her hot wine. A drink was the only consolation he had to offer. He stood at the very edge of the room, not getting too close to her, nothing like the man who once offered her his arm on the street. It was as if the sight of her frightened him.

"You can't be like this when he comes for you," he said, not looking at her face. "He planned that night for weeks, imagining all your joy, all the adulation. And instead, he got grief and disappointment. I know you loved her. But Rufus will never understand. She was just a pretty slave to him. You will have to mourn her in private."

Amara had been too upset to reply. She has avoided Philos since then, though she still took his advice. She wore her white dress when Rufus returned, lavished him with affection, professed her boundless loyalty, enthused about the house. She even apologized for her own grief, fearing that it might have marred all he had done for her. Rufus was gracious in reassuring her that he understood. He never mentioned her friend by name and neither did she.

Amara doesn't have to name Dido to think about her. When she is alone, she spends time standing in the atrium at the same place where Dido stood, trying to take comfort from the fact she was here, in this very house—she saw it, she touched it. Amara remembers their conversations, Dido's kindness, her surprising boldness when she performed, the way she sang, with a grace like no other. But at night, she cannot blot out her last memory, the blood on Dido's face, the pain and the horror.

Amara realizes her hands are shaking. She puts Pliny's letter away. Dido deserves more than private mourning. From her desk drawer, Amara takes a crude wooden carving, a small statue of the goddess Diana, armed with her hunting bow. She wraps the figure in cloth, ties around the label she has written. *I am the gift of Gaia Plinia Amara, Liberta.*

She gets up, walks down the stairs, looking across the open space. In the garden, painters will soon be starting work on a large fresco. Rufus had seen it as a delightful sign that she is so thrilled with the house, that she wants to make it special for them both, make it somewhere suitable for him to stay. He had been less certain about the myth she chose. It will be Acteon turning into a stag, while his own hounds tear him apart. Wouldn't she prefer scenes from the legends of Venus, rather than Diana? Perhaps the virgin goddess isn't *quite* the thing for a love nest? But Amara laughed, teasing him. *We can always have Venus in the bedroom.*

She steps down into the atrium. A young woman is waiting by the pool. Amara hurries over. The girl is early, and Amara knows she has very little time to herself. It is Pitane, the waitress from the Elephant, the one who owes Amara for her abortion.

"It's beautiful," Pitane says, looking round. "How well you've done! I can't believe it!"

"I'm sorry you can't stay longer or have some wine with me," Amara replies. "But I know what it's like. I'm grateful you spared the time to come at all."

"It's no trouble," Pitane says. "I'm on a run for supplies. They'll never notice."

Amara hands her the wooden statue, hidden in its cloth. "Could you give this to Paris for me please? It is for his master. Paris should tell Felix that I apologize the gift is too late for the Saturnalia. But it has not been sent with any less feeling. Can you remember all that?"

"Of course!" Pitane nods. "You're nicer than me I must say. If I got my freedom from a new master, I wouldn't be sending Sittius any fucking presents."

Pitane turns and walks across the atrium, slipping through the heavy wooden door. Amara stands alone, shivering slightly from the breeze. It is quiet here. She pictures Pitane, rejoining the noise and the chaos, carrying her Diana through the streets of Pompeii. And when her gift arrives, Amara knows Felix will understand what it means.

ACKNOWLEDGMENTS

A book is the product of the hard work of many people and I'm so grateful to the whole team at Head of Zeus. Thank you to Madeleine O'Shea whose thoughtful advice and enthusiasm made editing a joy, and to Charlotte Greig who took over the reins with aplomb and an endless supply of support. Thanks also to Anna Nightingale and Laura Palmer. Thank you to Holly Ovenden for the exceptionally beautiful cover art and a truly gigantic thanks to everyone in sales, publicity and marketing. Above all to Kate Appleton, Jessie Sullivan, Jade Gwilliam, Lottie Chase, Jennifer Edgecombe, and Avneet Bains. Last but not least, thank you to Anthony Cheetham, whose passion for this project is what led to the trilogy being commissioned.

Friendship runs through *The Wolf Den* and also ran through the writing of it. Thank you to Andrea Binfor for a lifetime of love and for traipsing round Pompeii with me for so many hours. And a massive thank you to Dan Jones for endless Pompeii advice, support, pep talks and encouragement.

Thanks also to Samira Ahmed, to Jason Farrington, to Jo Jacobson for "Pliny's" Ammonite, to Kristina Holt, to Anna, Trilby and Bethan for loving me in spite of the ginger cat, to Daniel Kiss for checking my translations, and to Kate Prout for putting up with a whole night of Pompeii documentaries.

Love and gratitude always to Juliet Mushens, for being the absolute best, both as an agent and a friend: your love and support means everything to me. Huge thanks also to foreign rights supremo Liza de Block and the team at Mushens Entertainment. Also to Buki Papillon, Jennifer Saint, Caroline Lea, Claire McGlasson and all my fellow writers at Team Mushens and the Debuts 2021 Twitter group.

Thank you too, to all the book bloggers and booksellers who have supported me, I am so grateful for all you do. In particular thank you to Dan Bassett at Waterstones Cribbs Causeway, Diane Park at Wave of Nostalgia in Haworth, Cody Duffy at Waterstones Liverpool, Julia Zarychta at Waterstones Victoria, Sarah Whyley at Heffers in Cambridge and to Kim Morris and team at West End Lane Books.

Closer to home, my Mum, Suzy Kendall, is my first reader and most enthusiastic cheerleader, my Dad, Sandy Harper, was my first and favourite storyteller, and my dearest son Jonathon fills every day with love.

And then there are my siblings—this book is for you. Thank you to Ruth for being a wonderful sister-in-law and for sharing so much of your own beautiful writing life. I have such admiration for you. Thank you to Eugenie for being the best sister I could have hoped for—you turned up, uninvited, at the hardest time and gave me hope. Whenever I feel down, I remember the way you were there when I needed you most. And thank you to my brother, Tom, for keeping me company throughout all the ups and downs, always understanding, never judging and for being a source of constant love and support. How lucky I am to be your sister.

Turn the page for an exclusive sneak peek
of Elodie Harper's second book
in the Wolf Den Trilogy:

THE HOUSE WITH THE GOLDEN DOOR

ELODIE HARPER

Available from Union Square & Co.
in September 2022

75 CE

PARENTALIA

1

*"Man alone of living creatures has been given grief . . .
and likewise ambition, greed and a boundless lust for living."*
—Pliny the Elder, *Natural History*

The painter stands balanced on a wooden platform, his brushstrokes hidden from sight as he brings the goddess to life. Amara watches him. The rest of the fresco is complete, a hunting scene encircling her small garden. Only Diana's face is unfinished. She breathes in deeply, enjoying the scents of spring. Narcissi lie scattered at her feet like white stars, and the air is sweet with them.

"Nobody could do justice to her beauty," the painter remarks, standing back briefly from his work to scrutinize it, before busying himself with the brush again.

Amara knows he does not mean the goddess Diana. She could have hired anyone to paint a god, but she chose this man, Priscus, because he was once the lover of her friend Dido and the only artist capable of drawing her likeness. "I know that you will," she replies. Or she certainly hopes so. The rest of the painting was done by his craftsmen at a far cheaper rate. It cost ten times as much to hire Priscus, the master of the firm, to immortalize her friend.

"She was the most exquisite woman," Priscus says. "There was a lightness to her unlike anyone else. I can still remember the way she sang."

Dido has barely been dead three months and Amara feels tears prick her eyes. She blinks, not wanting Priscus to notice. It is strange to have him in her home. The last time they met, she and Dido were enslaved. Priscus was a regular customer, paying their pimp to spend the night with Dido, while his friend Salvius paid for Amara's company in the bedroom next door. Now she is a freedwoman paying for *his* services. She suspects neither of them quite know how to treat the other after this change in fortune.

He stands back from the wall again, looking over his work. "I believe it is finished."

Amara steps forward. "May I see?"

"Of course," Priscus climbs down from the platform, finally leaving his painting in view.

Dido is standing with one hand to her heart, the other pointing across the garden. Amara gazes at her dead friend. Priscus has captured the perfect symmetry of her face, the softness of her mouth, and most of all her eyes, dark with a sadness she could never hide. Grief hits Amara then and she turns away. Priscus reaches out before dropping his hand, perhaps afraid his touch will offend her. It is a while before she trusts herself to speak. "I can never thank you enough for this."

"It has been my pleasure," he says. "It gives me some comfort to think her beauty is not entirely lost." Priscus stands next to Amara, leaving enough space between them to show his respect. "But can I ask you something? Why did you choose to remember her like this?"

He gestures at the walls surrounding them and Amara takes in the scene, so different from the woman he has just painted. A stag with a human face is being ripped apart by hunting dogs, their muzzles slick with blood, teeth sharp in wide open mouths. Through the stag's mangled body, white ribs are poking and the red of his heart. It is Acteon, transformed into a stag by the goddess Diana, only to be torn to pieces by his own hounds. The price he paid for seeing the goddess naked. Diana points at him as he dies, turning Dido's melancholy into a mark of cruel indifference.

"She had the purest heart," Amara replies. "Who else could Dido be but the virgin goddess?"

They both know she has avoided his question. Priscus bows his head in agreement, too polite to press further. "Of course."

Amara waits while he collects his paints, packing them carefully into a box, his apprentice taking apart the platform to carry back to the workshop. Afterward she walks them both across the atrium to the door. There is no need to hand over the money now. Rufus, her patron and lover, can be relied upon to pay an account at his own leisure. At the doorway, Priscus hesitates. "I hope you will not mind if . . ." he trails off, then collects himself. "Salvius asked me to pass on his good wishes for your health, and his heartfelt thanks to the gods for your good fortune. He holds you in great esteem."

Amara's face betrays no sign of the turmoil she feels at this reminder of her old life. She is conscious of Juventus, the porter, no doubt listening to every word, even as he stands silent at his post. "That is kind of your friend. Please pass on my thanks and good wishes for his own health." She nods, polite but distant, and walks away before Priscus can say anything more. The mention of Salvius has flooded her mind with unwanted memories. His hands on her body, his nakedness, the weight of him and then worse, not Salvius, but the fear and darkness of her old cell at the brothel, the violence and the pain. Her past is the whirlpool Charybdis, pulling her down under the waves where she cannot breathe.

Amara walks swiftly up the stairs to her private study, trying not to run, and shuts the door. Her legs are trembling. She sits down at the desk, hands flat on its wooden surface, trying to crush the rising panic. Her mind is playing tricks on her again, giving her the sense that she is not here, where her eyes tell her she is sitting, but back there, in Felix's Wolf Den. Blood thuds in her ears as she searches in the drawer for the box that always calms her. It is heavy in her hands. She sets it down and opens the lid. Inside is all the money she has earned since she came to live here, a mixture of loans she has collected and the generous allowance Rufus gives her. She runs her fingers through the coins, feeling their reassuring weight, listening to the sound of them drop, like the gentle patter of rain.

She arranged this room to be as unlike Felix's study as possible, placing the furniture at unfamiliar angles, making everything look different. The walls are white not red, small cupids balancing gracefully at intervals along the walls, one with a harp, another with a bow. Every small, pale figure, each careful brushstroke on their bodies, is more finely drawn than anything in the Wolf Den, yet somehow the images are less vivid than the bulls' skulls and black plinths she remembers. If she closes her eyes, Amara knows she will see them. There is something about sitting behind a desk that always makes her think of her old master. Even in her dreams, this is how she remembers him. The sharp lines of his body bent over the books, the tilt of his head glancing up, the strength in his hands.

A knock at the door startles her back into the present. "Who is it?"

Martha enters. Amara smiles but her maid only looks at the floor. "Shall I get you ready to see Drusilla, Mistress?" Martha's accent is so strong, Amara sometimes struggles to understand her.

Martha's shoulders are rounded, her whole posture hunched. At first Amara had thought the girl was shy, but now she recognizes it as the deliberate withdrawal of the unwilling slave. She herself used that same reticence against Felix. Amara has to stifle her irritation. *The girl does not know how lucky she is to be here in this beautiful house, not there, in the brothel.*

Martha is Hebrew, captured in Rome's recent offensive against Masada—or so Philos, the household steward, told Amara. It was Philos who chose which other two slaves should join him here on behalf of his master. Rufus, who owns Martha, has not said anything about her. Slaves are not people to him. He "loaned" all the servants to Amara along with the furniture, and it would no more occur to him to explain their different personalities than he would waste his time describing a history of the tables or lampstands.

Amara only hopes Rufus never slept with Martha, although the girl is pretty enough. It might explain why she is so unfriendly.

"Thank you," Amara says, rising from the desk. "You are good to remind me."

They walk downstairs to the first of Amara's private rooms off the atrium. Martha has already set out the dressing table. It is impossible for Amara not to think about her friend and fellow she-wolf Victoria when she takes her place in front of all the perfumes and cosmetics. She remembers all the cheap bottles Victoria used to line up so carefully on her windowsill at the brothel, the pains she always took to look her best. Victoria is so vivid in Amara's memory, the tumble of black curls over her shoulders, her husky laugh and the drawl of her sarcastic remarks, that it seems impossible she will not walk in to the room, demanding her own turn at the table. Martha starts to brush out her hair. Amara picks up a delicate glass jar, shaped like a flower, unstoppers it and holds it to her nose. Jasmine. It is the only scent Rufus likes her to wear. Martha huffs as Amara puts it down again and pulls at the comb. All this movement is ruining her attempts to style her mistress's ringlets.

When she has finished, Martha holds out the silver mirror. Amara always prefers to do her own makeup. She takes the kohl, redoes her eyes where it has smudged, but doesn't smear any paste on her skin. It was unaffordable while she worked at the brothel and now Rufus is used to seeing her barefaced. The only time she painted herself for him, he hated it. All the words he uses to describe her—*lovely, delicate, naive*—she takes as instructions rather than compliments. It doesn't matter that she worked in a brothel, that she outwitted the most violent pimp in Pompeii, or that she could move mountains with her rage. This is not what her lover wants to see, so she hides it all.

"Thank you," Amara says. "You can start work in the kitchen now."

"But don't you need me to come with you?" Martha looks nervous. "Master said it's better you don't walk out alone."

It is one thing having a discontented maid, Amara does not want a spy as well. "The streets do not frighten me," she replies, with a cold smile, knowing the girl will understand her. "I am quite used to walking them."

Martha bows her head, cheeks flushing, no doubt cursing the day the Romans dragged her from her homeland to serve a *whore*. Amara leaves her and walks across the atrium to the huge wooden door. Juventus hesitates a moment before letting her out unaccompanied, glancing round to see if Philos, the steward, is there to grant permission. "Philos is with the Master today," Amara says impatiently. "Perhaps you will let me out to attend the harp lesson Rufus has paid for?"

"Of course, Mistress," Juventus says, stepping aside.

It's a quieter street than the one she used to live on—the brothel stood at a fork in the road, facing one bar and a stone's throw from another—but even so, stepping out on to the pavement always makes Amara feel like she has slipped from a still pond into a fast-moving stream. She weaves her way past the billowing cloths that flank her doorway, strips of red, yellow and orange fabric flapping in the breeze. The house Rufus rents for her is fronted by a clothing store, one of several on the street. The shopkeeper, Virgula, nods as she passes, unperturbed at having a concubine for a neighbor. After all they both share the same landlord, a friend of Rufus who Amara is yet to meet.

The road is narrow but Amara owns her space on the pavement, her gaze cutting through to the middle distance, forcing others to let her pass. A man weighed down with an armful of leather goods huffs but stands aside. Amara does not acknowledge him. The days she had to meet any man's eye on the street are over.

It's not long before she reaches Drusilla's house. Pompeii's most desirable courtesan does not live far away, her road runs in parallel to Amara's. It's why she knows Rufus will tolerate her making the journey alone. This house is not rented, Drusilla owns it outright, and the beautiful glass workshop that fronts it is also hers. Amara lingers, looking in. The glassware becomes increasingly intricate the further inside you venture. Plain cups and scent bottles stacked on the counter give way to jugs shaped like fishes and an urn dripping in green grapes, a pair of nymphs acting as the vessel's arms. Amara's eyes are always drawn to the same place. A shelf carrying small statuettes of the gods. She thinks of the beautiful glass Pallas Athene from her parent's house, wonders who owns it now.

Amara feels her heart lift as she steps across the threshold into Drusilla's atrium. The porter inclines his head as she enters: she is always welcome here.

"There you are!" Drusilla calls down, leaning over the indoor balcony, her face dimpled in a smile. Amara beams back. Drusilla is—bar Dido—the most beautiful woman she has ever known. The pale yellow linen tunic she is wearing brings out the warmth of her skin, and her black hair frames her face like a laurel wreath. She could be Hesperia, Amara thinks, goddess of the setting sun.

Amara hurries up the stairs. She always enjoys Drusilla's company, even more so when they meet without their lovers present, when she knows everything her friend says is genuine. They embrace on the balcony, admiring one another's outfits, then head to Drusilla's bedroom where she keeps her harp.

"When is he going to buy you your own?" Drusilla asks, as they sit down together, Amara positioned to play the instrument, Drusilla close beside her to instruct.

"Today, if I let him," she replies with a sigh. "But I'm not good enough yet, I don't want him to hear me."

"But you could practice every day with your own. You would improve more quickly."

Amara knows it is true. She is finding the harp harder to master than she anticipated. Every time she plays the lyre for Rufus, however beautifully or skillfully, all he wants to know is when she will entertain him with the harp. There's no malice in the way he asks, it's all eagerness like a child, but his insistence makes her feel insecure. She wishes he could enjoy the instrument she already plays. "I'm not sure why he's so set on this," she says, patting the strings.

Drusilla strokes her lightly on the back, brushing her hair over one shoulder. "I think it's an encouraging sign," she says. "He's making his mark. Turning you into the perfect concubine to suit his tastes. If he invests enough money in you, he won't look elsewhere."

Amara feels a flicker of anxiety. It's a constant shadow, the worry of losing her patron's interest. "Let's try Sappho again," she says. "I nearly had it last time."

They play for an hour or more. Amara is a dedicated pupil, never complaining when Drusilla gets her to practice the same chords over and over. For her part, Drusilla is an exacting teacher, not only passing on her musical knowledge, but also her advice on how Amara should hold herself to look as attractive as possible when she plays.

"I think that's enough for now," Drusilla says, running her hand along Amara's arm. "You are getting tense. I was serious earlier. Let Rufus buy you your own instrument. You will learn faster."

Amara follows Drusilla to the couch. The maid, Thalia, has left them some wine and pastries. "All this effort," Amara remarks, helping herself to a bun, telling herself she will eat less later. "Can you imagine Rufus and Quintus spending their afternoons deciding how to please us?"

"Not Quintus, certainly," Drusilla says with a frown.

"But he adores you."

Drusilla shakes her head. "A man like Quintus will inevitably want the excitement of something new, sooner or later. And I worry it might be sooner." She toys with her wine glass. It is blue, no doubt bought from the shop she rents out, the red of the wine shining purple through the glaze. "I'm not in love with him, as you know, but a new man is always a disruption. I'm used to Quintus now."

Amara is not entirely sure she believes Drusilla when she says she does not love Quintus. It's hard to dedicate so much attention to pleasing a man without ending up feeling some affection for him. "I keep having to remind myself to ration out the tricks I learned at the brothel," she says, raising an eyebrow. "Leave Rufus a *few* surprises."

Drusilla snorts. "That one maneuver you told me about! I think even Quintus was shocked when I tried it."

They both laugh. Amara settles back onto the cushions, enjoying the freedom of friendship, the license to say what she likes. Her apprenticeship at the brothel was brutal, everything Felix forced her to learn came at the highest possible cost, but now, after she has escaped, it can almost seem worth the pain. "Priscus finished the painting today," she says.

"How do you think Rufus will react? When he realizes it's Dido?"

"Philos says he won't even notice," Amara shrugs. "She was just a slave to him."

"You discuss Rufus with Philos?" Drusilla's voice is sharp. "Is that wise?"

"Philos was my friend before, when we were both . . ." Amara hesitates, not wanting to say the word. "When we were both enslaved."

"But now *you* are not and *he* still is. Philos belongs to your lover. Be careful what you say. He might feel bound to repeat it to his master."

"I trust him," Amara says. "I don't believe he would do that to me." She hopes it is true. She feels too ashamed to admit the truth to Drusilla. That she is so lonely she cannot bear to be distant with Philos, to admit that he is Rufus's servant and not her friend. Who else is there in the house for her to talk to? "How is Primus?" She asks, changing the subject.

"Oh!" Drusilla claps her hands, face shining with delight. "He's doing so well with his letters! Such a clever boy. Come, come, I'll take you to see him. He will love to show off to you." She leaps off the couch, holding out her hand. Amara takes it and lets Drusilla lead her down the stairs.

They cross the atrium, heading out into the garden. Primus is roaming through the flowers, prattling about a bee, waving a small chubby hand, watched over by his nurse. He looks so like his mother. The same dimples when he smiles, the large dark eyes. Drusilla flings her arms out and the little boy runs over, hugging her round the knees. Amara smiles. She didn't even know about the existence of Primus until a month after Rufus freed her. Drusilla guards her child from all but her closest friends.

"What have you learned today?" Drusilla is asking him. "What can you tell Mummy?"

"Bees live in palaces of wax!" he declares, looking up at his mother and then at Amara, as if daring her to contradict him. "They turn flowers into honey!"

Drusilla gazes adoringly at her son as he relays his three-year-old's wisdom with a great deal of self-importance. Amara had been shocked when she learned who the child's father is. Popidus is a Pompeiian grandee and one so ancient Primus must be many years younger than his legitimate grandchildren. The old man does not recognize Drusilla's son as his own.

Sitting with her friend, watching the child play in the garden, Amara could almost imagine that her life is now one of blissful security. But even though he is absent, she can still feel Rufus's hands holding her up—and knows he has the power to let her fall. It is his money which brought her here, he pays for Drusilla's time, and Amara knows she would never have won such a valued place in her friend's life if she had a less prestigious lover. When they meet at the Venus Baths, Drusilla is always surrounded by other, less powerful concubines. Amara is one of many women in her orbit.

Time alone with Drusilla is precious but Amara doesn't dare linger. She needs to prepare herself for Rufus's visit in the evening. He has been busy this past fortnight with his family celebrating the Parentalia—a domestic festival commemorating the ancestors—which left him little time to see Amara. The festival has been an uncomfortable reminder of her peripheral position in Rufus's life, and her own orphaned, rootless status.

Amara rises, murmuring her excuses about Rufus to Drusilla, who accompanies her to the door. Drusilla leaves Primus behind with some reluctance, even though she will be free to join her son again in a matter of moments.

"Do you think Rufus would be pleased if you gave him a boy?" Drusilla asks the question just as Amara is poised to step out onto the street.

"I'm not sure," she says, startled. "I don't think so." It is hard for her to explain why, but she is almost certain Rufus would not like to see her as a mother. She is still scrupulous at avoiding pregnancy.

"It is always a gamble," Drusilla nods, no doubt thinking of the heartless Popidus. "Don't forget to mention the harp tonight. Go well, my love."

Drusilla slips back into her home. Amara stands on the threshold, loneliness creeping up on her. When she was enslaved, she would visit Drusilla's house with Dido. They would leave together too, walking the streets hand in hand back to the Wolf Den. The grief hits her so hard that for a moment she doesn't think she will be able to keep her composure. *I have my freedom now*, Amara tells herself. *That's all that matters.* She strides out onto the pavement, her face cold, betraying nothing of the loss she feels.